Charles Lambert is the author of several novels, short stories, and the memoir *With a Zero at its Heart*, which was voted one of *The Guardian* readers' Ten Best Books of the Year in 2014. In 2007, he won an O. Henry Award for his short story *The Scent of Cinnamon*. His first novel, *Little Monsters*, was longlisted for the 2010 International IMPAC Dublin Literary Award, and his sixth novel, *Prodigal*, was shortlisted for the Polari Prize in 2019. Born in England, Charles Lambert has lived in central Italy since 1980.

Praise for Charles Lambert:

'Charles Lambert is a terrific, devious storyteller.' – Owen King

'Charles Lambert writes as if his life depends on it. He takes risks at every turn.' – Hannah Tinti

'Charles Lambert is a writer who could one day attain classic status.' – Maggie Gee

'A writer who never ceases to surprise.' – Jenny Offill

'A seriously good writer.' – Beryl Bainbridge

BIRTHRIGHT

Charles Lambert

Also by Charles Lambert:

The Bone Flower
The Children's Home
Two Dark Tales: Jack Squat and the Niche
Prodigal
Little Monsters
The Scent of Cinnamon and Other Stories
Any Human Face
The View from the Tower
With a Zero at its Heart

BIRTHRIGHT

Charles Lambert

Gallic Books
London

A Gallic Book

First published in Great Britain in 2023 by
Gallic Books, 12 Eccleston Street, London, SW1W 9LT

A CIP record for this book is available from the British Library

Typeset in Adobe Garamond Pro by Gallic Books
ISBN 978-1-913547-28-8

Printed in the UK by CPI (CR0 4YY)
2 4 6 8 10 9 7 5 3 1

PART ONE

CHAPTER ONE

She is washing the feel of the evening's cooking from her hands when Aldo calls her into the living room. She wipes her hands on a tea towel, picks up her tray and joins him on the sofa.

He is pointing at the screen. 'Isn't it remarkable?' he says. She looks across and sees a photograph of a girl with a fringe almost covering her eyes and the kind of blue-and-white-striped sweater she thinks of as Breton. The photograph has that deckled edge that photographs used to have and is set at an angle, which accentuates its vintage air.

'I don't know what you mean.' Her fingers grip the tray. For a second she thinks she might faint.

Aldo pours her a glass of wine. 'Come on, Liz, don't tell me you can't see the likeness.'

She lays the tray carefully down on the coffee table next to his, picks up the glass.

'Likeness?' she says.

'It's the spitting image of you when you were that age.'

She sips her wine. 'How would you know what I looked like?' she says, her tone level, under control. 'You didn't know me when I was that age.'

'Well, practically,' he says. 'Don't tell me you can't see it. You could be twins.'

The photograph disappears and a blonde woman begins to speak, but Liz can't concentrate. She needs to breathe normally, her heart is racing. She closes her eyes for a second, then takes another sip of wine. Aldo continues to stare at the screen, shaking his head in disbelief.

Moments later, the presenter is replaced by an old woman, frail in an armchair too large for her, a cloud of permed white hair around a sunken face. Liz hears the woman speak a few words of affected English, the English her generation uses on the telephone, until her voice is masked by the confident, strident enunciation of a younger woman saying in Italian that she would never understand, that it was all so long ago, that she would rather be left in peace but she couldn't bear not to know, the words so contrary to what the old woman is trying to say, everything lost, or almost lost. Liz hates it when they do this, this layer of Italian distorting the still just audible English, so that all she can hear is the gap between the two, into which meaning tumbles.

'What is this programme anyway?' she says, because something, sooner or later, has to be said.

'It's about people who go missing. You've seen it a hundred times.'

'And hated it every time,' says Liz, with a shudder. 'It's so intrusive.'

'Look at that poor old dear,' says Aldo. 'She's crying.'

'I don't want to look at an old woman crying,' says Liz. 'That's exactly what I mean.' She stands up, crosses the room to the door leading out to the garden.

'I need some fresh air,' she says.

*

Late afternoon the following day, she walks out onto the terrace with a bottle of white wine and a glass, and finds the programme on her iPad. She's been putting it off all day, but Aldo is due

10

home in an hour and she needs to be alone. She sits down, sips the wine slowly until the glass is empty, refills it, then sighs and streams the programme from the beginning.

The journalist, young, blonde, with a tailored jacket and an air of concerned authority, is in a studio, with banks of people on phones behind her. The action alternates between urgent searches for people who have just gone missing, with photographs and details of where they were last seen and what they were wearing, most of them in their teens or terminally confused, and more leisurely trawls into cold cases of the past. The programme has the air of being a public service, cutting to anxious parents, or deserted husbands, or weeping siblings. Policemen chip in with details of where the missing person was last seen in a language no normal person would ever use. Neighbours say the missing person was always cordial, that no one would ever have expected him or her to disappear like that, from one day to the next. They all seemed so happy is the constant refrain. But Liz isn't convinced. Who wouldn't want to escape from that frigid sitting room, with its flimsy Empire-style chairs and faded artificial flowers and Padre Pio on the wall? Who wouldn't empty the family coffers into her handbag and make a run for it? What right do these people have to set the hounds of hell on her trail?

And then there she is. The girl. Liz wonders how many other photos have survived, small and curling, their colours subtly changed by time. She will have kept them all, Liz supposes, in a biscuit tin the way people used to do. I remember that sweater, she thinks. I never liked it.

A fact sheet appears alongside the photo. Name. Age. Height. When and where last seen. The clothes the girl was wearing when she disappeared. Liz lifts her eyes from the tablet and looks down the garden to the line of distant hills, blue-grey in the afternoon light, the setting sun lending them depth. I don't need this, she says, out loud, to no one. I don't need this.

And then she's back, the woman from last night, hunched and faded, lost in her armchair, her fuzz of hair around her skull of a face, twisting a tiny handkerchief in her hands, one of those embroidered handkerchiefs women used to tuck up their cardigan sleeves. So old now, so old she seems to be on the point of death. But of course she's old, it all happened so many years ago, the woman would have been middle-aged even then. The eyes chastising as ever, although larger now in that chaos of wrinkled skin and bone; the voice, despite being barely perceptible beneath the interpreter's jaunty Italian, with that slight metallic edge to it that she must have acquired as a kind of self-defence.

Liz listens more carefully this time, teasing the English out, as the woman talks about the girl, how much she was loved, how badly she was missed. It's a mercy her father wasn't there to mourn the loss of her, the woman says. He would never have got over it. He lived for his little girl, worshipped the ground she walked on. Liz picks up her glass, puts it down again, the wine untouched. How could she just have disappeared like that, from one day to the next, and in a foreign country, the woman says, our lovely daughter, in a country she loved so much, when she had her entire future in front of her. The woman's voice breaks at this point, she dabs at her eyes with the handkerchief in a way that strikes Liz as coquettish. Because none of this is true, she thinks, furious. It wasn't like that at all. She was all I had, the woman says, and Liz shakes her head. No, no, no. All of it lies, she says to the empty garden.

The next case is a fifteen-year-old boy, last seen on the outskirts of Milan three days before. His mother is too distraught to talk, but his father is in the studio. He's a good boy, he says. It isn't like him to make us worry. The photo shows a sullen adolescent, with a hoodie and ripped jeans, standing alone in front of a graffiti-covered wall. Everyone calls him Mikki, the fact sheet says, but his father uses his full name, Michele. When the man sighs, Liz hears an edge of irritation, a hint of anger. We can't imagine why he should want to run away from home, the father says, turning to the camera. At least get in touch, Michele, the man says, and there it is again, that note of barely contained rage. Your mother and I want you back. Let's start over, he says.

Liz sips her wine, snaps shut the iPad cover.

'Run for your life,' she says.

PART TWO

CHAPTER TWO

Fiona first came across proof of the other girl's existence when she was sixteen. She was searching in her mother's dressing table for a bracelet she wanted to borrow when she spotted a loop on a small velvet cushion in the top drawer. Curious, she lifted the cushion and there she was. The other girl. But she didn't know that then. She thought she'd found a photograph of herself.

It was a newspaper cutting, a girl in clothes she didn't remember wearing, a woman she didn't recognise, and above the photograph the headline 'Pot-induced madness, a modern mother's shameless antics'. And she thought, I don't remember this. But the woman wasn't her mother. And her mother wasn't modern. And, well, pot. She couldn't see her mother smoking pot. Her mother wouldn't let people smoke normal cigarettes in the house, she'd make them stand on the patio while she fussed around inside, pretending not to mind that they preferred their filthy vice to her company.

She wasn't sure what to do. The cutting had been hidden, so there had to be something wrong about it. But it had been worth keeping, and running the risk of its being discovered. She remembered being told by someone – Ludovico maybe, because this was the sort of clever-clever comment he would make – that the things people hide are the things they most want to be found. Maybe her mother had wanted her to find this. She sat on the bed and looked at herself, she lost all track of time, trying to understand what she'd discovered. She stared at herself in the photo and wondered if she'd been drugged and kidnapped, and that was how she'd ended up in the paper, but she didn't look as if she'd been kidnapped, although she might have been drugged, and you don't take a kidnapped child to what looked like a rock festival. She had a big smile on her face and daisies in her hair. She looked like a hippie and so did the woman with her, the woman the paper said was her mother, and she supposed that's why the paper – the *Sunday Express*, it had the name at the bottom edge, and part of the date – had thought she was using pot. She looked maybe nine or ten in the photograph, but she was hopeless with ages. Later, when she knew, she told her earlier self sternly that she had to stop thinking 'I' when she thought about the photograph because it wasn't her at all. It was someone else. Someone she didn't know.

It was the summer after her father died, and they were in England, and it was too hot to bear without a swimming pool or the sea. Before his death, they spent the summers in Italy, with Ludovico and his family in their villa in Liguria. It was modern and not very nice, and there were mosquitoes, but it was only a few minutes from the sea and the two families had met up there every August for as long as she could remember, long sun-baked summers, with everyone except Ludovico speaking Italian all around her so that she'd found herself learning it without even trying. They made fun of her when she answered them back in their own language, all those skinny boys and girls, tanned so dark they looked like Turks, the girls in tiny costumes she wished her mother would let her wear, constantly rubbing oils into their skins, the boys playing football along the edge of the beach until someone's mother told them to stop. She was almost as dark as they were by the end of the summer, and then it was the girls at school who made fun of her, but that was envy, because their parents hadn't taken them anywhere decent. And the food, fruit that tasted of fruit, the first time she'd eaten real fish with a head and tail on it, the glass of cold white wine she'd be given as though it were the most natural thing in the world for a thirteen-year-old girl to drink wine with her dinner. And Ludo always there to defend her when she needed to be defended, to peel her prickly pear with a tiny penknife he carried around with him so she didn't get the hair-like prickles in her fingers, to hold her by the waist as she learnt to swim, like a friend and then like a brother and then, one summer, more than a brother. But that hadn't lasted long, those moments — no more than three or four — when no one knew where they'd gone, when they'd sneaked away from the others to hide inside a beach cabin, giggling at first and then kissing, with Ludo's hands on her hard new breasts. And then Ludo's father had spoken to him, and her mother had spoken to her, and then the summer was over, and the summer after that a boy she'd never seen before that year had promised he would love her for ever if she let him put his penis inside her, and so she had, glad that she'd got that over with. She couldn't remember where Ludo had been, but she remembered wishing it had been him. Perhaps he'd had another girl that summer. He'd have been at university by then, maybe already in the States. She'd see him talking to their fathers sometimes, like an equal, about money and politics, because that was all their fathers cared about, and mostly it was money. Money was what bound them together, her family and Ludovico's. It was all about money in the end, but money was men's business; the women of the house had no part in it. His mother was always in the kitchen, shouting at the Filipino woman who looked after the villa with her husband.

Her mother would be reading a book in the shade somewhere, her white-gloved hands holding the book up close to her face because she didn't want to be seen in glasses, until the book fell to her lap and she slept, her mouth half open, and Fiona would find her when she came back up from the beach and take the book out of her hands and close it. And then Ludo would see her and walk across to talk to her and she'd tell him what she'd been doing that day, but not a word about the boy. Not that. Not a word about what the boy had done.

That summer, though, when she found the cutting, she was at home in England and nothing she owned was cool enough or light enough and she had no one to talk to. She hadn't understood why they shouldn't go to Italy, even if Daddy had died. She lay on the lawn, on a beach towel in a new bikini until she glistened with sweat. She missed Ludo, and the sea. She wondered if the other boy would be there, and what she might have done if he had been. It was her mother's decision, she'd told Fiona that it was time to free themselves of Ludo's family while they could. They didn't need to maintain a friendship with one of her father's employees, she'd said, her lip curling at the word friendship, as though it were something infinitely compromised. She said she didn't trust him, he would stab them in the back as soon as look at them now that Daddy was gone. Fair-weather friends, she said when Fiona insisted, quite the worst kind of people. Which was her way of saying foreigners. Fiona wondered if a letter addressed to the villa would reach Ludovico, but never wrote. She didn't know what to say, other than that her father was dead and she was unhappy, and he would already know that. Besides, she thought, if Ludo cared he would write to her.

What made it worse was that all her friends had gone somewhere nice for the summer and she hadn't been invited because her father was dead and no one knew what to say or do. She was stuck in the house with Mummy, who just kept bursting into tears, and closing curtains to keep the heat out. She mooched from room to room, lay around in the garden pretending to read a magazine, her transistor radio beside her head until she couldn't take another note of Abba and Kiki Dee, and stomped back into the house to snap at her mother and her mother's awful friends when they asked her how she was. She began to keep a diary. 'I do love her in my way,' she wrote, 'and I suppose she loves me in <u>her</u> way, although I don't know what that is, and I never have. She's always shown me off to other people as though she's got nothing else to be proud of but her daughter. Maybe she hasn't. She hasn't done anything at all with her life, really. She hasn't <u>lived</u>. She's been pampered from start to finish, or at least from the day she hooked Daddy, and so have I, I suppose. I'm spoilt. And I wish I wasn't. It's not my fault. I wish I was someone else.' And then she padlocked the diary with the key provided, and put it away in a drawer. Because Fiona had secrets as well.

She took the cutting into town the next day and found a shop that made photocopies. The youth in the shop, a year or two older than she was, looked at the photograph and then at her. 'You were really pretty,' he said, then added, with a hopeful grin, 'And you still are.' She didn't answer. At home, she put the original cutting back where she had found it. The copy she slipped into her diary, snapped shut the tiny padlock and put it away again. She tried not to think about it any more, but the girl with her crown of daisies kept coming back into her mind. Is it me? she thought, and if it isn't me, who is it? And if it is me, why can't I remember?

A few days before she was due back at school, she asked her

mother if she'd ever been taken to a rock concert. Her mother was reading a novel and didn't answer. Fiona coughed, then asked again, her tone more insistent. Her mother looked up from her book.

'A rock concert? Who on earth do you think would take you to a rock concert?'

Fiona shrugged. 'I don't know.'

'Well, if you don't know,' her mother said, returning to her book, and Fiona couldn't think what else to say.

The following day, during breakfast, her mother asked Fiona if she'd been rooting around in her drawers. Fiona giggled.

'Don't be vulgar,' her mother snapped.

'Well,' said Fiona, 'you should choose your words more carefully.'

Her mother sighed. 'You've been touching things in my dressing table, haven't you?'

Fiona shook her head.

'All right,' said her mother, detaching a sliver of grapefruit from its skin. 'But be sure your lies will find you out.'

'I'll be sure if you will,' said Fiona.

'What do you mean by that?'

Fiona shrugged again, her default reaction this summer. 'Nothing.'

'I'll be glad when you're back at school, young lady.'

'So will I,' said Fiona. She buttered a piece of toast, then threw it down on her plate with a gesture of disgust. 'I've had a hateful summer.'

'It hasn't been that much fun for me either,' her mother said. 'Having you moping around the house all day. I told you I would have been happy to have a friend of yours staying. You must have some friends who'd love to visit, surely. We have such a pretty village.'

'We could have been in Italy. We could have had a swim. I'm boiling.'

Her mother put down her spoon with an irritated gesture. 'I don't intend to have this conversation again.'

'And what you want is all that counts, I suppose.'

'As long as you're in my house, yes.'

'Well, I wish I wasn't.'

'You've made that perfectly clear,' her mother said. 'And now perhaps you'd like to answer my question.'

Fiona stood up, pushing her chair back as petulantly as she could manage. 'What question?'

'Good heavens, Fiona. Do you never listen?' Her mother rarely raised her voice, which explained the shrillness.

Fiona smiled. She'd managed to infuriate her. 'I've already told you,' she said. 'I've got better things to do than root around in your smelly old drawers.'

'And now you're just showing off.'

'Showing off?' Fiona laughed. 'I'm sixteen, for God's sake, not five.'

Her mother threw her napkin onto the table.

'Get out of my sight, before I do something I'll regret.'

'Like having me in the first place, I suppose,' said Fiona, under her breath. She walked towards the door.

'Wait a minute.'

Fiona turned to see her mother staring at her, the colour drained from her skin. In this mood her face grew tight and hard. 'What did you say?'

'You've never wanted me. Not the way Daddy did.'

'How can you say that?'

'Because it's true.'

'I think you'd better go to your room.'

Fiona ignored this, and left the house, slamming the door

behind her. She stood on the step, beneath what her mother always called, absurdly, the Doric portico, and stared down the drive towards the road that would take her into the world, where she knew no one and had no one, and cared for no one. 'I miss you, Daddy,' she said, listening to herself as she spoke, hearing the tremor in her voice, 'I miss you so much,' and then, turning back to face the door, louder now, hoping that she would be heard, she said, 'And I hate you. I hate you with all my heart. You're not my mother. I wish you were dead.'

CHAPTER THREE

Fiona tucked the photocopied cutting into her diary and, back at school, put it out of her mind. She was in the sixth form, in a bedroom with only one other girl. Jennifer had been thrown out of her previous school after a prefect caught her smoking a cigar in a potting shed with – in her words – the yummiest of the school's gardeners; arriving at Fiona's school, she trailed an aura of glamour.

The two girls became inseparable. Fiona had never been popular and Jennifer's reputation provided another sort of isolation. They studied together or pretended to, sitting side by side in the school library until another girl complained that their constant whispering and giggling distracted her and they were made to sit at separate tables, after which they began to take their textbooks into the patch of unkempt lawn behind the tennis courts, where one of them would make daisy chains while the other read pages of R. H. Tawney in a bored monotone. They ate side by side in hall, they spent their free time in each other's company, leaving the grounds of the school whenever the chance arose to do so, without explaining why. Life is too short for obedience and explanation, Jennifer liked to say, and Fiona was thrilled. They had pet names for each other – Fifi and Jojo, like performing seals – and vowed they would never use them in front of any other girl, a vow they kept until the end. One night, they kissed with their tongues poking into each other's mouths, but decided they preferred the real thing. Boys.

There was a dearth of boys. They tried to make up for their absence by talking about what they had done, and what they would do if they had the chance. What Fiona had done behind the *pedalò* was adjusted to suit her audience, the boy who had fucked her reclothed in the lovelier and more adult flesh of Ludovico. She added a touch of passion and several repeat performances, and was thrilled when she saw Jennifer's face, its flush of eagerness, the bareness of its jealousy. The other girl leant forward, voice lowered, determined not to be outdone. Her gardener, she said, had touched both breasts and had wanted to go all the way, and she had said no, because she'd expected to get a second chance, and she would have done if that bitch of a prefect hadn't reported her, and she would have said yes, which she would have said the first time if she had only known. He looked like David Essex, she told Fiona, repeating the name in a breathless way. The gardeners in Fiona's school – all of them, at the very least, in their thirties – were hopeless, she said. The nearest place with fanciable boys was the nearby town, the dead-and-barely-alive hole the school was attached to, a resting place for pensioners before they were called to their eternal home.

There were two types of boys in town, the ones from the equivalent school to theirs, who were brothers and cousins or knew brothers and cousins, and couldn't be trusted. And then there were the local boys, who couldn't be trusted either, although for more exciting reasons. They would gather outside Woolworth's and half sneer, half whistle as the girls walked past, then follow them in and stare while the girls lounged around the pick 'n' mix counter. Sometimes, a bolder boy would offer a girl a cigarette, which would always be refused, although there were ways of refusing, some of which were barely refusal at all. Outside,

26

they separated, like oil and vinegar, the girls heading off to the school, the boys regrouping for the next skirmish. Occasionally, a girl would hang around to talk to one of the boys, then walk down the street a little way, until they could turn into the lane behind the bins. When asked what had happened, she would shrug and say, oh nothing, but no one believed her. She was envied and condemned, in ratios determined by her popularity and whether the boy was considered worth it. Spots were a no-no, as was greasy hair. Tall was good, blue eyes were better than brown, clean teeth were a definite plus. Jennifer disappeared one afternoon for almost twenty minutes with a boy she'd singled out the week before, older and more soberly dressed than most. When she came back, she had a love bite just high enough to be seen with her collar turned down, and chapped red lips. I touched his thing, she whispered to Fiona that night, when they were both in bed and the lights were off. Fiona lay in the dark and wondered about Ludo, and his thing, and what her breasts must have felt like when he touched them, and if he would touch them again if he had the chance. And she hated her mother all over again.

'You need to meet my brother,' Jennifer said.

'You don't know how lucky you are. I'm stuck with my mother and that's it. She's my entire bloody family now that Daddy's dead. It's like some awful nightmare.'

'Not all families are perfect,' said Jennifer consolingly. 'Mine isn't either.'

'At least you've got someone to talk to.'

'Patrick? My brother? I don't talk to Patrick.'

Fiona flicked ash from her cigarette. They were crouched on their haunches behind the far wall of the kitchen garden, shivering, their blazers buttoned up, scarves knotted around their necks. Their bare knees, almost touching, looked vast and blue. It was late November and they shouldn't have been outside the main building, but they wouldn't be missed. They never were, unless a prefect or one of the more spiteful teachers had decided to make their life even more unliveable than it already was.

'I think he'd like you,' said Jennifer, appraising Fiona in a swift, unnerving way. 'I'm sure he would. You're just his type. You know, pretty.' She took a long slow drag on her cigarette, blew the smoke out in a perfect circle, her own breath cloudlike in the cold. 'You know what I'm going to do?' she said, as the circle broke into ragged scraps. 'I'm going to fix you two up.'

Fiona was too surprised to answer.

'He'll be home for Christmas. Come and stay with me for a few days and bingo, he's yours.'

'What if I'm not interested?'

Jennifer grinned. 'Oh, you'll be interested. He's gorgeous. I had a friend at my old school who was totally in love with him. And she'd only seen a photograph. He's even better in real life. He's got this dishy hair.' She mimed a fringe with her free hand, then swept it back. 'Mummy says he'll break every girl's heart when he goes up next year. He's got a scholarship to Balliol to read economics. He wants to be a banker, or something.'

'Mothers always say stuff like that,' said Fiona.

'Is that what your mother says about you?'

Fiona shrugged. 'Normal mothers. My mother doesn't count.'

'So she won't mind if you come for Christmas?'

'What she minds doesn't matter.' Fiona straightened up, her hand on Jennifer's shoulder to steady herself, grinding her cigarette butt into the frost-hard earth with determination, as though it was her mother's face. 'Not now Daddy's dead. It's what I want that counts.'

'So you'll ask her?'

Fiona shrugged again, her heart beating. 'Yes,' she said. She could have cried, she was so excited and so angry. 'If you're sure.'

Her mother would have none of it.

'Don't be silly. Christmas is a time for the family,' she said.

'What family?' said Fiona. She was in a telephone kiosk in the town. She had a pile of coins ready to be inserted, and one glove off so that she wouldn't drop any.

'I'm not prepared to listen to this nonsense.'

'I haven't had a family since Daddy died.'

'What a hurtful thing to say.'

'It's true. You know it's true.'

'I don't know anything of the sort.'

'You don't want me.'

'Of course I want you. You're my daughter.'

'I don't belong to you.'

'Actually, young lady, you do. Until you're eighteen.'

'I hate you. I wish I'd never been born.'

'And I wish I—'

'What? What do you wish?'

There was a long pause. Fiona imagined her mother, struck to the floor by grief, and felt a thrill of power.

'You wish I'd never been born, don't you?'

Her mother sighed. 'Oh Fiona, can't we just talk about this calmly?'

'What do you wish?'

'I wish you'd be reasonable, that's what I wish. Honestly. You're so like your father sometimes.'

'Is that why you hate me? Because you hated him too?'

'For heaven's sake, Fiona,' she said, her tone exasperated. 'Will you just calm down for a moment and listen to me? Of course I didn't hate your father. And I don't hate you. How can you say

such a thing? I love you. You're my only daughter and I love you.'
She said these last words slowly, with great care, as if afraid she
might be misunderstood.

'So you expect me to spend the whole Christmas holiday
cooped up in that house with you?'

'That house, as you put it, is your home, Fiona.'

'Well, I don't want it. You can bloody well keep it.'

'You will not use that kind of language with me, young lady. I
don't care how angry you are, I will not put up with it.'

Fiona pushed another 10p into the slot.

'You don't have any choice,' she said. 'Not if I come back for
Christmas. You'll have to listen to it for three whole weeks.' She
put the phone down. She hit the box with the heel of her hand,
said 'Fuck, fuck,' then headed back to school.

Jennifer found her sitting cross-legged on her bed, scribbling
in her diary, muttering to herself as she wrote. She didn't interrupt
her scribbling or look up until Jennifer asked her what she was
writing about. 'My fucking mother,' she said. 'She says I've got to
spend Christmas with her.'

'I thought what she wanted didn't matter,' said Jennifer.

'Don't you start.' She threw her pencil across the room,
followed by the diary. It hit the wall, and a folded sheet of paper
fell out. Jennifer picked it up,

'What's this?' she said, unfolding it before Fiona could stop
her. Jennifer looked at the photograph and then at Fiona. 'What
were you doing at a rock gig?'

'That can't be me.'

'Don't be silly. It's the spitting image of you.'

Fiona uncrossed her legs and let them dangle from the side
of the bed. She watched her feet swing backwards and forwards.

'So who's that woman with me? Because she certainly isn't my mother.'

Jennifer read the few sentences that remained of the article. 'I wonder what the rest of it says.'

'I don't know.'

'We could always find out.'

Fiona looked up. 'How?'

'Libraries, silly. That's what they're for. Look,' she said, holding it out, 'it's got the name of the paper and a bit of the date. It shouldn't be that difficult.' She folded the photocopy up and slid it into her skirt pocket. 'This might be just what we need,' she said. 'You'll see.'

CHAPTER FOUR

The woman at the town library hadn't wanted to let them use the apparatus, as she called it, but Jennifer had told her they were doing research for one of the school governors, a local benefactress, and the librarian had acquiesced, stepping away from the table with a truncated curtsey while Fiona smirked at Jennifer behind her back. For Fiona, all women of a certain age had become her mother, and so were worthy of contempt. Now she watched Jennifer pull out the glass plates and slip the microfiche into the space between, turning the knob on the reader as page after page passed in front of their eyes.

'Got it!' said Jennifer. Fiona craned in to read. Yes, there it was. The girl half asleep and sliding off the woman's lap. The headline. 'Pot-induced madness, a modern mother's shameless antics.' How badly she wanted the woman to be her mother, how badly she wanted to be the girl with her ragged crown of daisies. She read on.

> Among the many thousands of Rolling Stones fans at last week's free concert in Hyde Park, our reporter came across this young woman, with her nine-year-old daughter, Maddy. When asked whether she thought a rock concert was a suitable place for such a young girl, the woman, Heather Thomsett,

30, laughed and blew smoke from her reefer into the air. 'The music's great,' she told our reporter in a notably slurred voice, 'the sun's shining. What could be better for a growing girl?' Her daughter, feet bare and clearly in need of a wash, also appeared to be under the influence of the allegedly 'soft' drug, and did not respond to questions, although she did reply when asked her age. When it was pointed out to Miss Thomsett, who claimed to be 'happily not married', that her behaviour was not only immoral but also illegal, she denied that her reefer contained cannabis, claiming that the substance inside it was a form of medicine used by Chinese 'doctors' to relax muscles, and that her daughter was perfectly healthy and a free spirit, as she was. She added that her generation was a reaction against the previous one, which had done nothing but fight a 'useless' war, and that what the world now needed was peace and love. Unfortunately, Miss Thomsett was not the only 'free spirit' neglecting her duty as the mother of an impressionable child in order to indulge in the hedonistic pleasures of illegal drug use and over-amplified music. Explicit sexual activity was also observed among the crowd, possibly encouraged by the presence of Mr Jagger's new fiancée, Miss Marsha Hunt, in white leather hot pants …

Jennifer giggled, but Fiona hushed her. She took a notebook out of her pocket and wrote down the names and ages. Heather Thomsett, thirty. Maddy Thomsett, nine. The concert was in 1969, which would make Heather thirty-seven and Maddy sixteen now. Her own mother was forty-something, but she, like

Maddy, was sixteen. So Heather was twenty-one when Maddy was born, while her own mother was, what, thirty? None of it made sense. Cousins. Maybe they were cousins. How would that work? Her mother would be Heather's elder sister and they hated each other because Heather was a free spirit and her mother was a killjoy and the kiss of death. But Heather looked nothing like her mother. Her mother was washed out and dried up, skinny, pallid, with little patches of rouge that only made her look worse. She had thin lips and a beaky nose and colourless hair. Heather was tanned, no make-up to speak of, firm round breasts in a T-shirt, no bra, thick hair hanging free. How could they possibly be related? That left her father. Her father had a sister he'd never accepted? She had an aunt she'd never been allowed to know? She had always felt that a sister had been denied her, and now here was a cousin her own age, so like her they might have been twins and she had never been told. And her father had known, and played along. She would never forgive him. She would never forgive her mother.

'Well?' Jennifer said.

'She's me, isn't she?' Fiona pushed her chair back.

'But she can't be, Fifi,' said Jennifer, doubtful. 'You aren't called Maddy. Your mother doesn't go around with her nipples poking through her top. It's a coincidence.'

'A miracle,' said Fiona.

'It's an odd sort of miracle.'

Fiona turned round, her expression urgent. 'How do I find out who this woman is?' she said. 'Heather Thomsett. I mean, she must be somewhere. She must know something.'

'I don't know,' said Jennifer. 'But I'll tell you who could find out.'

'Who?'

'My brother. Patrick. He's a genius at finding things out.'

The following morning, a letter arrived from Fiona's mother. Fiona waited until she and Jennifer were alone, then sat on the bed, with Jennifer beside her, so that they could read it together.

My dearest Fiona

I am so sorry we never seem to see eye to eye on anything these days. We seem to do nothing but argue and I must admit that it is often hard for me to forgive you for many of the hurtful things you say to me, which I do not believe I deserve. But our last telephone conversation has made me realise how much you must be missing Daddy. I miss him too, of course, I was his wife and loved him very much, but I know that you had a special bond and I know that I can never compensate for the loss of that. However, I am your mother and I love you too, and I want you to remember that always, whatever might happen, even when we disagree.

I have thought a great deal about your wish to spend Christmas with your new friend and her family, and I can quite understand why you might wish to pass some of your holiday away from home, although it is painful for me to say this. I appreciate that it can be lonely here, where you have no real friends, and the only people you see are middle-aged women. You see, I do understand how you feel, although I must say that I wish you felt differently and that you wanted to keep your mother company. But enough of that. What I want to ask you now is that you try to make the same effort to understand me. I wonder if we can reach a compromise, Fiona. I am prepared to let you spend a week with your new friend, but I insist that we spend the few days of the Christmas period together. I think I have a right to expect that from you, as your mother. I promise you that I will make every effort to ensure that those days are festive. Christmas, my dear, is for the family, and you are all the family I have. Please think about my proposal and let me know.

Your loving Mummy

'She doesn't say what happens if you don't agree,' said Jennifer. 'And why does she keep calling me your "new" friend? It makes us sound like ten-year-olds.'

'What do you think I should do?'

'What do you want to do?'

'I don't know.'

'So don't do anything. Let her stew for a bit.' Jennifer read through the letter again. 'It's just like a business letter, isn't it? I can never compensate for the loss. I am prepared to let you spend. Does she always write like that?'

'She used to be Daddy's secretary,' Fiona said. 'She's never shaken it off. I'm surprised she doesn't put "Yours sincerely" at the bottom.' She sighed. 'Oh my God, I hate her. I just wish she'd leave me alone.'

Jennifer put the letter back in the envelope. They sat there in silence for a few moments before she continued. 'Can I ask you something?'

'Of course you can,' said Fiona warily.

'Why do you hate her so much?'

'What do you mean?'

'I mean, it's normal not to get on with your parents. Who does? But you *hate* her.'

'I don't know.' Fiona stood up, took the envelope from Jennifer's hand and threw it on the bed. 'I don't want to talk about it.'

Jennifer raised both hands. 'All right,' she said. 'Not another word.' She grinned. 'So shall I tell Mum you'll be coming?'

Fiona sank back onto the bed.

'I suppose it wouldn't hurt to do what she wants,' she said. 'Just this once.'

'A week, then? Or eight days?'

Fiona laughed. 'Eight days, of course!'

Why did Fiona hate her mother so much? She didn't know. She couldn't remember not hating her, or loving her, which came to the same thing. It was what you did with parents, you loved them or you hated them, there was no middle ground. She couldn't remember being held, or cuddled, when she was little, or having her cardigan buttoned up or her sandals buckled. She couldn't remember having her hand gripped as she crossed the road, or being lifted across some obstacle, or being comforted because she had fallen over and grazed her knee. She had seen other mothers kissing their children's scratches and grazes and making them better. Had her mother shown her love like this? If she had it had left no trace.

When Fiona tried to recall her childhood it was as though she'd been brought up by a stranger, or someone employed to do it, a nanny, an au pair. Her father, yes, her father had picked her up and thrown her in the air and made her squeal with fright and joy all mixed up together, and brought her presents when he came home from work or travelling, but her father had been away so often. She remembered him tucking her in and telling her she was his favourite girl, and when she was lying in the darkness of her bedroom she'd wondered how many other girls he had, and then dismissed the thought. Sometimes he'd come back and she'd pretend to be asleep until he'd gone and then wish she hadn't, wish she'd told him how much she loved him. But she couldn't remember her mother coming back into the bedroom after the light had been turned out, or sitting on the edge of her bed, or stroking her hair from her face. Maybe no one could, but how could she ask without seeming stupid? She couldn't even ask Jennifer – Jennifer would laugh, or feel sorry for her, which would be worse. She couldn't bear to be pitied because her mother had been disappointed in her. She would never forget one afternoon, she couldn't have been more than five or six, when Rosie, the cleaning woman, had given her a basinful of dripping just-washed handkerchiefs and helped her rig up a line between two garden chairs. You're a good little girl, Rosie had said, and had given her a bag full of clothes pegs. Now you peg up these hankies, my love, she'd said and Fiona remembered still how pleased and proud she'd felt as she took each handkerchief from the basin and gave it a shake, watching the drops of water burst on the flagstones, and then pegged one corner to the line. That's it, Rosie had said, as she stretched the handkerchief out to get rid of the creases, and pegged the other corner. Rosie had shown her how to use one peg for two handkerchiefs, and she'd loved that. And then her mother had arrived and slapped the peg bag from her hand so hard the skin was still smarting when she went to bed, or that was how she remembered it. What on earth do you think you're doing? her mother had said, and she wasn't sure if the anger was directed at her, or at Rosie, or at them both. We don't pay people to have you hang out the washing, she'd said, and she'd seized Fiona by the upper arm and pulled her back into the house. Fiona still remembered turning to see Rosie's face and the expression on it, of shock and hatred and contempt.

None of it for her, no sympathy, no pity, no attempt at defence; her mother had deprived her of that.

What made it worse was that Ludovico's mother had hugged her and held her face in her hands, covering her cheeks with big wet kisses and her skin with special creams against the sun, telling her how lovely she was and how the boys would never leave her alone. Call me Luisa, she'd told Fiona one summer, years ago now, but Fiona, shy, had shaken her head. *Va bene, chiamami Mamma.* Call me Mamma. She'd told her own mother how sweet Ludo's mother always was with her, and her own mother had sniffed and said, Well, what do you expect? She's Italian. They're so demonstrative. She hadn't understood what demonstrative meant until Ludovico had told her. It means you don't hide your feelings, he said, like English people do. So that was it, she'd thought. Her mother must have hidden the love she felt for her. But why? Was that Fiona's fault? Did she think someone else might steal it? But who would want it, other than Fiona? Who else would have any use for it?

She could imagine the sort of love her mother might offer, some dried-out powdery husk from the bottom of the sack, weighed and measured out because too much of it might make them both ill, or be common, or not be given back in kind, a love that was cramped and suffocated and deprived of light. She'd never felt more alone than she did when she was with her mother. She'd catch her lifting her head from her book to look at Fiona with a sort of bemusement, as though she wasn't sure whose property this odd, mysterious girl might be. If Fiona smiled, her mother would give a little shake of the head, as though she'd been thinking about something else, and then smile back, but Fiona knew when her mother was lying. She'd seen her do it to her father, small lies that served no other purpose than briefly to deceive, as far as Fiona could see. White lies, her mother might have said if she'd been challenged, but they weren't white, they were colourless, invisible, useless. Watching her mother: that was how Fiona had learnt to lie.

CHAPTER FIVE

Patrick met them at the station. He was standing beside a dark-blue Range Rover, reading a book. He seized Jennifer's bag with his free hand, swung it into the boot, then held out the same hand towards Fiona. Fiona took it, immediately realised her mistake and, blushing, gave him her bag. He smiled.

'You're Fiona, right? Jennifer's new best friend?'

She nodded, watching him throw her bag into the car beside Jennifer's, not sure if she liked him. She hadn't liked the way he said 'new', as though she might be replaced by an improved model before too long. Her mother had done that too. She inspected him as he closed the back of the car and locked it. He was good-looking, although not in the way she'd imagined. She'd been promised tall, but he wasn't much taller than Fiona. He was slim, as far as she could tell, beneath a duffel coat and a cable-knit sweater. His jeans looked new, his shoes as highly polished as the car. Did he want to make a good impression on her, she wondered. If he did, he hadn't quite succeeded. Even his smile had been a touch too sardonic for her liking.

'Who else would she be?' Jennifer shifted the passenger seat forward to let Fiona pass. 'You don't mind getting in the back, do you?' she said. 'It's probably safer. He's only just got his licence. He'll probably kill us all wherever we sit.'

'O ye of little faith,' he said. Inside the car, he turned round and gave her the book he'd been holding – *The Day of the Jackal* by Frederick Forsyth – then looked at her again, more appraisingly. 'I don't suppose you have to put up with a baby sister, do you?'

'Or a big brother,' said Jennifer. 'She's lucky.'

'I left Mum decorating the tree,' he said, starting the car. 'It looked like Miss Havisham's wedding cake when I left the house. God only knows the state it's in by now.' He glanced into the mirror, caught Fiona's eye. 'Perhaps you can help her tone it down.'

'I thought Miss Havisham's wedding cake was rotten,' said Jennifer. She shuddered. 'With spiders crawling all over it.'

'Don't be so literal.' He turned his head to look at Fiona directly. 'Is she like this at school, correcting people all the time? She must be a real bore.'

Jennifer thumped his arm, then lit a cigarette. 'The last one,' she said.

'You can put that out right now,' Patrick said. 'You know little sisters aren't allowed to smoke at home.'

'I'm not at home,' she said. 'Not yet anyway.'

'Well, think of Dad's second-best car as an extension of home.'

'See what I mean?' She passed the cigarette back to Fiona, who took it. 'Nag, nag, nag. He's worse than a parent.'

'*In loco parentis*. I do my best,' he said. 'You could at least open the window.'

She shrugged. 'I suppose I could,' she said, defiant. A moment later, she wound her window halfway down. 'Tell me if you get cold,' she said to Fiona.

'We're nearly there,' Patrick said. 'Don't worry.'

Fiona said nothing. She was curled up in the back of the car, wishing she were somewhere else. The intimacy of their bickering, even the irritation in it, left no space for her. This is what family is, she thought. It reminded her of Ludo, and his mother, and the friends she had made in Italy, and how she had come to depend on them for what her own mother and father had failed to give her. A brother, a sister; it didn't matter which. An ally, she supposed. She'd read somewhere that twins were believed to share a soul. There was a girl at school, Antonia, who had a twin brother and she claimed she could tell when he felt sick because she would feel sick too. I know when he's unhappy, she said, it's like a cloud inside me. Fiona didn't believe in souls, but how wonderful it would be to share a soul, to have that bond with someone, better than love, because love can fade or turn into hate; to have something that would always be there, that no human agency could break.

Patrick pulled up outside a gate set into a high red brick wall. 'Here we are,' he said. 'Home sweet home.'

The gravel drive was flanked by a paved area. A flight of steps led up to the front door, stone vases overflowing with ivy at the far ends of each step. Fiona could see her breath as she watched Patrick take their bags from the boot. Jennifer was blowing into her hands. 'It's freezing out here,' she said. Fiona was about to pick up her bag when the front door opened and a woman hurried down the steps.

'Don't bother with that,' she said, pulling her cardigan around her. She had an unlit cigarette in one hand. 'Patrick will look after the luggage.' She turned to look at him with a smile. 'Won't you, dear?'

'I have to put the car in the garage,' he said.

'The car can wait a few minutes,' the woman said. She opened her arms. 'Fiona,' she said. Fiona stepped forward, embarrassed. She tried to imagine her own mother greeting someone like this.

'I'm here too, Mummy,' said Jennifer.

'Of course you are, my dear. I'm just so pleased you've brought someone home with you.' She rested her hands on Fiona's shoulders. 'You've been so kind to help Jennifer settle into her new school. I don't know what she'd have done without you.'

'She'd have been fine,' said Jennifer. 'She isn't completely useless.'

'Take no notice.' The woman gave Fiona an encouraging squeeze. 'Promise me you'll take no notice of my daughter.'

Fiona nodded, smiled. 'Hello, Mrs Appleton.'

'No need to be so formal, my dear. You must call me Ruth.'

'Can I call you Ruth too?' said Jennifer.

'You can stop pretending to be jealous,' said Ruth, 'and help Patrick take the bags into the house.'

Jennifer took her round, opening and closing doors in a bored, dismissive way, taking the stairs two steps at a time. The house was large, larger than Fiona's although it felt smaller. It was so much busier, there were so many signs of life. Fiona wanted to slow her friend down, ask questions, pick up books and flick through them, examine ornaments and ask where they were bought. There was an elephant's foot with umbrellas in it. Jennifer caught her looking at it. 'Vile, isn't it?' she said, and Fiona supposed it was, but her heart was filled with something that wasn't envy; it was closer to wistfulness, a nostalgia for what might have been. Her own house felt like a showroom, a furniture store pretending to be a home. The dining room had the grandest bay window Fiona had ever seen, a curved wall made entirely of windows that opened onto the garden, and a chandelier the size of a pram. On the first floor were half a dozen bedrooms and two bathrooms, both with bidets, Fiona noticed, with a stabbing ache of nostalgia for Italy. On the second floor, the polished wood of the landing pale gold beneath an enormous skylight, Jennifer turned down a corridor and opened a door set apart from those of the other rooms. 'Come on,' she said. She led Fiona down a short flight of steps into a room with a dormer window and sloping ceilings, the smallest room so far, empty apart from a bed and a desk, its only decoration a row of posters on the walls. Genesis. Barclay James Harvest. 'This is my room,' Jennifer said, enthusiastic for the first time. 'My kingdom.'

Fiona picked up a troll from a shelf near the bed, stroked its shock of orange hair. 'I didn't know you were into progressive stuff,' she said, pointing at the posters.

Jennifer nodded, but showed no sign of wanting to talk about music. She sat down on the bed and patted the space beside her. 'This is where I hide,' she said.

'Your mother's nice,' said Fiona, sitting down, still holding the troll.

'She's a bit full-on sometimes.' Jennifer sighed. 'She wants everyone to be happy. All the time. It can be very wearying.'

'She was lovely with me.'

'You're new. She's got to win you over.'

'Well, that's better than being treated like a stranger in your own home.'

'Is that really what it's like for you?'

Fiona nodded. She lifted the troll to her mouth and kissed it.

'I'm not sure I want to call her Ruth,' she said. 'It feels a bit weird.'

'Just humour her, all right?'

'All right.'

'And don't forget to tell her how wonderful her Christmas tree is.'

The tree was eight feet tall, overburdened with decorations, dripping with glass balls. An angel stood on the top, a swirl of gold and gauze, like something from the frescoed ceiling of a church.

The tree at Fiona's house would be a mean-spirited costive affair, a string of lights. Her mother would have decorated it grudgingly, annoyed that Fiona wasn't there to help. She'd agreed, after some negotiation, to let Fiona stay with Jennifer for eight days, after which a car would be sent to bring her home. Fiona suspected the car was intended to impress Jennifer's family, and wondered if it would. She hoped not. She wanted them to despise her mother as much as she did.

'Dreadful, isn't it?' said Patrick.

She turned. He was standing in the kitchen doorway. He had taken off his duffel coat and sweater and looked surprisingly fragile in a checked cotton shirt. He had a glass of wine in one hand and a sausage in the other. Grinning, he held them in the air like trophies. 'See anything you fancy?' he said.

'Behave yourself,' said Jennifer from the stairs. Fiona ignored her.

'Yes,' she said, surprising herself. 'I do.'

He grinned at Jennifer. 'Ham sandwich all right?'

'That sounds fine,' Fiona said.

In the kitchen, she watched him slice and butter bread, liking the way he carved neat slivers of ham off the joint and laid them on the bread so that even the tiniest part of it was covered. She enjoyed the attention he gave to it, as though he were devoting himself not to the sandwich, but to her. At the same time there was something about his concentration, a manic edge to it, that made her nervous. When he asked her if she wanted it with mustard, she shook her head. 'I would have given you a sausage,' he said, and she wasn't sure what he meant, 'but that was the last one.' She wondered what Jennifer had said about her. She had been stupid to rise to the bait. Did she fancy Patrick? Is that what he'd meant? She'd thought so at the time, but now she wasn't sure.

'Come and keep me company,' he said, when the sandwich

was on a plate. 'Get some milk or something to drink from the fridge, if you want.' He nodded towards a door on the other side of the corridor. 'I'm in there.'

She followed him into a sitting room: chintz-covered armchairs around a low table, overloaded bookshelves on three of the walls, a large television set pushed against the fourth. Patrick threw himself onto an armchair and picked up a paperback from the table.

'Have you read this?' he said.

It was the book she had seen in the car. *The Day of the Jackal*. She shook her head.

'What's it about?' she said, sitting in the armchair nearest his. *Behave yourself.* The words still rang in her ears. What had Jennifer told him? she wondered.

'Oh, political assassination, subversion, hired killers. Forsyth can't write for toffee, but that doesn't matter with books like this. You just read on, it's like watching a film. This one is OK, but it's not as good as *The Dogs of War*. I mean, the story's all right, but it doesn't have anywhere near as much information.'

'What kind of information?'

He looked alive for the first time, unmocking. He really did want to talk about books. She felt herself relax. She picked up a quarter of her sandwich and began to eat.

'*The Dogs of War* is amazing. It's like a handbook on how to stage a *coup d'état*. It's filled with lists of all the things you'd need. It tells you what clothes you have to get hold of. How to smuggle arms, what type of boat to use, how to take over a shell company, how to shift money around from one country to another without it being traced. Banks, loads about banks. It's probably the most useful book I've ever read. I can't wait to put it all into practice.'

She couldn't tell if he was joking. 'So you're planning a *coup d'état*? Is that before or after you go up to Oxford?'

'Who knows? If the price is right. It would depend on that, obviously. I mean, I am a mercenary.'

She picked up the book. 'And this one?'

'Well, it's OK,' he said, 'but the only really useful thing in it is how to get a forged passport. Or rather, a real passport, but with your photo, in someone else's name.'

'Which would be useful if you're planning a *coup d'état*, I imagine.'

'I imagine it would.'

She looked at him. 'You sound as if you mean it.'

He laughed. 'The world has always needed people without principles to do its dirty work. I might be one of those. But I wouldn't tell you if I was, would I? I mean, I might not be telling the truth, whatever I say.'

'Well, obviously,' she said, amused. 'You can't be too careful, can you?'

'Walls have ears,' he said.

'So how do you get a forged passport?' she said.

'Now why would you want to know that?'

'You can never have too many passports,' she said. 'They're like pairs of shoes.'

There was a cough behind her head.

'So this is where you are.'

Jennifer was standing at the door. 'I hope I'm not interrupting anything.'

'No, no,' said Fiona. 'We were talking about books.'

'Oh yes,' said Jennifer. She looked at her brother and then at Fiona, her expression sarcastic. 'Patrick loves to read.'

Later that evening, after dinner during which Jennifer's father, a tall gaunt man with a shaven head, silently ate a plate of pasta dressed with olive oil from a small crystal bottle – Jennifer whispered to Fiona that he had, something wrong with his stomach – and Ruth talked incessantly and played with an unlit cigarette between courses, the adults went into the room with the television and closed the door.

'They've gone to watch *Kojak*,' Jennifer said. 'It's their guilty secret.' She stood up and began to collect the plates, then put them down. 'I'm not doing this by myself,' she said. Fiona began to stand up. 'No, not you. You're a house guest.'

Patrick pushed himself away from the table. 'Come on, house guest,' he said. 'Let's leave her to it.'

Jennifer sighed. 'Just take him away from here,' she said. 'Before I say something I'll regret.'

Patrick had already left the dining room when Jennifer called Fiona back. She turned and saw Jennifer wink. 'Have fun,' she mouthed.

CHAPTER SIX

Patrick took her through a room with paintings on the walls, an antique desk, a leather couch with a chair behind its head, a fireplace piled with logs. 'I need some fresh air,' he said, opening French windows onto the darkness outside. When she hesitated, he took her hand. 'Come on,' he said. 'I don't bite. Not immediately anyway.' He pulled her gently down a short flight of steps and across a path. She felt the softness of grass beneath her feet. 'Come on,' he coaxed. 'I'll take you round the grounds.'

She could have pulled her hand away, but she let herself be led across the grass as it slowly emerged from the darkness, and beyond it to a wall of trees. He speeded up as they walked; he seemed anxious to get somewhere before they were seen. They came to a tall yew hedge and, walking behind it, to an oval swimming pool, black and bottomless as the mouth of a volcano. 'Wait here,' he said, letting go of her hand and hurrying around the pool to a low brick building. He disappeared and then, as if by magic, the pool was bathed with light from below. When he came back, Fiona was shivering.

'Hang on,' he said. He went back into the building and came out with the kind of large plaid blanket people used for picnics. 'Come over here.' He beckoned her across to a wooden swing seat at the edge of the pool. He spread the blanket out and waited for her to sit down, then sat beside her and cocooned them both.

She could feel the heat of him down her left side. 'There, you see,' he said, as if to a child who needed to be reassured. She had no idea what he wanted. She didn't feel excited, although she did find him attractive, in a way. He was almost as old as Ludo, it occurred to her, and she felt an unexpected start of panic as though Ludo himself were there, in the darkness of the trees beyond the pool, watching her.

'Well, you've survived the first evening,' Patrick said.

'It wasn't that bad. Your parents are nice.'

'Nice? Mum never stops talking and Dad never says a word. The secret of a happy marriage apparently.'

'What does he do?'

'Dad? For money? He's a shrink. He talks rich women through their marital crises. Or lets them do it. He just eggs them on.'

'He must know how to listen,' she said.

'I suppose he must. He's had lots of practice. He certainly knows how to keep them coming back for more. That was his study, the room we came through. The one with all the books and the leather couch, à la Sigmund. Impressive, right?'

She nodded. The water in the pool was mint green from the lights set into its base, with an oily sheen. She couldn't imagine wanting to swim in it, couldn't imagine feeling hot. She shivered and pressed against him, pulling the blanket more tightly around her.

'And your father? What about him?'

'He's dead.'

'Oh right,' he said. After a moment, he continued. 'I'm sorry, I mean I knew that he was dead. Jennifer told me.'

'It's all right.'

'I meant, what did he do? Before he died?'

'He worked in business,' she said.

'Business? What kind?'

'I don't really know. Import, export. Italy. He never talked about his work at home. To be honest, he never really talked at all.'

'Fathers don't, do they? Maybe your mother talks too much. Like mine.'

'No, she doesn't talk much either. Not even when Daddy was alive. I hate going home. It's like being in a morgue.'

He fiddled beneath the blanket, momentarily alarming Fiona, and then, to her relief, produced a packet of cigarettes. 'Want one?' he said.

She nodded.

'Jennifer tells me you're an heiress.'

She shook her head.

'Not yet,' she said. 'When I'm twenty-one.'

'And what are you now, sixteen?'

She watched him light two cigarettes and give her one.

'Seventeen. I had my birthday a few days ago.'

'So, four more years to wait,' he said. 'And then?'

'And then what?'

'I mean, how much will you get?'

She took a drag on her cigarette and blew the smoke out slowly. 'Mummy says it's vulgar to talk about money,' she said in her best prim voice.

He looked at her, apparently not sure if she was serious. She liked that, his doubt, but his question unsettled her.

'Well, Mummy's right, I suppose,' he said. 'I'm sorry if I've been vulgar.'

'I'm joking, silly,' she said, suppressing her anxiety beneath a giggle. 'I honestly don't know. Far more than I could ever need or spend, apparently. That's what my mother says. She was furious it wasn't all left to her. She thinks she's been cheated. She thinks I'll fritter it all away.'

'And will you?'

'Of course I won't,' she said. She thought for a moment. 'I'll spend it on things I need. Useful things.'

'And what's the first useful thing you'll spend it on?'

She liked being teased, as though she were an old friend, or a sister. 'Oh, I don't know. A place to live. That's useful, isn't it? Somewhere my mother won't be able to find me. An island, maybe.'

'She'll find you,' said Patrick. 'There is no escape.' His tone was mock horror, a pantomime villain.

'Really?' said Fiona, amused. 'And how will she do that?'

'You can find anyone if you know enough about them,' he said. 'Even their name can be enough.' He tapped the side of his nose and added, with an air of mystery, 'I know people.'

She looked at him. 'In that case, maybe I should get a second passport.'

He nodded. 'Maybe you should.'

Next morning, she woke early, hot beneath too many blankets, the central heating already on. She lay in bed for a while, suddenly shy, and then, because she needed to pee and couldn't hold it any longer, she steeled herself to get up. Jennifer had given her a dressing gown the evening before. She slipped it on and crossed the still-dark landing to the nearest bathroom, then tapped gently on the closed door. When no one answered she went in. It was just after half past six. She locked the door behind her, turned on the light, took off the dressing gown and sat on the loo, looking around her at the bathtub, the bidet, drawings of women in traditional costumes on the wall, a framed diploma, a spider plant dangling in front of the curtained window. When she'd finished peeing, she walked across to the basin and opened the cabinet. Medicines she'd never seen before, most of them for stomach problems, a bottle of aspirins, cotton wool balls, TCP, a small bottle of olive oil, sticking plasters, tubes of antiseptic cream. Vaguely disappointed, she closed the cabinet door and saw herself in the mirror. Her hair was a mess, pushed up where she'd slept on it. I wouldn't like Patrick to see me like this, she thought, and then blushed. 'I'm ridiculous,' she said out loud to her reflection, but she couldn't stop herself smiling. He'd touched her cheek last thing before she went to bed, the slightest touch, but it had been enough to keep her awake and wondering if he would sneak into her room and, if he did, what she would do. But he hadn't come and she'd been relieved, then disappointed that she hadn't been put to the test.

She opened the cabinet again to see if there was a hairbrush or comb, moving the items around. When someone knocked on the door, she jumped and a bottle of pills fell into the basin, and broke. 'Oh fuck,' she said, beneath her breath. 'I'm coming,' she called out, 'wait a minute.' Panicked, she scooped the small blue pills and broken glass up with her hand, starting with pain when a sliver of glass cut deep into the ball of her thumb. 'Oh fuck, fuck, fuck,' she said. She dropped what she had scooped up into a bin beneath the basin and held the cut under the tap. 'Hang on,' she said, shocked at the amount of blood, feeling suddenly faint. She wrapped some loo paper round her hand and was about to open the door when she realised she hadn't put the dressing gown back on; she was naked apart from the T-shirt she slept in. Holding the paper in place, wincing as she curled her fingers into a fist, she grabbed the dressing gown with her free hand and tried to put it on, letting it hang behind her, bending to push her wounded hand into the sleeve, but the harder she tried the more tangled the dressing gown became. 'I'm nearly ready,' she cried.

But whoever it had been must have gone away.

She crumpled onto the edge of the bathtub, then pulled the dressing gown off her shoulder and threw it to the floor in frustration. She peeled the blood-soaked wad of paper away, wincing as it pulled at the cut. She went to the cabinet and took out the bottle of TCP, unscrewing the top with her teeth. You are so stupid, she said to the face in the mirror, pressing antiseptic-soaked cotton wool to the cut, counting as she waited for the bleeding to slow down and, finally, stop, placing a sticking plaster over the wound, feeling sick at the sight of it.

Before she left the bathroom she wrapped the broken glass and pills in a square of loo paper and put them in the pocket of the dressing gown. She would get rid of them later, under a stone in the garden somewhere. She would tell them she had cut herself with her nail scissors, nothing serious, an accident. They would believe her, they would have to. Her mother would be proud of her.

She found Jennifer's father perched on a stool at the breakfast bar beside the kitchen window, staring out. He was unshaven, his hair standing up at the back, in his socks, wearing suit trousers and a string vest. When she shuffled her feet, he turned to look at her with a fleeting air of bemusement. 'Hello,' he said after a moment. 'It's—'

'Fiona,' she said. 'Jennifer's friend.'

'Yes, of course,' he said. 'Fiona. Jennifer's school friend.' He was eating what he had eaten yesterday evening, spaghetti gleaming with olive oil, cutting it into small pieces and lifting them up with his fork in a way that would have reduced Ludo to hopeless laughter. 'You slept well, I hope?'

'Yes, thank you,' she said. She had the pills and broken glass hidden in her pocket. She felt like an intruder, although Jennifer's father was concentrating once more on his plate, as though he had forgotten she was there. She stood at the door, waiting, until he looked across again.

'I'm sorry,' he said. 'I suppose you'd like some breakfast?'

She nodded. 'I can get something for myself?' she said.

He nodded. 'Yes, why don't you?' He waved his fork in the direction of the fridge. 'You'll find juice in there,' he said. 'And milk.' He paused. 'For cereal,' he said patiently, pointing to a row of cupboards on the wall above the sink. 'I expect you'll find something in one of those.'

'Thank you,' she said. The fridge was American, with double doors; she'd never seen one so large. Her mother would have said it was ostentatious, like everything that came from America. She wasn't hungry. She looked at the milk and the Tupperware container of cheeses and the plate with its puddle of congealed blood and what was left of the previous evening's roast, and felt queasy. Where was everyone?

'So you'll be here for Christmas?' Jennifer's father said. Startled, Fiona closed the fridge.

'No,' she said. 'I have to go back to my mother's house for Christmas.'

He considered this for a moment. 'She lives alone?'

Fiona nodded. 'My father's dead,' she said, and then wished she'd kept her mouth shut. This is how shrinks work, she thought. They ask you a simple question and all you need to do is answer yes or no, but you tell them everything you know, you blurt it all out. Last night, with Patrick, she'd done the same thing. She'd told him about the girl in the photograph, everything she could remember, and he'd sat there, his arm pressed against hers, the blanket wrapped around them both, and let her talk. It was what he'd said about names, about knowing someone's name and how they'd never be able to hide from you if you did. Heather

Thomsett, she'd said. A teacher and her daughter, Maddy. Heather and Maddy Thomsett. And now Patrick's father was standing in front of her, waiting for her to continue, his eyes sympathetic, and she couldn't help herself. 'He died last year,' she said. 'He had a heart attack in his office.'

He nodded. 'It must have been very hard for you.'

'I was at school,' she said.

'Your mother told you?'

Fiona shook her head. 'No,' she said. 'The headmistress.' She felt tears welling up and prayed he wouldn't notice. She'd worked so hard to not think about that morning. Being called out of the lesson and taken by a prefect to the headmistress's study, a room she'd never entered before except under threat of punishment, and she'd wondered what they'd found, her cigarettes perhaps, and there was the woman standing up and hurrying over to her and hugging her, and all she'd wanted to do was push her away. 'My poor girl,' the woman had said. 'I'm afraid I have some very bad news for you,' and, for a moment, Fiona had thought, my mother's dead. If anyone else had died she'd be here, she'd be the one to tell me. And, for a moment, she'd felt a sort of gladness.

When she heard the truth – that her father had died that morning – she asked the headmistress where her mother was, why her mother wasn't here, her voice thick with tears, and the headmistress shook her head sadly, but also with what seemed to Fiona an edge of irritation. 'Your mother is very upset,' she said and then, 'It's only natural. You mustn't expect too much of her.' 'When do I go home?' Fiona said. She couldn't bear to be in the room a moment longer. 'We'll talk about that later, my dear. In the meantime, you're excused from lessons. I think you'd better go to the infirmary; Nurse will make you a nice cup of tea.' The woman stepped back. 'I'm not ill,' Fiona said. 'Just do as you're told, Fiona,' the woman said, visibly exasperated. 'Your mother has more than enough on her plate without having to worry about you as well.'

'What are you doing up?' said Jennifer, leaning against the doorframe in her nightie and slippers. 'I thought you'd be fast asleep.' She scanned Fiona from head to foot. 'Just look at you. You're dressed and everything.'

'I've been awake for ages,' Fiona said, relieved she would no longer be alone with the man, his unnerving concern.

'Well,' said Jennifer. 'I'm starving.' She glanced at her father. 'Hello, Dad. No patients yet?'

'They aren't patients, dear,' he said wearily. 'I do wish you'd remember not to call them that. You know how much I dislike the word.'

'Sorry, Dad.' She winked at Fiona. 'Clients.'

He looked at his watch. 'Good God, is it that time already?' he said, rubbing a hand over his unshaven cheek. 'It's about time I prepared myself for the fray.'

CHAPTER SEVEN

'So what happened last night?' Jennifer asked her as soon as her father left the room.

'With Patrick, you mean?'

'Of course!'

'We talked,' said Fiona. 'What do you think happened?'

'You could have done that in the house,' said Jennifer. 'Fine best friend you are, leaving me alone like that. I thought you were here to help me get through the hols without murdering anyone.'

'He wanted to show me the swimming pool,' said Fiona. 'I think he was just being polite.'

'Not really swimming weather, is it?'

'It looked absolutely freezing, to tell you the truth.'

Jennifer smirked. 'But I imagine he kept you warm.'

'We shared a blanket, if that's what you mean.'

Jennifer had filled their cups a second time when they heard her mother's voice, low, in the corridor outside. Jennifer raised a finger to her lips. He must have left this morning, her mother was saying. Before we were up. I'll go and see if he's taken the car, her husband said. He'll have gone up to town, she said. God knows what for. I hate it when he just disappears like this, without breathing a word to anyone. They were standing near the closed kitchen door, whispering, although surely they must have known they could be overheard, thought Fiona. She was about to say this

59

when Jennifer hushed her again. 'Not now,' she mouthed. 'Just listen.' Well, wherever he is, he's taken my pills, they heard her mother say. He's what? Which pills? My pills, she said. The blue ones. You know. The ones you gave me for my nerves. They're not in the cupboard any longer. Who else would have taken them if not Patrick? I'm worried that he knows he can sell them. He doesn't need money, her husband said, I gave him some money yesterday. Why in God's name would he want to sell your pills? Well, what's the alternative, Ruth said, her voice rising. Have you considered that? I don't even want to think about *that*.

At this point, Jennifer pushed her stool away from the breakfast bar as noisily as she could. Immediately, the conversation in the corridor came to a halt.

'Do you suppose they heard us?' said Fiona, abruptly anxious. 'Before?'

'You're the last thing they'll be thinking about if Patrick's gone off to London with a bottle of Mummy's little helpers.'

'I wouldn't worry about that,' said Fiona. She pulled the bundle of loo paper from her pocket. 'Is this what she meant?' she said, holding it out. Jennifer stared down.

'You've cut yourself,' she said.

Half embarrassed, half giggling, Fiona told her what had happened. 'It's my fault for being nosy,' she said, her tone apologetic, when Jennifer didn't respond.

But Jennifer began to laugh.

'He'll be in so much trouble when he gets back,' she said. 'I love it.' She looked around. 'We need something to hide them in,' she said. She picked up a mug. 'Quick, put them in here.'

'What about the glass?'

'All of it. We'll sort it out later.' She laughed again. 'They'll kill him for this!'

Fiona was shocked. 'Is that what you want?'

Jennifer looked at her. 'I want to see how he wriggles out of it. Because he will. He always does.' She paused. 'I wonder what he's really gone up to town for.' She studied Fiona's face. 'You don't know, I suppose?'

Fiona shook her head. 'No idea,' she said.

They spent the morning in Jennifer's bedroom, working their way through her record collection, emerging for coffee and a sandwich at lunchtime. Fiona was halfway down the final flight of stairs when Jennifer caught her arm. Fiona caught a glimpse of a middle-aged woman with pale-blue hair and a fur coat crossing the hall, pausing for a second to look at the tree. 'One of Dad's ladies,' Jennifer said. 'He doesn't like them to see us in the house. It interferes with their relationship if they know he has a family, he says. He's supposed to be omnipotent, like God.'

'I wonder how he'll explain the tree,' said Fiona.

'Oh, he doesn't *explain*. They have to work it out for themselves. It's called the talking cure, did you know that? They talk and he listens, and then they pay him. It's money for old rope, really.'

'Are they actually mad?'

'Mad? You mean smearing-their-poo-on-the-wall mad? No, of course not. He'd refer them if they were. They just have too much money and nothing to do. They're all women. Did you see that fur coat? I hate fur coats. It's like she's trailing blood.'

'He just has to sit there and listen. That sounds like my kind of job,' said Fiona.

'But you're going to be rich,' said Jennifer. 'You won't need to work.'

They had reached the bottom of the stairs and were almost in the kitchen when Fiona came to a halt. Jennifer turned back.

'What's up?' she said.

'You told Patrick, didn't you?' said Fiona. 'That I was going to be rich? That I was an heiress.'

'Did I? I may have done. I don't remember.'

'Well, someone did. He asked me how much I was going to get.'

'I didn't think it was a secret,' Jennifer said uncertainly. 'You don't mind, do you?'

'Don't be silly,' said Fiona, walking past her into the kitchen. 'Of course I don't.'

Patrick got back that evening, when they were having dinner, a more subdued affair than the evening before. They heard the front door open and then slam shut, followed by feet on the stairs, a second slammed door, muffled by distance, and then silence. Ruth, who had turned with a wry smile towards the hall, threw her napkin onto the table and stood up. 'That's it,' she said. 'I've had enough of this.' She looked at her husband, who sighed but didn't move. 'Well?' she said. Jennifer scratched Fiona's leg lightly beneath the table.

'You go and talk to him,' her husband said. 'I'll stay here with the girls.'

Ruth left the room, visibly exasperated. They listened to the tattoo of her heels on the stairs, and then, in the silence of the dining room, knuckles rapping a closed door and Ruth beginning to speak. At first, it was hard to make out what she was saying, but then she raised her voice. 'I said I'm coming in whether you like it or not,' she shouted. 'This is still our house, young man.' After which she must have gone in and closed the door behind her because nothing more was heard.

Ruth came downstairs, alone, as they were clearing the table. Her husband, still seated, raised an eyebrow, but she shook her head.

'Not now, dear,' she mouthed, then sighed, a weary sigh as if to say nothing could be done. She emptied the wine bottle into her glass. 'Waste not, want not,' she said, with forced cheerfulness, then beamed at the girls. 'Aren't you wonderful to give me a hand,' she said, watching them stack plates and put all the glasses but hers on a silver tray.

'Shall we put something to one side for Patrick?' said Jennifer, in a tone that, to Fiona's ears, sounded wilfully provocative.

'I don't think that will be necessary,' her mother said.

'He had something to eat in town?'

'Yes, I believe he did.' Ruth looked at her daughter, with a coldness that startled Fiona, then gave a little shake of her shoulders, as if returning to herself. 'Perhaps you girls would like to watch something on television this evening?'

'You aren't going to watch anything?' said Jennifer, glancing at her father.

Ruth shook her head. 'Not this evening. I have a splitting headache and your father's tired, aren't you, Oliver?'

He stood up. 'I'm afraid I have some paperwork to sort out before I can go to bed,' he said. He looked at his wife. 'You go ahead.' He folded his napkin. 'I'll be up later.'

Fiona lay in bed that night, unable to sleep, feeling the presence of Patrick less than a foot away from her on the other side of the wall. She'd sneaked into his room that afternoon and found herself in a mirror image of her own room, a single bed pushed tight against the wall behind which her own bed lay. She pressed the palm of her hand now to its cold, unyielding surface, feeling foolish, wishing she had the courage to tap out a message of consolation. But how could she make him understand that consolation was all she was offering? Was he awake as well? she wondered. Perhaps he was lying there, still smarting from his mother's accusations of theft, and worse; perhaps he was thinking of her and wondering what might happen if he tapped the wall. Would she tell him the truth, that she had the pills? She hadn't decided.

She and Jennifer had picked out the fragments of broken bottle with tweezers, then thrown them away at the bottom of the garden, in the yew hedge beside the pool. The pills they'd transferred to a small lacquered box of Jennifer's and hidden in her bedroom. 'You never know when they might come in handy,' Jennifer had said, winking. Fiona rubbed her wounded hand now, in the dark, just hard enough to feel the cut. She was about to press harder, to see how much pain she could endure, when she heard a door open onto the landing and, seconds later, a shuffling noise outside her own door. She lay still in the dark while something brushed against the carpet, was pushed beneath her closed door into the room. She lay there, her heart thumping, the blood in her hand throbbing behind the cut, until she was sure there was no one there to hear her, then eased herself out of bed and tiptoed across the room in the darkness, reaching out until her hand touched the door. Kneeling, she ran her hand across the carpet until she had found it, a piece of paper with one ragged edge where it had been torn from something else. She breathed out in a rush; she'd been holding the air in so as not to make a noise. She knelt there, silent, until her heart calmed down.

Only when she was back in bed did she think to turn on the bedside light and read what it said.

I know where she is.

*

When the first light came in through the window, she dressed as quickly as she could, not bothering to wash, slipping on her coat and scarf and picking up her heaviest pair of shoes. At the foot of the stairs, she sat and slipped them on, then let herself out into the garden, passing through Jennifer's father's study, walking down the three stone steps to the path and onto the lawn. A coating of frost sugared the grass; her feet left a track that could be followed and she was tempted to trail her scarf behind her, to rub it out, but that would only have made the path she had taken easier to see. Besides, it was her favourite scarf, pale blue, she had had it for as long as she could remember. She walked on a little further, until she was in the shadow of the small wood at the far end of the garden, and turned back to look at the house. She had worked out where her bedroom was in relation to the study door, but the window that interested her belonged to Patrick. Like hers, the curtains had been pulled open to the early light of the day. Maybe he was standing inside the room, just out of sight, watching her as she edged back into the covering darkness of the trees. If she waited quietly where she was maybe he would come down and tell her what he had found out. He knows where Maddy is, she told herself, and shivered with a deep, excited fright, as though she was on the point of finding not some girl she had never met but herself. She would find herself. Every word she'd read about twins and what made them special, their private language, their uncanny understanding of each other, would be worthwhile; all of it would finally make sense.

CHAPTER EIGHT

The next time she saw Patrick was almost three years later, two weeks into her first term at Oxford, at a college film club. She'd gone alone, she still knew hardly anyone apart from the three girls on her landing, all from the same school, none of whom she liked; desperately lonely, she welcomed the darkness of the occasion, the opportunity the film gave her to escape herself for a couple of hours. He was sitting next to her – he must have followed her in, she realised later, and maybe before that; maybe he had been following her for days. He offered her a cigarette, which she accepted because she knew almost no one and had no cigarettes herself because she had decided to stop, and then accepted the light, which he held at a short distance to give her the chance to see his face, and his eyes upon her, the wry look in them as he waited to be recognised, waited to see her reaction. Patrick, she thought. Runaway Patrick, in all his glory. Startled, but not really surprised, because this had been bound to happen sooner or later, she nodded her thanks and turned back to the screen, where a row of cardinals minced along a catwalk, aware that he had moved an inch or two closer. The film was Fellini's *Roma* and she was beginning to feel bored, however much she loved the language, so when he suggested in a whisper, his head so close she felt his breath on her skin, that they go and get a beer she followed him out of the room.

'I wondered how long it would take me to bump into you,' he said when they were seated with their beers. 'Jennifer told me you'd come up this year.' He unbuttoned his jacket, sliding it off his shoulders onto the back of the chair, shaking his arms free of it in a single move. She'd watched him at the bar, as neat and attractive as she remembered, bulkier than he had been three years ago, his hair shorter, better groomed, but otherwise the same. Waiting for the beers to be pulled, he'd glanced across at her and smiled, and the word wolfish came to her, a word she'd never used to describe a smile before that evening. Now, with the same smile, he was opening a packet of smoky bacon crisps and putting the packet on the table between them and it all came back, like food repeating, like acid in her throat. A rage she had thought she no longer felt, a rage she had fed until it had turned on her and she had found herself being consumed by it, and had put it to one side, began to rise and burn within her once again.

'I've been wondering that for three years,' she said. She tried to sound flippant; she didn't want to scare him off. Not yet. She wanted him to think he didn't matter to her, or not in the way he imagined.

'Surely not that long?' he said, raising an eyebrow as he sipped his beer. 'It feels like only yesterday we were snuggled up together by the swimming pool.'

'That would be the day before you disappeared, right? The day before you just fucked off.'

He looked contrite. 'I don't suppose we can just let bygones be bygones?' he said.

She sipped her beer. She felt him staring at her, seeking forgiveness or the first signs of it, some slight thawing, but she refused to meet his eyes. She kept this up until he sighed, at which point she couldn't resist a rapid glance, if only to see how sincere the sigh might be. Patrick doesn't do sincerity, she thought. She wasn't disappointed. He'd adopted the kind of expression a puppy adopts when it knows it has done something wrong but doesn't know what. 'I thought Jennifer had explained it all,' he said.

'She said you'd fucked off without telling anyone,' Fiona said. 'Not really much of an explanation.' She took a crisp from the packet and examined it for a moment. 'In any case I was there, remember? I was staying in your house. I didn't need to be told.' She could still see his bedroom window in her mind's eye, the curtains drawn back onto the emptiness of the room behind, the track she had left on the frosted lawn, which she retraced into the house, excited, expecting him to be there.

'I don't mean then,' he said. 'I mean later.'

Was this the moment to tell him that her friendship with Jennifer had begun to go wrong that morning? That Jennifer had accused her of lying, of destroying their family, not all of it that morning but in the days and weeks that followed? She could still see their mother crying and shouting, their father trying to comfort her. But what had stuck in her memory was the look that Jennifer had given Fiona when she didn't say what she knew, what she had done, when she kept her mouth shut as the furious woman ranted about her drug-using son, about a life being ruined, and her husband nodded and patted her head until she pushed him away and he became the focus of her rage. Jennifer, who had kept her own mouth shut because to open it would have been to implicate herself in the lie, in the trip down the garden to hide the glass, the pills she would flush down the toilet later that day that were still in her bedside cabinet, concealed in the pretty little lacquered box she had chosen with such care only hours before. Fiona was the only person she could blame. Not Patrick. Patrick hadn't been there. All Patrick would ever know was that he had been forgiven, as he knew he would be, and that she, Fiona, had been excluded, first from the family for reasons that weren't clear, and then, as the caul of friendship was slowly withdrawn, from Jennifer.

'Patrick,' she said. 'You had your little adventure, as Jennifer called it, you upset everyone, your mother hit the roof, and then you came home. And, magically, all was forgiven.' But you never told me what you'd discovered, she thought. You never told me where my sister was.

'Well, you're not entirely without blame, you know,' he said, lighting a cigarette, offering her one, lighting hers, watching her every move, the way she looped her hair back behind her ear to protect it from the flame. She knew this, she didn't need to see it. She knew when she was being watched. Nothing has happened between us, he seemed to be saying. Nothing has changed.

'Your mother's pills, you mean?'

He nodded.

'When did she tell you?'

He shrugged. 'I don't remember. Afterwards. Ages ago.'

'She promised me she wouldn't, you know that, don't you?'

'I didn't know that, but I'm not surprised.' He picked up his glass, then put it down again. 'She would say that. She's not very reliable.' He paused. 'It runs in the family, I'm afraid.'

'So what did you do?' Fiona said, ignoring this. 'Where did you go?'

'She didn't tell you?'

'We weren't really talking when you turned up again,' she said. 'Certainly not about you.'

'Nowhere special. Friends I had in London. A squat in Lambeth, in a council block. Overlooking the Oval.' He grinned. 'I saw lots of free cricket.'

'Is that where you were the day before?'

He looked puzzled.

'The day before you disappeared,' she said.

69

'Ah,' he said.

'The day you left me the note,' she said.

'Ah,' he said again.

'Yes,' she said. 'Ah.' But what she wanted to say was, not a day has passed since then that I haven't thought about that note and wondered what you'd found out. You know where she is, you said, and I don't, and I will never forgive you for that. Because ever since I've known that she exists I've needed her, it's crazy, it's like a hole in my heart, or no, worse than that, and now I'm being dramatic, melodramatic even, I know I am, Patrick, you spoilt little fucker, but this is something you need to know, this is something you need to hear, it's like being the shadow of someone who refuses to turn round and see you, actually see you, as though you're spread out on the floor behind yourself, behind her, a sort of darkness that she has made and that is all you are and all you'll ever be, moving when she does, and when she does turn you turn with her, you will never see her face to face. I'm fucking incomplete. Do you understand that, you bastard? Ah. Is that it? Is that all you have to say? Ah.

'I never had the chance to explain,' he said. 'I'm sorry about that.'

'You could have written,' she said. 'You could have called. It wouldn't have been difficult. A public telephone. Given that you're so good at finding people.'

'I was angry with all of you, I suppose,' he said. 'And then, when I found out that you'd taken the pills and said nothing, I was especially angry with you.'

'This wasn't about the pills. Anyway, I thought she'd only told you after. That's what you just said, isn't it?'

Impatient now, he stubbed out his cigarette.

'My God,' he said. 'I don't remember the order of events. I was actually doing a fair amount of drugs at the time.'

'Oh well,' she said, sarcastic. 'In that case.'

They stared directly into each other's eyes for the first time that evening, and then, in deadlock, turned away to glance around the half-empty room, the fruit machine, the juke box no one fed. She'd never been in this pub before; she wondered if it was one he used and if he had brought her here because he would feel on home ground. But that would give her too much significance. She wasn't important, he'd made that clear three years ago, by disappearing. She was about to leave when he touched her arm.

'So?' he said.

'So what?'

'So do you want to know where she is? Your mysterious twin?'

She looked at him as he swung back in his chair, arms crossed, one foot against the table leg. His lips were wet with beer. He was smirking. She had never so badly wanted to slap a face, or kick a chair away. If she had been able to find within herself the nerve, the self-wounding stupid courage that she needed, she would have shaken her head and said, no, I don't want to know, just fuck off. The sell-by date for that scrap of information is long past, she would have said, and then she would have left.

'Of course I do,' she said.

He lit another cigarette, not offering her one this time, taking his time to light it. 'And what will you give me if I tell you?'

She paused. 'I'll try to despise you a little less than I do now,' she said coldly.

'Well,' he said, 'that's a start, I suppose.' He finished his beer and stood up. 'I'm having another one,' he said. 'You?'

She emptied her glass. 'Yes.'

The next day she spoke to her tutor. 'I'm having problems with

PPE,' she told her. 'I'm not convinced it's what I want to be doing.'

'And what would you prefer to be doing?' her tutor said.

'Italian,' she said. She smiled shyly. 'My heart's in Italy.'

CHAPTER NINE

She forgave him. He knew so much, and was generous with his money and his time, and he distracted her from her loneliness. Besides, she found it amusing to think how annoyed Jennifer would be to discover that she and Patrick were spending time together. When he tried to kiss her outside college after their third evening together, she took his hand and led him along the road until they came to a doorway deep enough to offer protection. 'It's better here,' she whispered. 'No one can see us.' I could break your heart, she thought unexpectedly, and was thrilled. It was no more than he deserved. But being with him wasn't just an escape from loneliness or the pursuit of revenge; there was something about him, an air of subterfuge, of duplicity and risk, that appealed to her, even excited her. He felt like a risk worth taking, she thought; he knew things she would like to know.

Their second evening together, before she'd made up her mind about him, she'd tried to persuade him to tell her exactly how he had tracked Maddy down, whose help he had enlisted, what kind of people he had squatted with in Lambeth. He grinned at every question, poured her more wine. He'd taken her to the kind of restaurant students rarely used, and had put on a tie for the first time, his college tie. He'd asked her to wear something nice, and she'd bought a new dress for the occasion, telling herself as she picked it out – a sheath of olive-green raw silk that left her arms bare, the most expensive dress she'd ever owned – that Patrick wasn't worth it, but that she was. She deserved everything she could get. They were playing adults, she thought, as he filled her glass and told her that he intended to be immensely rich one day because living well was the best revenge. She'd never heard this expression before, and it struck a chord with her. Did you think of that? she asked him, but he shook his head. Some people say George Herbert said it, but they're wrong, he told her. Nobody knows. But why would you need revenge? she said. Revenge is like collateral, he said. You can never have enough.

She hadn't understood, but that was all right. He had a way with him, her mother might have said disapprovingly, which only made him more attractive in her eyes. My mother would say you're a bad boy, she told him, raising her glass, and he smiled, and nodded. I certainly can be, he said. Worse than you can imagine. If you'll let me, that is. He clinked his glass against hers. You must introduce me to your mother one of these days, he said. She let that pass. She was in no mood to talk about her mother. He paid with a cheque, and wouldn't let her see how much the bill came to; the menu she'd chosen from had been without prices, which struck her as tacky and exotic at the same time.

The third evening, she decided she would let him kiss her and then see how she felt. When she heard him moan and felt him press himself against her, trapping her in the doorway, she thought, I can do what I want with you now, and it wasn't until later she realised how odd that was; that the moment she was at her most defenceless, crushed between his body and the door at her back, his lips on hers, his hands on her waist and then her breasts, she should have that rush of power. She could have pushed him away, she knew that – he was barely two inches taller than she was – but that wasn't what she meant. It wasn't that kind of power.

Some of it had to do with sex, of course, a sense that his pleasure would also be hers, and that she could withhold it from him if she chose, although she didn't think she would. She liked his touch, his smoky, winey breath, the scent of him – bergamot, she thought, and an edge of sweat – the way his hair felt when she stroked it, gathered it in her hands, silky and strong. But there was also a sense that she had found her match. His power was her power, his revenge – his collateral — would be hers. She wanted to know more about him; she wanted him to know more about her. She also felt, and this was maybe the most powerful thing of all, that he was the bond between her and her sister. For that was how she thought of her now. Her twin sister. Maddy. All that she knew about Maddy she knew through him.

The first time they had sex, one afternoon a few days later in his room – he lived outside college with three other students in their final year – she wondered if it was true that twins shared sensations, emotions, were linked across space by invisible bonds. That everything her body told her, its every pore alert, its blood alive, Maddy would also be told. When he entered her, teasingly slow, his lips on her earlobe, his teeth against her skin, his agitated breathing a murmur she could almost make into words, she imagined herself as Maddy, feeling what she felt without knowing why. She gripped him, her hands behind his back, holding him inside her. Like that, she said, that's right. Like that. And then, because Maddy would surely be thinking in Italian, *così*. Beside the murmur, Maddy's voice in her ear. *Così*.

He told her all he knew: that Maddy and her mother had lived in Rome for nine or ten years, that her mother had taught in an international school there, the school at which Maddy had first studied, that they had lived at various addresses, that Maddy was a first-year political sciences student at Rome university. He had no current address for them, only the area. San Lorenzo. They had left the last place a couple of years ago but had never registered their new home with the local police, he said, and she wondered how in heaven's name he found these things out. Not only facts. To her delight, he showed her a photograph of Maddy that must have been taken during her last day at high school, surrounded by fellow students. They were in a square with a church behind them, blinking against the sun, laughing and waving at whoever was taking the photograph. Some of them were holding beer bottles in the air; others were smoking cigarettes and what were probably joints. They looked older than their contemporaries would look in England, more adult, without school uniforms, each in the clothes that he or she had chosen. Maddy was wearing jeans and a T-shirt with 'Psycho Killer' written on the front. So she's into new-wave stuff, thought Fiona, and was intrigued and a little upset, as though the choice of a type of music Fiona had never really liked had been designed to hurt her. She bought the album the day after seeing the photo, took it back to her room and played it incessantly until Patrick took it off the deck with a sigh of exasperation.

In the end she gave up asking him how he knew so much; it never crossed her mind – not even before the photo – that he might be lying. She understood that he would never tell her and this, perversely, made her trust him all the more. He had endless resources. He turned up one morning with a sports car and drove her to London, and bought her shoes and a bag from a place in Bond Street, and then afternoon tea with champagne in Fortnum's, and it could all have been so tacky, but he made it seem subversive, as though they were breaking some unwritten law. Maddy would understand, she told herself, thinking of the T-shirt. The car was too small to make love in properly, but he managed to bring her to orgasm in a lay-by just outside Oxford, with cars whizzing past. She wondered what Jennifer would say if she could see her now, her thighs apart and bare against the leather seat, her brother's hand inside her panties, his eyes locked on hers. She wondered what Ludo would say if he knew that she had found someone to replace him. She wondered if Maddy had gasped as she had done when she came, and how she would make sense of it, her rebel body.

The day after changing from PPE to Italian she wrote to Ludovico. I'll be spending my year out in Rome, she told him. I need your help to find a place to work and to live. He wrote back by return of post. Wonderful news, he said, I'll see what I can do. Two weeks later, he told her to contact a friend of his mother's, a literature professor at the university. They need a new *lettrice* for next year, he said. She asked her Italian teacher what *lettrici* did. You'll be assisting the academic staff, she was told, doing a little teaching yourself; it's a perfect opportunity to learn how things work in Italy. Her teacher smiled. Or don't work, she added. You're lucky to have such useful friends. But then, that's Rome. *Una mano lava l'altra*, she said. One hand washes the other.

When Fiona wrote to the professor in Rome, she wanted to ask if she might be able to teach in the political sciences faculty, but Patrick advised her against it. You'll find a way to get to Maddy, he said, as soon as you're there. She had never been to Rome; she pictured herself at the Spanish Steps, in Piazza Navona, with Patrick on her arm and then without him, alone in a city she didn't know. But what about you? she asked him. What will you do while I'm in Rome? He shrugged. Who knows, I might be anywhere, he said, waving a hand in the air; the City, Wall Street. The world will be my oyster. She was shaken. I thought you loved me, she wanted to say, but fought back the impulse, anxious not to look like a foolish lovesick girl. Did she love him?

Sometimes she felt she did, other times not. Mostly, she wasn't sure. She thought of the hour they had spent together huddled up beside his parents' pool, wrapped in a blanket, and wondered what he had wanted from her. Had he wanted to kiss her, to see how far she'd let him go? So why hadn't he kissed her, or tried to at least? Because he hadn't wanted her? And Maddy? Had they talked about Maddy that evening? They must have done, but how strange that she couldn't remember now. Sometimes she felt that all they really had was Maddy, who bound them together and held them apart at the same time. She looked a dozen times each day at the last-day-of-school photograph he had found for her, taking it out of the drawer she kept it in, beneath her diary. It could be me, she thought, except that I never look that happy. Her hair, the angle of her head as if the sun is shining in her eyes, the expression on her face, even the way she's standing, turned slightly to one side – all of it the same. Two girls, one girl, divided at birth. It came to the same thing, somehow.

And then there was Maddy's mother. Because if Maddy was her twin – and she had no doubt about that – then Maddy's mother was her mother too. Because the alternative, that her own mother was the mother of them both, was too awful to contemplate. Because if Maddy's mother was hers that would explain the hatred she had always felt for her mother, who was not her mother at all but had acquired her in some way, through adoption or worse, and was a usurper of the worst kind. Because she had been deceived all her life by her mother, who was not her mother and had never been her mother, who was a thief of lives, of her life, and a liar of the worst sort. There was something she had come across while she was working for her Latin A level, something Seneca had said: 'We are in the habit of saying that it was not in our power to choose the parents who were allotted to us, that they were given to us by chance. But we can choose whose children we would like to be.' How much more reason did she, Fiona, have to choose whose child she would like to be if the mother she rejected was an impostor and the mother she chose was genuinely hers?

Even if she would have to share her.

Her first Christmas away from Oxford she tried to convince Patrick to come home with her, for a few days at least. She wanted to show him off, she told him, but what she really wanted was to see her mother's face when Patrick appeared and took it for granted that they would sleep together. But Patrick refused. He said his own family would be expecting him. She didn't believe that what his family wanted would be reason enough for him to do something he didn't want to do of his own accord; that wasn't his style. When he turned her invitation down, they argued seriously for the first time. You're lying to me, she told him. Why would I do that? he asked her. When the truth is hard enough to accept, why would I lie? Lies are supposed to make life easier. I'm going home to my own dear folks. Jennifer's back from Exeter with some creep she's picked up there. Isn't that punishment enough for you? I can't believe you're letting me down like this, she said. You know how much I need you to be there with me. He tried to kiss her. When she pulled away, he shrugged. You'll be all right, he said.

The next morning he came round while she was getting up. She let him into her room in the T-shirt she wore to sleep in.

'I'm sorry,' he said. 'I behaved shittily yesterday.'

'Sit down over there,' she said, stepping away when he tried to kiss her. As soon as he was seated in the room's only armchair she lifted her T-shirt over her head, using the sight of her body to punish him. When he stood up and began to move towards her, she held out her arms to ward him off. 'I told you to sit down,' she said.

'I didn't mean it,' he said with a sigh, standing hopelessly in the middle of the room as she put on her bra and pulled a sweater over her head.

'What do you want?'

'I want to take you out,' he said.

'Out where?'

'I want it to be a surprise.'

'What makes you think I want a surprise?' she said, zipping up her jeans.

'Because you generally like surprises?'

She laughed; she couldn't help it. He made her laugh.

'I like nice surprises,' she said.

'I promise you this will be a nice one,' he said.

He had a different car this time. She didn't know very much about cars, but this one had a new fresh-leather smell and felt luxurious. She asked him whose it was, and he said it was practically as good as his, which didn't really answer her question. She relaxed in her seat and watched as the town gave way to rows of large houses set back from the road and then open country. He drove fast and well; she liked the look of his hands on the steering wheel. She reached over and touched his thigh with her nails, let them rest there for a moment, a tacit apology for her behaviour in her room earlier. When he asked her if she wanted a cigarette, she shook her head. She thought about asking him where they were headed, but decided she didn't really care. It was good to be in a richly upholstered, almost silent car with a man she almost always thought she loved, even if he did treat her badly at times. She wasn't perfect either. She would survive Christmas without him; it wouldn't be the first time she'd spent three weeks alone in the same house as her mother. There would be decent wine and whisky, in case anyone dropped in; she would take some grass home with her and hide in her room if necessary, as it would be. She could work on her Italian, although she didn't really need to; all those summers with Ludovico's family and friends had stood her in good stead. Maybe she could invite Ludovico to come over to stay with her for a few days. She wondered how Patrick would react if he did, if he would be jealous or indifferent.

He parked outside a small grey church on the outskirts of a village she'd never heard of. She stared with aversion at the thick yew hedge by the car. The countryside didn't appeal to her, dusty old churches even less. She was about to ask him why he'd stopped, puzzled and a little annoyed, when he turned to her and said, 'Here we are.'

'I thought you said it would be a nice surprise,' she said.

He didn't answer. He got out of the car and waited for a moment, as if to see what she would do, then walked along the road until he came to a break in the hedge. He paused and turned to face the car, a teasing look on his face. When he disappeared, she sighed and left the car.

He was waiting for her before the first row of tombstones. She turned to walk back to the car but he caught her arm.

'I want to show you something,' he said.

'I hate these places.' She looked around her, with distaste and an edge of unease. 'It's like the start of that horrible zombie film you made me watch.'

'*Night of the Living Dead?*' He followed her eyes. 'I was thinking more Gray's "Elegy". Not feeling elegiac?'

'Not one bit,' she said, but she let him draw her behind him among the stones. The graveyard felt abandoned, headstones tilted away from the mound beneath, tombs green with lichen, metal vases filled with wilting or long-dead flowers. She shivered, pulled her coat closer around her.

'Here we are.' He stopped beside a small headstone, glistening black with flecks of white. The lettering was still fresh. Sinking down on his haunches, he ran his hand along the top of the stone. 'You see?'

'I don't know what I'm supposed to be looking at,' she said.

'The dates,' he said. 'Look at the dates.'

'"RIP our Beloved Daughter Elizabeth Mary Bingham,"' she read. '"Now in the Arms of our Saviour Jesus Christ. Born 18 December 1959. Died 20 December 1975."' She looked at him. 'She was sixteen when she died. A year before I met you, almost to the day. That's awful.' She shivered again. 'She would have been my age. If she'd lived.'

Patrick clapped his hands.

'Exactly,' he said.

CHAPTER TEN

Patrick arrived three days after Christmas, when Fiona thought she would go mad with boredom. Her mother had given her clothes she would never wear, and overcooked food she forced herself to eat, because to push the plate away would lead to what her mother called a scene. There were people who dropped in, but Fiona barely knew them, and they left before she could decide whether they were worth the effort it would take. But the decision had already been made and was implicit in their presence in her mother's house. They were the sort of people her mother worked endlessly to attract, people who thought of themselves as county, who supported local hunts, who were convinced that Margaret Thatcher would sort the country out after years of socialist misrule, who regarded Fiona as an intriguing misfit and her choice to study Italian as a hobby, inoffensive as, although less useful than, embroidery. And to think she was at the very same college that Maggie had been to, one of them said when she thought Fiona was too far away to hear. Such a waste. Fiona sat in the chair that used to be her father's, sneakily filling her glass with whatever was to hand, listening to them talk about how young people these days seemed to think they should have everything on a plate, and a silver one at that. She despised them with all her heart. She caught her mother looking at her with a blend of menace and anxiety in her eyes, afraid she might start to extol the virtues of Fidel Castro, and she might have risen to the bait if her thoughts hadn't been about Maddy, and Rome, and Patrick. If she hadn't ruined her friendship with Jennifer, she could be in their house now, with Patrick in the bedroom next to her. Her mother caught her in the hall one afternoon, her nails digging into Fiona's arms. 'You're drinking too much,' she said. 'Don't think I haven't noticed. I suppose you want me to be ashamed of you.' Fiona shrugged, inwardly delighted. 'Have you met any nice young men at Oxford yet, Fiona?' some blue-haired matron asked her as she handed round the vol-au-vents, and Fiona nodded and simpered and thought of Patrick's teeth on her nipples, and wished the woman dead.

Patrick arrived when the turkey's carcase had been stripped of its final scraps of meat and transformed into broth. He turned up without warning, and caused a flurry in the bedlinen department, as her mother put it. The flurry was designed to make him feel uncomfortable, Fiona knew, and she was amused that it so signally failed in its purpose. She and her mother watched in silence as Patrick threw his case on the bed, opened it and presented them both with exquisitely packaged bottles of perfume. When she had a chance, her mother having gone to the kitchen to bully the cleaning woman, Fiona asked him why on earth he'd come and he said he'd missed her, which was the least he could say. He ignored her attempts to get him out of the house for the rest of the day, all his efforts going into charming her mother, but she finally got him to herself when her mother went to bed and left them alone in the drawing room with a bottle of Laphroaig her father had never opened.

'You still haven't shown me your bedroom,' he said, filling their glasses.

'So that's why you're here,' she said, amused.

'It's part of the reason, certainly. I really have missed you, you know. You. Us.' He sipped and smiled, and she wondered if the smile was for her or for the whisky.

'And the rest of the reason?'

He looked around the room, at the carriage clock on the marble mantelpiece, at the bookcase filled with Reader's Digest condensed novels. 'Your mother seems to have taken a liking to me,' he said.

'Well, you certainly put the time in,' Fiona said. 'You've barely said a word to me since you got here. I don't know how you can stand to be with her.'

He put his glass down, came over and kneeled beside her chair. He took her hand and kissed each finger and she watched his head bob up and down, resisting the urge to stroke his hair. 'Is that better?' he said when he'd finished, and she nodded that it was.

The next morning, she woke up alone. She went downstairs and found Patrick in the kitchen, laughing with her mother.

'Good morning,' she said. They turned their heads towards her in an awkward way, as if they'd been caught out, she thought, but brushed the thought aside.

Her mother filled the kettle. 'Coffee, dear?'

'We've been talking about your future,' Patrick said.

Her mother laughed. 'Don't be so silly, Patrick.' She smiled at Fiona. 'Of course we haven't.'

But Fiona was looking at Patrick, who raised his eyebrows and nodded.

'Patrick's been telling me all about his studies,' her mother said. 'It's so refreshing to meet a young man with his head screwed on the right way.' She glanced at him admiringly. 'You should listen to what he has to tell you, Fiona. You could learn a great deal. It isn't too late to change back to your first choice, you know.'

'Oh, don't worry,' said Fiona, 'I always listen to Patrick.'

'He understands how important it is to look after what you have,' her mother said.

'I'm sure he does.'

'Your mother's been telling me about your father.' Patrick took a bite from a slice of buttered toast. 'It must have been very hard for you both.'

Hard? It was hard not to laugh at the bare-faced cheek of this, the first time Patrick had mentioned Fiona's father beyond the occasional passing reference to his wealth.

'Oh, we don't need to talk about that any more,' her mother said, but her lingering glance at Patrick was more grateful than reproving. My God, thought Fiona, she's totally fallen for him. He is such a bastard.

'I'll take you down to the village,' she said. 'You need some fresh air.'

'But you haven't eaten anything,' her mother said.

Fiona took Patrick's hand and tugged him to his feet. 'Come on,' she said.

'I'd like to borrow Patrick for an hour or two this afternoon, if that's all right with you, my dear,' her mother said as they were leaving the kitchen. 'He's such a bright and well-informed young man. I need to pick his brains.'

They drove to Oxford two days later, as soon as her college would let her back into her room. Her mother stood at the bedroom door and watched her as she packed, but didn't speak, and neither did Fiona. She had never felt less interest in her mother, as though the prospect of meeting her real mother had wiped the slate clean of any affection she had ever felt for the woman who had brought her up. All Fiona could bring herself to feel was a condescending pity, because the woman still didn't know that her game was up. At least she'd had Patrick to play with, thought Fiona, with a sense of gratitude that he'd paid the woman so much attention, and of irritation that he'd paid her daughter so little.

She was leaving the house when her mother pushed something soft into her hand. 'I suppose you'd better have this,' she said, then kissed her hurriedly on the cheek before darting back into the hall and closing the door behind her. Fiona glanced down at her hand and found a black velvet pouch with a drawstring, the kind used for jewellery. She would have looked inside but Patrick pipped the horn and she slipped it in her pocket, unexamined.

'So tell me about Ludovico,' Patrick said.

'What do you want to know?'

'Your mother says he's like an older brother to you.'

'Stop fishing.'

Patrick laughed, pulling out of his lane to overtake the car in front. 'People ought to have their licences taken off them after a certain age,' he said.

'Is that the kind of thing you told my mother?'

He laughed again. 'Professional advice, that's all I gave her. How to invest more profitably her considerable fortune.' He glanced at Fiona. 'Which will soon be yours.'

'Well, I'm glad you found something in common.' She touched his arm. 'I haven't really thanked you for coming,' she said.

'I thought you thanked me last night,' he said. 'In bed.'

It was her turn to laugh. 'Don't be vulgar,' she said.

'You see, you are your mother's daughter.'

Fiona was silent after that. When they reached her college, Patrick carried her case up the stairs, waiting on the landing while she unlocked, but didn't open, the door. 'Don't get angry.' She turned to face him with a tight smile. 'I just need to be alone for a bit. You know, decompress.'

He looked at her, his face set, then put down her case and left.

At the turn of the stairs, he looked over his shoulder. 'I'll see you tomorrow,' he said.

She only remembered the velvet pouch when she was taking off her clothes to get into bed. She opened it and shook out what it contained into her palm. A ring. Two slim threads of differently coloured gold twisted together. How odd that her mother should have given her something so lovely in such a hasty, reluctant way, as though she didn't want to be associated with it. Fiona felt a qualm of guilt, and wished she'd opened the pouch at once, in front of her mother, and thanked her for it. She slipped the ring on, then lifted it to her mouth and touched her lips to it.

*

The next morning she stepped into the courtyard and found them standing together. Patrick and Ludovico. Her instinct was to step back into the darkness of the staircase, but she'd already been seen. She forced her face into a smile, her heart beating as though she'd been caught out, and walked towards them, hands raised in mock surrender.

'Surprise, surprise,' said Patrick. He took her by the shoulders, winked, then kissed her hard on the mouth. She saw, out of the corner of her eye, Ludovico fall back a pace.

'I guessed who he was the minute I saw him.' Patrick gestured towards Ludovico with his head. 'I saw him hanging around and I thought, that's going to be Fiona's Italian boyfriend.' He grinned. 'And I was right.'

Fiona waited for Ludovico to kiss her on both cheeks before speaking. 'What on earth are you doing here?' she finally said, her voice cooler than she intended.

'I had a meeting with a colleague. I thought I'd surprise you.'
He raised an eyebrow. 'Italian boyfriend?'

'Ignore him,' she said. 'He's trying to embarrass you.'

'I would consider myself a fortunate man,' said Ludovico, with a smile and a little dip of the head, the slightest possible attempt at gallantry. 'If that were the case.'

'Don't encourage him,' Fiona said. The last thing she wanted was to be drawn into one of Patrick's games. She looked at the sky, which was heavy with cloud, and then at them both, standing side by side on the gravel path, Ludovico towering over Patrick, his expression bemused but entertained, Patrick grinning with satisfaction. She took a deep breath, then smiled. 'OK, what would you two like to do?'

'How far away is the river from here?' said Ludovico. 'I need to see at least one punt before I leave.'

Fiona looked at Patrick, who shrugged, then nodded. 'To the river, then,' she said. 'Although your chances of seeing a punt this morning are fairly slim.'

They left the college and headed east, awkwardly along the narrow pavements until they reached the park, Patrick and then Ludovico taking the lead, Fiona avoiding anything that might seem to favour one of the two men over the other. The air was cold and damp, their breath formed instant clouds. The trees around them were bare of leaves, edged with frost. Ludovico had a donkey jacket on, and jeans tucked into boots, which gave him a foreign air. Patrick was wearing a leather jacket she'd never seen before, oxblood brown, zipped pockets, a stylised biker's jacket that looked and felt as though it had cost a fortune. When she asked him, he told her it had been made by a new Italian designer, a guy from Milan called Giorgio Armani. Ludovico snorted.

'Patrick thinks living well is the best revenge,' she said, recalling Maddy's Psycho Killer T-shirt, wishing she had stayed in her room. Ludovico snorted again. He still hadn't told her what he was doing here.

Patrick stepped in front of her to stroke the arm of Ludovico's donkey jacket with mock reverence. 'I suppose this makes you feel like one of the lads,' he said.

Ludovico shrugged, but didn't move his arm away. 'It keeps me warm,' he said. 'That's all I require from a jacket.'

Fiona had had enough of this. 'When did you get here, Ludo?'

Now it was Patrick's turn to laugh. 'Ludo?' he said. 'Is that what she calls you? Like the board game?'

Ludovico nodded, unapologetic. 'We've known each other since we were children,' he said. 'She has the right.'

'How sweet,' said Patrick, but his irritation was palpable. They had reached the river by this time. They paused on the bridge and stared into the icy water beneath them. Fiona had an urge to tuck her hands around their arms, to draw them into a union against the world, her lover and her oldest friend, but didn't dare, and then the moment passed and she wished with all her heart they would both disappear, and leave her alone. There was an extended silence, which was finally broken by Ludovico.

'You must come and visit us in Rome,' he said.

'Us?' said Fiona.

Ludovico looked at her. 'It's all arranged,' he said.

'What is?' said Patrick.

'I've found the two of us a rather nice place. You mean you didn't know? I thought you would have received my letter by now. It's an embassy flat, just round the corner from Piazza Farnese.'

'I haven't received any letter,' said Fiona. She turned to Patrick, who had stopped in his tracks and was staring at her with a mixture of hostility and surprise. 'I didn't know, honestly.' But she couldn't hide how pleased she was by this news.

'Really?' said Patrick.

'We could be in the heart of the country,' said Ludovico, looking around him at the bare branches, the cloud-filled sky. 'Little England never lets me down.'

'I didn't know,' said Fiona hopelessly. 'I didn't pick up my post yesterday. You just took my case up to my room and I—'

'So it's my fault.'

'I didn't say that,' she said.

'You did actually. You said—'

She interrupted him. 'I know what I said.'

'Oh dear,' said Ludovico. Fiona glared at him.

'We'll be sharing the flat with other people,' he said. 'An English couple.'

'How cosy for you,' said Patrick, blowing into his cupped hands.

'Oh, don't be stupid,' Fiona said, annoyed.

'I've got something for you,' Patrick said, staring into her eyes, ignoring the other man. 'Something I think you'll like.' His tone was teasing, flirtatious.

Ludovico coughed and made a show of looking at his watch. 'Well,' he said, 'it's time I was off. I have a car to deliver.'

Patrick looked at him. 'You hired a car? What a pity. I could have driven you to the airport. We could have got to know each other better.'

'Maybe next time I'm in Oxford,' Ludovico said. 'I'm often here.' He shook Patrick's hand, acknowledging the suppressed recoil of the other man with a brief smile, then kissed Fiona on both cheeks. 'I'll be in touch,' he said.

Fiona waited until he was out of sight before speaking to Patrick.

'You really embarrassed me,' she said. 'I hope you're happy.'

'It's not my fault if I get jealous,' he said. 'You and your Italian stallion.'

'Now you're being ridiculous,' she said, but the idea of Ludovico as a stallion, Italian or otherwise, made her smile, and then laugh. When Patrick tried to hug her, she slapped his arm away, then grabbed his elbow and pulled him close enough to kiss his cheek. 'Utterly ridiculous,' she said.

They walked back to her room, silent, arm in arm. She only asked him what he had for her after the door was closed behind them. He pulled a manila envelope from the inside pocket of his jacket. 'Here you are,' he said, with a flourish. 'Elizabeth.'

She didn't understand until she'd taken the passport from the envelope and opened it at the page with the photograph, and there she was, staring up at herself, just as she had stared at herself in the photo booth, and thought she was doing it for Patrick, and where it said 'Usual signature of bearer' on the opposite page she saw the name 'Elizabeth Mary Bingham' written in a hand that might have been hers. 'I didn't do this,' she said, not sure what else to say, unexpectedly anxious.

'It looks like your handwriting though, doesn't it?' he said, pride in his voice, and she nodded, because it did. It looked exactly like her handwriting.

Patrick was arrested during the Easter vacation and charged with a series of offences, including forgery, obtaining money by deception and credit card fraud. He was tried in Oxford magistrates' court and, given his lack of previous convictions and his impeccable family background, received a reduced sentence of nine months. The chief magistrate expressed a hope that he would think long and hard about the shame he had brought to his father, a highly esteemed professional whose life was devoted to helping those less fortunate than himself. When Fiona heard about this, in an angry and entirely unexpected letter from

Jennifer, who blamed the malicious influence of her ex-friend on her elder brother, weak-willed and blinded by love, she wondered if Patrick had been too shocked to smile.

CHAPTER ELEVEN

Elbows on her windowsill, a cooling cup of coffee in her hands, Fiona looked down at the sunlit square below. A half-dozen young men in cassocks were headed into the bar on the left side of the square, bright in the sun, jostling one another, giggling at the door. On the steps of the church opposite, three girls had stopped to sit and talk together, their heads bent low over what looked like a diary. As she watched, a moped pulled up at the petrol pump, tucked into an alcove directly beneath her window, and a woman filled her tank. She had the corner room, and she had spent hours this past week watching people walk from the square, with its clutter of cars, into Via Monserrato. She had bought a poster from a shop that sold film memorabilia, a dozen yards down the road from the petrol pump, of the last film she had seen with Patrick, which he had loved. *The Shining*. She had watched it and seen the menace of the twin girls in the corridor, and the wall awash with blood, and wondered why people always found twins so disturbing. She had said this to Patrick, and he had looked at her as though she'd asked him if the world revolved around the sun. But they are, he said, they're totally creepy. It's like one person split into two, and you don't know how, you don't know which part is which. It's Manichean, you think, and then maybe not. Maybe they're both bad. He held her by the shoulders then, the way he always did, and looked into her eyes. You ought to know that if anyone does, he said.

*

She'd spent the summer in London, in a house that belonged to the parents of a girl she'd made friends with after Patrick's arrest. The parents were on a year's sabbatical in Austin, Texas, and had left Nadia the keys and a substantial allowance to cover her living costs. Nadia, who hated solitude, had invited everyone she knew, including Fiona, to keep her company and to help her spend what she referred to, giggling, as her pocket money. The house, actually a ground-floor apartment, was in a side road behind Harrods and so many people were staying in it that the part of the bay window nearest the steps leading up to the front door was left slightly raised, with just enough room for a hand to slide under and lift the sash, then wriggle through into the sitting room behind. The three rooms inside the apartment had been converted into makeshift dormitories. Fiona found herself sharing a mattress near the fireplace with someone working the final shift in a local nightclub, which meant that she was woken around five every morning by a body flinging itself beside hers and a muttered apology as the girl, stinking of smoke and still half dressed, whose name she could never catch, tugged insistently at the unzipped sleeping bag until she had enough to cover her. But Fiona didn't mind. Anything was preferable to her mother's house. Even her mother had agreed, or had at least decided not to put up a fight. Partly to make some money, partly to escape the chaos of the flat, she found herself a job at a stall at Paddington Station, selling fruit and chocolates, from eight to noon. In the afternoon she set about creating an identity for Elizabeth Bingham. She opened a bank account, giving the address of Nadia's flat and showing a bill she'd picked up from the mat in the entrance hall as proof. She signed on and was thrilled when the first giro landed on the same sisal mat, and then so horrified at what she'd done that she immediately signed off. But her confidence soon came back. It was all too easy. She considered finding a doctor, but something put her off, some fear she might be identified by her teeth, her blood, her hair. She wondered sometimes what the real Elizabeth had looked like and would have done with her life. Had she had a boyfriend or died a virgin? Had her parents loved her? She must have had plans for the future, dreams.

But thinking about the real Elizabeth made her sad; she was the real Elizabeth now, she told herself. She paid her giro into her – Elizabeth's – bank account, and added her first pay packet from the stall, and was given a cheque book and a cheque card, which she signed with her new name. Elizabeth Bingham. Seeing the two words written like that, in her handwriting, immediately made her think of Patrick.

She would have liked to do this with Patrick. It had all been Patrick's idea, after all. But Patrick was in prison and there was no one else who knew about the passport, hidden away at the bottom of her rucksack, wrapped in her favourite pale-blue scarf, slipped into a small plastic bag with a zipper, and more valuable to her than her own.

Her instinct when she arrived in Rome had been to disguise herself to stop Maddy finding her out. She wanted the element of surprise to be hers. She spent the first morning darting between her bedroom and the bathroom, avoiding Ludovico and the other people in the flat. She tied her hair up, away from her face, but that made her feel more exposed; she wore it down and felt that she would be spotted as soon as she walked through the door into the little square outside. She applied extra make-up to look more Italian, and then less, because maybe Maddy would cover her face in foundation, and paint her lips red, and outline her eyes. But how could she know what Maddy would be or do?

Fiona might go out of her way to look different and find herself looking the same, irresistibly drawn to behave as her sister did, to favour the same colours, the same styles. Maybe her voice would give her away, assuming they had the same voice, or a gesture. Whatever she did, or said, or wore, might just as easily identify her as not. In the end, she washed her face, put on the clothes she had brought with her from England and left the flat.

Now, three weeks later, her fear of bumping into Maddy had been transformed into a nagging anxiety that she might never find her at all. She had started to teach in her first week, classes of over a hundred students, almost all girls, on the ground floor of an ugly modern block near the station. She had been given classes for all four years, and a two-hour close reading class in a small room with windows that wouldn't open, but had to bring her own chalk. After the first day, she went to bed, her head throbbing, and refused to speak to anyone, even Ludovico. By the end of the second week, she had realised the hopelessness of her task and begun to relax.

She was reading a magazine over a breakfast of yogurt and coffee when Ludovico came into the kitchen and said he'd fixed her up to do some lessons in the political sciences faculty. He was wearing a crimson silk gown hanging open over boxer shorts and a Chicago university T-shirt. Unshaven, his hair still tangled from the pillow, his legs still improbably tanned from the previous summer, his physicality unsettled her. She wished he wouldn't treat her as though she wasn't supposed to be aware of him; he made her uncomfortable. She'd touched no one since her final night with Patrick, who had refused to let her visit him and had stopped answering her letters.

Ludovico poured himself some coffee from the pot, already cold, and sat down. 'Just call this number,' he said, and gave her a piece of paper from his pocket. 'It's all arranged. They'll provide you with a seminar room from now until the end of the semester. You just have to advertise.'

'Advertise?'

'Stick a notice on the faculty board. Get people to sign up for it.' He sipped the coffee, grimaced. 'How long has this been here?'

'I didn't know making coffee for you every morning was one of my duties,' she said.

He blew a kiss at her. 'My favourite geisha,' he said. 'And now perhaps you'd like to tell me why you want to teach in the political sciences faculty so badly?'

And so she did.

The following day, she left her department and walked the half-mile to the main campus. She strolled around the stark white buildings, the patches of unkempt grass, looking at everyone in a rapid covert fashion, hoping she would not be seen, her heart beating, nervous with anticipation and a fear that what she most wanted she would get. Three times, she saw people glance as if expecting something from her, a greeting, a wave; she looked away quickly, hoping they would think she hadn't seen them. Eventually she found the political sciences faculty. Ludovico's contact was a researcher in the faculty; she used the man's name when a porter told her she needed permission to leave anything on the notice board. He produced from his pocket a box of thumb tacks. '*Ci penso io*,' he said, and she thanked him and watched as he pinned the notice up. He looked at her again with a puzzled expression before going back to his glass box near the door. She left the building, trembling, as though she had been exposed. One of the things that had struck her, during her reading about twins, was the notion that only one of the two was real, the true child; the other was evil, or a harbinger of evil. A fetch, they called the unwanted one in Irish folklore. Patrick had said something like that and it had shaken her more than she realised at the time. Now, in the territory of the other, she felt at constant risk.

She left the campus and caught the first bus for the station. She found herself thrust against the central doors, her face to the glass as the bus headed up the hill. Maybe I'll never find her, she thought, when a woman behind her began pushing to get to the door and it happened. There she was, her sister, her twin, standing at the side of the road, waiting to cross. Fiona's hand rose to wave, to capture her in some way, but already, as quickly as the girl had appeared, she was gone. She had been seen, she was sure of that; she had seen the face of the other girl, of Maddy, freeze with shock. Of course it would; unlike Fiona, she had no idea she was a twin. She had thought she was unique until a handful of seconds ago. When the bus pulled up at the stop, Fiona moved aside to let the woman pass, but stayed on board. There was no need to hurry, she told herself. Maddy would still be there tomorrow. Their double fate had finally been set in motion.

PART THREE

CHAPTER TWELVE

The first time Maddy saw herself she had just left a lecture and was crossing a road on her way home for lunch, and there she was. The glimpse of a face on a bus heading towards the station. She stopped, her heart pounding in her chest. A moment later, the face had gone. It must have been my reflection in the glass, she told herself, knowing how impossible that was. The face, her face, had been looking directly at her, and smiling, unsurprised, as though it had known she would be there; while she, Maddy, had been staring down the road, and only turned her head when she had the sensation of being watched. No, more than watched. Recognised.

Waiting to cross, she looked around her, wanting to ask the people near her if they had seen what she had seen. But the fear of looking foolish halted her. As her heartbeat slowed and her breathing returned to normal, she had the urge to chase after the bus, to look up at the window and see herself a second time, tap on the glass to find out what her other self would do. But already the bus was a hundred yards down the road. Beside her, an old woman holding a small white dog was observing her with an air of concern. '*Tutto bene*,' Maddy said, and the woman nodded and walked on, hugging her little dog. Lots of people look like other people, Maddy told herself. She must have been mistaken. How many faces can there be in the world, without repetition?

Billions of faces, each imagining itself to be unique. She tried to remember what had been on her mind when she saw – or thought she saw – the face. She had no idea. Even the subject of the lecture escaped her. She crossed the road, abruptly hungry, stopped at the baker's just as the *pizza rossa* was being taken from the oven, and bought enough for two.

Her mother was fast asleep where Maddy had left her that morning, sprawled in her nightdress on the sofa. Closing the door with a sigh, she went into the kitchen, unwrapped the pizza, still warm from the oven, and put half of it on a plate.

'Lunch,' she said, taking the plate across to the sofa, her voice as cheerful as she could make it.

Her mother opened her eyes, lifting her cheek from the damp patch on the cushion beneath her head. 'What is it?' she said, her voice still thick with sleep.

'Pizza,' said Maddy.

'Again.' Her mother struggled to sit up, pulling the hem of her nightdress down until her legs were covered.

'Again,' said Maddy. She gave her mother the plate and stood back.

'Can you cut it into strips?' her mother said. 'It's difficult to eat like this. And a napkin? Can't you give me a napkin? A paper one, anything. I'm not an animal.'

'If a napkin is what madam wants,' said Maddy, 'that's what madam will get.' She took the plate back into the kitchen.

'I'm sorry,' her mother said. 'I didn't mean to sound like that.'

'Like what?'

'Selfish,' her mother said. 'I've just had an awful morning, that's all.'

'Really?' said Maddy, bringing back the plate. 'What happened?'

'Oh, both lessons cancelled, the gas bill turning up. Stuff like

104

that,' her mother said, pushing her hands through her hair. Her cheek was creased from the cushion.

Maddy gave her the plate. 'Don't worry,' she said. 'It may never happen.'

Her mother took a bite from the first strip of pizza, tearing it with her teeth. 'Believe me, sweetheart,' she said, her lips red with sauce. 'It always happens.'

'I'll get that napkin,' said Maddy.

Maddy and her mother lived between the cemetery and the train station in a gloomy first-floor flat, their fourth in seven years. Two poky bedrooms, a kitchenette, a windowless bathroom and a living-room-cum-hall, where her mother currently sprawled on the only sofa. Her mother's bedroom smelt of cigarettes and an anti-wrinkle face cream she bought from Standa in large plastic jars. The bed was usually unmade. Maddy's room had a lock on the door and clothes hanging on a row of nails, and books stacked along the entire length of one wall in an order determined partly by their position in the alphabet and partly by their size. Many of them came from a second-hand bookstore at the other end of the tunnel beneath the railway lines, where Maddy often went for refuge. She had read almost all of them, and would read the others as soon as she had time. She was determined to make something of herself, but still didn't know what that something might be, other than that it would not involve her mother.

But whenever she thought this, this awful, ungrateful thought about her mother, her eyes prickled and she reached down to pinch the fleshiest part of her thigh as hard as she could in order to focus her sense of guilt on a more manageable pain.

Later that week, Gina, the only other English girl on her course, came across to Maddy after a seminar.

'So what was up with you yesterday?' she said.

'I'm sorry?'

'You walked right past me. Outside the library. You totally ignored me.'

'I was nowhere near the library yesterday,' said Maddy.

'You were,' said Gina. 'I saw you.'

'I just said I wasn't.' Maddy's tone switched from surprise to annoyance.

Gina stepped back. 'OK,' she said, raising her hands. 'My mistake.'

'No, really,' said Maddy, apologetic. 'It couldn't have been me.' And then it struck her. 'You say you saw someone who looks like me?'

'No. I said I saw you,' said Gina, with a cautious laugh.

'No, seriously, Gina. What was I doing?'

'I don't know. Walking somewhere? Pretending not to see your friends?'

Maddy let this pass. 'What was I wearing, did you notice?'

'Jeans? Jacket? Blue, I think.'

I have a blue jacket, she thought. 'What else do you remember? Did I have a bag or anything?'

'Look, I said I don't know.' Gina shrugged. 'Let's just forget it, shall we? I didn't see you.' She raised both hands in a gesture of surrender. 'I didn't see anybody.'

Maddy was about to tell her about the face on the bus, but Gina left the room before she could find the words she needed. She watched her go, then closed her rucksack. She was shaken to the core, and couldn't explain why. There is someone who looks like me, that's all, she reasoned, someone who is studying at the same university, someone who has a blue jacket, perhaps like mine. Sooner or later, they would bump into each other and the other girl would be as surprised, and amused, as she would be, because it was amusing, Maddy told herself, despite her doubts. Maybe we'll become friends, she thought, as she left the room. All these years in Italy and she had made no friends, no real friends. All the other kids at her first school had been embassy kids or UN kids or just rich kids, and her mother had been staff, somehow, and she had carried that with her, like a taint. And then the local high school, and never quite feeling part of it; there were so many things she just didn't know, small things that everyone shared from nursery school. Nobody had been cruel to her. She had just been incidental, somehow. The new girl. The foreign girl. The girl who never took anyone home.

She could do with a friend right now, the way her mother had been these past few months. Difficult, needy, petulant, as though she were the child in the family. She hadn't dressed in days, just lolled around in her nightdress, her feet bare, picking up dirt from the floor. Only an Englishwoman would do that, Maddy thought, and then felt bad because she was English too, although she could pass for Italian by now, and hated it when Italians criticised the dirty English in her presence. She never took anyone back to the flat, she was too ashamed. She wondered how her mother would react if she turned up with someone exactly like her, the two of them standing there, side by side. She'd probably think she was hallucinating.

She was about to leave the building when Gina ran up. 'I am so sorry,' she said, 'I really am.'

'Why? What is it?'

'I've just seen you, I mean her. Over near the bar.' She tugged at Maddy's arm, then pushed her away. 'Go on,' she said. 'If you run you might catch her. I think she was going in, but I didn't stop to look. I am so sorry,' she said a second time, but Maddy was rushing down the steps in the direction of the campus bar, her rucksack bouncing on her shoulder.

Inside the bar there was no sign of the girl, but the barman spotted Maddy and waved her over. 'Ciao,' he said. He held out a scarf, pale blue, her favourite colour. 'You'll be looking for this,' he said, in Italian, handing it to her.

Maddy nodded. '*Grazie*,' she said. She stretched her hand out across the counter and took the scarf.

CHAPTER THIRTEEN

Inside the scarf, which was cashmere, Maddy found the kind of label she remembered from her school in England. A strip of white cotton sewn onto the hem with italic letters stitched in red that spelt a name. She said it out loud. *Fiona Conway.* She stroked the label, like someone blind. She's English too, she thought, and now she has a name. She lifted the scarf to her nose to catch its scent – apple shampoo and some flowery fragrance she couldn't place – then pressed it to her lips. Hello, she said. Hello, Fiona. She sat through her next class without hearing a word, her pen idle in her hand.

Walking home, it struck her that she had come across the name before, somewhere in the faculty. She touched the scarf, as if expecting to find an answer in the texture of it.

She was about to let herself into the flat, key poised at the lock, when she heard her mother swearing at the television, one of those daytime programmes she couldn't bear. She retreated, turned down the stairs and went to Bar Marani, the only bar that still had tables outside this late in the year. She sat beneath the threadbare canopy of vines, lit a cigarette from an almost empty packet, ordered a coffee she didn't want. She took off the scarf and smoothed it over her thigh, her mother's voice still ringing in her ears. When she had finished her coffee she took out the reading from that morning's course. Ten minutes later, she was trying to commit to memory a passage of John Stuart Mill when she remembered where she had seen the name. She packed the book away, paid for her coffee, and headed back to the campus.

There it was, on the department notice board, an advanced English language course for second-year *scienze politiche* students. Taught by Fiona Conway, *lettrice di madre lingua*. The course began next week, on Monday, at 5 p.m. There was a space below for students to write their names. Maddy took out her pen, uncapped it and, hand trembling, added her name to the list. That evening, her mother prepared lasagne and was so loving and thoughtful Maddy almost told her about the other girl. But an inner voice advised caution, and she kept her secret to herself.

*

Fiona went back three, four times a day to see who had signed up for the course. No one at first, and then a trickle of names until the list reached double figures. Between one list checking and the next, she went to the bar, to the library, she sat on the steps of the faculty building and pretended to read her mother's most recent letter, its gossip about people she didn't know, its detailed descriptions of the weather, its vague recriminations about Fiona's living abroad. When people caught her eye she would take a second to judge them, to decide whether they thought they knew her or not, before turning away, still not ready to be approached, not sure what would be best to do if she were. All the time, she thought, Maddy, my sister, my twin, has been here, Maddy has walked up these steps, Maddy has stopped at this bar and ordered coffee. Maddy will have seen what I can see now, as I look around, as though her eyes were mine. Blood of my blood, flesh of my flesh, she found herself thinking, as though she'd been dragged into some new atavistic version of Fiona she didn't recognise. She was distracted by the slightest thing. She lost her favourite blue scarf one day, and started to cry in the middle of the campus, a barely suppressed wail that frightened her with its intensity. When she calmed down enough to return to the bar to see if she had left it there, a barman she hadn't been served by before examined her as the porter had done, then looked behind the bar and shook his head.

That same afternoon she saw a new name at the bottom of the list. Madeleine Thomsett. It wasn't until she was back at the flat and talking to Ludovico that it struck her how strange this was. At first it had seemed fortuitous, or fateful, but Ludovico agreed that no one born in England would sign up for an English course. It made no sense. Unless, Ludovico pointed out, she knew whose course it was. 'Maybe you aren't the only one with spies,' he said.

'I don't have spies.'

He shrugged. 'So what do you plan to do when this other girl turns up?' he said.

'My sister, you mean?'

'You can't know that, Fee.'

'I do know it,' she said. 'I feel it.' She paused. 'I've always known it. I've always known something important was missing. Not something. Someone.'

He shook his head. 'I don't want you to be hurt.'

'I'm hurt already,' she said.

'I don't think you mean that.'

'I know what I mean.'

He nodded. 'I'm sorry.'

She sighed. 'No, I'm sorry, Ludo. It's just that I need to know. I need to know my mother.'

'You have a mother,' Ludovico said gently.

She sighed and shook her head. 'How can you say that, Ludo?

You know her, you've seen how she treats me. You, of all people.'

'Well,' he said, standing up. 'Time I went, I suppose. Anything I can do, you only have to ask. You know that.'

'I know that, Ludo.'

*

Maddy spent the next few days worrying about when to arrive. Her instinct was to turn up early, to hide among the other students, to find a seat as far from the teacher's desk as she could. Late, she would be immediately exposed, all eyes on her as she looked for a place to sit, that double-take as they glanced from her to the teacher, and back. In the end, she found herself at exactly five o'clock in a classroom on the third floor of the department building, empty apart from a student she had seen around the place but never spoken to, who was sitting in a chair in the second row. He glanced at her with a cautious smile, edging the chair beside his in her direction. He was wearing a faded black T-shirt with 'Heart of Glass' on the front of it, and looked cold. The room was unheated. She adjusted her scarf, their scarf, and smiled back, then sat down on the chair he had offered her.

'*Siamo i primi*,' she said, because one of them had to say something and the fact that they were first in the room was indisputable. She didn't want him to assume she liked him, although she did, a little. She liked his uneasiness, which gave her confidence, and his eyes, which were an unusually bright blue. He shook his head.

'We have to speak English,' he said, spreading his forearms wide, palms turned up, elbows tucked into his waist. 'It's why we are here.' His accent, like his body language, was unmistakeably Italian, but she was used to that, and it had a London edge to it, which was less common but would explain the T-shirt. She liked Blondie, another point in his favour. He was apologetic and assertive all at once. How hard it must be, she thought, to be a man.

'Fine,' she said. 'I don't have any problems with that,' she added, and was amused when he looked startled – realising from her accent that she was English by birth – and then regretful, maybe because he'd hoped his own grasp of the language would be better than hers. She didn't enjoy this normally; she still dreamt of blending in. Most of the time she could pass for Italian with her dark thick hair worn long and a little tangled, her brown eyes, a slight sallowness to the skin until the sun gave it colour; but there were moments when she saw in people's faces that flash of recognition, and then of distance, when they understood that she was not Italian after all, and the space between them shifted, solidified, became a fragile but undeniable wall. How disappointed he was and how badly he hid it, she thought, and she felt a flicker of pity for him. She smiled again. To make it up to him – she might not have done it otherwise – she held out her hand. 'Maddy,' she said. He took it with an almost imperceptible shrug of relief.

'Matteo. *Piacere*. I mean—' he coughed, 'hi. Hi.'

She was about to ask him how long he'd been in London when she heard voices outside the room. With a flush of apprehension, she turned her head. A dozen students came in and occupied the first row of seats, so that she and Matteo were half hidden. More students filled the seats beside her. Abruptly, she wished she hadn't come. She'd been stupid to think that this was the easiest way for them to meet. If she hadn't been trapped in the second row she would have left, but that would mean drawing attention to herself, the last thing she wanted to do. She imagined the scene: Fiona walking in to take the class and finding her double stumbling around rows of chairs, tripping over rucksacks, the scarf around her neck like a mark of shame. The thought of it made her blush with mortification. She took a deep breath, uncapped her favourite pen, opened her bag and pulled out a notebook she had bought for the occasion, so concentrated on the task she didn't notice Fiona enter the room and sit down at the desk. And then she felt Matteo's eyes on her face, and heard him say, under his breath or almost, '*Incredibile.*'

Maddy looked up. Fiona was sitting, back straight, facing the group, her eyes raised above their heads towards a window at the back of the room; with the light behind them, the heads of the students would be no more than silhouettes. She was wearing a white blouse and a tailored jacket, grey, with padded shoulders, that made her look older than she was, but her hair was loose and she had more make-up on than Maddy would ever wear.

'Hello,' she said. 'I'm sorry I'm late.' She gave an apologetic smile. 'I couldn't find the room.'

Her voice was softer than Maddy had expected, hesitant. Maddy had an urge to reassure her but kept her head down. She wanted to hear the voice again, to compare it with her own, although she knew no one ever really knew their own voice, any more than you could see your own reflection without it becoming the face you expected to see. Perhaps what frightened her most was that Fiona would show her as she really was. That there would be no filters.

Fiona's hands were on the desk before her, empty apart from a thin brown folder that she played with as she spoke. She was telling them how important it was that they all used English to communicate. Mistakes don't matter, she said, her voice more forceful as she gained confidence. We learn from our mistakes.

This was familiar stuff to Maddy; she had heard her mother say the same things a hundred times and had always wondered why, if communication was so important, her mother never really listened.

Matteo was fidgeting beside her. 'I don't believe it,' he whispered, leaning across until his mouth was near her ear. 'I see double.'

'I know,' she said, surprised by the pleasure of finding an accomplice. 'It's just so weird.'

Fiona must have heard their muttering because she lowered her gaze from the window and stared directly at Maddy. She paused, raised an eyebrow and gave an almost imperceptible nod before continuing to talk about her plans for the course. Some of the students turned to see what she had been looking at, but Maddy had ducked behind a curtain of hair and was pretending to search her bag.

'All right,' said Fiona. 'I'm going to give you a text and I'd like you to read through it.' Her voice was calm as she stood up and opened the folder. She took out a handful of stencilled sheets and divided them into two, giving half to the student sitting by the door. 'Can you pass them along the row?' she said. At the far end of the second row, she gave the girl in the seat nearest to her the remaining sheets, looking not at the girl but at Maddy. Her lips hinted at a smile. 'I hope you'll find this useful,' she said.

Maddy took the sheets of paper, kept one and passed the rest to Matteo, who took one and then raised his hand. Fiona didn't notice at first, looking down at her copy of the text they had just been given and playing with her hair, twisting a single lock around her finger as Maddy did, although she couldn't know this – only Maddy could. She seemed to be trying not to look in their direction. Eventually, she lifted her head.

'Yes?'

'Can we turn on the light?' Matteo said, prodding Maddy's leg.

With a gesture that struck Maddy as improbably regal, Fiona raised a hand and indicated the switch beside the door. 'Perhaps someone could switch on the light,' she said. 'And then we can all get on with the lesson.'

Maddy tried to focus on the passage she was supposed to read, an article from *The Guardian* about the Treaty of Rome, which had nothing to do with anything they were studying. She wondered who had chosen it, and why. Fiona, she supposed. She could sense the other students wishing they hadn't come, that familiar frisson of boredom and resentment. She glanced sideways at Matteo, who pulled a face that made her want to laugh. She liked him, she decided, and thought he liked her.

She didn't speak during the lesson, other than to Matteo. She had the sense that Fiona didn't want the rest of the class to notice her. After forty-five minutes, with a brisk 'Goodbye, the next lesson will be a week on Thursday, same time, same place, different day. Is that clear? OK, see you next time,' Fiona picked up her folder and left the room. Matteo folded his sheet of paper into four and slid it into his jeans pocket.

'Coffee?' he said.

'I'll see you at the bar,' Maddy said. 'Give me five minutes.'

*

Fiona's first idea had been to find Maddy and to tell her everything she knew, to present herself as her long-lost never-met sister, because they had to be sisters, and then they would fall into each other's arms with joy, she thought, joy at the rightness of it all, and then she would be taken to meet her mother, her real mother, and her real life would begin. But Ludovico had warned her against this.

'Take it slowly. Don't scare her off,' he said, reaching across the table and taking her hands in his. They were sitting in the kitchen over takeaway pizza and beer. 'Think about it, Fee. A person you've never met before – who looks exactly like you – turns up out of nowhere and knows everything about you. Everything. It would make you seem a predator, even if you are her identical twin.'

'But why wouldn't she just be happy?' Fiona was near tears. 'I know I would.'

'Maybe she doesn't need you,' said Ludovico, who must have realised at once how cruel this sounded, and corrected himself. 'What I mean is, because she doesn't know she needs you. She doesn't know you exist.' He turned her hands over and stroked the palms with his thumbs. She wasn't sure if this comforted her or if she wanted to pull her hands away. She'd caught herself thinking about Patrick, and missing him as well. She didn't know what Ludo expected from her. Sometimes he behaved like a big brother, at other times like a lover. He continued, his voice low, placatory. 'Remember how long it took you to come to terms with it, Fee. You've had years to prepare yourself, to get used to the idea. You'll have to give her time.'

'What you mean is that she might not need me at all.'

He was silent for a while, his hands lying open and empty on the table. 'How could she not want you?' he said finally.

'My mother doesn't,' she snapped. He sat back in his chair. He was too tall for this small kitchen table, he looked ridiculous. There was no way she could say she was sorry, although she regretted her words immediately. She didn't want this to be all about her mother. And if it was all about her mother, she didn't want Ludovico to know.

'Listen to me,' he said. 'You need to be as surprised as she is. You can't believe it either, all right? It's too strange to be true.' He sat up straight. 'Whatever you do, however you play it, you need to be really careful. Let her bring the idea up if you can. Let her do the work, make the discovery. Resist her if you can.'

'Don't be ridiculous. It's so obvious we're twins. How could she not realise at once? It's as plain as the nose on my face.' She giggled. 'On both our faces.'

'Just let her do the work,' said Ludovico slowly. 'OK?'

CHAPTER FOURTEEN

Maddy caught up with Fiona outside the building. She was standing on the top step, looking down towards the campus, as though not sure which direction to take. She had turned up the collar of her jacket against the coolness of the air. Maddy paused behind her, then touched her shoulder. Fiona turned.

'This is your scarf,' Maddy said, unwinding it from her neck. 'You left it in the bar.'

'Thank you,' said Fiona, but didn't take the scarf.

'Please,' said Maddy. 'You'll need it. The weather's started to change.'

'Keep it,' said Fiona. 'Seriously. It suits you.'

Maddy nodded. 'Well, it would do, wouldn't it?'

Fiona smiled. 'I didn't expect to see anyone English at the lesson. You gave me quite a turn.'

'Not a nasty one, I hope,' said Maddy. This close, she could almost forget that they looked the same. The girl in front of her had been reduced to details, eyes, mouth, hair; was simply another girl. 'I didn't know what else to do. I saw your name on the scarf,' she said, her voice trailing off.

Fiona put both hands in her jacket pockets. 'What did you think of the lesson?'

'It was really interesting,' Maddy said, hesitating a moment too long.

'I don't know. I was scared of pitching it too high, too low. Then, when I saw you, I thought, oh fuck, what if they all speak perfect English.' Maddy's surprise must have been obvious, because Fiona added, hurriedly: 'I knew you had to speak English. You couldn't look so much like me and not be English too.'

'So you noticed the resemblance,' said Maddy.

'Well, yes,' said Fiona. She smiled. 'Just a bit.'

'Look,' said Maddy, 'I'm supposed to be meeting someone at the bar. Why don't you come along?'

'I can't. I'd love to, seriously, but I have to be somewhere else.'

Maddy couldn't believe how disappointed she felt to hear this, as though she would never see Fiona again. 'Oh, well,' she said. 'Another time maybe?'

Fiona touched her arm. 'No, really, I do have to be somewhere else. But tomorrow. Are you free for lunch tomorrow?'

'I can be,' said Maddy. 'We can get some pizza maybe.'

'Do you like Chinese?'

'I don't know,' said Maddy, surprised. 'I mean, yes I do.'

'OK,' said Fiona. 'There's a place near Via Merulana, I only just found it, I haven't been here that long, but it's not bad. For Rome, I mean. It's not up to London standards, but you wouldn't expect it to be, would you?' When Maddy didn't answer, she said, 'Don't worry. It's on me.'

'I wasn't worried about that,' said Maddy, although she was, at least in part. She was worried about her mother not eating if she wasn't there to keep an eye on her.

Fiona shrugged this off. 'OK, great, let's say half past twelve in front of Santa Maria Maggiore. It's just round the corner from there.'

'I'll be there.'

Fiona was about to walk down the steps when some thought halted her.

'Wait a minute,' she said. 'I don't know your name.'

'It's Maddy. Short for Madeleine. Like the bad woman in the Bible.'

Fiona held out her hand. 'Hello, Maddy,' she said.

Maddy watched her go, then walked across to the bar, tying the scarf around her neck once more. Matteo was sitting outside, his jacket buttoned up to the neck, writing in a notebook. He stood up when she approached. He was taller than she expected, and more attractive. But she couldn't get Fiona out of her head. They had been so close, their bodies almost touching. A closeness she had felt as a warmth on the skin, suddenly gone, unbridgeable. As though she had stared into a mirror and seen no one, not even herself.

'So tell me more,' said Matteo, rubbing his hands together.

Maddy sat down at the table. 'I don't know what to say,' she said, the complicity she'd felt with Matteo in the classroom entirely gone. She had never felt so alone.

'Take your time,' he said. 'I'll get you something to drink.'

'Coffee,' she said. As he was about to enter the bar, she called after him. 'No, make that wine. A glass of red wine.'

When Matteo returned to the table she told him about the first time she had seen Fiona, and then about the scarf. He listened, silently, then shook his head. 'It can't be a coincidence,' he said. 'You're like twins. You are twins.'

'What do you mean?'

'You didn't know about her, but maybe she knew about you.'

'That's crazy.'

He shrugged. 'It may be crazy, but it's also crazy, more crazy, to imagine that you walk along a road in a foreign city and you see an identical twin you don't know you have go past on a bus.' He paused. 'And you think she recognised you. You said that, yes?'

'Yes,' she said. She sipped at her wine, which wasn't particularly good. She hadn't wanted wine, but she hadn't wanted anything else either. I'm like Mum, she thought. When I don't know what I want I go for wine. 'But I could be wrong. She didn't know my name.'

Matteo shrugged again. 'You don't know that. All you know is that she said she didn't.'

Maddy was silent for a moment. She wanted to cry.

'Look, I don't know anything,' said Matteo, placating now.

'It's not your fault,' she said. 'I'm just a bit shaken, that's all.' She touched his hand. 'Besides, you're right. It is strange.'

'Maybe she's a spy,' he said, with a laugh. 'MI5. Or is it MI6? *Dio mio*, you English are complicated.'

Maddy smiled.

'Well, I'll find out tomorrow, won't I?'

'Tomorrow?

'We're having lunch. She's taking me out for lunch.'

'Cool.'

'Chinese.'

'Even more cool.'

'Your English is very good, you know.'

He squeezed her hand and then let it go. 'I need to keep it up,' he said. 'I need all the practice I can get.'

Maddy let herself into the flat as quietly as she could, breathing out with a sense of reprieve when she found the living room empty. She had put down her rucksack when she heard a noise in her own bedroom, of furniture being moved. She hurried across, pushed open the almost closed door, to find her mother lying on her back on the floor, one hand wrapped round the leg of a chair. Her nightdress had ridden up to reveal pale mottled thighs. She stared at Maddy in a sort of fury.

'Don't just stand there, sweetheart,' she said. 'Help me up.'

Maddy didn't move. 'What are you doing in here?' she said. 'You know you're not allowed in here without my permission.'

'For Christ's sake, help me get up off this fucking floor.' She tugged at the chair again, dragging it across the floor, lifted the leg and banged it back down on the tiles in what looked like the start of a tantrum.

'You don't need my help,' said Maddy. She turned to leave, the room or the flat, she wasn't sure. All she knew was that she had to get out of this.

'Maddy, sweetheart,' her mother pleaded. 'You can't leave me like this.' She started to cry, harsh throat-wrenching sobs from deep down inside her.

Maddy relented. She reached her mother and grabbed her arm, pulling her into a sitting position. Her mother moaned. 'Ouch, that hurt,' she said, but Maddy got behind her and took her under the arms, heaving her up. She felt her mother's weight pull on her back, her shoulders, but she'd done this before. It was the only way. She used a knee to support her mother while she adjusted her grip.

'Be careful, can't you?' her mother whined.

'I'm trying to be,' said Maddy, although she wasn't. She wanted to hurt her mother as much as she could without its appearing obvious. She wanted to punish her.

As soon as her mother was on her feet and able to stand alone, Maddy took her by the elbow and began to bundle her out of the room. 'Don't pull me,' her mother said tetchily. 'I'm perfectly able to walk without being dragged about like a sack of coal.'

'It didn't look like that when you were sprawled on the floor.'

'I'm not drunk, you know,' her mother said, finally settled in the corner of the sofa she regarded as hers.

'I didn't say you were, Mum.'

'You thought it though, didn't you?'

Maddy said nothing.

'You thought I was too drunk to get up,' said her mother, heated now and on the attack. Her voice rose. 'I haven't touched a drop of wine all bloody day.' She waved a hand at Maddy. 'Smell my breath if you don't believe me. And don't call me Mum all the time. I do have a name, you know.'

'I don't think anything,' said Maddy. 'But I'd still like to know what you were doing in my bedroom.' She'd have to start locking the door when she left the flat, she thought. Up to now, she'd only used the lock when she'd been in the room, but that was no longer enough. She had nothing to hide, but that only made things worse. Maddy preferred her mother to think that her daughter had secrets. She added, after a sufficiently long pause, 'Heather.'

'I wasn't doing anything,' her mother said. 'Can't I even walk around in my own flat any longer without being cross-examined? I do pay the rent for it, you know. Or had you forgotten?'

Maddy chose to ignore this. She took off her scarf and coat, threw them on a chair.

'Where did you get that?' said Heather.

'Get what?'

'That scarf?'

Maddy looked at it as if for the first time. 'It was a present.'

'Who from?'

'A friend.'

'Someone I know?'

'No.'

'Of course not. I don't know any of your friends. You never bring them home,' her mother said. 'I wonder sometimes if you're ashamed of me.'

Maddy picked up her coat. 'I'm going for a walk.' Heather

didn't answer. 'Is there anything you want me to get?' Silence. 'I don't know. Food. Drink.'

Heather raised her eyes, which were damp, and lifted a hand. 'Love me, darling,' she said, 'that's all I want.' Her voice was almost inaudible. 'I know I'm not the world's best mother.'

Maddy hesitated, then sat down beside her mother and took her hand. 'I do love you,' she said. She stroked the fingers, swollen, the nails edged with dirt. She didn't flinch when the hand reached out and took the edge of the scarf and jerked it as though it were the only hold on the world she had. 'Of course I love you. You know I do,' she said, in a low voice, almost a whisper, not sure if she wanted to be heard. 'You're my mother.'

CHAPTER FIFTEEN

Maddy was already outside the church when Fiona arrived. Maddy didn't see her until she felt a tap on the shoulder. She turned around and there she was, herself, the same shock as before. They smiled simultaneously, Maddy feeling her face change as the face in front of her changed, the tightening around the mouth, the wrinkling of the nose. So this is who I am, she thought again, and wondered if Fiona was thinking the same. Fiona looked up towards the gilded vault beneath the open portico.

'Isn't this place fabulous?' she said. 'Is it true they used the first gold from the New World to do the ceiling?'

Maddy nodded. Who cares? she thought.

Fiona slipped her arm through Maddy's, then pulled her close, a gesture of affection that startled and unsettled Maddy. 'Hungry?'

'Starving,' lied Maddy. She was too on edge to be hungry.

'I booked a table,' said Fiona as they crossed the square, darting between the cars. Maddy was better at this than Fiona; she'd had more practice. 'I don't think I needed to but I didn't want to run any risks.' On the other side of the square, she took a deep breath and squeezed Maddy's arm again. 'I want everything to be perfect.'

A few minutes later they were sitting at a small table in an almost empty restaurant. Maddy knew the place, but had never eaten there. Chinese food for Maddy was a shabby restaurant she used to be taken to by one of her mother's boyfriends – the one she'd thought then was her father – where she would eat boiled rice with sweet red sauce on it and bits of pineapple floating around the plate, and he would smoke and complain that he had better things to do with his evenings than babysit. But that was years ago, back in England. She could barely remember him. I wonder what he'd think if he could see me now, she thought, watching Fiona read the menu, seeing her as suddenly separate. I wonder what you would think of me if you knew.

'They do a lunch special,' Fiona said, lifting her eyes. 'What do you fancy?'

Maddy stared at the menu, not taking it in. 'Yes, that's fine with me,' she said.

'Wine?'

'If you like,' she said.

'A half-bottle maybe,' said Fiona.

'Fine.'

'It's probably not very good.'

'No really, it'll be fine.'

Fiona ordered for them both. It was the first time Maddy had heard her speak Italian and she was selfishly pleased to hear that Fiona had an accent. When the waiter walked off, there was a silence, broken when Fiona spoke. 'So,' she said. 'Here we are.'

'Tweedledum and Tweedledee,' said Maddy.

Fiona pulled a face. 'That's a bit harsh.'

'Or those horrible twins in *The Shining*.' Maddy shuddered. 'Have you seen it?'

Fiona nodded. 'In Oxford.'

'You like horror?'

'I like freaky twins,' said Fiona. Maddy must have shown her shock because Fiona added, instantly: 'Just joking. I had a boyfriend who loved Stanley Kubrick. He probably still does.'

'You live in Oxford?'

'I'm a student there,' she said. 'I'm reading Italian.' She picked up the menu then put it down again. 'This is my year out.'

'And you're working at the university?'

She shrugged. 'Sort of. It's a bit complicated. Italian bureaucracy. I mean, I haven't been paid yet and I've been here for over two months. Thank God Mummy's helping me out,' she said, investing 'Mummy' with all the contempt she could find.

'Where are you living?' said Maddy, ignoring this.

The wine arrived. Fiona filled both glasses before answering. 'I think we may need another half-bottle,' she said, sipping from hers. 'Sorry, distracted. I'm in a flat near Via Giulia. It's an embassy thing. I'm sharing with another guy and a couple of English students who are here to get lots of Italian practice, which is a bit of a downer for me, although I hardly ever see them, to be honest. Still, I would actually like to speak some Italian sometimes. It is what I'm here for, after all. It's a bit run-down too but, you know, beggars can't be choosers.'

'I love Via Giulia,' said Maddy. Did she sound as envious as she felt, she wondered. She was about to say something about beggars not living near one of the loveliest streets in the capital when two bowls of soup arrived.

'I love Chinese soup,' said Fiona, dipping her spoon into the bowl. 'All these eggy bits.'

What am I doing here? Maddy asked herself, already knowing the answer. Because we could be twins. Because we have to be twins.

'What made you choose to study Italian?' she said, because one of them had to say something.

Fiona looked up from her soup. 'No, really. That's enough about me,' she said, unexpectedly categorical. Maddy sensed that her mood had changed and wondered why. 'What are you doing in Rome?'

'I've been here for years. My mother moved here when my parents split up, she had a job at a school for expat kids just outside Rome. She'd always wanted to live abroad and the job came up, so—'

'So you were an expat kid? How romantic.'

'I suppose I was to start with, although I've never really thought of myself as an expat. I hate the word.' Maddy paused for a moment, deciding how much to say. She'd already lied about her parents splitting up. 'Then she left the school and that meant I could leave too, which was the best thing that could have happened, to me anyway. It meant I could go to a normal school and begin to live here like everyone else.'

'And now you're doing political science.'

'Yes.' She paused again. 'I applied to Oxford, you know. To do PPE.'

'How weird.'

'Weird?'

'Yes,' said Fiona. 'Because PPE was my first choice.' She smiled. 'I used to drive Mummy mad by talking about Cuba all the time. Then, I don't know, I suppose I changed my mind and switched to Italian.' She put down her spoon. 'So why didn't you go? We might have been in the same college.'

'Oh, you know, money,' said Maddy, trying to sound as though the lack of it were a minor irritation. 'I actually won a scholarship, but it wouldn't have been enough.'

'Your father left you, you said.'

'Well, they left each other really,' said Maddy. 'There have been one or two others since then, but no one for long.'

The second course arrived – chicken with cashews, beef in black bean sauce, boiled rice. Fiona served them both. Maddy watched her measure the quantities out, her bottom lip trapped by her teeth, and was unsure if what she was witnessing was niggardliness, a fear of not getting her full share or an overdeveloped sense of justice. Perhaps she had learned to behave like this from Mummy dearest, the woman Maddy had never met already a caricature, and she thought about the slapdash way she and her mother ate at home with a twinge of affection, almost pride.

'I'm so glad we're doing this,' said Fiona as she put the spoons down and pushed Maddy's plate towards her. 'The two of us together as though we've always known each other.'

'So am I,' said Maddy, but she turned from Fiona's searching eyes and glanced at the till, where the waiter and a girl were muttering together. The girl performed a parody of a double-take before realising that she was being watched. She gestured to the waiter to leave her, then turned back to her book.

In silence, they began to eat.

'So what are we going to do about it?' said Fiona after two or three long minutes had passed.

Maddy jumped, discomfited. She had been thinking about Matteo, about how much she would tell him. 'About what?'

'About why we're here. We can't just pretend we're not practically twins, can we? I mean, look at us.' Her tone, thought Maddy, was almost hostile. Back off, she wanted to say, I've stolen nothing. But that was how it felt, as though some essential part of her had been stolen. Of course we should talk about this, she thought, but how can we? We barely know each other.

'So are we?' Fiona said.

'Are we what?'

'Twins?' Fiona's hostility had been replaced by an odd pitch in her voice, almost of fear. 'We certainly look like we are.'

'I don't see how we can be,' said Maddy. 'Where are you from?'

'London.'

'There you are,' said Maddy. 'I'm from Cambridge, more or less.'

Fiona looked surprised. 'But is that where you were born?' she said.

'Well, no,' said Maddy. 'I was born in London too. But I grew up in Cambridge.' It's not quite the truth, she thought, but it will do.

'There you are,' said Fiona. 'And how old are you?'

'Twenty,' said Maddy, her heart sinking. 'What about you?'

'Twenty,' said Fiona with a smirk of triumph.

'Look,' said Maddy. 'This is crazy. There's no way we can be twins. This is just a massive, insane coincidence, I don't know, like seeing two people at a party in the same dress. There are probably thousands, millions of people who look like us, we've just never bumped into them.' She paused. 'Maybe you're my doppelgänger.'

'Doppelgänger? Aren't they supposed to be evil?'

'Well, they're supposed to bring bad luck,' said Maddy. She didn't say that she'd looked the word up the day before in the encyclopaedia her mother had carried with her from flat to flat like an icon. There were other words, she'd discovered, to talk about strangers who appeared to be twins. Fetch, they said in Irish legend. A supernatural double and harbinger of impending death. 'But who's to say who's who? I mean, who's first? Are you my doppelgänger, or am I yours?'

Fiona paused, as if to consider this.

'When were you born?' she said finally.

'December.'

'December what?' said Fiona.

'What do you mean?'

'What day, stupid.'

'You first,' said Maddy, although what she wanted to say was,

131

Can we just stop this right now? 'You tell me first.'

Fiona hesitated, then shook her head. 'Have you got a pen?'

'No.'

Fiona called the waiter over, asked him if she could borrow his pen. He looked perplexed for a moment. He was Chinese, like the girl at the till, and his Italian wasn't perfect. Maddy was scared. Everything was happening too fast, she'd lost control, although she'd never had control, not since she saw Fiona's face on the bus as it went past, Fiona looking down at her as though she'd been expecting this moment, and now the Chinese boy was taking his pen from his pocket and uncapping it, giving it to Fiona, who wrote a number on her paper napkin, then folded it in two and passed the pen to Maddy.

'Write down the day,' she said.

'What?'

'Your birthday. December the what?'

Maddy hesitated, pen poised over her own napkin, less convinced than ever that this was what she wanted, as though this rush to know would destroy them both, what bound them, what kept them apart. She felt that she was being bullied. I don't even like you, she thought.

'Go on,' said Fiona, a touch of impatience in her voice.

Maddy waited a few more seconds, then wrote the number 12 on her napkin.

'Show me,' said Fiona, unfolding her own napkin, reaching across for Maddy's.

'No,' said Maddy. 'You show me.'

'OK, together. One … two … three,' said Fiona. And so, together, they put their napkins on the table, cluttered with empty serving dishes, half-empty glasses, the remains of a meal they had lost their appetite for, a half-bottle that had once contained acidic local wine and now contained nothing at all because Fiona had been right. A half-bottle had not been enough. There was a moment's silence before Fiona clapped her hands.

'Sister,' she said.

CHAPTER SIXTEEN

Maddy took a cigarette from Matteo's packet. It was late afternoon and she had still not gone back to the flat in San Lorenzo. She was cold, but not cold enough to want to be at home, where her mother would be ensconced in her corner of the sofa, awake and petulant, or noisily asleep. They were sitting at a small round table just inside the campus bar, her coat around her shoulders, her scarf unknotted and hanging loose.

'So what happened then?' he said, passing her the lighter. 'After she said you must be sisters. Wow, you will have been really freaked out, I think. What did you say?'

'I said it was impossible.'

Matteo shook his head. He looked anxious in a way that touched her. He had soft, slightly mournful eyes, despite their blueness, the skin beneath smudged grey as though someone had passed a sooty thumb across it. She wasn't sure how much she wanted to share all this. But he had sought her out, as though he knew how much she needed him, or someone. A person she could talk to, a friend, she supposed. And perhaps he needed her as badly. There was a gentleness to him, an openness she couldn't help but trust.

'Is it impossible?' he said.

'How can we be sisters?' said Maddy. 'We have different mothers, for a start.'

'Do you? I mean, how do you know this?'

Maddy flicked ash into the ashtray with such ferocity she detached the burning tip of the cigarette. 'Oh fuck,' she said, close to tears. 'I didn't mean to do that.'

'OK,' said Matteo. 'It has nothing to do with me. I'm sorry. It's not my business who is your mother, or her mother.'

'No,' said Maddy, after a moment. 'I'm sorry. I'm not angry with you.' She reached for the lighter, found Matteo's hand on hers, obstructing her but that wasn't his intention, she knew that, he was on her side. 'I just want to finish my cigarette.' As gently as she could, she withdrew her hand.

He sat back. 'The same mother and the same father,' he said, 'if you're twins.'

Maddy sighed. 'I'll tell you what I told her.'

'If that's what you want to do,' he said.

'I don't know what I want, to be honest. No, that's not true,' she said, her voice rising. 'I know what I want. I want to go back to the morning I saw her, and take a different road so that I don't see her. I want her not to have happened. I want to be me and *basta*.' She paused, shaken by what she had just said, because every word of it was true and she hadn't known it until this minute. 'But I can't. I can't.'

He spread his hands in a gesture of helplessness. She could see he would have liked to take hold of her again. But she could speak more easily if she pretended he wasn't there.

'I told her that I'd been born in London, and I was a really difficult birth, my mother said. It took hours of labour and then I was so bruised and ugly, when the nurse gave me to Mum she took one look at me and said you can have her back.' She had heard this story a hundred times, in gorier detail than she was prepared to repeat, but before today she had shared it with no one and now she had told Matteo, whom she barely knew. She would think about this later, with a thrill of betrayal. 'I don't remember any of this, obviously. The first thing I remember is feeding swans in a park with some man who might have been my father and having one of them try to attack me and him chasing it off.'

'Swans?' said Matteo.

'*Cigni*,' said Maddy. 'I'm sorry, I forgot you weren't English.'

'Thank you.' He smiled.

'I can carry on in Italian if you want?'

'No, please,' he said. 'I love listening to you speak English. You do it so well.'

He was teasing her, she realised, and, unusually for her – always alert to the merest hint of disparagement – she liked it.

'Where was your mother?' he asked.

'I have no idea.'

'So?' he said, encouraging.

'So,' she said. 'That dad or a later version walked out on us when I was nine. I never saw him again and I've no idea if he ever tried to see me, although I doubt it.' Did she? She had nothing but fond memories of him. The truth was that her mother had poisoned him for her, a poison that – she saw this now – had also been inoculation against his loss. 'My mother taught in a primary school, but she stopped work when I arrived and never went back, I don't know why. I suppose she could have started again when her boyfriend moved on, but she said she'd had enough of kids. She started teaching English in a language school. That's where she met Nello.'

'Nello?'

She nodded. 'He was a student. He came from Sicily but he was living in Rome. He needed English for his job, but I don't remember him ever saying what that was. I asked Mum once and she said he was a lying bastard, but I don't think she was talking about his CV. Although he probably lied on that too. Anyway, he moved in with us, and Mum was cool with that because he was a bit like my own dad, the same type. She's always gone for that type. The smooth type.' Maddy looked appraisingly at Matteo. 'I wonder if she'd like you. I think she might.'

'I'm not so flattered by this comment,' said Matteo.

Maddy smiled.

'Anyway, when I was about ten Nello had to move back to Rome – I don't know why, he was living off Mum in Cambridge, he didn't lift a finger in the house. So Mum found a job at St Cuthbert's here in Rome and here I am, ten years later, sharing a flat with her.'

'And Nello?'

'Is God knows where,' said Maddy. 'Because we certainly don't.'

'Your mother has had bad luck with men,' said Matteo, offering Maddy another cigarette. She took it.

'People make their luck,' she said, leaning towards the lighter in Matteo's hand.

'This isn't always true,' he said. 'Sometimes people have no choice for their destiny. We study political science, we know this.'

She ignored this. 'He found us a place to live and then he moved in with us, because he still didn't have a job, and it was just like being back in England except that he'd bring his friends round and I hated them. They'd smoke dope in the flat and drink beer and argue about politics and sit around waiting for my mother to feed them. She's always hated cooking, but they'd sit there and watch her fill the pan with water and throw the pasta in and then complain. All they did was complain, but it was always, you know, what can you expect, she isn't Italian. She doesn't know what al dente means. I'd hear her crying at night, with Nello beside her, so fucking drunk he didn't even hear her, and I couldn't do anything.' She paused. 'It was awful. And then the police came round one day when he wasn't in, and when he found out he just disappeared. And then we had to leave the flat because it was an illegal sublet. And Mum couldn't get her deposit back. Thank God we still had money coming in from the house in England.' She shook her head.

'And all this time you went to school each day, like a normal girl?'

'Well, I was a normal girl,' she said, with a smile.

'You know what I mean,' he said.

'I went to the school my mother was teaching at, to start with anyway. That's what kept her together, I think, the fact that I was getting what she called a proper education. An English education. She could never have afforded to send me there if she hadn't been working for them. It's crazy how she wanted me to be English so badly. She wanted me to grow up and make something of my life.' She stubbed her cigarette out, half smoked. 'She's never been happy here. The one good thing I can say for her is that she's given me the freedom I need. She's always been a hippie, even when she made me wear my uniform. She'd drag me to rock things, festivals, all that stuff, but if I didn't have my school skirt on properly she'd go totally bonkers. Crazy, isn't it? Still, uniform or not, she's let me be me, as far as that's been possible.'

'And she's never spoken about a twin.'

'God, no.' Maddy shook her head. 'The last thing she's ever wanted is another child.'

'So she might have given one away?'

Maddy was silent.

'I'm sorry,' said Matteo, again.

Eventually, because her silence had become unbearable and because she felt sorry for Matteo – who was clearly mortified and may have been about to leave the bar, which Maddy would do anything to avoid – she nodded.

'I suppose she might.'

CHAPTER SEVENTEEN

Maddy hadn't said all this to Fiona. Sitting together in the now-empty restaurant, she had given the other girl a tailored version of the past, in which her abandoned mother made only rational choices and the rough edges of their life in Rome, and before, were smoothed away. No Nello, no friends of Nello. No evictions, or debts, or unexpected tussles with hardship. No alcohol. She made herself sound free more than anything, free of ties and parental constraint, free to be herself. Above all, she made it sound as though her mother loved her, and Maddy became convinced as she spoke that this was the truth of it, despite the tantrums and the weeping fits, the lies and recriminations; that underneath this lacerated garment of pain her mother had draped them in was a body of love that was innocent, naked, shared, pain-free. Free, that was the word she found herself returning to as she spoke, so that by the end of it, when Fiona had finally seemed satisfied, Maddy wasn't surprised to hear her say, in an awed and breathless voice, 'My God, I envy you so much.'

'So tell me about you,' Maddy said, and it was hard not to sound smug.

'Oh, my life's nothing compared to yours,' said Fiona. 'I'm just a well-bred boring little rich girl. Boarding school. Holidays abroad, in Italy actually. The usual.' She shrugged. 'Would you believe I even had a pony called Silver?'

'You haven't said anything about your father.'

'Well, we do have that in common, in a way,' Fiona said. 'Except that mine didn't run away, he died. He made Mummy very rich and then he died.'

'She wasn't rich before?'

'Oh no,' said Fiona. 'She's the granddaughter of a chambermaid.' She shuddered. 'She's the only person I've ever come across who talks about other people being above their station, as though they were trains or something. I think she managed to trick my father into marriage, and as soon as she'd got him she started to treat him like part of the furniture, until he died of boredom, or to spite her maybe. But that didn't work either because she got all the money in the end. Well, not quite. She's looking after it for me, in theory anyway, until my birthday.'

'When you'll be twenty-one.'

'Exactly.'

'And then what will you do?'

'I'm not quite sure,' said Fiona. 'I know what I'd like to do.'

*

Maddy was running through this conversation in her head as she walked up Via Tiburtina towards the flat. She couldn't imagine what it must be like to be rich, or to be about to be rich, although she'd spent the entire walk back from the Chinese restaurant to the campus putting herself in Fiona's shoes, as people say. In Fiona's flesh. What would I do if I had all the money I wanted, she'd asked herself, as she'd walked through the central atrium of the station, and she still didn't know. To be no more than weeks away from wealth, from great wealth if Fiona was to be believed; what an extraordinary feeling that must be. What would she do? She would find a way to wipe her slate clean, she'd thought, and the vision of that, of a gleaming empty slate she could write her life on, her life alone, had brought her to a halt. The perfection of it, the cruelty. 'I don't know how,' she'd said, out loud, in English, in the bustle of the station as the first wave of commuters moved through, because no one ever listened, the world was impervious to her as she was to the world, 'but I would wipe my slate clean.'

It had started to rain, a light rain, barely more than a moistness in the air, but everyone around her was opening bags and unfurling umbrellas. She turned up the collar of her coat. When the rain grew heavier, she turned left and nipped into a shop just by the closed and shuttered market to buy some wine and bread rolls; the bread they had would be stale now and waiting to be thrown out. On an impulse, knowing she couldn't afford it, she picked up a packet of chocolates she knew her mother liked. She looked at the packet as she waited to pay the old woman at the till, sitting there in her coat and hat, as though she'd just dropped in. She wondered if Fiona had ever tried them. She would give one to Matteo the next time she saw him, to eat with his coffee. She hadn't told Matteo that Fiona had asked her round to her flat near Via Giulia for dinner that weekend, and that she'd accepted at once. She wasn't sure why she'd kept this to herself, but she thought it might have been because she felt ashamed, and didn't know why.

Her mother was watching the evening news. She turned her head briefly to acknowledge Maddy's arrival. 'What a sodding awful world this is,' she said when Maddy had taken off her scarf and coat, drenched through with rain, and was carrying the shopping into the kitchen.

'Why? What's happened now?' she said, coming out with a glass of wine for her mother and another for herself. She'd decided to keep the chocolates for herself.

'I thought you were studying politics,' said her mother, looking at the glass with distrust.

'I am,' said Maddy.

'You never tell me anything.' She took a cautious sip. 'The world's going to hell in a handcart, people are getting kneecapped left, right and centre, it looks like the United bloody States is about to be run by a ham actor, and you never tell me anything.'

'Good God, Mum, I didn't know I had to keep you informed on the whole world's political developments as well as feed you.'

Her mother didn't answer. She took another sip, then pulled a face. 'What's this supposed to be?' she said.

'It's all I could afford.'

'That's right. Rub it in.' She emptied the glass. 'Remind me what an awful mother I am.'

'That isn't what I said.'

'Oh, don't worry,' her mother said. 'I can read between the lines.'

'That isn't what I said,' Maddy repeated carefully.

'You'd never have been this insolent if we'd stayed in England.'

'If we'd stayed in England I wouldn't be anywhere near you. I'd be at Oxford. I'd have a fucking grant.'

'Don't swear.'

'Oh, I'm so sorry,' said Maddy.

Her mother held out her glass. 'Give me another glass of this filthy wine.' Her tone was half pleading, half ironic; the tone she used when she wanted to make peace. Maddy took the glass and went into the kitchen. The washing up from the previous evening had been done, she noticed, although the plates were still in the rack. There was an odour of something rotten she couldn't place, which might be coming in from outside. The kitchen looked onto a small terrace, the flat roof of the trattoria below, surrounded by other buildings. When they had moved into the flat three years ago, Maddy had imagined a table, wicker chairs, some citrus plants in Sicilian ceramic pots, a swing seat maybe. She imagined evenings spent around the table, talking about books, and music, and film, and the infinite wealth of the world with people who listened to her, appreciated her, and her mother reborn, attentive to the needs of their guests and of her daughter. Then she found a dead rat behind a fold-down picnic table some previous tenant had left there, and the vision died. Perhaps that's what she could smell now, some rodent that had crawled behind an abandoned scrap of furniture to die and then rot in peace.

'There's soup,' her mother called and Maddy looked across at the stove and saw a saucepan, and a wooden spoon positioned haphazardly on the adjacent gas ring. She lifted the lid and looked inside and there was the start of a minestrone, some roughly chopped vegetables, the stock cube intact, a slew of greyish water. Beside the stove was an opened can of borlotti beans and a half-used packet of linguine. 'You just need to add the pasta,' her mother called out. 'And hurry up with that wine, sweetheart,' she added, after a pause and what sounded like a giggle. 'It's not totally undrinkable.'

Maddy couldn't stop thinking about Fiona, her maybe sister. Matteo was right. If they were twins they must have had the same mother and, if they did, whose mother would it be? The one beside her on the sofa, roots growing out, minestrone stains on her jumper; the one whose income of private lesson earnings, already scarce, seemed to be dwindling to nothing; the one who worked best with alcohol inside her, or thought she did, who ate when food was prepared for her and only then, who left the flat as rarely as possible and allowed no one in because no one could be trusted any longer because the world and everyone in it was shit, whose last relationship had ended in blood and tears over two years ago; the one who loved her daughter, because Maddy knew she did, despite all this.

Or that other one, the mysterious Mummy, of humble origins she despised, wily and snobbish and unloved. A woman who would deny her own daughter her inheritance, although Fiona hadn't quite said that. But also, thought Maddy, a woman who had provided for her daughter, a woman who had paid for everything needed to make Fiona's life run smoothly, a woman whose friends had found a room for her daughter in an embassy flat – whatever that was – in the loveliest part of Rome, while she was living above a trattoria and a chiropodist's, with a rubbish tip for a terrace. There is no justice, she thought, but whoever said there was. You didn't need a degree in political science to discover that. She didn't expect justice, but she would have liked a little more, well, comfort. Comfort would be nice.

And so the evening drew to a close, with Maddy curled up beside her mother on the single sofa, the television tuned to something about people going missing that the woman, now grumbling in her sleep, professed to enjoy, although she was rarely awake to watch it. As soon as it was over, Maddy turned the set off and wondered what to wear to the dinner Fiona had invited her to. She wanted to look different from Fiona, but she had no idea what sort of thing Fiona preferred. She had seen her at work, in that horrible jacket, and at lunch she had on faded jeans and what looked like a man's shirt over a plain cotton T-shirt, as though she'd been afraid of revealing too much about herself. But what would she wear for dinner in her own flat, Maddy wondered, something smart or casual? Tomorrow morning, she would look through her own clothes – wardrobe being too grand a word for the pile of roughly folded garments on a bench beneath the window, the coat hangers dangling from a row of nails hammered into the back of the door – and she would find something Fiona would never think of wearing. She would be the anti-Fiona, she said to herself in the silence left by the turned-off television. She would be Maddy, and no one else.

CHAPTER EIGHTEEN

'That'll be her,' Fiona shouted. 'Let her in, will you? I'll be out in a sec.' She looked at herself in the mirror, fought back panic because everything she had chosen – the dress, the tights, the pearls, her hair – was wrong and there was no time to do anything about it. A moment later, she was in the hall, and Ludovico was looking from one to the other with an expression of astonishment. 'My God,' he said. 'You're identical.'

Fiona stared at Maddy. Tight black jeans, a green sweater underneath a leather jacket, massive silver earrings that made her neck look even slimmer than it was, her hair in a ponytail. She looked so pretty, so herself. And here I am, she thought, dressed like my mother with a string of pearls round my neck.

'I know,' she said. She gathered her hair in both hands and held it behind her neck. 'Now look.' Ludovico nodded slowly as Fiona let her hair fall back onto her shoulders and slipped her arm through Maddy's. She led her into the sitting room. Ludovico had lit the fire while she was setting the table, the room had that pine-cone smell she loved. Maddy, she noticed, had arrived empty-handed. She took her over to the sideboard. 'Would you like a glass of wine? There's this rather nice red,' she said, picking up a bottle, 'unless you'd prefer white?'

'No, no, red is fine,' said Maddy. Fiona poured her a glass.

'Let me take your coat,' she said. Maddy slipped it off and

handed it over, then lifted the glass to her mouth and took what looked like a grateful sip. Fiona glanced at the label. 'Armani,' she said. She remembered Patrick's leather jacket and the way he'd talked about Giorgio Armani as though no one had ever heard of him. Fiona had learnt a great deal since then. She held it up to see if it would fit her. But of course it would. They were the same size. 'Very nice.'

'I've had it for ages,' said Maddy; she sounded apologetic. 'It's second-hand, from Porta Portese.'

'We must go together,' said Fiona enthusiastically. 'I adore flea markets! You can show me where all the bargains are.' Calm down, she told herself. Ludovico was watching her from the door, a wry expression on his face. He walked across as Maddy sipped her wine, and held out his hand.

'Well, as Fiona obviously isn't going to present me, I'm Ludovico. I live here too.'

'Introduce, Ludo. We say introduce,' said Fiona.

A door at the far end of the room opened and Alice and Robert walked in, giggling, their arms around each other in what was obviously a postcoital tangle. Fiona wished she'd been able to persuade them to eat out, but they'd been told by Ludovico – who would not be forgiven for this – that someone was coming to dinner who looked exactly like Fiona and they'd refused to leave the flat. She left them for a moment to fill a pan with water and put it on to boil, then hurried back into the sitting room. Maddy seemed lost, shrunk into herself, and Fiona's heart went out to her. She reached over, rested her hand on Maddy's. Startled, Maddy looked down. The two hands, naked of jewellery and coloured varnish, were indistinguishable, as Fiona had known they would be. She remembered the ring her mother had given her, how she had almost put it on, and was glad now that she hadn't worn it.

'It's lovely to have you here,' Fiona said.

Ludovico nodded.

'It certainly is,' he said. 'It's like a special offer in a supermarket. Two for the price of one.' Alice and Robert giggled.

'You make us sound like tarts,' said Fiona. 'Doesn't he?'

Maddy shook her head. 'I think he's trying to be nice.' Her voice sounded odd. She'd barely opened her mouth since she arrived. Fiona noticed Alice staring across the table at Maddy, bemused, not entirely friendly. This dinner was an awful idea, she thought. Please God, don't let me scare her off.

She'd decided to keep her cooking to a minimum and had chosen for starters salami already sliced in the shop, the most expensive *salumificio* in Campo de' Fiori, and spicy olives in little bowls. A silence fell on the table as people ate. The salami and olives were soon finished, as was the wine she'd poured before they sat down. Ludovico picked up the bottle and filled Maddy's glass, then his own, and then, apparently as an afterthought, Fiona's. Fiona, irritated, picked up the empty bowls and headed for the kitchen. She could hear Ludovico talking to Maddy and a furtive giggle from Alice. She threw a trayful of ravioli into the pan of boiling water, put the sauce on to warm over a low heat and stood there, tapping her fingers on the edge of the table. When she came back into the sitting room with the serving dish, Maddy was saying, 'I'm a student. Political science.'

'He doesn't want to know that,' she said, putting the dish on the table. 'He wants to know if you've got a boyfriend.'

'You know me too well.' Ludovico looked at Fiona, and then at Maddy. 'Well,' he said. 'Do you?'

'Do I what?' she said.

'Have a boyfriend?'

She shook her head.

'He's a natural born flirt,' said Fiona, handing round plates of ravioli. 'I wouldn't let it worry you.'

'It doesn't,' said Maddy, smiling for the first time since she'd arrived.

'So, Maddy, you were telling us about yourself,' said Fiona, a little too brightly.

Maddy took a deep sip of wine, finishing her glass, then paused, as though weighing her options, thought Fiona. She looked at the now-empty bottle and nodded at Ludovico, who stood up and fetched a second bottle from the sideboard. She watched him refill their glasses, smiling, his eyes on Maddy as she spoke, her eyes on his. This wasn't what Fiona had planned, this feeling that she had been excluded. She pushed her ravioli around the plate and barely listened to Maddy; she'd heard it all before only days ago, at lunch. She was only drawn back into the conversation when Maddy said, 'I've known Fiona for a week.'

Fiona laughed. 'Actually, not even that.'

'No, not even that,' said Maddy. 'So here I am. I'm here because we look alike and Fiona thinks we're twins. Isn't that right, Fiona?'

'Maddy thinks we're a freak of nature,' said Fiona, not looking at her, her eyes fixed on Ludovico.

'I never said that.'

'A weird coincidence,' she said, turning to Maddy, her tone more strident than she intended. 'Like two people turning up in the same dress. That's what you said, isn't it?'

Maddy said nothing.

'And then you decided I was your doppelgänger.' Fiona smiled, but it was no good. Maddy hadn't been forgiven for what she had said at lunch – that one of them was evil. She knew more about twins than Maddy ever would. 'You see, I've done my homework too. I know all about doppelgängers, and fetches, and all that stuff.'

'Did I say that? I don't remember.' Maddy looked embarrassed.

Nobody spoke. Ludovico filled their glasses once again. Alice and Robert began to fidget. After a moment or two, Fiona stood up.

'I'll get the salad.' She was glad she hadn't prepared a main course. They didn't deserve it. She went down on her haunches to take the salad bowl from the fridge, and would have burst into tears if they hadn't been waiting for her. She took a deep breath, then straightened up and carried the salad to the table, along with another bottle. 'This is it, I'm afraid,' she said, putting the bowl beside the candlestick, passing the corkscrew to Ludovico. 'You don't mind using the same plates, do you?'

'You aren't at all alike, you know,' said Ludovico to Maddy. 'You look alike,' he said, opening the bottle, and sniffing at the cork before pouring her a glass, 'but, believe me, you really aren't.'

*

Fiona was sitting on the sofa when Ludovico got back. Alice and Robert had disappeared into their room and she was finishing the final bottle of wine. She had the onset of a headache.

'You waited for the bus with her?' she said. He poked the last few embers of the fire into life, then took the glass from her hand and drank what was left of the wine.

'Of course,' he said. When she didn't respond, he sighed. 'Are you angry with me?'

'Why should I be angry with you?'

'I've no idea.'

She took the empty glass back from him. 'Thank you,' she said.

He ignored this. 'She seems very nice.'

Fiona snorted in disbelief. 'Is that it?'

'Is what it?'

'Is that all you've got to say?' She sat up, and then stood up. She was furious, with the evening, with herself. 'You meet my mysterious twin sister, from whom I was separated at birth, you spend the entire evening flirting with her, and all you've got to say is that she seems very nice.' She walked across to the table, emptied Alice's glass into hers. 'You spend too much time speaking English, Ludovico, that's your trouble.' She put the glass down in irritation. '"Very nice",' she mimicked. '"Very nice".'

'Well, isn't she? Am I supposed to not like her?'

She pulled out a chair and slumped into it with a sigh. It was useless to lose her temper with Ludovico. She stared up at the chandelier, noticing the dust on it for the first time. 'I don't know if she's nice or not. I can't make her out. There's supposed to be this – oh, I don't know – this alchemy between twins, or do I mean chemistry? Whatever it is, we're supposed to understand each other like that.' She clicked her fingers. 'But we don't. Or I don't. Maybe she does.' She looked at him. 'Did she say anything about me? She did, didn't she? What did she say?'

'We didn't talk about you,' he said gently. 'She wanted to know about my work, so I told her. We talked about the stars.'

Did she believe him? She wasn't sure. She wished she did. More than that, though, she wished that Maddy *had* wanted to talk about her, had shown some curiosity, some need to know, as she would have done. There were so many questions she would have asked.

'OK,' she said. 'I'm going to bed.' She looked at the table. 'Leave the dishes. I'll worry about them tomorrow.'

CHAPTER NINETEEN

'It was horrible, Matteo,' Maddy said. They were in the campus bar, at their usual table. They had fallen so easily into this routine, as though they had known each other for years rather than days. How strange friendship is in Italy, Maddy always thought, so sudden and precarious and deep, all at once, as though there was no time to lose in case the moment passed. She looked at him gratefully as he stirred his coffee. It was Monday morning, the weather had changed for the worse, and they had a half-hour break between lectures. Maddy had changed her scarf for a heavier one in a different colour, a woollen scarf that belonged to her mother and had the scent of her on it, musky, a blend of cigarette smoke and anti-wrinkle cream; an odour as familiar to Maddy as that of her own skin. 'I don't know why I went. I don't even think I like her. She was all dressed up like a society hostess. She barely spoke to me.'

'I worried about you,' he said. 'You didn't call.'

'Neither did you.'

'Really, I did call.' He paused. 'She didn't tell you?'

'You spoke to my mother?'

'She was your mother? She didn't say.' He lit two cigarettes, passed her one.

'We don't have a maid, Matteo,' Maddy said.

'I know that,' he said. 'It's only that, well, she didn't seem to know you. I thought perhaps she could be some friend who was dropped in.'

'*Had* dropped in,' said Maddy, without thinking. When Matteo repeated her words in a reprimanded way, she took his hand. 'I'm sorry. She should have told me you'd called.'

'The first time? Or the other times?'

She squeezed his hand. 'Oh dear. I really am sorry.'

'That's all right. How was the food?'

'The food was bought in expensive shops, so it was good. So was the wine. She didn't *prepare* anything, she just threw some salad in a bowl and did some *burro e salvia* for the pasta.'

'But you ate well?'

'For God's sake, Matteo, it isn't all about food. You are *so* Italian!'

He grinned, amused and apparently flattered. 'Who else was there?'

She was going to tell him about Ludovico, who had walked her back to Largo Argentina, but stopped herself. Ludovico had half hugged her, kissed her on both cheeks and, more importantly, given her his number, which was also Fiona's number as Maddy had realised when she was on the bus and thinking about him. Did he flirt with everyone, as Fiona had said, or was that just intended to keep Maddy in her place? If he found her attractive, Maddy thought, he would also find Fiona attractive – an idea she still found difficult to accept; that they would appeal automatically to the same people. But perhaps he knew Fiona well enough for that not to matter. He said how different they were, after all, as people, even if they did look alike. Fiona is empty, she thought, and vindictive too. I'm not like that, she told herself, and he will have seen that. She liked the way he'd spoken to her as they walked, in Italian finally, his accent not exactly Roman; the way he told her about the research he was doing at the Institute for

Astrophysics – I spend my days looking at stars, he'd said – his doctorate in Chicago, the two years spent at an English boarding school. He didn't mention Fiona, and she was grateful for that.

'The people she shares the flat with, an English couple. Very into each other.'

'Didn't you tell me she shared with Italians?'

'Did I? I don't remember.' She finished her cappuccino. 'Anyway, she doesn't. Apart from an old friend of hers, who spoke English all the time.' She paused for a moment. 'I haven't told my mother about her.'

Matteo said nothing.

'I'll tell her when I feel I need to,' she said, on the defensive.

'That's your decision to make,' said Matteo, but she could feel his disapproval. It's the Italian mother thing, she thought, but it was more than that. He saw her as duplicitous, or cowardly perhaps. Why couldn't she just be protecting her mother? she wanted to say. Because that was also true. It hurt that he might think badly of her.

'It's time we went,' he said, looking at his watch.

'We still have ten minutes,' she said.

'I'd like you to take me home,' he said.

'Have you forgotten how to get there?'

He laughed. 'No, stupid. Your home.'

She shook her head. 'I can't do that,' she said.

'You don't trust me,' he said. He shrugged. 'OK.'

'It's not OK,' she said, suddenly furious. 'It's not at all OK. It's totally fucked, to be honest.' She pushed her hands through her hair. 'I just can't believe she'd never have told me,' she said, and her voice broke; she was on the point of crying.

'They were only phone calls,' he said, anxious.

'I don't mean you,' she almost screamed. 'This isn't about you, Matteo. It's about her, my mother. She had twins and she kept one and she gave the other one away to some other woman and she has never once thought to tell me about it in twenty years.' She sniffed back tears. 'Twenty fucking years.'

'You can't know that,' said Matteo, uneasy now, trying to reassure her. 'Maybe you need to ask her.'

Because the alternative was what, she thought – that the adopted twin is me?

She nodded, wiped her eyes with the end of her scarf. 'Maybe I do.'

*

At ten on Sunday morning, Fiona was wandering around the stalls of the market at Porta Portese, hoping Maddy would be there. Last night had been a disaster, she knew that, but all they needed to do was talk and for them to be together, as sisters, and everything could be saved. What she wanted now was to put her arm through Maddy's and to walk from stall to stall, rooting through piles of second-hand clothes for something that might have a designer's label sewn inside. She didn't want to argue or interrogate or challenge. She wanted people to notice them, and nudge each other and say, look, they're identical, with that mixture of curiosity and wonder, because it was wonderful that two people should be indistinguishable from each other. Equally, she wanted other people not to matter, she wanted the world to reduce itself to her and Maddy. She wanted them to have a private language, impenetrable from outside, the way twins did. She wanted them to be one.

Leaving the market, she spotted a stall selling dolls, arranged in tiers like spectators in an arena. Modern baby dolls sat next to Victorian ladies, their features painted on porcelain, their dresses a riot of lace and ribbons, their legs sticking out like stalks. She picked up a pair of rag dolls from the front of the stall. A fat man in a fisherman's waistcoat put down his *Corriere dello Sport* and nodded at her.

They looked as if they had been made by hand. Their hair was wool and their faces were embroidered in cross-stitch. Their clothes were sewn directly onto their bodies. They had the same crooked infantile smile and the same straw-coloured hair. A double thread of cotton held the right hand of one to the left hand of the other. Fiona asked how much the man wanted for them. It was more than they were worth, but that didn't matter. She bought them both.

The following day, Monday, Fiona was distracted, felt that she was teaching badly, and then decided not to care. As soon as the lessons were finished, she headed to the campus bar, then retraced her route to the political sciences faculty. She sat on the low wall at the top of the steps, pulling her coat around her. Maddy would be bound to pass sooner or later and she would give her the present. After a while she began to shiver, she hadn't expected the weather to be this cold, she'd dressed like a student, like Maddy. The ochre sweater she had on she'd bought at Porta Portese the morning before. She'd shown it to Alice, who'd given a wry smile and said 'Copycat'. Fiona had pretended not to understand. The colours are totally different, she'd snapped.

She was about to go when she noticed the student who'd been sitting next to Maddy at the lesson. He was walking up the steps, alone. She thought of following him in the hope that he might lead her to Maddy, but he'd already seen her. When he stopped and smiled, she stood up. 'Hello,' she said.

'Hello,' he said, cautiously.

'You're in my class, aren't you?'

'Yes,' he said. 'But the lesson is Thursday, right?'

'Yes, yes,' she said, hurriedly. 'I'm just here to see someone.'

'Oh,' he said, then, 'Maddy, I suppose.'

'She's a friend of yours?'

He shrugged. 'I suppose so.'

She took a deep breath. 'Because I have something for her,' she said. 'Something I promised to give her, and, you won't believe this, I've lost her phone number and her address.' She pulled what she hoped was a whimsical face. 'I know, crazy, isn't it? I had them on this piece of paper and I must have thrown it away by mistake.' Don't explain, Fiona, she told herself. The more you say the less convincing you are.

He lifted his palms. 'I'm sorry,' he said. 'I can't help you.'

'Oh well, never mind,' she said. She looked behind him. 'Perhaps she'll be along herself.'

He shrugged again. 'She may not have any classes,' he said. 'I don't know what her programme is today.'

'No, of course not.' She smiled. 'Thank you anyway.'

He stood there awkwardly, then smiled back. 'See you on Thursday.'

'Thursday?'

'At the lesson.'

'Yes, of course,' she said. 'Silly me.'

Half an hour later, she decided she was wasting her time, and stood up to go. At the bottom of the steps she heard someone call out 'Maddy'. She froze, then turned to the voice and saw a girl she didn't know running towards her. The girl came to a sudden halt only feet away from Fiona. Her hands flew to her mouth.

'Oh my God,' she said. 'It's you, isn't it?'

'Me?' said Fiona.

'You aren't Maddy. You're the other one.'

Fiona held out her hand. 'My name's Fiona.'

'I knew you were English.'

'And you are?'

'Oh right. Sorry. Gina.' She took Fiona's hand.

'So you're a friend of Maddy's?'

Gina nodded. 'This is just so strange. I can't get over it. You're identical.'

'That's what everyone says.'

'I saw you a couple of weeks ago. You looked right through me and I went off and shouted at Maddy. I was furious with her.' Gina laughed. 'How was I to know she had a twin?'

She had said 'twin' as though it were beyond dispute. Fiona wanted to hug her. 'You haven't seen her around, have you? I was supposed to be meeting her.'

Gina shook her head. 'Try her at home,' she said.

'I'll do that,' said Fiona.

'I'm going to San Lorenzo,' Gina said. 'I'll walk with you if that's all right? It's nice to have a bit of company.'

'Fantastic,' said Fiona. She stepped back, waited for Gina to lead the way. A few minutes later, they walked past the point where Maddy had been standing only two weeks earlier, although it seemed a lifetime ago, Fiona's life divided in two by that moment, that flash of recognition from the passing bus. If it had been like that for Fiona, who already knew that Maddy existed, how much stranger it must have been for Maddy, who knew nothing. Fiona had a rush of sympathy for Maddy. Maybe she was expecting too much from her, too soon. She thought about the rag doll, pushed deep into her bag. Maybe she should wait before she gave it to her, before she told her about the other doll lying on her own bed, its woolly hair resting on her pillow.

'Your English is amazing,' Fiona said, coming to a halt at a corner because she had no notion which direction to take. Beside them, a man was selling cut flowers from the back of a van. She had an urge to buy some for Maddy, to wander the streets with a bunch of yellow tulips until she found her.

'My father's English. He makes me speak it at home,' said Gina, looking pleased.

'Like Maddy's Italian,' said Fiona. 'I mean, that's really good, isn't it?'

Gina slipped her arm through Fiona's and began to walk towards a street market a block or two away, pulling Fiona in until she fell into step. 'Maddy's been here for years.'

'Yes,' said Fiona.

'But where have you been? You just popped up out of nowhere!'

'I'm sorry?'

'I mean, you are twins, aren't you?'

Fiona nodded.

'It's crazy. She's never even mentioned you.'

'Oh, you know,' said Fiona, easing her arm away. 'Families.'

'All right, all right,' said Gina, loosening her grip. 'Be mysterious. I don't mind.'

Fiona extricated her arm. 'Well, we might as well say goodbye here,' she said.

Gina looked startled. 'Oh,' she said. 'OK then. *A presto!*' She waited for Fiona to move off. Fiona hesitated, then turned right, walking along the side of the square that held the morning food market. By this time, mid-afternoon, everything had been packed away apart from one stall, where an old woman with a scarf over her head was stacking boxes into the back of a van. Fiona paused and glanced behind her. Gina was where Fiona had left her, staring at Fiona with a bewildered expression. When Fiona waved, she raised a hand in a half-wave, then shrugged and walked away. Fiona looked around her. A little further on, she saw a bar, a patio surrounded by a low wall. She walked towards it, her heart beating with anticipation.

She had just reached the bar when she heard a cry from behind her. She turned to see a woman being pushed out of the way by a man, who ran away, leaving the woman staggering like someone drunk. She got to her feet and fell over again. Fiona's instinct was to help, but someone from the bar pushed past her and was hurrying towards the woman, now on her knees and reaching for a handbag. She pulled up the collar of her coat and turned away.

*

When Maddy closed the door behind her, she sensed immediately that something was wrong. She walked through the living room and checked in the kitchen and bathroom, but her mother was nowhere to be seen. She was about to call out her mother's name, *Heather*, but didn't want to wake her if she was sleeping, although she only slept on the sofa during the day. She always said she hated the light in her bedroom. Carefully, Maddy opened the bedroom door. The room was empty, the bed, surprisingly, made. She couldn't remember the last time she had found the flat empty. She'll have popped out to do some shopping, Maddy told herself, but why would she do that? Everything she needs is already in the flat. She checked the cupboard where the wine was kept, and the fridge. Nothing had been touched since that morning. The sink was empty, so she hadn't eaten anything or, if she had, she had washed the plates up and put them away, which was hard to believe. She's dead, Maddy thought with a rush of panic, but she knew at once that made no sense. If she were dead she'd be in the flat. She'd be slumped on the sofa, stretched out on the floor; if it had happened outside, in the street, someone would surely be waiting to tell her. People don't just die. But the thought had shaken her so hard she collapsed on the nearest chair, heart pounding, stunned that a part of her should have felt relief.

She only moved when the phone rang.

Her mother was sitting outside Bar Marani, under the canopy of leafless vine. Her legs were wide apart, her upper body slumped forward, her forearms resting on her thighs. She looked like an exhausted boxer between rounds. She had a smear of dirt on her left knee and a leather handbag she never used dangling between her calves. The girl who worked there was holding a damp cloth to her forehead. When Maddy walked through the gate, her mother lifted her head, then pushed the girl away. 'There was no need to call you,' she said, in English, and it was hard to tell if she was angry or contrite. 'I wish people wouldn't fuss. I'll be all right in a minute.'

Maddy apologised, but the girl folded the damp cloth in half, then shook her head. Crouching beside her mother's chair, Maddy took her hand. The knuckles were scraped raw. 'You've fallen down,' she said, her voice soothing. 'I was worried.' Hesitant, she touched her mother's knee. Heather was wearing a skirt and had ripped her tights, grazing the skin. What she had thought was dirt was dried blood. Her mother winced.

'Careful,' she said.

'We need to get you home,' said Maddy. 'Can you stand?'

'Of course I can stand,' her mother said, but she didn't move until Maddy slid a hand under her arm. She let herself be lifted a little from the chair before sinking back. 'Oh God, Maddy, give me a minute.'

The girl came back with a glass of water and a smaller glass of brandy. Heather nodded. '*Il brandy*,' she said, hand reaching out. '*Mi dia il brandy.*' She drained the glass.

'Oh Mum,' sighed Maddy. 'Time to get home now.' She

looked around, hoping to see someone she knew, but the other tables were occupied by women her mother's age or older, shopping bags at their feet, their faces concerned, their curiosity undisguised. A stocky white-haired woman Maddy recognised from the building opposite began to tell the other women what had happened as though she and her mother were no longer there. That one there was just about to go into the jeweller's shop down the road, the woman said, pointing at Heather, when some lad pushed her out of the way and she fell on her knees right into the gutter, screaming that she'd been robbed. But she hadn't, the woman said, I watched her get up and then fall over again. Like someone who's had a glass too many, she said, her voice lowered. She shook her head slowly. So there she was, down on the floor again, the woman continued, her tone a mix of contempt and pity. You should have seen her hang on to that old bag for dear life, the woman said. She's got something valuable in that, I said to myself. She leant forward until she could poke Heather's shoulder with a bony finger. 'Haven't you, dear?'

Maddy fought the urge to slap the old woman's hand away. Her mother had started to weep uncontrollably. A great hollow space of pity and love opened up inside Maddy, unplumbed since she couldn't remember when, and she felt a wave of guilt she could not bear as she wiped beneath her mother's eyes with the sleeve of her coat. She was rougher than she'd intended, so that her mother was startled and then, to judge from her expression, hurt. 'I'm sorry, Mum, I'm so sorry,' she said while her mother examined her face as if for the first time, then turned away. Don't do this to me, thought Maddy, letting her hands fall to her mother's arms, to her lap, easing the old black handbag out of her grasp. I look like you, I have your eyes, your skin, your mouth, she told herself, although her mother's eyes were watering now, her mother's skin was blotchy and marked by broken veins, her mother's mouth was swollen and loose. I am your daughter, I know I am. You are my mother, and only mine.

'Do you love me?' she said.

Her mother lifted both hands and took Maddy's head between them. The skin was cold and rough, she had trouble straightening her fingers because of the grazes on her knuckles. She held her daughter still, as hard and steady as she could.

'I love you more than anything else in the world,' she said. 'My darling, darling child. You're all I have.'

CHAPTER TWENTY

Maddy helped her mother out of her clothes, easing the ripped tights down over her hips and legs, then sat her on the edge of the bathtub with her dressing gown over her shoulders. She bathed her mother's knee with warm water, picked out the pieces of gravel from the broken skin with tweezers while her mother stared up at the ceiling, gripping the sides of the tub with both hands, her feet so white and bloated in the eddying water that it hurt Maddy to see them. She patted the newly bleeding graze on the knee with alcohol-soaked cotton wool.

'Ouch, that stings!' her mother cried.

'I can't help it,' said Maddy.

'I'm not blaming you, sweetheart,' her mother said, that same unexpected fondness in her voice.

'I know that, Mum.' She waited to be corrected – *my name's Heather* – but her mother sighed.

'I felt so foolish,' she said.

'You're home now,' said Maddy. 'I'll get you tucked up on the sofa and then I'll make you a cup of tea.'

'I should be looking after you.' Heather stroked Maddy's cheek. Her voice was filled with pleasure. Maddy hadn't heard her sound this contented in ages. An understanding between them had been reached, an intimacy she wasn't sure she could handle.

'Yes, well,' she said, standing up. 'Let's get your dressing gown back on before you get cold.'

Her mother struggled to her feet and stepped out of the bath, wincing as she put weight on the injured leg. 'Yes, matron,' she said and Maddy realised that the moment had passed, and regretted this, and could do nothing to bring it back.

'What were you doing out?' Maddy asked ten minutes later, when her mother was sitting on the sofa with a glass of red wine, the offer of tea having been turned down.

After a few moments Heather said, 'I wanted to sell some jewellery.'

'What for?'

'What do you think? We haven't got any money, Maddy.'

'We never have any money,' said Maddy.

'Well, this time, we really haven't got any money.'

Maddy had been expecting this for weeks, since Heather's income from lessons had dried up, but she hadn't dared mention the subject. To bring it up would have meant bringing up Heather's drinking, and how much that cost and what it did to her, the rows, the hangovers, the missed appointments, and that would have led to an argument from which neither would have emerged unscathed. For months now, Maddy had done the food shopping, wandering from store to store on the hunt for cut-price pasta and canned tomatoes, buying the cheapest fruit and vegetables from the market before the stalls closed, turning off lights her mother left on, making a hundred small economies in order to put this moment off. If only we hadn't given up the house in Cambridge for good, she thought. That had been her mother's idea, a bad one, spurred on by a fugitive post-Nello boyfriend whose name Maddy no longer recalled. All she remembered now of the miracle money-making scheme the man had proposed was that it involved rabbits.

'If only you'd let me get a job,' she said. 'I could find work in a bar or something.'

'I don't want you to neglect your studies,' her mother said.

'I wouldn't. I'd find the time, honestly.'

'I don't want to argue about this, Maddy. You know how I feel about it.' Heather's tone had changed, hardened. 'Besides, you know how impossible it is here. They don't even let you keep your tips in most places. You'd end up working for nothing.'

'Lots of people study and work,' insisted Maddy, although she recognised the truth of what her mother had said.

'I just told you there's no need for that. All I need is something to tide us over until I'm feeling a bit livelier.'

'Livelier?'

'Don't be like that,' Heather said, plaintive now. 'I can't help feeling a bit run-down.'

'You aren't run-down, Mum.' Maddy fought to hold back her anger. 'You drink too much, that's all.'

'I know I do,' her mother said, to Maddy's surprise.

'I didn't mean to sound—'

'You sounded fine,' said Heather. 'None of this is your fault.' She poured more wine into her glass, then put it down on the floor beside the sofa with exaggerated care. 'I've got some rings and a few other things, a necklace, a couple of Victorian brooches; they belonged to your grandmother. I never wear them, and I just thought, if I could just not feel any pressure, you know, for a few weeks, then maybe I could pull myself together.'

'So you wanted to sell them?'

'It was just an idea. I thought I'd see how much they were worth.'

Maddy picked up the bag.

'Why on earth did you use this bag?' she said, starting to root through its contents. 'It's horrible.'

'It's the one I use to keep my personal things in,' Heather said anxiously, her hand reaching out.

Maddy handed the bag over. 'Show me what you wanted to sell,' she said. 'I didn't know we had any family jewels.'

'They're nothing special.'

'That's OK,' said Maddy. 'I'd still like to see them.'

'I said there's nothing special, sweetheart. Just drop it, will you?'

Maddy knew better than to insist.

'And get me an aspirin, there's a good girl. My head's splitting.'

Maddy was coming out of the bathroom with two aspirins in her hand when the phone rang. Heather, half asleep, still clutching her bag, was startled into wakefulness; a look of desperation flickered across her face. Maddy touched her knee. 'Don't worry,' she said, 'I'll get it.'

'*Pronto*,' she said.

'It's me, Matteo.'

She shook her head at her mother, mouthed, 'It's for me.'

'I just wondered if you were all right.'

'I'm fine,' she said. 'How about you?'

'Listen, Fiona's been here on campus to find you. She remembered that I was with you at the class last week. She wanted to know where you lived. I said I didn't know, I just sat beside you, that's all. But then I saw her talk to someone else on our course. Gina something.'

'Gina Scarpone.'

'That's her.' He paused. 'Is she your friend?'

'No,' said Maddy.

'Who is it?' said her mother.

Maddy covered the mouthpiece with her hand. 'No one.'

'A boy?'

'For God's sake, Mum.' She lowered her voice. 'We need to talk.'

'OK.'

Putting the phone down, she heard him say, in a voice he must have picked up from B-movies, unctuous, faintly menacing, 'Don't worry. Your secret is safe with me.'

*

Fiona didn't go straight home. She didn't want to see anyone she knew, didn't want to make conversation with Ludovico or, even worse, the other two in the flat. She stopped for a coffee in a bar near the station, her thoughts a tangle of resentment and doubt, and determination. When she left the bar, she reached inside her bag for cigarettes and felt the paper in which she'd wrapped the doll. She'd forgotten all about it, her reason for seeking Maddy out, although it had never been more than an excuse. But now it seemed that the only useful thing she could do would be to deliver it into her hands.

She set off back to San Lorenzo, walking fast to warm up. By this time Maddy would be shopping for dinner, or having a drink or an ice cream somewhere with friends. What did she do in the evenings? Fiona wondered. Did she lock herself in her room and study? Did she eat with her mother, or alone? Surely, in Italy, they would eat together. They would sit at a table, with a proper meal on their plates, and they would talk about their day. Her mother was a teacher, she would have stories to tell about the children in her class. Maddy would say what she'd been reading. How different from Fiona's home in England, with her mother distracted by the radio and Fiona taking her plate into the next room and eating off her lap, the television on, or a book propped up on a cushion beside her. She hated the radio as much as her mother loved it, the endless voices effortlessly confirming what the woman thought, the trivial stories of everyday folk, the music so bland it was immediately forgotten. Did Maddy listen to the radio? Fiona wondered. Did she still like new wave? Her friend, the boy with the bright-blue eyes, was wearing a Blondie T-shirt at the lesson. Did Maddy still wear her Talking Heads T-shirt or had her tastes moved on? So many questions.

By the time she reached San Lorenzo it was dark. She looked at her watch. A few minutes past five. She'd been wandering around for hours. She was tired, and hungry, and cold. She remembered the bar she'd seen earlier, the one with the open patio, and wondered if anyone would be brave or foolish enough to sit at one of the tables outside. Perhaps she would stop and have a hot chocolate, warming her hands on the cup, and wait for Maddy to pass by. Some story she couldn't place came into her head about sitting on the banks of a river and waiting. No, it wasn't a story, it was a proverb Patrick had told her one evening in a pub in Oxford. If you sit by the river long enough, he'd said, it's a samurai thing, you will see the body of your enemy float by. But that wasn't at all what she meant.

She turned a corner into a short cobbled road and saw the bar at the far end. She was almost there when she heard a man speaking English. She stopped walking, then crossed to the far side of the road and walked the length of the bar, darting around the corner to the entrance, where she could hide behind a brick column next to the steps leading up to the patio. The man she had heard was Maddy's friend, the one who had said he barely knew her and didn't know where she lived, and he was talking to Maddy, who had her back to Fiona. The two of them were leaning forward, their heads together, but Fiona was close enough to hear what they were saying. They were laughing about one of their courses, about a professor they both disliked, and Fiona decided that she would walk up to their table and tell them that she had just been passing and had heard them talking and wasn't that an extraordinary coincidence, all of which was true, or almost true. 'Of all the gin joints in all the towns in all the world,' she would say, and see if Maddy picked up the reference, and how wonderful it would be if she did.

She was about to leave the shelter of the brick column when the waitress came over to their table and asked Maddy how her mother was, after being pushed over like that; she said, it's just awful when you fall down in the street, and asked if she'd lost anything, there were so many delinquents about these days and Maddy reassured the waitress, but Fiona had stopped listening by that point. The woman she had seen being pushed over was her mother? She had been that close to her own mother, and done nothing? She leant back against the wall, her heart in her throat. She had seen her mother. How had she not known? How had that bond that must exist between them not been felt? And now what do I do? she thought. Still skulking behind the column, she watched the woman walk away, saw Maddy pull a face, then shake her head when her friend said something Fiona didn't catch.

Fiona was on the point of leaving, her plan to reveal herself striking her now as foolish, ill-conceived, her idea of presenting Maddy with the doll absurd, when she heard her own name mentioned, and Maddy's mother, her mother, was forgotten. The man said something about Fiona being Maddy's 'new friend'. Fiona couldn't tell what Maddy thought of this; their voices had gone low and she strained to hear what they were saying. She thought she heard him repeat the conversation they had had this morning. She touched the rag doll in her bag. Maddy said something about the lesson that Fiona didn't catch, but that didn't matter. Then she saw Maddy move her head away from his and sit back in her chair, and say in a clear voice, so that nobody could misunderstand her, Fiona gives me the creeps. As if he hadn't heard, she said it again. She gives me the creeps, she said.

Fiona felt sick. Her whole body began to tremble. Maddy was flirting with the boy now, she could see that from how they were sitting, his face all smiles, her head closer to his again. Fiona pressed her forehead against the cold brick of the column, then moved away, staggering a little because one of her legs had gone dead. She needed to get away from them as fast as she could. She had a sensation like heartburn, of pure hatred, a jet of hatred that flared in her throat. She had never been this hurt before. I can't let this happen, she told herself. Whatever it costs, she said to no one, she's not going to get away.

CHAPTER TWENTY-ONE

'Don't turn round,' Matteo said.

'What?'

'I think I saw her in the street, just behind you.'

Maddy froze. 'How did she find me here?' She covered her face with her hands, then let them fall. 'Did she see you?'

'I don't think so.'

'Is she still there?'

He shook his head. 'She just left. If it was her. I can't be sure.'

'Quick. Give me a *gettone*. I need to make a call.'

A woman's voice answered. '*Pronto.*' Alice, thought Maddy, instantly relieved. In Italian, she asked for Ludovico. 'Hang on a sec,' Alice said, her own Italian apparently exhausted. 'Who is it?' '*Un'amica,*' said Maddy. She heard her put the receiver down, listened to the silence of the room and then the sound of footsteps and someone picking the receiver up. For a second, she wondered what she was doing. And then she heard Ludovico's voice, curious, distant, and felt calm.

'Hello,' she said. 'It's me. Maddy. We met on Saturday.'

'Of course we did,' he said. 'What a pleasant surprise. But I'm afraid Fiona isn't here.'

I know that, she almost said. She's sneaking around San Lorenzo, looking for me.

'Actually, I wanted to speak to you. I realised I hadn't given you my number and so I thought I'd call and—'

She waited for him to say something. When he didn't she decided to take the initiative: 'I don't suppose you'd like to meet up for a pizza sometime?'

'I would like that very much,' he said. 'But I'm really the one who should invite you.'

'It's not too late,' she said, surprising herself.

'In that case,' he said, and then laughed. 'Thursday evening?'

'Thank you. That would be great.'

'Do you like motorbikes?'

'Yes,' she said. 'Yes, I do.'

'Excellent. Where shall I pick you up?'

'Piazzale Tiburtino. Eight o'clock?'

'I'll be there.'

Matteo was waiting for her. 'So you made your call,' he said.

'Yes,' she said. 'I called Fiona's flat. I wanted to see if she was there.'

'And was she?'

'No, you were right,' she said. 'Well, not proved wrong, at least.'

'Small comfort,' he said. 'I love that expression. I use it all the time.'

They sat in silence for a minute or two.

'So who did you speak to?' he said.

'Oh, no one,' said Maddy.

'No one?'

'A flatmate,' she said hurriedly.

'Because you had a nice long chat,' he said. 'I thought you didn't like the other people in the flat. The lovebirds, you called them.'

She took a deep breath. 'It was the other one,' she said. 'I told you about him. He's an astrophysicist. He's known Fiona all her life. Anything else you want to know?'

Matteo raised his hands. 'OK, OK. I was just curious.'

'I'm sorry,' she said. 'I'm really on edge today. I think it's Fiona's fault. I feel as though I'm being stalked.'

'Stalked?'

'You know – followed, spied on. What hunters do to their prey.' She sighed. 'It doesn't matter,' she said when he looked puzzled. 'I just wonder what she wanted.'

'Maybe she wants to get to know you better,' he said, in a tone of fake sincerity.

Maddy burst out laughing. 'Oh God, did I really sound like that?'

'Worse. You sounded like someone on afternoon TV.'

'Really?' She laughed again. 'Not that I ever watch afternoon TV, of course. That's my mother's thing. Which reminds me.' She finished her beer. 'I have to get back home. She'll be thinking I've been kidnapped or something. Not that I'd be much of a prize.'

'Let me come with you,' he said.

She stood up. 'Not today,' she said. 'Another time, I promise.' She put her hand into her pocket. 'Oh fuck,' she said. 'I've forgotten my wallet. I've come out without any money.'

'Don't worry, I'll get it.' He walked into the bar. It occurred to her that she could simply slip away – she'd find an excuse later – but he deserved more than that. When he came back to the table, sliding his wallet back into his pocket, she looked up at him.

'I don't deserve you,' she said. 'All I do is take.'

He shrugged. 'You're forgiven,' he said, and smiled.

She stood up and slipped her arm through his, then kissed him on the cheek. 'You can walk me to the door,' she said, 'but that's as far as it goes. Is that OK with you?'

He nodded, then gave her a mock salute. '*Agli ordini, signora.*'

When Maddy entered the flat, her mother was waiting for her, standing by the kitchen door, one hand on the doorframe to steady herself, the other held out and clenched into a fist. Maddy was filled with a tenderness she didn't know what to do with. She was awkward with love.

'You shouldn't be on your feet,' she said.

Her mother shook her head. 'I'm fine, sweetheart,' she said. 'You have to stop worrying about me.' Slowly, her fingers uncoiled. 'I wanted to give you this,' she said. 'I should have given it to you years before now.'

Maddy took the ring from her mother's palm with a cry of surprise and joy. It was exquisite, two strands of differently coloured gold woven together into a single band. 'It's beautiful,' she said, her voice breaking.

'I had it made for you,' her mother said. 'A long, long time ago.'

CHAPTER TWENTY-TWO

Maddy got there early, but Ludovico was already waiting for her, leaning against his bike. She hurried across, pulling her jacket about her. It was the jacket she'd worn when she went to dinner; she wondered if he'd notice. He was wearing black jeans and a pea coat; he was taller than she remembered. The motorbike beneath him was enormous, like some vast armoured insect. She felt a moment's trepidation. When he spotted her and straightened up to wave, she saw that it was a Moto Guzzi, and her first thought was how much it must have cost. She'd had money on her mind all day, money and unpaid bills. Her mother had spent the afternoon looking through old letters from the handbag she had when she fell, weeping on and off, sipping from a carton of wine, and refusing to talk about either, which meant that Maddy had thought about nothing else. She would have gone to the faculty library to work but she was scared she might be seen by Fiona after the lesson.

When she reached him, he took her by the shoulders and kissed both cheeks.

'You look lovely,' he said, and she was tempted to say that he did too, but men didn't always appreciate that sort of comment, so all she did was smile and stroke the seat of the motorbike, where Ludovico had been leaning.

'It's beautiful,' she said.

'She's my baby,' he said. He took a step back, to include in the same gaze both the motorbike and Maddy, then spread his arms. 'Together, you make a perfect pair,' he said. Disconcerted, she felt herself blush. This is the kind of thing you say on a first date, she thought. Is that what he assumed this was? A date? She told herself to calm down, she was jumping to conclusions, conclusions she might not want. But it didn't help. He was even better-looking than she remembered, which didn't help either. He stroked his chin, in mock contemplation. 'Now where shall I take you this evening?'

'Anywhere you like,' she said; she hated being teased.

'Hungry?' He didn't seem to have noticed.

'Enough,' she said, softening.

'In that case I know just the place,' he said.

He got on the bike, heaved it off the stand, turned round and patted the pillion. 'Jump on,' he said.

'I don't have a helmet.'

'Neither do I,' he said, reassuringly, she supposed.

She hesitated. 'I've never been on anything bigger than a scooter before.'

'You're safe with me,' he said. 'Nothing will happen that you don't want to happen. Trust me.'

She climbed onto the pillion, a little agitated by what he had just said. Had he realised how easily his words might be misinterpreted? Had that been his intention, she wondered, that she should misinterpret him? The engine beneath her was still warm; she could feel its heat through her jeans.

'You will drive carefully, won't you?' she said.

'You'll need to hold tight,' he said, ignoring this. 'There's a sort of handle you can use. Alternatively, you can put your arms around me. Which is better for both of us. Safer for you, and a greater pleasure for me.'

Laughing now, because his flirtatiousness was so unwarranted, so theatrical, she put her arms around his waist and linked her hands.

'Perfect,' he said. 'Now hold on. I'm afraid we won't be able to talk until we arrive, but if you want me to stop, just bite my ear.'

She laughed again. 'I didn't expect you to be this much fun,' she said.

'People always say that,' he said, manoeuvring the bike onto the road. 'They think that because I'm an astrophysicist I will be dry as dust.'

'As cosmic dust,' she said.

'Indeed,' he replied, and those were the last words she heard as he moved off, accelerating noisily, under the railway lines. She wished she'd thought to tie her hair back. The motorbike passed easily from lane to lane as if to mock the almost stationary surrounding cars. Her initial fear was replaced by an exhilaration she'd never felt before, her heart and lungs seeming to open out, made larger by the rush of air as the bike speeded up.

Breathing more easily, she tightened her hold, felt her breasts press against Ludovico's back, shook her head until her hair was out of her eyes and mouth, and she could see where she was. They were heading away from the centre of Rome, away from its history and wealth. The Moto Guzzi she was sitting on was probably worth as much as these soiled apartments, their crumbling balconies loaded with the overflow of the rooms behind them. She had a sudden revulsion at the idea of poverty, theirs and hers. Clinging to Ludovico as the bike moved effortlessly on, she was struck by a vision of Fiona in the flat she shared with Ludovico, Fiona in her little black dress and pearls, and behind her the fireplace and the chandelier, and the matching bowls with olives, and Alice and Robert ignoring her, their well-bred tongues probing each other's mouths, and the whole picture was so dripping with comfort and warmth, and the indifference that only wealth could bring that she actually felt nauseated, and had to swallow hard until the feeling passed.

He pulled up outside the kind of place Nello used to bring them to when they first arrived in Rome, usually run by friends from his past who would look over Heather as though she were a souvenir brought back from some exotic journey. The ten-year-old Maddy they'd pick up and kiss in a way she hated, while her mother said how physical Italians were, how spontaneous they were, what a welcome change from the constipated English. She'd shudder at the thought of it. They'd be given plates overflowing with offal in various sauces and pestered until they tried it. Heather would make a fuss about her weight and barely touch the food, although she'd empty the carafe of wine soon enough, while Nello cheered her on. She couldn't remember now who paid on these occasions, although she'd bet it was her mother; all she remembered was the texture of tripe in her mouth the first time she was forced to eat it, the sponginess of it against her tongue, and the rising acidic bile in her throat as she tried to swallow.

Ludovico was holding the door open for her. 'Thursday,' he said, 'is gnocchi.'

'I'm not that keen on gnocchi,' said Maddy, walking into the long narrow room. At the far end was a brick-built oven with a blazing wood fire inside it. The walls were panelled halfway up in stained pine, with prints of Rome and photographs of football players covering the space above. After the street, the room was almost unbearably hot.

'Give me your coat,' said Ludovico. He had already draped his over the back of a chair. He was wearing an ironed white shirt, tailored to his frame, and blue jeans with a narrow belt. He made Maddy, in jeans and a striped sweater with a high neck and a glittery thread woven into the wool, feel overdressed and cheap. He placed her jacket over the chair opposite his and then pulled it out for her to sit. He took the chair opposite, his back to the wall. Normally, this was where she would sit – she liked to see the rest of the room and to feel herself protected – but he had given her no choice, her field of vision was restricted to him as he smiled and fiddled with his napkin, his eyes skimming the room. For the first time, he seemed lost for words. She wanted to say something that would amuse him, as he had amused her, but nothing came.

'So you don't like gnocchi,' he said, when a middle-aged woman in an apron had thrown two menus on the table and given them a basket of bread. 'Let's see what else they've got.' He lowered his head to read the menu and she took this opportunity to look at him closely for the first time. He'd been to the barber's since she last saw him; his hair was clipped around his ears in an almost military cut, which made his fringe look longer. He had a habit of pushing it off his forehead. When he looked up from the menu, his eyes were bright, as dark as Matteo's were blue.

'Made up your mind?' he said.

'There's too much choice,' she said.

She hadn't planned to talk about Fiona, but Ludovico brought her up as they were eating their first course. Neither had ordered gnocchi. 'Fiona's worried,' he said. 'You weren't at her lesson this afternoon.'

'Why should she be worried?'

'Well, maybe not worried.' He stopped to think. 'Maybe in a mood would better describe it.'

'She could have come this evening,' said Maddy, although that was the last thing she would have wanted.

'Hardly. I didn't tell her.'

'You didn't tell her?'

Ludovico shook his head, then grinned. 'Should I have done?'

'I don't know. I thought you were friends.'

'We are. That doesn't mean we have to do everything together.'

'I suppose I thought there might be more than that.'

'Really?' He raised an eyebrow. 'Is that what she said?'

'No,' admitted Maddy.

'I'm totally uncommitted, to Fiona or to anyone else for that matter. I'm a free man in Rome. I haven't been in a relationship since Chicago. Which is one of the reasons I'm not there now.'

Maddy blushed, she could feel the heat rise in her cheeks. 'I'm sorry. It's really none of my business. I wouldn't want you to think, oh, I don't know.' Her voice faltered. 'I'm jumping to conclusions, that's all.'

'That's dangerous, you know.'

'I know,' she said. 'I really know nothing at all about you. Or Fiona, come to that.' She put her fork down; she'd lost what appetite she had. 'How did you meet?'

'I've known her for years, since she was a child. We're practically family, to be honest. My father worked for her father, he represented him in Belgium and then here in Italy. I don't know how they met, I never asked. I think my father was with him when he became rich, they were associates in some way. Buying, selling, objects at first and then just money itself as far as I could tell. My father was always cagey about his work. They'd come and have holidays with us, Fiona and her parents. We had a place just outside Rapallo and they'd stay in the summer until her father died and her mother stopped bringing her and the holidays stopped. She used to hang around with me and my friends, and then it became a bit awkward.'

'Awkward?'

He finished his pasta, pushed the plate away. 'Some friends thought she was fair game and made a pass at her, and when it all went wrong she'd tell her father, and then my father would blame me.'

'Maybe she wanted to get at you? For not looking after her?'

'I don't know.' He paused. 'I used to think she wanted to make me unhappy because I was never unhappy.' He smiled. 'I practically never am, you see. It's a failing in me.' He shook his head. 'I really do try. I force myself to be miserable sometimes, but no, it just doesn't happen.'

'You are cosmic dust.'

He smiled. 'Exactly. That inconsequential.'

The woman came and took their plates away. They ordered lamb and green salad, amused that they had chosen the same dishes, and another half-litre of wine.

'So Fiona spoke Italian before she came here?' she asked Ludovico as soon as they were alone.

'Yes,' he said. 'She had a Genoese accent when she was fifteen. Now she speaks it like someone who's studied Italian at school.'

'So why did she switch to Italian?'

He paused. 'I think she wanted to come to Rome.'

'She could have come to Rome in any case.'

'She wanted to live here, I think. She wanted to have an excuse to live here.'

'Is that what she's said?'

'Not exactly.' He looked around the room. 'Do you like it here?' he said. 'The decor's rigorously proletarian, don't you think?'

'Is that why you brought me here?'

He looked stricken. 'Of course not,' he said. 'That was the furthest thought from my mind.' He shook his head. 'You surely don't think—'

'That you're slumming on my behalf?'

'Slumming?'

'Seeing how the other half live,' she said. 'Getting a cheap thrill out of squalor. Is that what you're doing with me?'

He was speechless, she could see that, for the first time this evening. She should have felt satisfied but she didn't. She felt abruptly guilty.

'You do me an injustice,' he said at last.

'All right,' she said. 'We didn't come here to talk about Fiona, or at least I didn't. But we seem to have talked about nothing else.'

'That wasn't my intention,' he said, his tone still apologetic.

'I know that,' she said. 'Look, let's start again.'

'I'd like that.'

'Tell me what happened in Chicago,' she said. 'Your last relationship.'

'My God,' he said, 'do you really want to know?'

'I really do,' she said.

He shook his head. 'I think I'd rather tell you a little more about my work, if that's all right with you? I'm more comfortable talking about the stars than affairs of the heart.'

'In that case we'll need some more wine,' she said.

CHAPTER TWENTY-THREE

When Maddy left the flat on Saturday morning, Matteo was leaning against a wall at the corner of the street. He was reading a book, absorbed.

'What are you doing here?' she said.

'I was just passing,' he said, then laughed and closed the book. 'I began to just pass—' he checked his watch, 'about thirty minutes ago.' He looked down at his feet, and then back up at her. 'I didn't see you yesterday. I thought I would. I wanted to tell you how the lesson with Fiona went.'

'You could have rung the bell,' she said, although she was glad he hadn't. Her mother had been complaining about people using the intercom and then not answering when she got up to see who it was. The house rule now was to ignore it, and Maddy was happy to comply. Nobody visited them unless they had bills to deliver.

'Do you want a coffee?' he said.

'If you're offering,' she said. Had he noticed she always let him order, always let him pay? She hoped not; she wanted to avoid that conversation.

'Of course,' he said. 'I'm a perfect gentleman.' He offered her his arm. His jacket came open; he was wearing his Heart of Glass T-shirt again, the one he had on when they first met. She wondered for a moment what his mother thought when she washed and ironed it, but Matteo's mother, she knew, would never do that kind of housework. They'll have had an English au pair when Matteo was a child, and then a series of foreign women, Filipinos, Romanians. She slipped her arm through his. He had no idea.

'So what have you done since I last saw you?' he said when they were sitting at a table and had ordered coffee.

'All of two days ago!'

'Three,' he corrected her. 'It was Wednesday that we saw each other last.' After a pause, he continued. 'I really missed you at the lesson. It wasn't very useful, to tell the truth.' He lowered his voice. 'She isn't a very good teacher. You'd be much better. Maybe we should kidnap her and you can take over. No one would know.'

Maddy leant forward. 'Maybe I should take over everything.' Her voice was conspiratorial. 'Her life, her flat. Her money. I'd be such an improvement on the original.'

'I think you would,' he said, unexpectedly serious.

When their coffee arrived, she sat back.

'Yes, well, that position is already occupied.'

'Yes, we will have to get rid of her first, obviously.'

'I think people will probably notice if she just disappeared.'

'But she won't disappear, right? You will. And who will miss you? Apart from me.'

Maddy looked at him. He seemed perfectly serious. She laughed.

'Did she say anything to you? About me, I mean.'

'Yes. She asked me where you were. I said I didn't know.' He heaped sugar into his coffee. 'I think that all she wants from me is information about you.' This time, he laughed. 'I feel used.'

'Women,' she said. 'We're all the same.'

'She was dressed like you,' he said suddenly.

'What?'

'She wore what you wore the first lesson, more or less. I think she wanted to look like you. Some of the other guys noticed. Maybe some of them thought she really was you.'

'I expect she just wanted to look more relaxed,' said Maddy, without believing it. She knew what Fiona was trying to do, although it made no sense. She had everything; Maddy had nothing. Fiona had no reason to be envious.

*

She would have told Matteo about the dinner with Ludovico if he hadn't been so sweet to her. She would have welcomed the chance to put what she felt into words, to see if any sense might be found in it. She'd asked Ludovico what his research involved. He was reluctant at first; she had to encourage him to talk about his work, not in Rome but outside it, in Frascati, at an institute she'd never heard of. She couldn't hear the word Frascati without remembering a visit there, soon after she and her mother had arrived, a little trip on the local train, a villa on the hill. How excited she had been until the motive for the trip had been revealed. They were there to sample the local wine, or Heather was, and she would never forget how disastrous that had turned out to be. But she didn't want to think about her mother now. She listened as Ludovico's manner became increasingly animated, his vocabulary more precise, not really taking much in, her eyes fixed on his, on his hands as they moved in the air, shaping the universe for her, on his mouth, the attraction she'd felt initially becoming stronger the longer he talked. And then, for no reason, he stopped and apologised. 'I'm boring you,' he said and she denied this immediately. How could she be bored if she was barely listening? She was riveted not by his words, but by his every movement, the dark hairs on his knuckles, his eyelashes, his teeth when they caught his lower lip, then let it go. She was confused, and excited, and a little scared that what she felt might not be shared, and a little scared that it might be shared, because what would it mean to be in love with a man like him, she wondered; what would it mean to be in love with a man who might mistake her for another woman? Who might be looking at her, apparently with love for her, and seeing someone else? Throughout the meal, she felt the presence of Fiona there at the table, seated beside her, as though his eyes might flicker to the left and find her there, and be confounded. As though each were constantly in the orbit of the other.

That was when her attention returned to Ludovico. He was talking about one of his projects, a group of stars called Algol. For centuries people had believed it was a single star that varied in brightness every seventy hours, like a long slow pulse – they thought it was alive, he said; astronomers called it the Demon Star, although the English term ghoul is closer to the original Arabic. Secretly, he told her, he always thought of it as ghoul. He said he loved the word, the way it sounded, his lips pouting out in an unrequited kiss. Ghoul. How badly she'd wanted to kiss him back, right there in the trattoria, pushing the plates to one side like people in a film.

It was centuries later, he continued, leaning forward, his elbows on the table, that someone discovered there were two stars, bound together like conjoined twins, he said, his large, strong hands weaving before her eyes – two stars orbiting and eclipsing one another. So you can't see them both at the same time, she said, and he was so surprised – because she hadn't uttered a word before this – that he lost his thread. Algol, she reminded him. The Demon Star. Two stars, she said, and added, bound together like twins. And then, as if he'd only just realised the significance of what he'd been saying, he sat back, startled, and shook his head. Actually, he said, that isn't the case. Algol has more than two stars. A third was discovered some years later, and there may be more in the same system. There almost certainly are. That's what I'm looking into, he added rather lamely, that possibility. That there are more than two.

Outside the restaurant, he watched her zip up her jacket. 'I've enjoyed this evening very much,' he said. 'Not everyone lets me talk about my work. In fact, no one does. I hope you weren't too bored.'

'I wasn't bored at all,' she said.

He stepped closer, reached over to adjust her collar. She caught his hand and moved it to her lips, pressed it against them, hardly aware of what she was doing. He lowered his head and kissed her cheek, and then, when she turned her own head, the corner of her mouth. The second time their lips met as they should.

'I wish we had somewhere to go,' he said, his breath warm, ticklish in her ear.

She pulled back; she wanted to see his face. She smiled, nervous now, not wanting to show it, wanting it to continue. To hide herself from his eyes, she brushed her lips against his cheek, abrasive with stubble, shivering at the feel of him, the feel of his body as it moved with hers, his arms around her, his hands on her lower back. When he lifted his head away from hers, so that all she had of him, of his skin, was suddenly denied her, she felt bereft.

'I want to see you again,' he said, his voice above her, both close and distant, as though he were speaking to someone else.

'Yes,' she said.

He stepped back, lifted her chin and kissed her again. 'And now I'm going to take you home,' he said, 'before you change your mind.'

I won't do that, she thought. 'All right,' she said, her voice as strange, as broken and far away to her as his. She smiled, her heart still beating fast in her chest, and touched his cheek, as if to make sure he was real. 'Thank you,' she said.

Seated behind him as he manoeuvred the motorbike into position, she waited until the engine was ticking over, then placed a hand over his heart and felt it beat as fast as hers.

He left her on the corner.

'I'll be fine from here,' she said.

Later, lying in bed alone, she thought, you could so easily have smuggled me into the flat. It was past midnight by the time we were back in San Lorenzo; it would have been even later by the time we reached the centre. You could have taken me to your bedroom in that wonderful, enormous flat and no one would have known, Fiona would never have known. And if she did find out, what harm would that do? You aren't a couple, are you? You told me you were just friends. Why should you lie? And then she thought, if we make love, will you be thinking of me or her? You say you've never slept with her, you protected her, that was all, but I'm not convinced. I wish I was. We're Algol, she thought. Algol, ghoul. Two stars orbiting and eclipsing. Will you be comparing our bodies, the way we move, the noises we make? Which one of us will be more passionate, more enterprising, more inventive? Which one of us will give the most, the best, require the least? How will you measure one against the other? Or will she simply not be there when I am there? Is that how it works?

Because you can't have both.

There would be no point.

CHAPTER TWENTY-FOUR

Two days after the lesson, when the hurt of not seeing Maddy there had begun to pass – although not what she had said about Fiona giving her the creeps, the injustice of which still brought tears of wounded rage to her eyes — a letter arrived for Fiona. It was Saturday morning, around eleven, and Ludovico had been to Campo de' Fiori to buy fruit and pizza. Fiona was reading Doris Lessing in the sitting room when he came in and frisbeed an envelope across the room towards her. It landed at her feet. She picked it up, examined it for a moment, then put it down on the cushion beside her.

'It was in the post box downstairs. I thought I'd save you the effort of fetching it,' he said. 'It's from England.' He hovered by the door, shopping bags in his hand, until she looked up from her book.

'Yes?' she said.

'Nothing,' he said. 'Just curious.'

She would have opened it in front of him if she hadn't recognised the writing.

'Coffee?' he said.

'No, I'm fine.' She stood up as casually as she could, slipped the letter into her book. 'I'm going to prepare a couple of lessons.'

'Well,' he said, 'if you change your mind.'

She nodded. Ludovico had behaved strangely these past few

days, over-attentive, with that ironic courtesy he'd picked up in England, which must have gone down an absolute bomb in Chicago, she thought, but didn't wash with her. He was hiding something. He'd been too affectionate, kissing her when it wasn't called for, giving her a hug when they passed each other in the corridor. At the same time, there was something in his manner that made her think he was avoiding her. It reminded her of when she'd thought he might be in love with her. That was years ago, she'd been no more than fourteen, but she'd found herself comparing him with Maddy's friend Matteo, weighing up the pros and cons. Ludovico's height against Matteo's eyes. Ludo's easy manner against Matteo's cautious, almost timid formality. The fact that Ludo knew all there was to know about her, or thought he did, while Matteo knew nothing. The fact that Matteo belonged to Maddy. And now, she thought, locking her bedroom door behind her, throwing herself on the bed and taking the letter out of her Lessing novel, now, like a hooded snake rearing up from a basket to the music of some invisible charmer, there was Patrick.

The letter was a single sheet of lined paper, ripped out of an exercise book. It was written in Patrick's neat but quirky hand, slightly pedantic, with odd little flourishes and loops below the line and the letter 'e' like the working end of a tiny trident lying on its side. It was less than half a page long. How the hell had he got hold of her address? she thought, but then she remembered; that was how Patrick worked. She read it quickly, threw it on the floor, then picked it up and read it a second time, more carefully.

My dear Fiona

I want to thank you for your letters and I also want to apologise to you for the fact that I have not written back before now. It has been, as you can imagine, difficult for me to adapt to life within a prison cell, although I have been treated very well, and certainly better than I deserve, by everyone. I am pleased to be able to tell you that I am likely to be released well before the end of my sentence as a result of my good conduct, and, I like to think, my work in the prison library, where I have been able to use my academic skills for the good of the community in which I find myself. I am looking forward very much to visiting you in your new home, and even more, to spending some time with our darling Elizabeth. She owes us both so much, as we do her. She's our collateral! I know <u>for certain</u> that you are aware how much she means to me, as of course do you. We shall be soon together, my dear, and living well. Until then, I remain

your very own
Patrick

Everything about this letter was wrong. The scrappy paper, so unlike fastidious Patrick, the affected handwriting, the overall tone – so false, so insinuating, so hackneyed, like something her mother might write – the underlining of 'for certain', which felt like a threat, the coyness of 'my dear' and the final 'your very own', which made her squirm, the way he talked about Elizabeth, as though she were a child they had made between them and now shared. Above all, the word 'collateral', because she realised now that Patrick remembered that conversation as well as she did, that revenge was their collateral, that living well was the best revenge. Just to be sure, he'd reminded her of it in those last few words. 'And living well.' This letter will have been read and vetted, she thought, and they will have understood nothing. They will think they have helped a deserving well-educated young man from a respectable background avoid a life of crime. The whole letter intimidated her, made her feel sick with anxiety. She screwed it up, then smoothed it out again. She needed to show this to someone, to weaken the force of it. But who? She thought of Maddy. This is what sisters are for, she thought, to share things with. A real sister would understand. In the absence of that, it would have to be Ludovico. She folded the letter in two and left her bedroom.

The kitchen still smelt of coffee but Ludovico must have filled his cup and taken it somewhere else. She knocked on his door, then, when there was no response, opened it slowly. The bed was made, the room empty. She walked through to the sitting room, expecting to see him at the table, but the room was empty apart from Alice, sprawled on the sofa in her dressing gown, reading a magazine.

'I was looking for Ludovico,' Fiona said.

'He's just gone out with Robert, to help him get something for my cold.' She sniffed dramatically.

'I thought Robert was here to learn Italian?'

'Don't be cruel. He's only a beginner,' she said. 'I don't want him buying the wrong thing and then me feeling even worse. It was sweet of Ludovico to offer.'

Fiona had turned to go when Alice called her back.

'What is it?'

'I forgot to tell you,' she said. 'That friend of yours who looks just like you?'

'What about her?'

'Well, she called the flat a couple of days ago?' Everything Alice said sounded like a question. 'When you were out?'

'When exactly, Thursday?'

'No, before that. Tuesday?'

'I was here on Tuesday.'

'Monday, then. I don't know. Does it matter what day?'

'Did she leave a message?'

Alice smirked. 'No. She spoke Italian of course, but I recognised her voice. I thought it was you showing off, to tell you the truth, because you really do sound exactly the same. Anyway, she said she didn't want to speak to you.'

'She didn't want to speak to me?'

'She wanted to speak to Ludovico.'

'Are you sure?

Alice nodded, pleased with herself. They heard a key turn in the lock of the front door. I don't believe you, thought Fiona.

'That'll be my medicine,' said Alice.

*

Ludovico read the letter, then shook his head, folded it in four and gave it back to her, watching her while she slipped it into her pocket. 'I never liked him,' he said. He stood up and shifted the wood in the fireplace, then filled her glass. 'This only confirms what I thought.'

Fiona stared out of the window towards a wall of trees. She wanted to say that Ludovico didn't know Patrick. But what would be the point of that? She had turned to Ludovico for comfort and he had given it. He had brought her to this cottage behind Frascati, one of the half-dozen houses his family owned or had the use of, scattered around Italy like way stations along a pilgrimage of wealth. She'd spent the occasional weekend in the cottage before, with her parents and Ludovico's, before her father's death and her mother's self-punishing refusal to return to Italy. She'd been introduced to the family in the big house, the

Palladian villa down the hill. She'd walked through the woods and collected acorns and worried that a wild boar might emerge from the undergrowth, because Ludovico had told her, in his teasing big-brotherish way, how likely this was. The woods are full of them, he would say, knowing how terrified she would be. He'd said it again this afternoon, as they walked from the car to the front door, and she'd slapped his arm harder than he'd expected. 'I'm not a scaredy-cat any longer,' she'd told him. He'd laughed, repeating 'scaredy-cat' as though the expression were new to him. She watched him now as he poked at the fire and was glad that she'd agreed to come. She felt safe here, despite the wild boars. She felt safe with Ludovico.

'You will look after me, won't you?' she said, not sure how far she was joking. 'If he turns up.'

'I thought you were a couple,' he said.

'We were,' she said. 'That doesn't mean I want to see him now.'

'How does he know where you're living?'

'I wondered about that too.' She shrugged. 'The only person who could have told him is my mother. She fell in love with him last Christmas. She thought he was a very nice young man. She doesn't know he's in jail, I don't think. I certainly haven't told her. There's always his sister, Jennifer. He might have asked her to get in touch with home. It's the kind of thing he'd do.' She paused, curled her legs tighter beneath her on the sofa. 'Thinking about it, he might have done what he did when he found out where Maddy was. Used his friends, I mean. Now that he's been in jail, he's probably better connected than ever. That's what scares me.'

'And Elizabeth? Who on earth is Elizabeth?'

She'd realised the moment she handed the letter over to him that he would ask her about Elizabeth. She'd tried to think of a plausible explanation, but nothing came to her. She would have to tell him the truth. He listened silently as she told him about the Forsyth novel, the country cemetery, the photo booth. When she finished, he shook his head.

'So this was all his idea.'

She nodded. 'Yes,' she said, 'totally.' She'd been worried he might think badly of her. Because she hadn't resisted, she'd let Patrick go ahead. And because no one had made her do the rest of it, the dole giro landing on the doormat, the national insurance number. She'd been excited, and a little scared. She was as responsible for Elizabeth as Patrick was. But Ludovico didn't seem to notice any of this.

'He's sick,' he said. 'Sick and dangerous.'

She nodded again. 'I just hope he doesn't come to Italy.'

'You don't know when he's going to be released?'

'No. I suppose I could find out.'

'Don't do that. If he hears you've been asking questions he might think you really want to see him. It's odd that he doesn't ask you to write back, isn't it?'

'He ignored all the letters I did write,' she said. 'I don't think letters from me are what he wants.'

'So what does he want?'

'I don't know. That's why I'm worried.'

Ludovico shook himself. 'I need some fresh air.' He nodded towards the door. 'Coming?'

They headed away from the villa, towards the highest point of the park. It was dark by this time, and Ludovico took her hand to lead her along the path that bordered the remaining areas of wooded land. The air smelt of smoke from fires in the scattering of nearby cottages, and moist earth; it had rained earlier that day. Neither of them spoke. Fiona was conscious of the feel of Ludovico's skin against hers. Her eyes had adjusted to the darkness; there was no need for him to guide her steps, and she felt that he knew this as well as she did, but neither he nor she was willing to break the bond their hands had made. After ten minutes or so, they were brought to a halt by a flare of light to their right, followed almost immediately by a muffled boom.

'Fireworks,' he said as a rowdiness of coloured stars filled the sky. They stood, enthralled like children. Flowers opened effortlessly into a myriad of twinkling spores, waves of colour rolling through the infinite dark beach of the air above them, rosettes like polyps bursting into smaller polyps or dandelion clocks, and then, after all that colour, a brilliant whiteness and a noise so deafening Fiona's hands flew to her ears. And then it was over.

'Do you know what illuminates the night?' he said when the silence returned.

Fireworks like these, she thought, but didn't say. She shook her head.

'Poetry.'

'That's beautiful,' she said. She'd expected him to say love.

'It comes from a film. French, I think. I don't remember which. But I've never forgotten it.' He moved closer to her, put his arm around her waist as they stood side by side, staring at the sky that, seconds before, had been the most living thing in the whole world and was now emptiness. 'I'll look after you,' he said. 'Don't let him scare you.'

She leant into him, encouraged. 'I know you will,' she said, her voice quiet. She felt him stiffen and then relax. He shifted his body until it was facing hers.

'No,' she said. 'No, Ludo.'

'I care about you very much,' he said.

'I know that,' she said.

'Poetry,' he said again, as though the word were a poem itself, as though the simple idea of poetry would persuade her of his earnestness.

She stepped back slightly until he had to loosen his grip. 'You mean a lot to me, Ludo, you know that, but—'

'But?'

'But no.' She pulled away. 'Not like that. Not any more.'

Back at the cottage, she found it hard to relax. Ludo revived the fire, then opened a bottle of wine, offering her a glass she didn't really want. He went into the kitchen and she heard him fill a pan with water, heard the dull sound of a wooden spoon moved against metal. She didn't know what she felt about him. Instinct had pushed him away, but now, in the warmth of the cottage and of his care, she wondered if she'd been right to trust it. If I'd had time to think, she told herself, I might have let him kiss me, and all the rest of it. But then it struck her that his bringing her here to the cottage might have had that end in mind, and she was angry, as though she'd overheard someone insult her.

And then the conversation with Alice, her sly insinuations, came back to her from the place into which Patrick's letter had pushed it. She put down her glass and went to the kitchen. He didn't hear her coming. He was turned away from her, bent over something she couldn't see.

'Why didn't you tell me Maddy wanted to speak to you?'

'Fuck,' he said. He turned, held up a bleeding finger. 'You made me cut myself.'

She watched him cross to the sink and hold his finger beneath the flow of cold water. 'Give me a paper towel,' he said. He pointed towards a dresser against the opposite wall. 'The roll's over there.'

She watched him wrap the paper around his finger, watched

the blood soak through and the towel be discarded and replaced. She could have helped in some way, but she was too angry; it gave her an obstinate satisfaction to see him fumble with the roll of paper, trap it beneath his armpit, open the cupboard beneath the sink with his foot and throw the blood-soaked towel into a bin. When he looked at her, pleading, she set her face against him.

'For God's sake,' he said. 'Can't you see I need some help?'

'Why did she want to speak to you?'

'Why don't you ask her?'

She hadn't expected this. She'd expected denial. She turned to go.

'Don't be stupid, Fee.' He moved away from the sink, staggered as though he were about to faint, then rested his good hand on the table. 'Fee,' he said again, plaintive this time. 'I don't know why she wanted to speak to me. How do you know she didn't ask for you first?'

'Alice said she wanted to speak to you.'

He pulled out a chair, sat down. 'And you believe Alice, but not me.'

'Don't blame Alice.'

'I'm not blaming anyone.' He peeled the towel away from the cut and winced. 'I think you may have to drive us back.' He looked at the chopping board, at the handful of olives he'd been slicing. 'And finish preparing the dinner as well,' he said, with a wry smile.

'Don't change the subject,' she said, but she could feel herself relenting. It was true that Alice was untrustworthy, and a stirrer. She didn't much like Fiona either, although she'd never said this. Fiona had caught Robert looking at her a few times, weighing up her sexual worth the way men did, and Alice would have caught him too, and blamed Fiona. She knew how these things worked. She'd seen Patrick do it with women in the street, in bars, the flicker of the eye drawn sideways as though it had no choice. In any case, why would Maddy want to speak to her, if she thought she was creepy? She couldn't get that out of her head. I suppose I give *you* the creeps as well, she was about to say when Ludovico raised both arms, flinching as the paper towel caught on his cuff. 'Come here,' he said. 'Come here, and we can make up.'

She shook her head, but couldn't suppress a smile. 'Don't be ridiculous,' she said. 'I'm not going to forgive you just like that.'

'Whatever I have to do,' he said, 'I'll do. I'm sorry about earlier. You just looked so frightened.'

'You think you can get away with anything,' she said.

He nodded. 'I know,' he said. 'I'm terrible.'

She cooked, with Ludovico's guidance, and when he suggested they sleep at the cottage and return to Rome the following morning, she agreed. She didn't want to drive at night, the cut was deep enough for him to plead incapacity, and, in any case, they'd both had too much to drink. After they'd eaten, he gave her one of his T-shirts to wear during the night and a clean towel, then led her to the room she always slept in, a small room on the first floor, opposite his. I know where it is, she almost said, but she let him lead her anyway. She was scared of being alone inside the cottage in a way she didn't understand. As though there were someone else with them, someone who might do her harm. She stood there, a step behind him, as he turned on the light. Scaredy-cat, she told herself. But she felt unsettled by the conversation with Ludo, by the whole day, from Patrick's letter on. Scraping the uneaten food from the plates, she'd seen the screwed-up paper towels beneath the sink, dyed scarlet by his blood, and felt her stomach heave. 'You'll have to make up the bed,' he said, holding his wounded finger up as proof of his helplessness, 'but I'll keep you company.'

'I'm sorry I made you jump,' she said as she shook out a sheet to make sure no spiders were concealed within it and laid it on the single bed.

Ludovico sat down in a small armchair by the window. 'I'm sorry I didn't tell you your sister spoke to me.'

She slipped a pillow into its case. 'That's the first time you've called her my sister.'

'Is it?'

'I still don't believe it,' she said, shaking out and tucking in a second sheet. 'I mean, I know it's true, but I don't believe it. Does that make sense?'

'There are blankets in the wardrobe,' he said. 'You'll need them. At least this bedroom's over the fireplace downstairs, so it's been warmed a little.' He nodded towards the door. 'My room's freezing.'

She stopped what she was doing. 'You don't want to talk about her, do you?'

'Don't be silly,' he said. 'We can talk about her all you like, if that's what you want to do.'

She sighed. 'I don't want to talk about her,' she said. 'I want to talk *to* her. But I'm not sure she likes me.' *She gives me the creeps.* 'I don't think she wants to talk to me. Do you?'

'Do I what? Want to talk to you? Of course I do.'

'Now you're being silly.'

He nodded. 'I'm sorry. It's not a good time to joke, I know that. But I mean what I say. I can listen to you. But that's all I can do. I don't know anything more than you do about her. Probably a lot less than you do. I don't even know what you want from her.'

'I want a sister,' said Fiona, her tone more stubborn than she'd intended, as though Ludovico had wilfully denied her this. 'I want her to be a sister to me.' She paused. 'And I want a mother.'

'You have a mother,' he said gently.

'A real mother,' she insisted.

'More than you want a sister?'

'Yes. No. Oh, I don't know.' In her bewilderment, she began to cry. She turned her face away. Ludovico rose from the armchair and hugged her, gently resting his injured hand on the back of her head and guiding it to his chest, holding it there until she was calm.

'Don't cry,' he said. And then, more quietly, as though someone might be listening: 'You're shivering.' He pulled her closer to him, stroked her back. 'Everything will be all right,' he said, his voice low, comforting, as she let herself go.

CHAPTER TWENTY-FIVE

Back in Rome, Fiona divided her time over the next two days between her own department and the campus. She would finish her lessons and walk the half-mile that separated the two, her thoughts on Maddy, on Patrick, on Ludovico, barely stopping to eat. She imagined conversations in which Maddy took back what she had said about Fiona being creepy, accepted every claim that was made on her, in which Patrick apologised for his horrible letter or Ludovico explained himself, and the world was gradually set to rights. Maddy would welcome her and accept her sister's love, Patrick would simply melt away. Ludovico? What did she really want from Ludovico? Fraternal love, or something more? She would catch herself arguing aloud with whoever had crossed her mind, only falling silent when she felt the eyes of others on her.

It wasn't until Wednesday morning that she caught sight of Maddy, crossing the campus, thirty or so yards away from her.

She called out her name, saw Maddy freeze and then turn. She ran across, her heart beating, unsure what to say although she had rehearsed this moment a hundred times. As soon as she could, she took hold of Maddy's arms, kissed her on both cheeks.

'I missed you at the class,' she said, breathless, trying to ignore the way Maddy had stiffened at her touch. 'Why didn't you come?' But that was too intrusive. Maddy backed off, avoided

Fiona's eyes. Fiona tried to lighten her tone. 'Are you coming tomorrow?'

'It isn't really for me,' said Maddy. 'My English is already pretty good, don't you think?'

'Of course it is,' said Fiona. 'I didn't mean that. I'd just welcome a little moral support.' Was that the tone she needed? Oh please, she thought, don't shut me out.

Maddy looked evasive. 'I've got so much to do these days. Exams, you know.'

Fiona tried another tack. 'I don't suppose you can spare the time for a coffee?'

Maddy shook her head. 'Not really. I have to go to a class.'

'You can't miss it, just this once? You missed my class.' Oh fuck, she thought, why did I have to say that?

'I don't need your class,' Maddy snapped. Then, in a softer tone: 'I'm sorry. I didn't mean it to sound like that.' She looked at her watch. 'Oh what the hell, I'm late already.'

'Fabulous,' said Fiona. 'After all, we are in Italy. I mean, everyone's late in Italy, aren't they?'

In the bar, Fiona paid for a coffee for Maddy and a cappuccino – her third cappuccino that morning – for herself. She carried the cups to the table and took off her parka while Maddy watched her. Fiona sat down, searching for something to say. The last time she had seen Maddy was at the bar in San Lorenzo, drinking beer with her friend, the one with the bright-blue eyes, saying that Fiona gave her the creeps. She wondered where he was now. I wonder if she thinks I'm creepy now, Fiona thought.

'Your boyfriend was a bit cagey,' she said.

'I'm sorry?'

'After the class,' she continued, knowing she should let the subject drop. 'When I asked him where you were.'

'Matteo?' Maddy said. 'He isn't my boyfriend, and he wasn't

being cagey – he just didn't know where I was.'

'He isn't your boyfriend?'

'No.'

'So who is?' Fiona said, her tone teasing, as though they were as close as she would have liked, as twins should be. She bit back the question she really wanted to ask. Why did you want to speak to Ludovico and not to me?

'I don't have a boyfriend right now.' Maddy drank her coffee. 'What about you?'

'Well, yes and no,' Fiona said. If you want to play games, she thought, let's play games. She sipped her cappuccino, an eyebrow raised.

'Really?' said Maddy.

'You met him. In my flat. When you came for dinner. That was such a nice evening. We must do it again.'

'Ludovico?'

'You remember his name,' said Fiona with a trace of ill-concealed sarcasm. 'Well done! I'm hopeless with names.'

Maddy looked apprehensive. 'Yes and no, you said?'

'Oh, let's not talk about men,' said Fiona. 'They're so boring in the end, aren't they?'

Maddy nodded. 'I suppose they are.' She looked at her watch, still uneasy, pushed her empty cup away from her. 'I really should go.'

'No, don't go yet,' said Fiona, unable to hide the urgency in her voice. This isn't how it's supposed to be, she thought. 'We still have so much to talk about.'

'I don't think we do,' said Maddy.

'Please don't be so, well, difficult,' said Fiona, feeling her sister, her lifeline, slipping away. Before she'd had time to think about what she was saying, she blurted out: 'Look, what are you doing for your birthday? Our birthday? Do you have anything planned?'

'Birthday?' Maddy was startled.

'I was thinking,' said Fiona, desperate to backpedal or soften the impact of what she had said, knowing already that it was too late. 'Maybe we could do something together.' She paused. 'You know, celebrate together. Your friends, mine, Ludovico, a family thing, I suppose. Your mother.'

'My mother?' said Maddy hotly.

Fiona ignored this. 'We could have so much fun,' she said. When Maddy didn't answer, she looked at her. 'You have told her about me, haven't you?'

'No,' said Maddy. 'And I don't intend to either.'

Fiona's heart sank. She hadn't expected this. 'You can't deny her that,' she said. You can't deny *me* that, she thought. 'She has a right to know.' She waited a moment, battling to contain her anger, before continuing in what she hoped was a reasonable voice. 'I mean, if she has adopted you, she needs to know that you know. She might not even be your mother. It's your responsibility to tell her. You both have a right to know.'

'My responsibility? I've had enough of this,' said Maddy, standing up.

'No, no,' said Fiona, her voice rising. 'Don't just run off and leave me.' She reached across and grabbed Maddy by the sleeve. 'You can't,' she cried. 'You're all I've got.'

'You're crazy. You haven't got me.' Maddy stared around her, as though searching for an exit. 'I'm not yours to get.'

Fiona was desperate now. 'Please, please, Maddy,' she begged. 'Just sit down again and let me explain.'

Maddy stopped, but didn't sit down. Fiona still had hold of her sleeve. 'Let me go. There's nothing to explain.'

'But we're sisters, Maddy, we can help each other, don't you see?' Fiona was pleading now. 'Don't just think about yourself. Think about me. Maybe I need your help.'

Maddy snorted. 'You? How can you need my help? You have everything.'

So that's it, Fiona thought. I'm just some privileged bitch muscling in on her life. No wonder she thinks I'm creepy. 'I don't want to sound like a poor little rich girl,' she said, in a tone she heard as bleating and tried to correct. 'It's just that I'm so unhappy. I feel so alone.'

'I thought you had a boyfriend,' said Maddy, caustic now.

Fiona's fingers tightened on Maddy's sleeve. She raised her head and stared into Maddy's eyes with such fierceness Maddy was shaken. She turned away.

'I wish I did.'

Maddy slumped back into her chair. Fiona let go of her sleeve. Now what? she thought. I've ruined everything.

'I don't understand. Why do you want to do this?' Maddy said. 'Seriously. I know about all this,' and she pointed at her own face and then at Fiona's, 'but we hardly know each other.'

'We're family,' said Fiona.

'Oh, fuck family.'

'You can't mean that.'

'I don't want more family,' said Maddy. 'I want less. Why can't anyone understand that?'

Fiona reeled back, shocked. 'What do you mean, less? You're saying what we have doesn't matter?'

'I'm saying that being separated at birth, if we were, might mean we're sisters, but it doesn't mean we have to be friends.'

This was worse than Fiona had ever imagined. 'You don't want to be my friend?'

'Oh God. I don't know what I want,' said Maddy. 'I want you to leave me alone.' But something seemed to have broken in her, a resolve to hold Fiona at bay. There was a weariness that gave Fiona hope.

'I've got something for you,' Fiona said. She'd been carrying the rag doll around in her bag so long she'd almost forgotten it was there. 'A present.'

'I wish you wouldn't,' said Maddy. 'You're just making it all so difficult.'

'Here you are,' she said, holding the parcel out.

Maddy stared at it, obviously confused, uncertain what to do.

'Just take it,' Fiona said, pushing it into her hand. 'You don't need to open it now. Just take it and open it later. Think of it as an early birthday present. Or whatever.'

'All right,' said Maddy.

*

Later that day, Maddy called Ludovico from the bar phone but put the receiver down when she heard Fiona's voice. She went back to the flat and sat with her mother for a while, watching afternoon TV – families destroyed by hate, united by miracles and acts of faith – but it didn't distract her as she'd hoped. She had moved the phone beside her on the sofa, hoping that Ludovico would call. If not Ludovico, Matteo. She needed to talk to someone. She had put the present, unwrapped, in her room.

When her mother began to snore, she took the empty wine cartons out of the bin, folded them and carried them down to the skip. In the street, she felt that she was being watched, but resisted the temptation to turn round, telling herself that she was being foolish; worse than foolish, paranoid.

Still, the sense of being watched – or more than that, accompanied – stayed with her as she turned the key in the main door of the building, walked up the stairs to the first floor, where she lived, turned a second key and let herself into the flat, her mother turning her head from the screen to briefly nod as she entered the room. It felt like Fiona was always there, at the edge of vision, until Maddy turned and found there was nothing but her own face staring back at her, as if the whole world mirrored her emptiness, to taunt her with it.

*

Fiona was back in the flat that afternoon, half dozing on the sofa, when the phone startled her awake. She let it ring for a moment to see if Alice or Robert might emerge from their bedroom, then walked across the room to pick it up, said 'Pronto', and heard a click as the receiver was replaced. Who could it be but Maddy, wanting to speak to Ludovico? She suddenly wished that she had Patrick with her. Patrick would know exactly what to do. She had a sudden urge to hurt Maddy in some way. She remembered her own suggestion that they share their birthday, one happy extended family. How stupid she had been. She had offered Ludovico up as bait. She blushed to think of it. Would she even tell him what she'd done? She wasn't sure. She thought back to how he'd been in the cottage that night, how he'd snuggled up against her, his bare skin against her T-shirt, which was actually his and bore his scent, and had stroked her into silence, acquiescence it felt like now. She'd waited for his hand to move, but he'd held off, and now she wondered why. What would she have done if he hadn't? Would she have let him, or would she have told him to try it on with Maddy? Wasn't one of them as good as the other? If you can't have me, have her. Would she have had the courage, or the foolishness, to say that? But maybe she was making all this up, on the strength of a couple of phone calls, on the fleeting expression of a face, the tone of a voice. Maybe Ludovico was still her best friend in the world, as he always had been, and meant nothing to Maddy, as Maddy meant nothing to him.

Besides, it wasn't Maddy she was after. She knew that now. She thought of Maddy's mother, of her mother, alone, and felt that her heart would burst if she couldn't have her.

'What are you doing in the dark?'

She started.

'I was thinking about you,' she said.

He threw his coat on an armchair and sat down beside her. 'Should I be pleased?' he said.

She nodded. 'I need your help,' she said.

He took some persuading but she managed to win him over in the end. She'd turned to face him, a hand on his sleeve and told him her plan. He'd listened in silence. When she had finished, he shook his head.

'You're crazy,' he said, but she brushed that aside.

'She's my mother too,' she insisted. 'I have every right to see her.'

He sighed. 'So see her,' he said. 'Ring the doorbell and tell her who you are. Why all this subterfuge?'

She squeezed his forearm a touch too hard. 'Because Maddy won't let me, don't you see? She's just being so possessive. She wants to keep her all to herself.'

He sighed again. 'And you expect me to take her out of Rome so that you can go round to her house and do what exactly?' He threw up his arms as far as her grip would let him. 'Surprise!'

Fiona slid from the sofa and sank to her knees before him, her eyes on his face as he watched her, exasperated, with half a smile because she was being ludicrous, she knew that, she was behaving like a child who wanted her own way, and she didn't care, not if it helped her get what she wanted. 'She hates me.'

He laughed. 'Who hates you? Maddy? What in the name of God makes you think that she hates you?'

She shook her head, as if to say you don't understand, please try to understand, then rested her elbows on his thighs. 'All I need is a few hours alone with my mother, without Maddy around. That's all I'm asking. And I can't do it without you.'

He raised an eyebrow. 'So you've made up your mind that she's your mother,' he said.

She swallowed and nodded, her eyes damp, her face a paradigm of pleading. 'I *know* she is.'

He looked at her, still half amused, which gave her hope. 'And you want me to keep Maddy occupied while you scare her mother half to death. You really are crazy.' He paused. 'You don't even know where she lives.'

Fiona pulled away from him, sat back on her haunches. 'I'll find her. I know what she looks like. I know she lives in San Lorenzo. I know the bar she goes to. I'll find her, I know I will. She's my fucking *mother*, Ludo. Why can't you see that? Why won't you help me?'

Ludovico's expression changed to one of concern. 'This is doing you no good, Fee.' He touched her cheek.

'So help me,' she said. 'Please, Ludo, please.' He stood up, moving her to one side as though she were without volition, a doll to be played with and discarded, and all her body's strength drained from her. 'Please,' she said again, her voice the merest whisper, as he left the room.

When he came back ten minutes later, his face set, he told her that he would take Maddy away for the weekend if that was what she wanted. She nodded fervently. As for the address, he said that he would see what he could do. He had a friend, an old girlfriend of his who worked in university admin. She would have access to student files, he said. He would call her in the morning. She owed him a favour, he said.

'And then you'll call Maddy?' she said.

'You've given me no choice,' he said, but he didn't sound as though he minded much. For a moment, she was piqued. Was he doing this for her, she thought, or for Maddy?

'How do you know she'll want to come away with you?' she said, and to her relief he grinned unexpectedly and he was Ludo again, her childhood friend, her accomplice, and he said, 'I have my methods.'

She was about to ask him where he would take her, but of course she knew that he would take her to the cottage in Frascati, as though their own visit the previous weekend had been nothing more than a dress rehearsal, and for a moment she felt a twinge – no, more than a twinge – of jealousy. If you can't have me, she reminded herself, you can always have her.

'I'll make it up to you,' she said. 'I promise.'

He shrugged. 'Don't worry about that,' he said.

CHAPTER TWENTY-SIX

The next day was Thursday, the day Fiona taught her weekly class on campus at five o'clock. At ten past five, Maddy rang the bell beneath Fiona's flat. She waited a few seconds, then rang again. When nobody answered, she looked up at the windows, the glass black in the brightness of the late-afternoon sun. She hadn't expected to find Ludovico at home, but she was still disappointed. She walked across to the bar – she might as well have a coffee before she got the bus back to San Lorenzo.

Pausing outside the bar, she glanced back at the building in which Fiona and Ludovico lived and at the imposing archway two storeys tall; Roman buildings are strata of life, she thought, layered as lasagne, the *piano nobile*, the floors above more modest and then, at the very top, a floor of garrets for the servants, with sloping roofs and windows just large enough to let air circulate. Fiona had said that her mother was the granddaughter of a maid, or her daughter, she couldn't remember now. And here she was, living on the *piano nobile* with two spoilt brats and her on-off boyfriend. Maddy couldn't stop wondering who was lying, Fiona or Ludovico. And the money Fiona would soon inherit, like a constant buzz in the background, the unfairness of it. This is my city, she thought, not yours.

She was about to go into the bar when she saw a movement at one of the windows. There was a second twitch of curtain as she stared up and whoever was looking down at her in the square below must have realised she had noticed, and stepped back, and adjusted the curtain so that the window once again reflected the sky, bright blue and banked with cloud, and nothing else.

*

Fiona spent most of Thursday in the flat, curled up on her bed, wrapped in a blanket, convincing herself that she was too ill to go to work. She called the faculty to say she wasn't well enough to do her class. She ate bowls of cereal until the milk ran out and read *Jane Eyre* for the twentieth time. When the doorbell rang, she jumped but didn't answer. There was no one she wanted to see, and nobody else was in the flat. She crawled out of bed and peered down into the square to see who it might have been, but recognised no one. She threw herself back on the bed, picked up her book after checking her watch. She should have been at the lesson ten minutes ago, she saw, and she had a comforting sense of her own naughtiness. Patrick would be proud of her.

She was fast asleep when someone tapped on the door.

'It's me,' said Ludovico.

'Hang on,' she said. But he was already in her bedroom. He sat down on the bed.

'I've got her address,' he said and gave Fiona a scrap of paper. She slipped it inside her book.

'And Maddy?' she said. 'Did you speak to her?'

'She asked me to call her back in twenty minutes,' he said. 'But don't worry, I'm sure she'll say yes.'

'You've spoken to her?'

'I just told you. She was cooking dinner for her mother.'

'What time is it? How long have you been home?'

'Dinner time *chez* Maddy,' he said. 'I'll get you a drink.'

*

Fiona watched him as he spoke, the way his body shielded the phone from her, strained to listen as his voice dropped to a whisper. 'OK,' he said, and 'OK' again and then something she didn't catch. He laughed and she thought, he isn't acting, and then she thought, he's such a brilliant actor, as he blew a kiss into the phone.

*

The phone rang when Maddy was tipping pasta into a colander, blinded by steam. 'Get that, Mum,' she shouted. 'It might be for me.' Heather grumbled but took the call. 'It's a man,' she said. 'I didn't catch his name.' Matteo, Maddy thought, wiping her hands on a cloth. He'll be calling to tell me how the lesson went with Fiona.

'So now I've met your mother,' said Ludovico. 'Telephonically, at least.'

'Look,' she said, hurriedly, wondering if he would realise how shocked she was, and how delighted, 'this is a really bad moment. Can you call me back in twenty minutes? I've just drained the pasta and it's going to get cold. My mother will never forgive me.' This was a lie; her mother was in the process of falling asleep, her head rolling slowly back towards the cushion and then jerking forward with a grunt.

'Why don't you call me when you've finished?' said Ludovico.

'No,' said Maddy, 'you call me.'

When he called back, exactly twenty minutes later, she picked up the phone.

'Hello again,' he said.

'Hello.'

'I want to see you,' he said. 'I want to show you where I work.'

'I thought you said you work in Frascati.'

'Exactly.'

'You want to take me to Frascati?' she said, startled.

'Yes. This weekend. I want to spend the weekend with you.'

'The whole weekend?'

'That will depend on you,' he said.

'And where will we sleep?' she said; her first thought, blurted out and immediately regretted.

'I know a place,' he said. 'You needn't worry about that.'

'I'm not sure,' she said.

'What can I do to make you sure?'

'Where were you this afternoon?' she said.

'At work,' he said. 'Why?'

'Oh, nothing,' she said. She paused. 'I'm not sure,' she said again.

'Nothing will happen unless you want it to,' he said, and she remembered the way he'd said those same words, or words just like them, before he'd taken her to dinner. She'd wondered then what he meant, but this time the sense was clear, and she wasn't sure what to do with it. She was thrilled, and unnerved, and, somewhere to one side of that, like a figure lurking in a doorway, was the thought of Fiona. What would Fiona want to happen? she thought. She pushed this hurriedly from her mind to concentrate on what Ludovico was saying. 'We can just admire the view, drink wine, eat pasta. I know a place in Frascati that's famous for its *porchetta*.'

'Really?'

'You see,' he said. 'I knew I'd find a way to convince you.'

*

She found Matteo next day on campus. He was sitting on a wall near the library, sharing a cigarette with Gina. She felt a shiver of anxiety, as though a net were being drawn around her. She waved and called out 'Ciao', and they turned to greet her. This is where I belong, she thought, with people my own age, who know me as I am, who don't cheat on others. She'd told Ludovico that she would think about it, and tell him that evening, and he'd agreed. He'll think I'm playing hard to get, when all she wanted was to trust him, and now she didn't. I'll tell him no, she decided. She walked over to Matteo and Gina.

'Hello, stranger,' said Gina. 'That twin of yours, did she find you?'

'She's not my twin,' said Maddy, decisively. Out of the corner of her eye, she saw surprise on Matteo's face.

Gina laughed. 'You're identical. Saying you aren't twins won't make her go away.'

Maddy sighed. 'I've had enough of this. I don't want to talk about it any more, OK?'

Gina raised both hands in a gesture of surrender. 'OK, OK. Not another word,' she said.

'Sorry, I didn't mean to snap,' said Maddy. 'It's just that, well, the whole situation, it's all a bit overwhelming.'

'So you are twins?'

'Gina!'

Gina pulled an imaginary zip across her mouth, then picked up her bag. 'Well, I'd better get going,' she said. 'Lectures on Hannah Arendt wait for no man. Or woman.'

As soon as Gina had left them, Maddy turned to Matteo, who had listened to this exchange in silence. 'What was she like at the lesson yesterday?'

He shook his head.

'What lesson?' he said. 'She didn't come.'

CHAPTER TWENTY-SEVEN

'I saw a curtain move,' Maddy said. 'At the window.'

'But what were you doing there? I don't understand.'

Maddy hesitated.

'I'd been to the women's bookshop,' she said. 'It's just round the corner from where she lives.'

'I know where the women's bookshop is,' he said, which surprised her. Matteo was full of surprises. 'So you happened to pass the building where your possible sister lives and you saw a curtain move.'

'Yes.'

'Now help me with this, Maddy,' he said slowly, with a half-smile. 'Why should a curtain not move? You told me she shared the flat. It could have been anyone. The loving couple, the astronaut.'

'I know,' said Maddy. 'I'm being stupid.'

'You didn't ring the bell, did you?'

She shook her head, ashamed of herself. The astronaut, she thought. An hour ago, she wasn't sure she'd ever see Ludovico again; she was too angry, too hurt. Now, knowing that it might have been Fiona at the window, she felt exposed and stupid.

'So why shouldn't you have been there?'

'I don't know,' she said, her face firm. 'Let's drop it, shall we?'

'That's pretty,' he said.

'What is?' she said, startled. He took her hand in his and lifted it. She felt herself relax.

'This is,' he said, touching the ring.

She smiled. 'My mother gave it to me. She had it made for me when I was a child.'

'And she's only just given it to you?'

'My mother's strange,' laughed Maddy.

'All families are strange,' said Matteo.

When Maddy got home that afternoon, she found her mother fraught and tetchy. Her legs were hurting, she said; she lifted her nightdress and showed Maddy the scabs. She's like a child, thought Maddy, this need to be comforted and looked after, these fits of rage and sulking when she doesn't get what she wants. Gently, dropping into a crouch in front of her mother, she pulled down the hem of the nightdress until her knees were covered. Her mother stroked her hair. 'I'll just sit down for a bit,' she said, and Maddy nodded, straightening up.

'Yes, you do that,' she said. 'I'll make you a cup of tea.'

'I'd rather have a drop of wine,' her mother said, even her voice like that of a child.

'It's a bit early for wine, isn't it?' said Maddy.

'Just half a glass,' she said, 'to give me a bit of go.'

Maddy found the opened carton of wine, and poured out half a glass. Her mother took it and Maddy watched her restrain the urge to empty the glass, watched her take a cautious sip, and then smile up at Maddy as if to say, you see, I don't actually need this.

'I may be going away this weekend,' said Maddy, still on her feet. She wouldn't relax until she'd spoken. 'Just for one night.'

'Who with?' said her mother.

'No one you know. A friend.'

'I don't know any of your friends,' her mother said. 'You never ask them home.'

Maddy looked at the stack of gossip magazines beside the sofa, at a plate with day-old crusts of bread balanced on the arm. She imagined Matteo looking for a place to sit that wasn't covered with her mother's detritus, Ludovico furtively checking that his glass was clean.

'He's an astrophysicist,' she said.

'He?' Her mother looked at her, suspicious. 'I thought you said she was a girl?'

'I didn't say that. You assumed it.'

'Well, be careful. You don't want to have your life ruined by some unwanted child.'

'Thank you,' said Maddy.

Her mother ignored this. 'How old is he? I don't want you hanging around with old men.'

'Good God, Mum. He's twenty-seven. He's hardly a pensioner.'

'That's seven years older than you are. It's obvious what he's after.' She drained her glass and held it out to be refilled. 'I suppose this was his idea, this dirty weekend?'

'Get your own bloody wine,' snapped Maddy, ignoring the glass, ignoring the whimper her mother made when Maddy picked up her coat. 'The only dirty thing around here is you,' she yelled as she left the flat.

She was about to put the receiver down when a man's voice answered.

'Ludovico?' she said.

'*Sì.*'

'*Sono io.*'

'Maddy,' he said, his voice dropping to a whisper.

'Can you talk?'

'Yes,' he said, but she could tell he was lying, and not only from his tone; she could barely hear him.

'OK, you don't need to say anything, just listen to me,' she said. 'I'm on for the weekend, all right? I can't wait to get away.'

'All right,' he said. He was speaking so quietly it was hard to tell if he was pleased or not, but she found to her surprise that she didn't care.

'I'll meet you at the same place we met last time, OK?'

'OK.'

'What time?' she said, unexpectedly doubtful.

'Ten o'clock,' he said.

'In the morning?'

He laughed. 'Yes, in the morning.'

'*A domani*,' she said.

'Until tomorrow.'

Putting the phone down, she heard what sounded like a kiss. Her heart was pumping. She would have to go back to the flat, she knew that; she would have to make peace with her mother. But not just yet. She left the bar.

It was a few minutes after seven, between the end of work and the start of whatever the evening might offer. It had been dark for a couple of hours by now, she had some reading she needed to do for a seminar on Monday, her head was aching after the scene with her mother and already, wishing she hadn't lost her temper, she was beginning to regret her decision to spend the weekend with Ludovico. The truth was that she had nowhere to go, no refuge, no place that wasn't mean and cramped and – how else to say it? – blighted by her mother's presence. She thought with unexpected rage of Fiona in her perfect high-ceilinged apartment. Her thumb rubbed against the back of the ring her mother had given her. At least I have this, she thought, my ring, and she was touched, and remorseful, as always, at the thought of her mother.

She reached down into her pocket to see if she had any loose change hidden in the fluff, and found a *gettone* she thought she'd already used. She could call Ludovico and tell him she'd changed her mind about tomorrow, but she wouldn't do that. She realised all at once how badly she wanted to see him, be with him. She wondered what he'd be like, what kind of lover he'd turn out to be, if she let him. She imagined him generous, and slow, taking her needs into account; an ideal lover, she told herself, amused, excited against her will. Because she didn't know what she'd do when the time came. She hadn't made love with anyone for almost a year, and her last boyfriend had been hopeless – greedy, incompetent, out for himself. She thought of the last time they'd fucked, cramped in the back of a car he'd borrowed from his older brother, newspapers covering the windows, the heater on, his muttered curses as he tried to get inside her jeans, her fear some maniac would force his way into the car and kill them both like those poor couples near Florence. She couldn't bear that again.

Standing outside the bar, she felt a cold wind blow along the road. She was hungry – she'd barely eaten all day – but not for food. She needed to smoke. When a man walked past, smoking, she stopped him and asked him if he had a cigarette to spare. He nodded, opened a packet, took out a single cigarette, held it out in a teasing, faintly threatening manner, so that she was forced to reach for it, forced to appreciate that the offer might be conditional. He's old enough to be my father, she thought, remembering what her mother had said. She almost didn't take the cigarette, but that would be stupid. It was only a cigarette. She put it between her lips and waited for him to light it, avoiding his eyes as he fumbled for a lighter. She wondered if Fiona had ever asked a stranger for anything because she had no choice, and if that was what she – Maddy – was doing now: asking a stranger because she had no choice. He held the lighter to her face and she felt his eyes examine her. When the flame blew out before she had lit the cigarette, she pushed her hair behind her ears, smiling a little and shrugging, then cradled the hand with the lighter in hers. When he asked her if he could offer her a coffee or something stronger, an *aperitivo* maybe, she said yes, but not here, she knew a place a couple of streets away.

Five minutes later, sitting inside a bar she never used, he asked her what she did and she told him the truth, that she was a student. He said he worked in a bank, which might also have been true, judging from his clothes: beneath his coat, a grey suit, white shirt, tie, knitted waistcoat. He was shy, but insistent. Student of what? he wanted to know, what year, what faculty? Her name, she told him when he asked, was Fiona. The name came out naturally, as if it were hers. He asked her if that was a foreign name, sincerely curious for the first time, and she said, yes it is, I'm English. He bought them both beers, and offered her another cigarette. He wasn't bad-looking, she thought, although he must have been forty at least. He complimented her on her Italian – it's perfect, he told her, better than his – and she told him she studied the language at Oxford, she was only here for a year, aware that she was changing her story to suit her new name, her new self, but he wasn't listening. He was looking at her in a way that ought to have alarmed her; eyes flickering from face to breasts, a sort of vacantness in them, as though everything but his desire for her had been filtered out. She ought to have been scared, or offended, but instead she felt both absent and absurdly safe, as though she had slipped out of her own skin and into the protective skin of the other. Anything bad that might happen, she thought, would happen to Fiona, who deserved it.

When they finished their beers, he bought two more. She

glanced at her watch, then shrugged. It must be hard to be a student, he said, coming back to the table with the glasses. I never had any money, he said. Neither do I, she said. I never have a penny. Maybe I can help, he said. A pretty girl like you, you shouldn't have to worry about money. Like Fiona, she thought. Fiona didn't worry. So why should I? Help me how? she said. Oh, I don't know, he said. He offered her another cigarette, which she took. If you're nice to me, he said, maybe I can be nice to you.

Ten minutes later, the man, who had told her to call him Luigi, was outside the park on the other side of Via Tiburtina, holding the bottom of the wire fencing high enough for Maddy to slip beneath. Safely through, she held the fencing up for him. He was edgy, but keen. He'd already slipped some money into her pocket; she didn't know how much. She didn't care. She moved into the centre of a clump of bushes, sheltered by the pines that encircled the park, where the earth had been flattened by others. But she wasn't going to lie down, it was too risky. She didn't want him on top of her, pinning her to the ground. She leant against a tree, and waited, as Fiona would; every bone in her body was Fiona's, every drop of blood in her veins belonged to Fiona. Maddy was in some safe place far from here, far from the bark of the pine as it bit into her back, far from the scent of it in Fiona's nostrils. Just as Fiona would, because Fiona deserved this, she opened her coat and let him thrust his hands inside her sweater from below until they reached her breasts, let him force his way beneath her bra, then fumble with the clasp until she reached behind herself to help, let him ease it away from her to stroke her breasts, bunch the sweater up to bare them, graze them with his day-old beard. She let him open the zip of her jeans and slide his fingers into her panties and then, when he found the moistness, into her. *Così*, he breathed into her neck, her ear, his tongue in her ear, his teeth on her earlobe, *così*, as he slid his penis into her and then groaned, and hurt her, hurt her badly, lunging too hard, forcing himself in, because she wasn't ready. Maddy wasn't ready, because Fiona was nowhere to be found, and it was Maddy who pushed him away and told him, in English, to fuck off. Just fuck off, will you, she said, and he was excited by this, this foreign woman saying fuck.

Sì, he said. *Sì*.

CHAPTER TWENTY-EIGHT

Maddy put a ten-thousand-lire note on the kitchen table, beside her mother's untouched coffee. 'You'll be all right, won't you?'

Her mother nodded. She was picking at a slice of bread from the day before, rolling the stale crumbs into small grey balls. Maddy couldn't tell if she was sulking or hungover.

'Do you want me to get some shopping in before I go?' she said.

'No,' said her mother.

'It's no trouble.' Maddy couldn't quell the guilt she felt at leaving her mother alone for a night. Even worse, she was anxious her mother might ask her where the money came from, and what she had done to get it. But her mother barely glanced at the note, crumpled and smoothed out, or at Maddy's faded rucksack, dumped near the door.

'I don't know what I want yet,' her mother said. 'When I do, I'll get it myself.'

Maddy paused before speaking. 'I'm sorry about what I said to you yesterday. I was angry, that's all. I was wrong. I'm sorry.' She would have said this the evening before but her mother had already shut herself in her room by the time Maddy came home, and Maddy had been relieved not to have to speak to her. The man had left her in the park and she had waited to make sure he was gone before fastening her bra and pulling her clothes back into place. The first thing she'd done was check that the money was still in her pocket. She'd left the park then, lifting the fence herself and wriggling beneath it, and stood on the pavement, the note in her hand, her eyes filling with tears. She would have screwed the money into a ball and thrown it away, but common sense told her not to be stupid. Money was money. Without warning, she felt sick and bent over to throw up, her hands on her knees, shaking with a sudden chill, but the sensation passed as quickly as it had arisen and, straightening up, she headed back towards the lights and traffic of the Tiburtina, her jeans rubbing against the soreness between her legs as she walked.

Her mother looked at her. 'I don't know what you're talking about,' she said, and for a moment Maddy believed her.

'I'll be off then,' she said. She walked across and gave her mother a tentative kiss on the cheek. 'Be good,' she said. Her mother grunted. 'That's what you're supposed to say to me,' said Maddy, trying to make light of the situation. 'And if you can't be good, be careful. That's what you're supposed to say.'

'You'd better be getting along,' her mother said. 'You don't want to keep him waiting, whoever he is. Men hate being made to wait.'

Maddy stepped back. 'Look, Mum. Heather. I won't go if you don't want me to,' she said. 'You only have to say.'

'You don't need my permission,' her mother said, deliberately not understanding. 'You're a grown woman by now. You're practically twenty-one.'

Maddy picked up her rucksack and swung it onto her shoulder. It was light enough to carry in one hand. She'd packed a change of clothes and the notes she needed to read through for the seminar on Monday. She wished she could take some money with her, for emergencies – it would be up to Ludovico to pay for everything else – but all the money she had was on the table, and it was better that way. She'd rather her mother used it than her; it made it cleaner somehow. She still had her *gettone*, just in case.

'Bye, then,' she said. She paused at the door, one foot already on the landing, and finally, when it was almost too late, her mother relented.

'Come here, you stupid girl,' she said, and held out her arms.

She'd expected to see the motorbike, but Ludovico was leaning, legs crossed at the ankles, against the side of a small brown car, which made him look even taller. He was double-parked. 'Hurry up,' he said, but his tone was relaxed, his movements leisurely as he lifted the rucksack from her shoulder and bent to kiss her firmly on both cheeks, his free hand brushing her waist. He opened the door for her, watched until she was seated, then walked around the car. He was wearing blue jeans and the coat he'd worn the night he took her out. The sleeves were too short, she noticed this time; his wrists were bony and dusted with dark hair. He had a large, unexpectedly flashy watch and a sticking plaster on his index finger.

'No bike today,' she said, settling into her seat, watching him do the same. He's too tall for such a small car, she thought, as he folded his long slim legs into the narrow space available to them. He fidgeted under his seat for a moment, moving it slightly back, then turned and smiled at her, his hair grazing the roof of the car. She wondered why on earth he didn't have something better than a clapped-out 126. Was it inverted snobbery? she wondered.

'I didn't like the look of the weather,' he said. 'There's something in the air, do you feel it? I know I do. I'm meteoropathic, and I'm fairly sure that word doesn't exist in English, but you know what I mean. I'm like a cat,' he said, and grinned. 'So, what do you think? A storm on the horizon maybe.'

'I don't know,' she said. There was something catlike about

him. A sense of danger, a prickly quality in his manner, the way a cat would lash out and scratch the hand that stroked it. 'I'm no good at predicting the weather,' she said. 'I just wait and see what happens.'

'That sounds like an excellent policy,' he said, pulling out into the traffic. 'Maybe we should all do that.'

'You don't?' she said.

'No, I'm hopeless, I always try to guess what's coming. Most of the time, I'm wrong. I'm a victim of contingency.'

'There are worse things to be a victim of,' she said, remembering the evening before, the soreness still there as her jeans moved against her skin. She'd bathed with care this morning, smeared herself with a cream she'd found in an almost squeezed-out tube in her mother's beauty case – essence of calendula, for rashes and irritated skin, it said. Glancing at Ludovico's hands on the wheel, she imagined them touching her, and flinched. She wished she knew what she wanted. All she knew was that she wanted to be prepared for what might happen – to not be the victim of contingency.

Outside Rome, it wasn't long before they saw a prostitute, a middle-aged blonde woman in a tight miniskirt, stilettoes, fake fur jacket, sitting on a plastic crate beside a small bonfire. A few hundred yards further on, two younger women shared a cigarette beside a lay-by. Ludovico glanced at Maddy to gauge her reaction – something she sensed rather than saw – then shook his head.

'Have you ever paid anyone for sex?' she asked him before he could say anything, say something wrong.

'No,' he said. 'I can't think of anything I'd less want to do.'

She didn't know what answer she had wanted, but this would do.

'My mother says that all wives are whores, one way or another.'

'What a strange thing to say. Do you think she's right?'

Maddy looked out of the window, saw a girl no older than she was tugging a skimpy elasticated bright-red skirt over her thighs as though she was quite alone somewhere else, unnumbered miles away from this busy road, some private place where she could not be seen or touched, a village, a dirt track, a tiny room teeming with children. 'Of course I don't. My mother's an old hippie. They all say that kind of thing. No marriage, no mortgage. No ties. Marx thought marriage was a prison. A bourgeois prison. That's probably the only thing my mother knows about him.'

'So you're interested in politics?'

'I'm a political science student, Ludovico. Of course I'm interested in politics. The way you're interested in stars. You wouldn't be taking me to see where you work if you didn't care about them, would you?'

He paused. 'Is that what I said, that I'd take you to see where I work?'

'You know it is.' For a moment, she was apprehensive.

He nodded slowly, as though some suspicion had been confirmed, then grinned. 'Lunch first, though?' he said.

'Yes,' she said, relieved. 'Lunch first.'

*

Fiona waited for an hour after Ludovico had left the flat before catching the bus to San Lorenzo. Maddy would never take a taxi, she thought, and today she wanted to be Maddy, or as close to Maddy as she could get. She wanted to be the daughter her mother had chosen.

The flat was fifty yards from the bar with the patio, where Maddy had said she was creepy. Fiona flipped up the hood of Ludovico's parka against a burst of unexpected rain. She had tried to wear the sort of clothes that Maddy wore, but everything she had chosen felt wrong somehow. She stood outside the building, a three-storey place with a trattoria on one side of the main door and a chiropodist on the other. Inside were four flats. The name THOMSETT, handwritten on a strip of paper and taped to the buzzer, was next to 'Interno 1'. She glanced down the road, then pressed the buzzer, her heart in her mouth. She began to count. She'd reached four when she heard a woman's voice.

'*Chi è?*

'It's me,' she said.

There was a click. She pushed open the door and found herself in a gloomy hall, a bicycle leaning against one wall, a narrow staircase ahead of her. She felt along the wall for a light switch, pressed it and went up to the first floor. Two doors led off the landing. She looked at the bells. The one on the right had two names, faded and scribbled, the one on the left nothing. She pressed the bell on the left. The door opened and she saw a woman with dyed red hair, wrapped in a dressing gown.

'Forgotten something, have you?' she said, turning her back on Fiona. 'Apart from your keys.' By the time Fiona was in the room, the woman was sitting on a fold-out sofa with an ashtray, cigarettes and a lighter, and a mug half full of what looked like milky coffee beside her. A television in the corner of the room was on, with the sound turned off. Fiona looked around her. The room had no window, but part of the wall to her right had been knocked out to admit light from the kitchen. A table, a dresser, the side of a fridge. Two doors, one to the left and one on the opposite wall, were the bedrooms, she supposed. The place was dark, and cold, and stale-smelling, as though the windows were never opened. It was an awful place to live.

'I'm sorry,' she said. She stood there, the door behind her. She had an urge to turn round and leave, pretend that she had never come here. She had no idea what to do next. What had she imagined? That her mother would recognise her? Recognise a daughter she had abandoned twenty years ago? She looked at the woman on the sofa. I have no idea who you are, she thought. How stupid I've been.

The woman glanced up, a momentary doubt clouding her face. Fiona froze. This is when I have to tell her, she thought. But the doubt vanished as suddenly as it had appeared. 'What are you doing here anyway?' her mother said. 'I thought your new boyfriend had taken you away for the weekend.' She picked up the mug of coffee. 'Be a love and put some more hot water in this, would you?' she said, her voice softening.

Fiona looked at the woman in front of her, at her mother, and her heart opened, as simply and automatically as that. She slipped the parka from her shoulders, caught it with her hands, stood where she was, afraid to move, as though any movement might break some spell, some spell that protected her, or the woman in the dressing gown – that protected them both. It wasn't supposed to be this simple. A mother. A room. A daughter. Surely she would remember what Maddy had been wearing when she left, however careful she'd been to wear the slightly tarty sort of clothes that Maddy wore, that she would never choose for herself. Surely a mother would know her own daughter, whatever clothes she wore. But why would her mother expect Maddy to be anyone other than Maddy? Who else could she, Fiona, be, if not Maddy?

'I changed my mind,' she said. She hung the parka on a hook beside the door and took the mug.

The kitchen was bare, tidy but with an air of grime about it. Fiona looked around for a kettle, then saw a small saucepan on the cooker, with a puddle of water at the bottom. She filled it, turned on the gas, still shaken by the shadow of doubt that had briefly darkened her mother's face. Waiting for the water to boil, she glanced back into the room and saw her mother's head nodding, on the point of sleep. She seemed so lost, so defenceless. How could Maddy have left her in this state, alone and confused? She glanced around. No sign of food. She opened the fridge. Milk, sliced bread, a packet of what might be ham. How could people live like this? Empty one-and-a-half-litre wine bottles – Marino – were lined up beside a French window that looked as though it opened onto a terrace. She saw a jar of instant coffee on a shelf, and spooned some into a second cup, then filled them both with boiling water from the pan. She was about to ask her mother how much sugar she wanted, if she took milk, but stopped herself in time. Leaving the kitchen, she saw a ten-thousand-lire note on the table. She would have to do some shopping. She remembered the market at the end of the road. Perhaps they could go together, she thought, and that image excited her. She guided the mug of coffee into her mother's hands, then sat down beside her, holding her own mug to her chest. There was so much she wanted to ask, but she was scared that her voice might give her away. Would her mother notice if the girl she thought was her daughter – who was her daughter – sounded different? She was babbling to herself, she realised that. But how sad this flat was; for a moment she understood why Maddy was so hostile to any approach that might require intimacy, or hospitality. How could anyone be invited here? She imagined Ludovico sitting on the sofa, his knees sticking up, sniffing at the stale air and the chemical smell of some cheap cosmetic, and under that, what? Sweat? Blood? Dust? Did dust smell? Oh Mum, she thought, and on an impulse she put down her coffee and took her mother's mug away from her and held both the woman's hands in hers and stared into her mother's eyes and felt such an outburst of love she had tears in her eyes. She examined each line of her mother's face, although her skin was smooth for her age; she looked at her mouth and her nose, the faint down on her cheeks, her eyelashes without make-up, the roots of her hair, the hennaed red of it, to understand who this woman actually was, and to find herself there, as a living part of her. She felt she knew her already, yet what she saw was unknowable. She wanted to stroke the woman's cheek, get closer to her, behind sight, beyond touch. She wanted, she realised, to tell the woman who she was. I'm the daughter you lost, she wanted to say. She would have done if it hadn't been for the suddenly startled look in her mother's eyes, a look that might have been a sort of recognition, or worse, refusal. She shook her head with a sort of bewilderment as the woman stared at her, and then moved her hand within Fiona's hand and stroked the ring with its double twist of gold, and smiled, reassured.

'I love you,' Fiona said.

Soon after that, her mother went to sleep. Fiona disentangled the fingers of their two hands and stood up. She would need to do some shopping before the market closed or they would have nothing to eat, apart from a scrap of ham and some probably stale bread. She was worried her mother would wake up hungry. She needed to be looked after, that was clear. She was ill, run-down, a touch of flu perhaps although she didn't have a temperature – Fiona had checked. She stood up carefully, went into the kitchen to pick up the note on the table. She was sliding it into her pocket, when her mother spoke.

'Get some more wine, would you, sweetheart.' When Fiona didn't immediately answer, she added: 'And don't forget your key this time.'

Fiona hesitated. 'I'm not sure where it is.'

'Well, take the spare one.'

Fiona glanced towards the door, hoping to see the key hanging on a hook. No luck. 'What do you want for lunch?' she said, keeping her voice as low as she could. The more quietly she spoke the less likely it was that her mother would notice a difference and be suspicious.

'I don't mind. Pizza. Pizza's fine. The usual.' Her mother looked at her from the sofa. 'What are you waiting for, sweetheart?' Her voice was plaintive. 'I'd come with you if I hadn't hurt my leg.'

'I'll go and get some wine and pizza then,' she said.

'The key,' her mother said. 'For God's sake, Maddy. Anybody would think you didn't live here.'

This was the first time she had uttered Maddy's name. Fiona flinched as if stung. She looked around, hopeless, as her mother struggled up from the sofa, disappeared through a narrow door off the kitchen, came back with a set of keys.

'Don't lose these too,' she said, but her tone was affectionate. Fiona took the keys and turned towards the door, then, with a little shiver from deep inside, turned back and hugged her mother hard.

She found a large bottle of Marino in a shop round the corner, slices of pizza from a takeaway place near the market. A place that made copies of keys caught her eye as she was shopping. It only took a minute to have one cut. She'd have bought some fruit, some mandarins perhaps, or apples, but she didn't want to spend more than she needed to. It wasn't her money to spend. It had stopped raining; she wondered what the weather was like at the cottage. Looking down the road as it dipped, she saw the cypresses of the cemetery and beyond that hills, which must be the hills around Frascati. They would have arrived by now, unless Ludovico had stopped to eat in the town. She imagined them there, in one of the places he had taken her to. She'd tried to think of Ludovico's keenness to help her as a sort of sacrifice, but she knew it was only partly that. He liked Maddy, or the challenge of

Maddy, maybe more than he liked her, she admitted to herself, and made an effort not to be hurt. After all, letting herself into the flat – using my own key, she thought, with a tremor of glee – she was finally where she wanted to be. She was finally home.

CHAPTER TWENTY-NINE

After lunch, a plate of pasta and half a litre of local wine between them in a slightly musty *cantina*, Maddy lit a cigarette and leant back in her chair.

'What did you mean, when you asked if I was interested in politics?'

He looked startled. 'I'm sorry?'

'You made it sound as though I shouldn't be,' she said. 'As though politics was too much for my poor little female brain to deal with.'

He grimaced. 'I don't remember saying that. Maybe it was because Fiona gets so bored by any talk of politics.' He lowered his eyes and then glanced up, appealing. 'I suppose I expected you to be the same.'

'Because Fiona and I are the same for you?'

'I don't think that.'

'It sounds as though you do.'

'I know it does.' He stared at her with a look so agonised, so unexpected she wanted to reach across and pat his arm. This is what men do, she told herself. They turn us into mothers. Mothers or whores, she thought, wincing at a memory of the night before.

'Fiona told me she was studying politics. PPE, she said.'

'She was for a while, but she changed as soon as – well,' he paused again, as if to correct himself — 'as soon as she could.'

He called the waiter over and ordered coffee for them both.

'She told me you applied to Oxford?'

Maddy nodded. So they've talked about me, she thought, gratified. 'Yes, I won a scholarship.'

'But you didn't take it up?'

'It wouldn't have covered all the costs.' She paused. 'What did you mean about Fiona changing course? What made her change?'

He sighed again. 'Do we have to talk about Fiona?' She let him take her hand in his, turn it and smooth out her fingers until the palm was open. He traced her lifeline with the finger that had the plaster on it; the edge of it tickled her skin. She was about to ask him how he'd cut himself when he said, 'I read palms, you know.'

'So tell me about Fiona's palm,' she said. 'Although I suppose it'll be just the same as mine, so why bother?' I won't be put off, she thought, I won't let him off the hook. But she was immediately ashamed. 'I'm sorry,' she said. He smiled and shrugged, as if to say, don't worry, we all make mistakes. She let him stroke her palm with the tips of his fingers, a coaxing almost hypnotic movement that both calmed and aroused her, until she remembered something she'd read about tickling the bellies of trout until they allowed themselves to be flipped onto the bank, where they would die.

And then the coffee arrived.

They headed out of the town centre along a road that skirted the park of an imposing villa. After five minutes, a narrow road on their left doubled back. During lunch, she'd been amused and irritated, intrigued and provoked by him; now, as the road entered the park, she felt that she'd rather be somewhere else. He's trying to impress me, she thought, or intimidate me, and this made her angry. At the same time, she was fascinated by him, by the way he moved, by his wrists as he turned the wheel in his funny, unpractised way, by some quality in him that was fine and strong, by the incongruity of the over-large watch. She didn't know what to do with him, that was the truth of it. Why wouldn't he talk about Fiona? Because they were lovers, as Fiona had said? She didn't believe this any longer. She didn't believe a word Fiona said. Because he was genuinely indifferent? But she knew that wasn't true; she'd seen them together, seen how they worked as a team without even noticing, as people do who've grown up side by side, protected from the world outside. She's had so much, thought Maddy, a decent home, and love, and money, and a place at Oxford that she could have had, and, well, Ludovico. She closed her eyes and felt his presence beside her. His whole body had a fragrance she couldn't place, intrinsic to him.

He pulled up in front of an ochre two-storey cottage, its windows shuttered and withered geraniums dangling from tubs by the door. There was a long wooden table with its benches upturned and stacked on top, and a generally neglected look to the place.

'Come on,' he said. 'Let's get inside before it starts to rain again.'

'So this place is yours?' she said.

'It belonged to my maternal grandmother. Well, not belonged exactly. She had the right to use it, and she passed it on.'

'The right to use it?' Maddy put the bag of groceries she had carried in from the car onto the kitchen table. The table was large, old, marble-topped.

'She was related to the family that owned the villa.' He opened the bag and took out meat, tomatoes, half a loaf of bread, some mandarins in a net, two bottles of wine. Maddy watched him put these away. 'I believe a mistress was involved, and a bastard son, or nephew, I should say. A papal nephew. Popes aren't allowed to have sons.' He walked across to the empty fireplace. 'Let's light a fire,' he said, rubbing his hands together. 'I'll get some wood.'

'So you have papal blood?' Maddy said.

'Blood is blood,' he said. 'All blood is the same.'

She didn't answer this, because it was both obvious and untrue, and Ludovico knew this as well as she did. She looked around. It was the kind of room she had always wanted to live in, with lime-washed beams, and furniture that became more beautiful the more it was used. A high-backed armchair beside the fireplace, an old-fashioned radio on a shelf above the fridge. She thought about the flat in San Lorenzo – the television always on, the peeling veneer of the table her mother had covered with magazines, the poverty of her life there, even the air used up, exhausted. She was filled with envy and a sort of rage she could barely contain. She would kill for this, she thought.

'Help me get the wood,' he said, holding out his hand for her to take.

The wood was stacked beneath a canopy at the side of the house, covered by a sheet of tarpaulin. He pulled it back, shook it out. 'Watch out,' he said, 'there may be mice.'

'I'm not afraid of mice,' she lied.

'There's a basket over there,' he said, pointing behind her.

She carried the basket across and watched him lift the pieces of wood from the stack to fill it, loving the way he layered the wood. That level of concentration for a task so inconsequential, so trifling. She wondered again what he'd be like in bed, and then, in a rush of disgust, she remembered once again the man from the evening before, his haste, his awkwardness, his indifference.

Ludovico wouldn't be like that, she told herself.

He straightened up, pulling his sweater off over his head. 'Look after this for me, will you?' he said to her. She hugged it to her while he rolled his shirtsleeves up. 'There are dry twigs and branches over there, in that kennel thing,' he said, pointing beyond the woodpile, 'to start the fire. I used to know the word for it, but it's gone.' He stretched his shoulders back, moving his arms in a half-hearted workout, then pushed his dirty hands through his hair, and smiled. 'I need a shower,' he said, 'before I prepare your dinner.'

'I thought we were going to see where you work,' she said.

He smiled again.

'We are,' he said.

'When?'

'Right now.' He made a wide sweeping gesture with his arm.

She looked around her, at the woodpile and the wilted geraniums, at the drive with the tufts of weed pushing up through the gravel, at the bare trees and the faded ochre of the house, beautiful despite neglect, or perhaps because of it, because of its need to be cared for, and loved. She breathed in the scent of him, dark and clean and woody, from the sweater.

'You mean this is where you work?'

He nodded, emphatic. 'It's where I do all my best work. I wrote my thesis here.' He grinned like a boy and her eyes filled, unexpectedly, with tears. 'It's where I'm happy and whatever I have to do, whatever it is, I do it best where I'm happy.'

She tied his sweater round her waist. 'Kindling,' she said. 'It's called kindling.' She grinned back. 'I'll go and get it.'

CHAPTER THIRTY

When her mother fell asleep after lunch, Fiona crept into the room that had to belong to Maddy and closed the door behind her. She looked around. A single bed. A desk with a typewriter on it. A window onto the courtyard of the trattoria below. A wardrobe. Inside, she found her favourite blue scarf, hanging from a hook. She held it to her face. The scent of the room was different from the rest of the flat, less cloying, as though the windows were opened more often. She sat down and stared at the wall outside, thinking: this is what she sees, every day. She picked up a neat stack of paper on the desk, glanced at the top sheet: notes on nihilism, in Italian. She put them down and opened a desk drawer. She was looking for a diary, but all she found were pencils, paper clips, Sellotape, staples, an address book, a troll that unexpectedly brought Jennifer to mind. She picked up the address book, checked for her own name and Ludovico's, was disappointed, put it back where she'd found it.

The next drawer had a photo album. She leafed through it quickly, before returning to the early pages where her mother looked no older than Fiona was now and Maddy was still a little girl, although it was hard to believe that the child staring into the lens was Maddy, and not Fiona. Fiona at the zoo. Fiona feeding a rabbit with a lettuce leaf. Fiona and other children her age playing on swings while their mothers watched. Fiona sitting on the lap of a shirtless man with long hair, a joint in his hand. A school portrait of Fiona holding a book about polar bears. An alternative, hidden past. Maddy had stolen these moments from her, she thought. It felt to Fiona as though she had never had a childhood, had loitered in the wings like an understudy, watching the show as it unfolded, waiting to enter, her lines never spoken, overheard in the mouth of another. In one photo, taken outside a pub, the little girl was sitting on a bench with a bottle of pop and a straw sticking out of it, lost and ecstatic all at once, it seemed to Fiona as she eased it out of the mounts and pressed it to her heart. Swiftly, she removed two other photographs, one of them with her mother and one without, and slipped them into her pocket. She would put them in her bag later.

In the lowest of the three drawers, beneath a bulging yellow folder with '*Documenti*' written across the front, she found a parcel wrapped in bright-red paper and recognised it immediately. She took it out and held it in her lap for a few moments, burning with hurt, and then, recklessly, tore the parcel open to free the rag doll. 'Hello, Fiona,' she said. She hugged the doll to her, then crossed the room and lay on the bed.

She woke when her mother called her name. No, not her name. Maddy's name. 'I'm coming,' she said, picking up the doll.

Her mother was in the kitchen, still in her dressing gown, filling her glass from the half-empty bottle. Fiona looked at her watch. Five o'clock. She'd slept for more than two hours on Maddy's bed; she felt bizarrely rested. She held the doll out. 'I've got something for you,' she said. Her mother looked surprised, and then confused.

'What on earth is it?'

'It's a doll,' Fiona said. She wanted to add, she's one of a pair, they're identical, like twins, to see what might happen, but she didn't dare.

'What have I done to deserve this?' her mother said, still puzzled.

'Nothing,' said Fiona. She shrugged, smiled. 'Everything.'

Her mother took the doll from her. 'Well, thank you,' she said. She studied the doll for a moment, then gave Fiona a clumsy hug. 'Thank you, sweetheart.'

Fiona went out for more wine, some cheese, a loaf. The money was almost spent, but she still had just enough for two small chocolates filled with cherry liqueur. When she came back, her mother had put on a creased Laura Ashley dress and sandals with coloured glass on the straps, and combed her hair, and put on some eyeliner which made her look like a flower child, and Fiona almost cried with joy. They spent the rest of the evening watching television, some endless variety show on RAI. How many hours of television she must watch, Fiona thought, whole evenings passed like this, and she was furious with Maddy, who had let it happen.

She watched her mother fill her glass from the first bottle, and then unscrew the second, with a sly sidelong glance at Fiona, as if she expected to be told off or to have the bottle taken away from her, moved out of reach, and Fiona was tempted to do that, because she couldn't bear to see her mother killing herself like this. She thought of her other mother, thousands of miles away from this dingy smoke-filled room, sitting alone in her tasteful home, a book on her lap, a glass of sherry on a nearby table. What would she think of this ageing, overweight hippie, this drunk, this single parent? What words of condemnation would she have for the bare bruised legs and unsuitable sandals? For the ashtray perched on the arm of the sofa, which needed to be emptied before it spilt over the cushions? Fiona started to get up to do precisely that, but her mother caught her sleeve. 'Where are you going?' she said. 'You were doing so well.'

'What do you mean?'

Her mother looked at her, a slow and appraising look that chilled Fiona to the core.

'Nothing,' she said. She patted the sofa. 'Don't leave me. It's so nice to have you here beside me,' and Fiona fell back.

'I was just—'

'It's all right, sweetheart,' her mother said. 'Everything's all right. I'm not stupid, you know.'

Before Fiona could speak, her mother continued. 'I'm so glad you're here. I haven't had such a lovely evening for ages.' She squeezed her daughter's arm, clumsily pulled her in close enough to be kissed. 'I've missed you.'

*

Ludovico liked to cook. Maddy sat in the armchair with a glass of wine, the heat of the fire on her legs, and watched him. She felt more at ease than she had in weeks. She was thinking about happiness and how there was no place in the world that made her happy, how her happiness was independent of place and whether this was a good thing or not, and she was on the point of saying this a dozen times, but something stopped her. He'd been putting some wood on the fire ten minutes ago and she'd seen a log slip and thought it might burn him. She'd grabbed the poker to push the log back into place and her arm had brushed the bare skin of his and she had felt its texture, its heat, as vivid and profound as a shockwave, a dry, resilient electric quality that had left her shaken, as though some alien element had touched her, burnt her almost, indelibly left its mark. She could feel it still.

'Do you like avocado?' he said.

'Yes,' she said.

'Because Italians can be very purist about their food.'

'You speak as though you weren't Italian,' she said.

'I'm Italian when I need to be.' He waved his knife at her.

'And wouldn't it be a good idea to be Italian now?'

'Because I'm preparing a meal for a beautiful woman, you mean.'

She laughed, amused, flattered. Is that really what he sees when he looks at me? she wondered. A beautiful woman? She didn't see herself as a woman, not really. Heather was a woman, Fiona's mother – whoever she was – was a woman. She felt untested, unsure in comparison. 'No. I just meant, here we are, in Italy, in the grounds of a papal villa, drinking some very good Italian wine.'

'In that case we can both be Italian,' he said. 'Or we can pretend to be, which is just as good.' He put down the knife and raised his glass to her. '*Allora, parliamo italiano?*'

She raised her glass back. '*Va benissimo.*'

When they had finished eating and Ludovico had opened a second bottle of wine and they had already drunk more than half of it, he reached across the table and took her hand.

'I like your ring,' he said. 'I noticed it when you came round for dinner.'

'You can't have done,' she said. 'I didn't have it then.'

'Really? I could swear I've seen it before. Are you sure?'

She corrected herself. 'Well, I did have it, in a way, but I didn't know I did.'

'You're being mysterious.'

She shook her head. 'My mother had it made for me when I was a child but for some reason she's only just given it to me.' She shrugged. 'My mother's strange.'

'I'd realised that.'

She looked at him. 'What do you know about my mother?' she said, more sharply than she intended.

He looked embarrassed. 'I'm sorry,' he said. 'I don't know why I said that. Your mother is none of my business.'

'That isn't what I asked,' said Maddy. She pulled her hand away. 'I asked you what you know about her.'

He tried to take her hand back but she wouldn't let him. She reached for the packet of cigarettes, lit one from the candle Ludovico had put in the centre of the table.

'Nothing,' he said, hopeless.

'Fiona's talked to you about her, hasn't she?'

He sighed. 'Do we have to talk about Fiona?'

'Not if we don't have to talk about my mother.'

'It's a deal,' he said. He poured her another glass of wine.

'She'd love this place,' Maddy said.

'I thought—'

'Don't be so pedantic, Ludovico,' she said. 'I thought it was a beautiful woman's prerogative to change her mind as often as she liked.'

He acquiesced with a nod.

'It's got a hippie feel to it,' she said. 'She'd like that. A bit run-down. In the country, but not really in the country, so she wouldn't have to walk too far to get a drink.'

'Ouch,' he said. 'Maybe we shouldn't talk about your mother after all.'

'Yes, I'm sorry. I shouldn't have said that.' She paused. 'Because she really would love it. Why do I always spoil things?'

'You haven't spoilt anything for me.' He reached out once

again to take her hand; this time, she edged it towards him.

'Why have you brought me here?'

'To show you where I work.'

'No, seriously.'

'Because I like you very much. Because I want to know you better. Because I think you're beautiful. Because I'd like to make love to you.'

So you must think she's beautiful as well. You must want to fuck her – sorry, make love to her – as much as you want to fuck me. Maddy bit these words back, but she could taste them in her throat. Why do I always spoil things? she repeated to herself. She looked at him, his eyes so dark they seemed all pupil, the shape of his face, his lips. She looked at the way his hair fell over his forehead, at his neck and the 'V' of hair on the pale skin where he had left his shirt open. The room was warm and she was suddenly tired. She picked up her glass with her free hand and rested it for a moment on the back of his, then drained it and put it down, her eyes still on him. When he walked round to her side of the table and took her shoulders as if to lift her, she stood up, her head swimming slightly, and put her hands on his waist. She raised her head for him to kiss her, and he did, and she was on the point of crying – with relief, with fear, because she was a little afraid, with desire, perhaps with love – when he turned and led her across the room and into another room she hadn't seen up to now, but had always known would be here, had always known would be where the evening ended.

CHAPTER THIRTY-ONE

Sunday morning, Maddy woke up alone. Her first thought – before panic, or loneliness, or resentment – was that she was sore. Her hands reached between her legs and the memory flooded back of Ludovico's gentle lips and tongue against her, inside her, and the unexpected roughness of his beard, and her dread that he would ask her why she flinched and tensed and moved away a little despite his gentleness. But he didn't ask; he just slowed down, his touch even lighter than before. How sweet he was, she thought, how tenderly he treated her, so that everything that had followed had been right. There was no other word for it.

This is the first time I have made love, she thought. This is the first time I have been in a real bed with a real man, and the first time I have made love. She moved her hand across beneath the covers to see how long he had been gone and found the sheet still warm. She lay there, feeling her skin against the sheet, her body new to her. She heard a noise in the next room, of cups and cutlery, and it comforted her. She was not alone – but she knew that already. She raised her hand to her heart and felt it beat and remembered doing exactly this to Ludovico during the night, the covers pulled back, propped on one elbow, her hand as light as she could make it, letting it settle on his chest, feeling the whisper of hair beneath her palm, and then the life of him, regular, potent, the indomitable pulse of his blood beneath her touch, available only to her.

He opened the door with one hand, a tray in the other. 'Coffee?' he said. He was wearing a dressing gown that was too small for him, which left his legs bare, and made him look both boyish and virile.

'Lovely,' she said, sitting up, moving a pillow behind her. She had a slight headache from the wine of the evening before, but that would pass.

He put the tray down on the table next to the bed, then stood beside it, hesitating.

'You should come back to bed,' she said. 'You'll get cold.' She paused. 'In your sweet little dressing gown.'

'Yes,' he said, with a smile. 'I've had it since I was fourteen, which makes it half as old as I am. It is a bit – what's the word? Skippy?'

'Skimpy,' she said, laughing.

'Skimpy, skippy.' He shrugged. 'You know that if I get back into bed I can't be held to account for what I do.'

'I'll take that risk,' she said.

This time he asked her if he had hurt her.

'Just a bit,' she said, because there was no point in lying.

'Oh Maddy. I didn't mean to,' he said, concerned.

'Don't worry,' she said, and, because she was not prepared to tell the truth, she added: 'I'm fine. I borrowed someone's bike a couple of days ago, that's all, and I slipped and—'

'Maybe if I kiss it better?' he said.

'I don't think that's a very good idea.' She laughed. 'It didn't work last time, did it?' She sat up, stroked her arms. 'I need a shower.'

'Is that something we can do together?'

'I don't think we'd better.'

'In that case, I'll prepare some breakfast,' he said. He picked up his dressing gown, then decided not to wear it. She watched him leave the bedroom, naked, the paleness of his back in contrast to the dark hair of his legs. How beautiful he is, she thought.

*

Sunday morning, Fiona woke up in Maddy's bed. She lay there, confused and shivering in her bra and panties, beneath a rucked-up blanket and bedspread that had half slipped from the bed. The noise of crates being moved beneath her window had woken her. She'd gone to bed without closing the shutters, without brushing her teeth, her clothes were thrown across the chair. She hadn't planned to sleep here, although she had known she would if she had the chance. She lay still, getting her bearings, holding her breath until she realised what she was doing, and sucked in air. The last thing she remembered was hoisting her mother up from the sofa, and then both of them falling back onto it in a sniggering heap. She sat up and looked around. There was a book beside the bed she hadn't noticed the evening before. She picked it up. *Sophie's Choice*. Oh, my God, she thought. She put it down again.

Through the door, Fiona could hear her mother's breathing, heavy, irregular. Her room overlooked the street, the trattoria. Fiona wondered how she could sleep there. She had helped her to bed the evening before, helped her out of her dress and knickers, and into some men's pyjamas she'd found on the bed. Hold your arms up, she'd said, and her mother had sleepily obeyed. She knew more about her mother's body after a day than she did about her other mother's after twenty years, she knew the creases and folds, the full soft breasts, the stretch marks she and Maddy had made, the last real thing they had done together. She'd kissed her mother good night on the forehead, the way a parent kisses her child, reassurance that she would still be loved when she woke, that she would not be alone. Her mother had murmured something into the pillow that might have been 'I love you', or might not, but that didn't matter; whatever it was, it would do. Fiona had been acknowledged, and maybe more than that. What had Heather meant when she said, *I'm not stupid, you know?* Had she been on the point of recognising Fiona, had she understood? Why hadn't she said so then? Fiona lay in bed until she felt cold and then pulled on her clothes from the night before, because she had no other clothes to wear, apart from those that belonged to Maddy, and the thought of wearing those – of lying, because that is what it would amount to – revolted her. She would never lie again, she told herself.

Now, on this first morning of her new life, she went into the kitchen and searched out coffee, unscrewed and refilled the coffee pot, washed cups and spoons. She opened the door to the terrace and looked up at the surrounding buildings. I could be happy here, she thought, her head thrown back, staring at the handkerchief of cloudless blue sky far above her. I belong here. I won't let anyone take this from me.

'You'll get cold out there,' her mother said. Fiona turned round.

'I'm coming in now,' she said. She couldn't remember the last time she had felt this happy.

After their coffee, Fiona convinced her mother to leave the flat. They walked until they reached the cemetery, where her mother came to an abrupt halt. 'This place depresses me,' she said. She pulled away from Fiona, her tone querulous now. 'I want to go home. I'm tired.' Fiona, filled with guilt, hugged her mother to her. All she had wanted was to make her happy. How stupid she'd been to bring her to a place of death. Death is so far away, she'd thought. A flash of memory carried her back to the graveyard she'd visited with Patrick, but she pushed it to one side. The last thing she needed now was to worry about Patrick.

Home in the flat, her mother said, 'Why are you treating me like this?'

'Like what?'

'As if I mattered. What I want. What I feel. As if they mattered. After all I've done to you.'

Fiona was thrilled. What a monster Maddy must be. You'll pay for this, she thought. But who did Heather think she was talking to?

'You do matter,' she said. 'You've done nothing.'

'Well, you don't always behave as if I do,' her mother said, looking carefully at her.

'I will from now on,' Fiona said. 'I promise.'

Her mother nodded. 'Come over here next to me,' she said, patting the seat of the sofa. 'I want to tell you something.' When Fiona hesitated, she tapped the seat a second time, playful but impatient. 'Get a move on, before I change my mind.'

As soon as Fiona was beside her, she took her daughter's hand, held it almost too tightly. Then she loosened her grip and touched the ring.

'I had this made for you a couple of weeks before you were born,' she said. 'I was enormous, like a beached whale.' She smiled. 'I went to visit a friend of mine near Bristol, on the coach. I filled two seats, I remember, and the driver asked me if I'd be all right and when was the baby due, and I told him not to worry about it. My friend had a cottage just outside town, she sent someone to pick me up in a clapped-out old car and I thought I was going to fall through a hole in the floor of it, it was so rusty. I only went all that way because this friend was amazing at making jewellery. She was older than me, an artist. I hadn't known her that long, we shared a squat when I first got to London. I was your age.' She paused. 'Twenty years old, and pregnant, and all I could think of was getting these rings made for you. I must have been crazy. I didn't even have any money.' She said 'rings', thought Fiona, oh my God, she said *rings*. 'She kissed my hands and gave me these little velvet pouches and I tried to give her what I had in my bag, which was almost nothing but I couldn't not try, could I? She wouldn't take it, she wouldn't take a penny. She said I should save my money for you. She said she'd made the rings for you, and that they were special because you were special.' She opened her eyes. 'I wonder what she'd say if she could see us now. If she could see you.' She clutched Fiona's hand even harder than before, then let it go with a sigh. Her eyes filled with tears.

'Why is it special?' asked Fiona gently.

'Look at it,' her mother said. She took Fiona's hand and lifted it to her face; her own face, blotched and puffy, was suddenly illuminated. 'You see? You see how it's made of two separate threads of gold twisted together? Not just twisted, united. Separate but inseparable, she said. I hadn't even told her about you. She was extraordinary. She always said she had the gift of second sight, and I believe she did.' And then, without warning, her face became sad again. 'She was right about everything.'

All Fiona had to do now was say, But if one thread is me, then who is the other one? That's what Maddy would have said. But her mother's honesty had trapped Fiona in her deception.

'About everything?' she said.

Her mother shook her head. 'I've said enough for one day.' She let go of Fiona, straightened up. 'And now I think, after all that, I deserve a little drink.'

*

The rest of the day Fiona passed in a state of grace. Her hand kept returning to the ring, to the new-found weight of it on her finger. She sat beside her mother on the sofa, watching a programme identical to the one she had watched the evening before, when the ring had simply been a ring her other mother had given her. She sat in the place that now felt hers, seeing the same actors advertising the same films, the same dancers on the same stage, and it was perfect, absurdly, almost cruelly perfect because she had never experienced this before. At one point she thought she might cry with joy. That was when she hugged her mother, so hard her mother cried out in mock complaint and pretended to push her away, which was also a gesture of love, Fiona knew. How could Maddy not know this, not know how fortunate she was – no, more than fortunate. Blessed. With infinite care, as though nothing in the world were more precious, she prised her mother's glass from her fingers when the woman nodded off, her mind buzzing with the questions she would ask when the right time came. When her mother woke, Fiona suggested they listen to some music and her mother, surprised, watched Fiona root through the LPs stacked against the wall and put a Rolling Stones album on the deck beneath the TV.

'I don't remember the last time I listened to any decent music here.' She took the sleeve from Fiona's hands. '*Let it Bleed*,' she said. She sighed and then, to Fiona's delight, began to sing along. 'You won't remember,' she said between one track and the next, 'how could you? How could you remember? Just before this album came out, when Brian Jones had died, I saw them. You were there, sweetheart, or were you? So long ago now. It was awful, it really was, it was just so sad.' She was slurring a little now. 'Mick read this wonderful poem by Shelley. I used to love Shelley.' She stopped and began to sing again, her eyes closed, rocking backwards and forwards. 'We were in one of the tabloids,' she said. 'They printed my name. That's how I lost my job.' She took Fiona's hand. 'That's when it all started going wrong.' A choir began to sing, and her mother closed her eyes again and joined in, her voice loud and tuneless and on the verge of breaking into a cough. When the song finished, she wiped her eyes on her sleeve.

'I haven't always been like this,' she said. 'I want you to know that.'

Later, when Fiona was sure that Heather was quite asleep, she tucked the rag doll between her mother's arms and breasts, and kissed her forehead as lightly as she could. She put the screw top back on the bottle of wine and took her own glass into the kitchen, emptying the wine that remained into the sink. She checked that she still had the spare key in her pocket and the photographs she had taken from Maddy's album in her bag, then left the flat.

CHAPTER THIRTY-TWO

Maddy and Ludovico spent the morning in the woods behind the villa. They walked in contented silence apart from the whisper of fallen leaves beneath their feet, the cooing of pigeons and an occasional rustle in the undergrowth that Ludovico said was probably rats. They saw no one. When Maddy mentioned this, Ludovico told her that the woods were almost always deserted. An ideal place to hide a body, he said, and she remembered her conversation with Matteo about kidnapping Fiona, and shivered. After an hour or so, Ludovico took her hand and they left the path to clamber over exposed roots and push through bushes as the ground rose before them. The trees gave way to a clearing, the villa below them at the foot of what looked like a giant staircase, flanked by two tall columns. She looked down, stepping back when she felt dizzy.

'It used to be a sort of artificial waterfall, technically a cascade,' said Ludovico. 'But they turned off the tap to save money.' He pointed to the foot of the staircase. 'That's called the Theatre of the Waters, which is unfortunate now that there is no water. Il Teatro delle Acque. It's got a *ninfeo*, I don't know how you say that in English.'

'Nymphaeum, I think.'

'It's pretty cool,' he said, which made her smile. 'Even without water.' He took her hand again, led her to the top of a narrower staircase running down one side of the cascade.

'Are we allowed to go down there?' she said.

Ludovico looked surprised. 'Why shouldn't we be allowed?'

'I don't know.' She glanced around. 'Isn't all this private property?'

'I live here,' he said.

'I suppose you do,' she said.

At the bottom of the steps, he dropped to one knee. 'My lady,' he said, sweeping his arm out to follow a curve of baroque grottoes in need of repair, each with its dirt-encrusted water god and clutch of nymphs. We're trapped, she thought, by who we are and there is no way out of that, no exit allowed. This was his world, she thought, and Fiona's. The world her mother had denied her. She glanced across at the facade of the villa, that poem about fate and hubris running through her head, a poem her mother used to recite when she was in the mood, with Maddy fidgeting between her knees. '"Look on my works,"' she said under her breath. When she caught a glimpse of movement at one of the windows, she flinched.

'There's someone there,' she said. Her first thought was Fiona.

Ludovico looked at her. 'They'll be here for the weekend,' he said. 'Just like us.'

'We're being watched,' she said.

'How flattering.'

'Won't they mind us wandering round their garden?' she said.

'I told you. I have as much right to be here as anyone else.'

She looked at the villa, but the face at the window had disappeared. She shivered.

'Cold?'

She nodded. He put an arm around her shoulder, turned her in to face him, to hold her close, but the idea that someone might be watching them had unsettled her, and she wriggled, then pushed him away. They'll think I'm Fiona. How many times had she been here, wandering around these crumbling grottoes and moss-covered nymphs, the toys of the rich, with Ludovico beside her?

'Let's go back to the house,' she said when he looked at her, his face concerned.

'Hungry?'

'Starving,' she said.

After lunch, and a bottle of wine, and an hour spent making love, she began to tell him about her mother, who had been in her thoughts all weekend. She hadn't planned to, she'd decided a long time ago that it was better to keep the truth about her mother to herself, to replace her with an anodyne all-purpose mother when anyone asked, to say as little as possible, to lie when necessary – strategies she'd developed over years.

But then Ludovico said, your mother, tell me about your mother, and there was something about the way he asked her, some inviting of trust and assurance of good faith in his voice, that softened her and left her both weak and open, and so she did. She told him not the version she'd told Fiona but the truth, as she remembered it. They were sitting together on a sofa in front of the fire, both sleepy after their lunch and the wine and the sex, so that sometimes her voice seemed to belong to someone else as she talked about the way her mother used to let her skip school because she hadn't woken her up in time, and the nights she slept in her clothes on her mother's bed because she had no clean pyjamas to wear and her mother was stoned, and the evenings her mother locked her out of the bedroom because she had friends in there with her, men with untidy hair, who would appear in the kitchen in their pants and T-shirts, or jeans and bare chests, who would look at Maddy in the morning as they ate their bowls of cereal like people who hadn't eaten normal food for days and finished the milk before she'd had a chance to drink any, who would stare at her as though they'd never seen a child before, and ask her mother who she was, and whose she was, so that she knew from an early age that she was her mother's, because her mother always said so. She's mine, she'd say, and sometimes she sounded proud, and sometimes she sounded weary, and sometimes she would look at Maddy for a moment before answering as though she needed to remind herself before she spoke. And Maddy would wait until the moment had passed and then stare into the fridge to see what she could find. She was hungry, often, she told Ludovico, who had taken her hand in his and was staring not at her, which made her feel safer, but at the flames, and she was often cold. In Cambridge, she told him, the wind comes direct from the Urals. There were meters in those days, you had to feed them constantly with money if you wanted to stay warm.

She told him about a bedsit they lived in for months, near Mill Road, a single room, with a single bed they both slept in, her mother's arms wrapped round her to stop her rolling out, and a single gas ring they used to boil water on, and how one day her mother had found a five-pound note at the bottom of a pocket, which was a fortune in those days, and Maddy had been so excited because she thought her mother would put some money into the meter and they would finally be warm, but her mother had gone out and bought cider and cigarettes and she had taken her hand and they had walked across Parker's Piece, she remembers the walk so well, past the lamppost at the centre where someone had daubed the words 'Reality Checkpoint', her mother dragging her as she dawdled, until they were in the room of a man she'd never seen before, and they had turned the TV on and left her in front of it with a packet of crisps and a glass of coke, and disappeared into another room. She had eaten her crisps and finished her coke and the programme they had left her with was some American cop show, she couldn't remember which, *Kojak* maybe, and then it had come to an end and another programme had started and she had gone to sleep and when she woke up the TV was humming and the screen was an electric field of grey and white dots.

She told him about another time, a year or two later, in another place where her mother and she had separate bedrooms, she must have been nine or ten by then, and the man her mother was living with told her to empty their rubbish in a council bin a few doors down the road and to make sure no one was looking and she'd wondered why, and as soon as she was outside the house she'd taken a look inside the bag and found syringes and she'd thought her mother was ill, and hurried back to ask her, and her mother had told her to mind her own business, and then started crying and hugged her so hard she thought she'd cracked a rib. They'd moved out soon after that, but the same man would come round and shout outside the windows of their new flat, and they'd had to move again.

She told him about the times when she was small, barely school age, and she would be sent into shops to steal stuff while her mother stood at the till and distracted the shopkeeper, and how the one time she'd been caught her mother had shouted at her and smacked the back of her legs in the shop and told her she was a bad girl.

She told him about the times she sat in hospital corridors while her mother spoke to doctors.

She told him about the time she was told to watch while two men fucked her mother on the kitchen table, one of them telling her as he did it that it was important she learn how to do it and that she'd be grateful to them one day, and the way her mother had looked at her as though she had never seen her before, which was the worst thing.

She told him about the time her mother took her to the zoo, and she got lost, and didn't remember how she was found. What she remembered was watching a monkey watch her back, and, hours later or maybe not, her mother treating her to fish fingers and chips in a place with a glass wall and enormous fish behind it, the irony of which had struck her even then.

She told him about going on demonstrations and being frightened by the police horses, the heat and smell of them, their enormous hooves and the noise their shoes made as they hit the tarmac, and deciding that one day — when she was big enough to do what she wanted — she would be a policewoman and arrest her mother.

She told him about the first day at a new school, one new school after another, and how she used to read books about girls like her in boarding schools and how she used to wish she could go to a boarding school and stay there even for the holidays, and for Christmas, because Christmas was something her mother didn't do, she thought it had been ruined by capitalism and so Maddy almost never had a present and, when she did, it was something she needed, or something her mother had found in the street.

She told him about the good times too, about the days she came back from school and her mother had made her tea and they had eaten it together, and she had helped her finish her homework and the two of them had watched TV sitting side by side on the sofa as we're doing now — she said to Ludovico, who squeezed her hand but didn't speak — and then played games until it was time to go to bed.

She told him about the concerts her mother took her to, and how she would be lifted onto someone's shoulders and waved around until the singer saw her and waved or blew her a kiss, and how excited her mother would be by that, as though the kiss had been intended for her. And other concerts, in fields, where her mother would sit in a circle with her friends, who were almost always men, and she would smoke and drink wine straight from the bottle then pass it round, and how Maddy would be offered a sip or a toke, and she would always refuse and sometimes her mother would say she was a good girl and sometimes she would laugh and say, you're no daughter of mine. She told him about the time she saw a man with a fake hand, with the veins painted on it, holding it out and it was full of pills, and how she had nightmares about him for months afterwards, how the pills would change her shape, make her grow as tall as a tree or shrink to nothing, all of it mixed in with her memories of *Alice in Wonderland*, which she'd just read. She told him about the days, whole days, she spent reading books, her own and her mother's, battered novels and poetry, because her mother loved poetry, and understanding almost nothing of what she read, but not giving up, never giving up.

She told him about the times she wished she had a sister.

When her voice stumbled and she started to cry, without realising at first, as though some thread that tied her to the world's needs had grown so thin it had ruptured without her knowing, Ludovico put his arm around her. 'You're with me now,' he said softly as her sobs became more intense. 'You're safe with me.' When he hugged her to him, she didn't resist, she barely acknowledged him. 'She can't hurt you any more,' he said. 'I won't let her,' but, unexpectedly, she sat up straight, breaking free from him, and shook her head. 'That isn't why I'm crying,' she said. 'You don't understand. I just feel so terrible.' She looked into his eyes. 'I love her, oh my God, I love her so much.' Her expression, if she could have seen it as he did, was one of anguish, and then self-blame. 'I should never have told you all that,' she said.

'You did what you had to do,' he said.

She shook her head, more fervently this time. 'I didn't have to do it. I've never done it before, not with anyone. I've been a total shit.' Her face was fierce. 'I want you to forget everything I've said.'

He sighed. 'I can't do that.'

'You've got to,' she said.

'You've opened up to me,' he said. 'How can I forget that?'

She stared at him. When she spoke her voice was broken, her speech slow.

'You must never tell anyone what I've told you. You must promise me that.'

Ludovico looked at her evenly. 'I would never do that,' he said.

CHAPTER THIRTY-THREE

Sitting beside Ludovico in the car, Maddy felt inexplicably anxious to get home to her mother. They were silent for the first part of the journey, Ludovico hunched forward, apparently unused to driving at night, Maddy's eyes half closed against the headlights of approaching cars. Later, she wouldn't remember who brought up the subject of Fiona, but, drawing close to the outer suburbs of Rome, slowed down by the Sunday-evening traffic, they found themselves talking about her once again.

'I wonder if she's ever been in love,' said Maddy.

'I wouldn't know,' said Ludovico.

'She had a boyfriend last year at Oxford, she told me,' said Maddy.

Ludovico nodded.

'They saw *The Shining* together. She said he liked Kubrick.'

'Yes, that's the kind of thing he would like.'

'Do you know him?'

'I met him once or twice, before he was arrested.'

'Arrested?' She was startled.

'That's right.'

'What for?'

Ludovico paused, tried to overtake the car in front, but pulled back as the car accelerated. 'People are crazy,' he said.

'Are you talking about that car?'

He smiled. 'That too. No, I was thinking about Fiona's boyfriend.'

'What was he like?'

'Oh, arrogant, good-looking, charming in a way I didn't much like but that's only my opinion, comes from a very good family, no reason at all to do what he did.'

'Which was?' Here it was again, that envy she couldn't keep in check at hearing the words 'good family', at how easily Ludovico said them, as though the value they bestowed were shared by her.

'Bad cheques. Not just, what's the word? Bounced. Actually forged, and forged very well, I believe. He told the court he was a conceptual artist, which didn't help. Sociopath would have been a better description, in my opinion.'

'Where is he now?'

'Still in jail, as far as I know. Even his parents' string-pulling couldn't keep him out.'

'So why did he do it, do you think?' She was fascinated by the idea that Fiona might have been involved.

'Why do people do things?' Ludovico said. 'Why did that trade union guy get shot? Why do people bomb stations and kill hundreds of people? We're surrounded by lunatics doing inexplicable things. There's always a reason and it's never good enough, it never explains anything.'

Maddy studied Ludovico's profile in the darkness of the car, waiting for him to speak. But he was focused once more on the road.

'Did Fiona know?' she said.

'No,' he said, and then, after a pause, 'At least, I don't think so. Not officially.' After a second longer pause, he sighed. 'To be honest,' he said, 'I'm sure she did.'

Maddy wondered why he should want to protect her. 'What do you mean?'

He sighed again. 'She wasn't surprised. She was always happy to let him spend his money on her. I think she must have known it wasn't his to spend. I think she liked the idea that it was stolen.'

'Is she still in touch with him?'

'No. She told me that he dropped her like a hot brick as soon as he was jailed. I don't know if she was pleased about that or not.' He turned to look at her. 'I wonder how you would have felt.'

'Why do you have to compare us?'

'That's not what I meant.'

She didn't answer. She stared out of the window at the arches of an aqueduct, lit from below. How extraordinary that it should still be here, she thought, after all these centuries.

'I'll probably regret this,' she said, 'but, well, I know you like me—'

He interrupted her. 'I more than like you.'

'I just can't help wondering if you've ever liked her in the same way.'

'Fiona?'

'Yes.'

'I told you. I know her too well.'

'But what does that mean? If you know someone better, you lose interest?'

'Now you're being obtuse,' he said. 'You know that isn't what I said, or what I think.' He paused for a moment, then turned his face her way. 'The fact that you look alike—'

'That we're identical twins, you mean.'

'All right, that you're identical twins. It means nothing to me. When I look at you, I see you, Maddy, not Fiona, not some copy of Fiona, not some wouldn't-it-be-nice-if-you-were-Fiona. I see you. Is that so hard to understand?'

'I'm sorry,' she said. 'I'm being stupid.'

'Where do you want me to drop you off?' His tone was cold, level.

'I said I'm sorry. I'm a fool.'

He smiled, but had turned away. 'No, I'm sorry.' He touched her leg, let his hand rest there for a moment. 'Would you like me to come back with you?'

She shook her head. 'Another time.'

'I'd like that.'

'It's late,' she said.

He looked at his watch. 'You're right.'

'That's a very impressive watch,' she said.

'I have a thing about watches,' he said. 'I've lost count of how many I've got.' He laughed. But the mood of the weekend was broken. It seemed days rather than hours since she had told him about her mother.

She was about to close the door when he said her name, so quietly she almost didn't hear him. She bent over to look back into the car. 'Don't go like that,' he said. He patted the seat beside him. 'Come back here.'

'What do you want?' she said, suspicious.

'I want to kiss you,' he said.

*

Her mother was asleep in front of the silent television. Maddy walked over to turn it off but stopped when her mother stirred and reached out, still half asleep. 'No, don't,' she said, with an edge of urgency in her voice. 'I want to watch what's on.' Maddy sat down next to her. She took her mother's hand and placed it on the cushion between them. 'It's all right,' she said quietly. 'It's only me. I'm home now.' She stroked the hand until it was still and her mother had relaxed once more into sleep. She sat beside her on the sofa, thinking about Ludovico. She lifted her own hand and held it to her nose to see if she could detect the scent of him, and found the faintest aroma of smoke. On the screen, two German women, identical twins, were dancing. Maybe we could make a living like that, she thought, taking our clothes off and kicking our legs in the air for money, like freaks.

'Turn it off,' her mother said, awake again. 'I've had enough for this evening.'

'Not just yet,' said Maddy.

'Why won't you do what I tell you the first time?' said her mother, struggling to get up from the sofa. 'You never do what I tell you. Why do you make me say everything twice?'

'In a minute,' Maddy said. She's lost all track of time, she thought. Poor thing, she's forgotten I've been away all weekend. 'I've only just got back.' She looked at her mother, anxious.

'What are you talking about?' her mother said. She stood up and pulled her dressing gown around her pyjamas. Maddy wondered if she'd dressed at all these past two days, or eaten. There was a rag doll she'd never seen before, face down, half hidden by a cushion. Where on earth had that come from? she wondered. She looked at the floor for an empty plate, but found nothing. An ashtray, filled with butts. An empty one-and-a-half-litre wine bottle, the kind with a screw top. So she must have been out of the flat at least once, thought Maddy, and wondered what else she had bought. She'd live on pizza if Maddy let her. The room smelt of the usual cream and of something else Maddy couldn't place, familiar to her but not in this context. She reached for her ring. Oh God, she said to herself, it isn't on my finger. I must have left it at the cottage. She remembered taking it off to shower, putting it in a bowl beside the basin. How stupid she was. Ludovico will suppose I've forgotten it on purpose, it struck her, but she knew – or thought she knew – that wasn't true. She could feel him now, his skin on hers, that last kiss in the car a sort of searching, she couldn't explain it any better than that, a searching inside her for something he could take away with him and keep. She could feel his lips on her lips, the roughness of his beard, the softness of his mouth, his tongue just touching hers. I've given myself to him, she thought, and for the first time in her life those words, to give oneself, had meaning for her.

'Turn it off,' her mother said.

Half an hour later, Maddy went into her room. She closed the door behind her, alone for the first time in two days, leant her body against it, weak with relief and exhaustion, before reaching to turn on the light.

Her bed had been used. The blankets beneath the bedspread were rucked up and the pillows had been placed against the wall, as though someone had been reading. She knows she can't do this, Maddy thought, outraged, she knows this is my room and she isn't allowed in here, but then, triggered perhaps by the wretchedness of the hastily made bed, a memory came of her going into her mother's bedroom as a child, scared by a bad dream, or simply lonely and unable to sleep, reaching up to the handle of the door and tiptoeing across the bare floor to the bed, and climbing in, careful not to make a noise or pull at the bedclothes, only to find it empty, empty and cold, because her mother was sleeping somewhere else and hadn't thought to tell her. She remembered curling up in the place where her mother should have been, pressing her face against pillows that smelt of her mother, because even that small thing – that smell – was better than going back to her own bed, where she would be even more alone and the bad dream would be waiting for her. That's what she must have done, thought Maddy now. She must have woken up and found herself alone in the flat and come into my room for warmth, because even the empty bed of another is warmer than your own when you're alone. She sat on the edge of the bed to take off her shoes and thought about the loneliness of her mother, and then – because how could she not? – about Ludovico, her secret. She lay back and stared at the ceiling, thrilled and scared at the thought of Ludovico, and their weekend together, isolated from the world, their acts unknown, the distance they had made for themselves. He was in Fiona's flat now, but only hours ago she had been sitting beside him, watching a fire they had built themselves, their skin still warm from the other's body, the other's breath.

CHAPTER THIRTY-FOUR

Outside the lecture room, Matteo put his arm through hers. 'Let's get a coffee,' he said. 'I need something to keep me awake. I didn't have much sleep.'

Maddy shook her head. 'I really need to be getting home,' she said. 'Give me a call later.'

'Your phone isn't working,' said Matteo. His voice was cold. 'Did you know? I called half a dozen times this weekend. It makes a funny noise as if it's not connected.'

'I wasn't at home this weekend,' she said.

'Maybe you haven't paid the bill,' he said.

'My mother probably took it off the hook,' said Maddy. 'She didn't want to be disturbed. She hates the phone.' She looked at her watch. 'I'd better get off.' She was about to kiss Matteo's cheek but noticed a just perceptible flinch. She stepped back.

'Be in touch,' she said, walking away.

A few minutes later, already off campus, she heard footsteps behind her. She turned round and saw Matteo.

'How can I be in touch if your phone isn't working?'

'You tell me,' she said.

'I'm right, aren't I? You haven't paid the bill?'

Maddy was about to deny this, but all her strength left her. 'Oh God, Matteo, I ruin everything. I've been an absolute shit for no reason at all.' She was on the point of tears.

'Come on,' he said. 'Coffee.'

They went to Bar Marani, sat under the bare tangle of the vine. Matteo offered her a cigarette and she took it, grateful. Her mother was fifty yards away, and probably had no cigarettes, and Maddy wondered if she had spent all the money she'd been left two days before. When the girl arrived, Matteo ordered cappuccinos for them both.

'Thank you,' she said.

'So you haven't paid the phone bill,' he said again, and this time it was not a question.

She shook her head, in confirmation. 'I don't know what to do.'

'Do you want to talk about it?'

'Not really,' she said and then, because this was a lie, she said, 'Yes, I do. If you're sure you want to listen.'

He stared at her, the brightness of his eyes as startling to her as ever. 'I'm all ears,' he said, as the girl came back with the cappuccinos. 'Spill the beans.'

She smiled. 'Sometimes your grasp of English is unnerving. I wish you'd make a mistake sometimes.'

'I think you're trying to avoid the subject,' he said.

Ten minutes later she had told him what she knew. She told him about the house her mother had inherited – who from? Matteo asked, but she didn't know – when Maddy was a baby, a house her mother had rented out and used the money to live on whenever she was out of work, which was too often, or when no man was around to help her pay the bills. And then the house was sold because another one of her mother's boyfriends knew someone who could make them rich and the money the house made – or part of it, because her mother surely couldn't have been that stupid – was invested in some half-baked scheme. And now, although her mother had refused to answer her questions, it seemed that something had happened to whatever capital was left after her so-called investment because the money had dried up, and her mother was incapable of working because she was always drunk or hungover, and there was no man on the scene and hadn't been for years now and Maddy – close to tears again – was terrified she might have to leave university and find a proper job. But what kind of job? She had no skills to speak of, apart from her language, she had no qualification to teach. 'I'm not like my twin,' she said, with a flare of bitterness. 'She's the lucky one.'

'You don't believe that,' said Matteo.

She looked at him. She had said too much, and was enormously relieved.

'Actually,' she said, 'I do. I think she's fucking lucky and I resent her for it. I want what she has, her money, her easy life, her place at Oxford, and I can't have them. I hate her, if you want to know the truth. I hope I never have to see her again. Even better, I'd just like to slip into her life and let mine go to hell.'

He stared into his empty cup, then turned back to face her. 'Another cappuccino?'

'Yes,' she said. 'That would be lovely. You'll have to get them though. I haven't got any money on me.'

He shrugged, then waved to the girl and mouthed his order. 'Look, Maddy,' he said, his tone cautious. 'If I can help.'

'With money, you mean?' She paused, then, unexpectedly, waved both hands in the air. 'No, wait a minute. I know what we could do. That idea you had. We kidnap Fiona and hold her to ransom. Have your parents got a cellar we could use? I bet they have. We cut off her earlobe and post it to darling Mummy if she doesn't pay. I saw a place this weekend we could bury her. Nobody would ever guess.'

He gave a bemused smile, then shook his head. He doesn't want to upset me, she thought. I've told him more than I've ever told anyone about the state we're in, I've been recklessly confessional and indiscreet, and I should feel guilty but I don't. He offered her a cigarette, which she took. 'I mean, if you need to borrow some money. To pay the phone bill. I can lend it to you. You don't need to worry about paying me back.'

'That isn't how borrowing works, Matteo,' she said gently.

'But I'd be doing myself a favour in any case,' he said. The second cappuccinos arrived. He waited until they were alone before continuing. 'How can I get in touch with you if you have no phone?'

She sighed. 'Oh God, all right. But, please, just this once. These mustn't be your problems, Matteo.' She sighed again. 'I hate myself for letting you do this.'

CHAPTER THIRTY-FIVE

Maddy found her mother standing in the middle of the living room with a bucket and a mop. Her hair was pushed into a floral bathing cap Maddy had last seen on a holiday when she was thirteen. When she closed the door, her mother raised her head, her expression both apologetic and challenging. 'I thought this place needed a thorough clean,' she said.

'You could have waited for me,' said Maddy. 'I'd have helped.'

'At least you've remembered your key this time,' her mother said, disgruntled as always by housework.

'I always remember my key.'

Her mother laughed. 'Not this weekend, you didn't.'

'I just told you. I wasn't here this weekend.'

'This isn't a hotel, you know.' She looked worn out, irritated. 'You should see your face. That's no way to treat me. I'm still your mother.'

Maddy threw her bag on the sofa. She'd seen her mother like this too often, convinced that someone had left something rotten on the stairs or that the shopping had been done and Maddy must have hidden it to make her look foolish or, worse, insane. I've seen *Gaslight*, she'd said more than once, I know what you're up to, and Maddy had no idea what she meant until she caught the film one afternoon in a local cinema, retitled *Angoscia*, and was shocked that her mother should think her capable of such ingenious subterfuge.

'I'm not treating you like anything,' she said. 'I'm just saying I wasn't here. But don't worry. Everyone makes mistakes. Like that cap you've got on your head. Where did you dig that out from?'

Her mother's hand flew up to her head and felt the rubbery flowers of the bathing cap. It was obvious she'd forgotten all about it. Gingerly, she pulled it off and threw it towards the sofa. It landed on the floor, like some gaudy, primitive life form.

'I'm not stupid. You don't need to stand there with that simpering goody-two-shoes look on your face.'

'I know you aren't stupid, Mum,' Maddy said, and sighed. 'It's just that sometimes I don't know what you want from me.'

'Well, a hand with this filthy flat would be useful.'

That isn't what I meant, she thought. 'Just tell me what to do, and I'll do it,' she said, bridling at the word filthy. She'd spent hours last week cleaning the living room and kitchen, washing the floor her mother was now washing again, badly, with water that was dirtier than the tiles.

'You can tidy your bedroom up if you want,' her mother said, as though doing Maddy a favour. 'Given that I'm not allowed into it.'

'You were in it while I was away,' snapped Maddy.

Her mother looked at her sharply. 'I was what?'

'You slept in there,' Maddy said.

'I did no such thing.'

'Well, someone did,' said Maddy. And then it hit her. Of course. Of course. Someone did sleep in her room. But it wasn't her mother. And it wasn't her.

'You said I forgot my key?' she said cautiously, her heart pounding in her chest. She took the mop out of her mother's hand, guided her to the sofa. She picked up the floral cap and placed it in the woman's lap. 'Look, why don't you sit down and let me finish this? I'll make some coffee, all right?'

Her mother nodded. 'I don't know what to do with you sometimes,' she said, twisting the cap in her hands. 'You come in here all snappy and unpleasant, and now you're fussing over me as though I were incapable. I'm barely old enough to be your mother, don't forget that.'

'I won't, Mum.'

'And don't keep calling me Mum. I thought you'd finally stopped. That's twice you've done it now. You know how much I hate it.'

'Sorry. Heather.'

'That's better.'

Maddy made coffee for them both, then sat beside her mother on the sofa. Last night, they were sitting like this and the television was on and what had her mother said? Turn it off. I told you to turn it off? Told who? She must have been here all weekend.

'Do you remember I told you I was going away for the weekend?' she said in a low voice, as gently as she could manage.

Her mother sipped her coffee. 'Well?'

'And then I came back?'

'Without your key,' said her mother.

'Without my key. And then what did I do?'

'What do you mean?'

'No, really. Heather. Just listen to me. What did I do?'

'Is this one of those tests they do with people they think have gone mad? I was there when they asked your great-aunt what the name of the prime minister was. I told them, I don't know the name of the fucking prime minister. Are you going to try and lock me up as well?'

'It's not a test, Mum. Heather. I promise you.'

Heather looked at her sideways, suspicious, then took a second sip of coffee and sighed before speaking.

'All right then, here goes. You looked round the room with this snooty look on your face and I thought, who the hell does she think she is, and then you gave me a hug and I didn't know what you were after. Make up your mind, I thought. Or maybe that was later.' As she spoke her voice took on the tone of someone reading from a script, as though she had thought about what she would say in case she was asked. I'm right, thought Maddy, and then, her heart sinking: she knows I'm right.

'What did I say?'

'You didn't say anything.'

'Nothing?'

'Not a word.'

'Didn't you think that was, I don't know, odd?'

Her mother laughed unexpectedly. 'Well, you *are* odd, you know. You're my daughter.' She paused.

'And then?'

'And then you sat down next to me and held my hands and looked at me as though you'd never seen me before. Which gave me the creeps, if you want to know the truth. I thought, who is this? This isn't Maddy.'

I could tell her now, thought Maddy, own up for us both. But she didn't. At this precise moment, what her mother knew and felt was less important than finding out what had happened. 'How long did I spend in my room?' she said.

'And then you said you loved me,' her mother said. 'And I thought, she never tells me she loves me.'

I do, thought Maddy, but you don't remember.

'And then you gave me that doll.' She glanced around her, anxious. 'Where is it? Where have you put it?'

'In my room,' said Maddy. 'How long did I stay in there?'

'I don't know. You came and went. You made me go out for a

walk, I don't know why. You made cheese on toast, but there was too much cheese on it for me, and I didn't eat it. I was watching TV most of the time. And then the news started and I told you to turn it off, it was too upsetting, and you wouldn't, so I said at least the sound, just turn the sound off, and you did. And then we listened to some music for a bit, and that was lovely. I must have gone to sleep for a while. And when I woke up, you'd turned the sound on again. And everything was back to normal.'

Maddy took the cap out of her mother's hand. She'd pulled off one of the flowers and Maddy took it and lifted it to her face as though it were real and had scent.

'Where's your ring?' her mother said.

'My ring?' said Maddy, taken aback. 'It's in my bag. I took it off. I was scared of losing it.'

'It looked so lovely on you. I was just so happy seeing you wearing it. The ring I'd had made for you.' Her voice was sentimental. 'I thought you didn't like it. You hardly ever put it on. I notice things, you know. You think I don't, but I do. And then I saw it on your finger and I was just so happy.' She must be drunk, decided Maddy. She's rambling. At this point nothing she said would make much sense. 'I'd waited all these years to tell you about it,' she said.

'Tell me about it?'

'Why I did it. The two threads of gold. What it means.'

'You told me? When did you tell me?'

Her mother looked suddenly distressed. 'Yesterday. Saturday. I don't remember.'

'I was wearing my ring over the weekend,' Maddy said carefully, and it was not a question. She understood now why Ludovico was so sure he'd seen it before. He'd seen it on Fiona. 'You told me what it meant. What did you tell me?' She grasped her mother's arm. 'Heather,' she said, to make sure that her mother was listening. 'Heather, what did you tell me?'

'I don't remember now what I told you,' said her mother. 'You're confusing me.' Her eyes were welling up with tears. 'I wish you'd just leave me alone.'

'What did I say? Can you remember what I said?'

Her mother looked at her, distraught. 'I don't remember. Yes, I do. You didn't say anything. You just hugged me. I thought you'd never let me go. You even bruised me.' She lifted her pyjama top, ran her fingers around her waist. Her flesh was white, blotchy. Maddy could see no sign of bruising. Oh Mum, she thought, but didn't say.

'I thought you'd never let me go,' her mother said a second time, as if to herself.

Maddy looked around her room, afraid of what she might see. She remembered finding the scarf on the chair that morning, as if it had been placed there for that reason. But of course, she realised now, it had been. How could she not have known? That scent in the flat, of apples and flowers. Fiona's scent. She looked in the bin beside her desk and saw the bright-red paper that must have been wrapped around that horrible, creepy rag doll. She opened the desk drawer where she kept her photo album. Had it been moved? She couldn't tell, but felt despoiled either way. She'll have opened the drawer and looked in, she'll have touched stuff that isn't hers and now will never be mine, Maddy thought. She took out the album and leafed through it, and found two, then three gaps, the four small corner mounts framing rectangles of paper that were darker than the paper around them. The missing photographs had been taken when she was younger – days out with her mother and whoever her mother was with at the time, picnics in the local park, sitting outside pubs, her bare legs dangling from a bench, her small hands holding lemonade in a bottle with a straw and a packet of crisps – but she couldn't recall which ones exactly, and now she would never know. Moments of her life, and of her mother's life, that had been taken from them both, and would never be given back. What made her choose these and not others, Maddy thought and then: What did Heather tell her? What the ring meant, she said. The rings. Two rings. So what do the rings mean? Now that bitch – that nosy, interfering bitch – knows things that I don't know, rooting around in my life like some fucking animal, touching my stuff, stealing whatever takes her fancy as though everything I had, my whole life, was some kind of pick 'n' mix counter in Woolworth's.

Maddy felt sick suddenly, physically sick. She closed the album, sat down at her desk and picked up the notes she'd been making on nihilism, interrupted by her weekend away, notes she could barely recall having made. Nihilism, that's rich. She'd wanted to contrast it with humanism, she remembered now, with humanism and, oh my God, with love. With love and Ludovico. How far away the weekend felt now.

And then the thought she must have been pushing away from her, to protect herself, finally made itself heard. How did Fiona know I wasn't here? Who knew I'd be away apart from me and my mother? Ludovico. No one else, not even Matteo. Ludovico must have told her. She looked at the bed in the corner, the bed she had slept in in half a dozen different homes, her bed. She lay on my bed, her head on my pillow, her skin against my sheets, knowing that I was with Ludovico in his. She had us both exactly where she wanted us, where she could hurt me most, and I had no idea.

She crossed the living room, ignoring her mother on the sofa, where she was leafing through a magazine, everything forgotten, and lifted a pair of scissors from the hook beside the sink. She took them into the bathroom and cut her hair, the fringe first of all, cut it back almost to her hairline, and then, bending over the bathtub, lifting whole hanks of the rest of it, great swathes of dark-brown hair that fell into the tub, growing more careless as she cut, filled with a sort of exultation as she guided the blades with her other hand, felt the cold iron scrape against her scalp and then a stab of pain above her left ear where she must have broken the skin, tugging and hacking until nothing was left of Fiona, until she had made the distance between them irrevocable, unbridgeable. When she had finished and the tub was filled with her hair, she stood up straight and looked into the mirror.

Maddy stared back at her, horrified, thrilled by what she had done.

PART FOUR

CHAPTER THIRTY-SIX

Aldo insists they both watch the programme the following week and Elizabeth sits beside him, her food untouched, while the journalist dredges up forgotten murder cases and introduces the anxious relatives of the people who have disappeared in the last seven days. Some of the missing are children, others are too old to know any longer where they live, their desperate families holding up photographs or items of clothing, the numbers to call scrolling constantly across the bottom of the screen. Mikki, the fifteen-year-old boy last seen outside a bowling alley in Milan, has been spotted in a variety of cities, which is proof, according to Aldo, that young people these days look identical, however convinced they are of their uniqueness. Liz nods, but isn't listening. She's wondering what other photos the woman has, and whether she will allow them to be shown on television. She has spent all week trying to guess what on earth has possessed the woman to expose herself like this. What does she hope to achieve, after all these years? Revenge? A chance to be forgiven? Each time the camera shifts to something new, some new disappearance, some new discovery, she tenses, wishing she were alone, or that Aldo would let her turn to another channel. He hasn't mentioned the girl all week, which gives her hope that she has slipped his mind, although not hope enough to feel at ease. She only relaxes when the programme comes to an end. Aldo looks at her plate.

'You haven't touched your dinner,' he says.

'This programme upsets me,' she says. 'I told you that last week. I don't understand why you like it so much.'

He stands up, takes her tray off her lap.

'It's a public service,' he says. 'Imagine if one of the boys had gone missing. We'd be the first to get in touch with the programme to ask for help. I would, anyway.'

'I don't want to argue about it,' she says, more snappily than she intends.

'Neither do I,' he says, coldly. He takes their plates into the kitchen. When he comes back, she is ready to apologise but he picks up the remote control without looking at her. He is sulking, and she can't blame him. It's obvious that she has something on her mind, and just as obvious that she has no intention of sharing it with him.

She's been tempted, of course. All week she's thought to herself, and if I told him? Just came out with it? I'm not who you think I am. But that's nonsense. She is exactly the person he thinks she is, the person he's known and lived with for over thirty years, and has had twin boys with, and nothing that happened before they met, no lie she has told him or evasion she has engineered or supposition she has allowed to survive, can alter that. She is who she says she is. Elizabeth. Liz. His Liz.

Another week passes before the programme returns to the case of the missing English girl. There has been a significant development, the journalist says. They show the photo again, and the details, arranged like information on a record card. Name, age, where last seen. How tall she was, how heavy, as though anyone could have known, as though it mattered now. The clothes the girl had on the last time she was seen, but how is that possible? Liz wonders. She can barely remember what she was wearing yesterday. She thinks about the boys. Their last visit home was a month ago. What were they wearing? she asks herself. She has no idea. How do people remember things like this? And then there is the last place the girl was spotted. The record card says San Lorenzo. She's sure that's new. Is that the development the woman talked about? The first time she's sure that it had just said Rome. Someone must have remembered, and phoned the helpline. Why can't people mind their own damn business? she thinks. They're closing in.

'So here she is,' says Aldo, with a sideways glance. 'The mysterious missing girl. Remember?'

Liz nods.

'I wonder what the news is. They must have found something out.'

'I wonder.'

He looks directly at her. 'I can't get over it,' he says.

'Oh, for God's sake, Aldo.'

'I thought you weren't interested,' he says.

She makes an effort to laugh. 'I'm not going to be provoked,' she says. 'There's no point in trying.'

'San Lorenzo? That's just by the university, isn't it?'

'You know it is,' she says.

'*Calma*,' he says.

'I'm perfectly calm,' she says. She has almost convinced herself of this when the television studio disappears to be replaced by a desk and a book-lined wall and there is Ludovico, bald now, thinner than ever, but still recognisable, still charming, his polished television manner coming to his aid. She's seen him a handful of times before on the kind of post-primetime shows that require his presence, and has managed to conceal from Aldo that she used to know him. She watches him in a sort of daze, weak with anxiety, barely listening to what he says, knowing that he will be careful, as he talks about his memories of the English girl he shared an apartment with, all those years ago, and had known as a child. She was like a sister to me, he says. We grew up together. Our families were close friends. His tone is nostalgic, his voice the same as it has always been, soothing, an ironic edge to it. No, he says, she never lived in San Lorenzo; as far as he knows she had no friends there, how strange that someone should imagine they remember having seen a girl there after all these years, a girl who looks so much like any other girl, and his tone throws a shade of doubt on the sighting. He's still protecting me, she thinks, when Aldo laughs, a humourless laugh that sets her teeth on edge.

She looks at him.

'I can't stand these people,' he says.

'Which people?'

'These people who think they know everything. These go-to expert types who don't actually know anything beyond their own vanity.'

'I think you're being unfair,' she says. 'You're doing what you accuse him of doing. You don't know him.'

'Neither do you,' he says. He shifts in his seat. 'I mean, let's face it, what has he just contributed to the search for this girl? Nothing. He's had another fifteen minutes on television, that's all. It's probably written into his contract. I bet he barely even knew the girl.' He puts on an affected voice. 'We were close friends.'

'Now you're talking nonsense.'

'You seem very keen to defend him.'

She is about to get up and leave the room when the woman appears on the screen. She is sitting in the same armchair as before, but wearing a different blouse. They must have gone back and wanted more. She looks tired, anxious. Has she always been like this, Liz wonders, as the woman starts to talk.

This time she talks about the money. She explains how

much her daughter inherited, or was due to inherit, and how her disappearance happened days after she'd come into her inheritance. And the money disappeared as well, she says. The journalist asks her what she means. Well, says the woman, her account was closed and the bank wouldn't tell me where it had all gone. She never cared about money, the woman says, and Liz smiles to herself. She had a friend who may have advised her, the woman says, a young man she knew at university, but she can't recall his name, she had no way of getting in touch with him. All this happened so many years ago, she says. I'd let bygones be bygones if only I could see her one last time. She looks at the camera. I know you're there, dear. I know you're alive and safe. You're my daughter. The journalist asks if she suspects foul play and the woman thinks for a moment, then shakes her head.

'She's lying,' says Aldo.

'Who knows?'

Aldo looks at her. 'Come on, Liz. A girl comes into a fortune and then disappears and you don't think there's something suspicious? And she's your only daughter? She's hiding something. It's obvious. I bet that family friend of hers had something to do with it. And the money just disappeared as well? If you don't think that's suspicious, you're crazy. What's that thing you English say? Follow the money.' He takes a breath, a swig of wine. 'Follow the money,' he says again.

'Not everyone cares about money,' says Liz.

'People who have grown up without it do,' he says. 'But I wouldn't expect you to know that.'

'Well, then,' says Liz, ignoring this. 'She obviously had no reason to care. Because from what her mother says they were absolutely rolling in money. Maybe that was the problem. Her mother. Money. Maybe she wanted to get away from them both.' Her voice rises. 'Maybe her mother was obsessed by money.'

'All right, all right,' says Aldo.

'What I mean is that we know nothing about these people,' says Liz hotly. 'Nothing.' She's about to try to leave a second time when the scene shifts to another room, book-lined as Ludovico's was, and a middle-aged man sitting in an armchair, a younger man opposite him. He nods when the younger man asks him if he knew Fiona Conway. Yes, he says, but I knew her twin sister better. We were students together in Rome. My God, thinks Liz, it's Matteo. After all these years, Matteo. Her twin sister, the interviewer repeats, sitting forward in his chair. Yes, she had a twin sister who'd lived in Rome for some years before Fiona arrived. What was her name? Maddalena, but she called herself Maddy. I don't recall her surname. She lived with her mother. Her mother? Matteo pauses. *Their* mother, I always thought. And where is she now? Matteo shakes his head. I wish I knew. We were very close, very close indeed, and then she disappeared. Like her sister? Exactly, Matteo says. So you think they may have planned their disappearance together, the interviewer says.

Before Aldo can stop her, Liz has picked up the remote control and turned the television off.

Aldo says nothing for a moment. They sit side by side on the sofa in silence. Liz is shaking with fury.

Then Aldo speaks. 'I was watching that.'

'Well, you shouldn't have been. It's morbid and unhealthy.'

'I'm sorry?'

'You heard what I said.'

He reaches across and prises the remote control from her hand. She watches him, aghast, as he turns the television back on.

'I can't believe you did that,' she says, but he doesn't look at her. He is staring doggedly at the screen. Matteo is still talking. She stands up, leaves the room and then the house. She stands in the garden and stares up into the night sky, her stomach suddenly churning. She is about to return to the house when something catches her eye, a movement high above the poplars at the foot of the garden, a circling that must be a bird, black against the deep blue of the sky, a circling that halts before diving, faster than falling, a vertical dive as though it is being dragged to the earth by some force it can't resist. A moment of utter stillness, of emptiness, and then it rises once more, a hawk of some kind she sees now, in its talons some small creature she can't identify, but for which she feels an immediate, hopeless sympathy. Her heart stops for a moment, as though the beat of it were no longer hers, and then starts again as the hawk swoops high into the sky and then low, a spot that shrinks to nothing, absorbed by the dark.

Follow the money, she thinks and then says, out loud, into the silence.

As though the money mattered.

PART FIVE

CHAPTER THIRTY-SEVEN

Fiona was eating a biscuit and waiting for the coffee to bubble up when the phone rang. She heard Ludovico answer. Seconds later, he came into the kitchen.

'Your mother's on the phone.'

Fiona's heart leapt. Heather had tracked her down. How was that possible? Had Maddy told her? Did Maddy know?

'She wants to know if you're all right. She's says you haven't called for weeks.'

Oh, thought Fiona, with a surge of disappointment. That mother. She put down her biscuit and went into the sitting room.

'Hello,' she said.

'I thought you promised you were going to call me once a week at least,' her mother said. 'I've been getting worried. It isn't fair, you know.'

'It's better if you call me,' Fiona said. 'You know that. We agreed.'

'Yes, well, I suppose we did, but you did promise,' her mother said, and sighed. 'Anyway, I hope you're all right.'

'I'm fine,' she said, softening a little. How strange to be talking with this impostor, she thought, after two whole days with her real mother.

'I worry about you, my dear,' her mother said. 'I can't imagine what it must be like living in Italy these days. What awful times.

As though the Irish weren't bad enough. It used to be such a delightful country before all these bombs and murders and people being kidnapped and held to ransom. I can't get that poor Getty boy out of my head, losing an ear like that. What monsters they must have been to do that to a child, just for money. You are being careful, I hope.' She could imagine her mother shuddering, as much with distaste as pity.

'Oh, I don't know,' she said. 'It's quite exciting, actually.'

'What an awful thing to say, Fiona.'

'Well, you asked me,' Fiona said.

'There's no need to use that tone,' her mother said. 'It's only natural that a mother should worry about her daughter, especially when she's about to become very rich and a target for that sort of thing. I hope you aren't running around telling everyone.'

'Of course I'm not,' she snapped. 'Look, Mummy—' there, she thought, I've said it, 'you really don't need to worry about me, all right? I'm absolutely fine.'

'I can't help worrying about you. All alone there. It's such a chaotic city. All those pickpockets.'

'I'm not all alone. I've got Ludovico,' she said, thinking, that's rich, coming from you, after you sent me to schools for years where I knew no one and had to look after myself, and I could have been at home, with you and Daddy, or with my real mother. 'He'll make sure I'm all right. You know what he's like.'

'I suppose he will. You certainly do need looking after. I can't believe you'll be twenty-one and independent so soon.' Her mother paused. 'By the way, I hope I didn't do the wrong thing when I gave your address to that old school friend of yours, you know, the one you visited at Christmas. She said she wanted to get in touch with you, and I couldn't think of any reason not to. If you'd telephoned me earlier I would have told you all about it.'

'Jennifer, you mean?'

'Yes, that's the one.'

'No, that was fine.'

'Did she?'

'Did she what?'

'Get in touch,' her mother said. 'Are you not quite awake, Fiona?'

'No,' said Fiona. 'Not yet.'

'Well, she seemed a very pleasant, polite young woman when she came round with her brother, so I'm sure she will, sooner or later. Maybe you could call her? She was so nice, they both were, I had a lovely long chat with her brother. It was so nice to see him again. I think he may be sweet on you, you know. And he knows such a lot about banking and finance and all that sort of thing. I wouldn't be at all surprised if he didn't make a name for himself one of these days in the City. I must admit that I picked his brains quite shamelessly. Can I say how disappointed I was that you hadn't kept in touch with them? You have to cultivate friendship, Fiona, it doesn't just happen, you know, you have to put the effort in. Friendship is so important, especially if you're an only child.'

'Yes,' said Fiona, thrown by a combination of rage and anxiety. *Came round with her brother?* 'Look, I'd better go. This will be costing you a fortune.'

'That doesn't matter. You are my daughter, after all.'

'Right. Anyway, look, I have to go.'

'Before you run off, dear, have you thought about your birthday at all? It would be so lovely if you could come home and celebrate it with your dear old Mummy.' Her voice took on a lighter pitch. 'And you'll have lots of things to sign as well, don't forget. All those papers. It doesn't just happen, you know. Inheritance is hard work, and so confusing unless you know what's what. I've been talking about it with Mr Furling, your father's accountant. You remember him, don't you, dear? Such a useful man when it comes to money and making sure it doesn't fall into the wrong hands.'

'I really do have to go, Mummy, so lots of love,' she said hurriedly. 'And I'll do what I can.' She put the phone down but not before she'd heard her mother say 'God bless you', which only made it worse. I would rather die than spend my birthday with you, she thought.

Ludovico was waiting. '"I'm not all alone. I've got Ludovico."' He said this in what he imagined to be a voice that resembled hers, high-pitched, whiny. 'That's good to know. I'm delighted to be appreciated.'

'Fuck off,' she said. She looked at him, irritated. 'So how was your weekend? Tell me about it.'

'It was good.' He sighed. 'Fiona, we need to talk,' he said. 'Not about my weekend. About yours.'

She smiled. 'I've found my mother,' she said.

'And she's found you,' he said. 'So how did she react?'

Fiona didn't answer at first. She couldn't shake the feeling that she'd ruined everything. How strange her silence had been, she thought now, how perverse and dishonest and cowardly it was that she hadn't confessed to her mother. But confessed was the wrong word. People confess when they have done something wrong, and tracking down the mother she had never known wasn't wrong. That was why she had come to Rome, why she had set up the weekend, why she had used Ludovico as bait. Honest, that was the word she needed. She hadn't been honest. She saw that now. She felt ashamed.

'I didn't tell her,' she said.

Ludovico laughed, incredulous. 'Are you serious?' He laughed again. 'And she didn't realise?' He shook his head. 'My God, she's even worse than I thought.'

'What do you mean?'

'Well, Maddy told me she was practically an alcoholic, but I never imagined she wouldn't recognise her own daughter.'

'I am her own daughter,' Fiona said coldly.

'I didn't mean that.'

Fiona took a deep breath. 'So you and Maddy talked about my mother. She accused her of being an alcoholic?'

He nodded.

'And what else? About me? Did you talk about me?'

'Not really.'

'And did you fuck her?'

'Yes.'

'And was it good? Is she better than I am?'

'I never fucked you, Fiona. Had you forgotten?'

'Oh no, that's right,' said Fiona. 'One of your near misses. Well, I'm glad she was more accommodating than I was. I hope you feel you got your money's worth.'

'Don't be vulgar,' Ludovico said.

'Metaphorically speaking, of course. Unless you actually did pay her? You didn't, did you?'

'She's right,' Ludovico said. 'You're nothing like her.'

Why did this hurt Fiona so much, after what she'd just said? Had she imagined Ludovico would allow himself to be endlessly provoked without responding?

'I think you two need to talk,' he said.

'Well, perhaps you can arrange something as you're so lovey-dovey with her.'

He nodded. 'Perhaps I can,' he said.

Fiona was crying when the phone rang. Her intuition told her that it was Maddy calling Ludovico. She lay there, waiting for someone to answer it. But no one did. She looked up at the faded motifs on the ceiling and waited for it to ring again, determined that this time she would pick it up and tell her sister enough to destroy Ludovico's chance with her for ever. She wished them both dead.

It was dark and she was asleep when the phone rang again. She got off the bed, momentarily unsure where she was, and hobbled from her room into the sitting room, wincing as sensation returned to her leg. She picked up the receiver. '*Pronto*,' she said.

'Hello,' said a man's voice. 'It's me.'

She was about to say 'Who's me?' when it came to her. Oh God, she thought.

'Hello, Patrick,' she said. 'Where are you?'

'Guess,' he said.

'You're out?' she said, unsure how successfully she'd masked the anxiety she felt. Well, of course he's out. He's visited my mother.

'I certainly am,' he said. 'Try not to sound too pleased.'

'That's good.'

'Yes, well,' he said. 'You didn't write back.'

'You didn't give me time,' she said. 'Where are you?'

'Is the telephone you're holding anywhere near a window you can look out of?'

Please God, she thought. Not that. Not yet.

'Yes,' she said.

'Does the window overlook a square with a bar in it?'

'You're in the bar, aren't you?' she said.

'Just look out of the window,' he said, 'and you'll see.'

He was standing just inside the entrance to the bar, holding the phone in one hand, waving up towards her with the other, a familiar grin on his face. She felt sick. He hadn't even needed to track her down; her mother had done all the dirty work for him.

'Come on down and I'll buy you a coffee,' he said.

She stepped back from the window. 'Give me a minute,' she said. 'I'll be right there.'

They sat at a small table at the back of the bar. Patrick had already ordered a bottle of wine by the time she arrived, and filled two glasses. She glanced at the label. Brunello. She was surprised the bar even had a bottle that expensive. He jumped up when she reached the table and kissed her on both cheeks. She was relieved; she hadn't been sure what he might do, whether he would be angry with her. He put his hands on her shoulders and held her at arm's length. 'You look fabulous,' he said.

'So do you,' she said, although this wasn't true. He'd lost weight and was pale to the point of looking greyish. His clothes, expensive-looking as ever, brand new, were too big for him; he had a waifish quality that Fiona found herself responding to, despite herself.

'Liar.' He grinned. 'I feel like Oscar Wilde after eighteen months in Reading Gaol.'

She smiled, despite herself. 'I thought he had to do hard labour. You told me you worked in the library.'

'So you did read my letter,' he said, sitting down and gesturing that she should do the same.

'Of course I did. I told you, you didn't give me time to reply.' She sat down opposite him and sipped the wine. 'And now you're here.'

'Like the prodigal son,' he said, his grin even broader than before, which only made his face look thinner. 'Come back to claim his birthright.'

She tapped the pockets of her jacket. 'Well, I haven't got it,' she said as lightly as she could.

'We'll have to see about that,' he said.

Neither of them spoke for a moment, until Fiona asked him

where he was staying, hoping that he would say that he'd found a room in some nearby hotel; even better, that he had no plans to stay.

'I was thinking you might be able to help me out with that,' he said, and that was when she saw the leather weekend bag just behind his chair.

'I don't know,' she said, immediately anxious. 'I don't live alone, you see.'

'I know you don't,' he said, his tone level. 'You share with that old friend of yours, what's his name? Ludovico. And another couple, English I think. I don't know their names yet. But I can find them out. You know I'm good at that sort of thing. By the way, how is your sister? Was she pleased to see you?'

Fiona ignored this. 'I'll have to speak to them,' she said. 'I can't just invite you to stay in the flat.'

He reached across and took her wrist in his hand. 'You mean they get to vet your boyfriends? They decide who sleeps in your room?'

She resisted the urge to pull her hand away; she didn't want him to realise how scared she was. 'I didn't know you were still my boyfriend.' She paused, gave a hesitant smile. 'I thought you'd given me my freedom. Isn't that what you told me when they sentenced you? You said I needn't wait.'

'Yes,' he said evenly, as though reason were on his side, his fingers tightening slightly around her wrist, or perhaps that was just her imagination. 'But I'm not in prison any more.'

There was a note for her, from Ludovico, on the kitchen table. She wondered how long it had been there. She left Patrick in her room, then went back to see what it said. It was short and to the point. 'I've taken Maddy to Frascati,' it said, 'to give you time to sort things out with your mother. We'll be there for two days, so

304

don't waste time. We <u>must</u> talk when I return. L.'

She went back to her room. 'You can stay in Ludo's room for the next few days,' she told Patrick, picking up his bag from the bed before he had a chance to contradict her. 'He won't be here.'

For a moment she wanted to pour out what she felt to Patrick, her anger, her jealousy, her sense of injustice at not being able to have what she knew she deserved. He would have understood; these feelings were grist to his mill. So they hadn't even wanted her with them, she thought, they hadn't even given her the chance to say no. Well, that was all right. She wouldn't have gone in any case. She couldn't have stood the sight of them together, Ludovico moon-eyed, Maddy checking her out all the time to see how she felt.

Maybe Patrick's arrival in Rome was providential.

CHAPTER THIRTY-EIGHT

Fiona let herself into the flat with the spare key. In her hand, she had a bunch of yellow tulips she'd bought from the man with the van. 'Hello,' she said brightly. 'I'm back.'

Her mother put down the magazine she was reading and looked up at her from the sofa. 'You don't need to pretend any longer,' she said. 'I know who you are. I don't know what name they gave you, but I know who you are.'

Fiona closed the door behind her, her heart pounding, too scared to speak. Her mother was silent behind her, waiting. Finally, she turned.

'I'm glad,' she said. 'I'm so glad you know.' Then: 'How do you know?'

'Your sister has chopped all her hair off. That's how. She looks like a street urchin. You don't, thank God.' Heather's tone was weary, aggrieved. 'She blames you, and to be honest so do I. What you did at the weekend was unforgivable. You thought you could pull the wool over my eyes and, do you know, you almost did. I knew, and I didn't know. Does that make sense? It's a good thing you've given me time to calm down. Do you realise what a shock all this is?' She shook a cigarette out of her packet. 'So what is your name? Maddy told me, but I've forgotten.'

'Fiona.'

'Fiona?' She lit the cigarette, exhaled with a sigh. 'What sort of name is that?'

'My grandmother's name. It's Scottish.' She added, lamely: 'She was Scottish.'

'Your maternal grandmother then. Your father was English through and through.'

'Yes.' So you knew my father, she thought. And then, of course you did. And then, so who is my father?

Her mother sighed again. 'I suppose you think it's all my fault. That I didn't want you. That's what you think, isn't it?'

'I've never thought that,' said Fiona, urgently. 'As long as I've known about you, I've always known you must have had your reasons.'

'Always? So how long have you known?'

'I found out a few years ago. I wasn't sure at first, but then—' She stopped. She didn't want to talk about Patrick. She'd left him sleeping in Ludovico's room, a pot of coffee waiting to be heated, a note on the table to say she'd be back that afternoon.

'And what does your mother think about all this?'

Fiona fought back tears. This was the hardest part, when every bone in her body was crying out, But you're my mother.

'She has no idea I know,' she said, 'I never told her.' Her tone was as cold as she could make it, cold and bitter and contemptuous. 'Anyway, it's got nothing to do with her. I'm old enough to do what I want. She'd only try and spoil everything. She always does.'

'You shouldn't talk about her like that,' Heather said. 'She doesn't deserve it. She brought you up. I didn't.'

Fiona heard regret, a softening of tone. 'Please don't be angry with me,' she said. 'I'm not to blame for any of this.'

'You sounded so like Maddy just then,' her mother said. 'When you were talking about Anne.'

307

'You know her name?'

'Of course I do.' She sighed. 'I didn't just give you away to the first person who walked through the door.'

'All these years, you've known about me?'

'Don't say it like that, sweetheart. I feel bad enough already.' She stubbed out the half-smoked cigarette, struggled to her feet. 'Give me those flowers before they start wilting. They need to be put in water. If I can find a vase for them.' She touched Fiona's arm. 'They're lovely,' she said, taking the flowers. 'I love tulips. They're my favourite.'

Fiona watched her carry the bunch of tulips into the kitchen. Oh God, she thought, there isn't a vase. Why didn't I think of that? Why is it that everything I do is wrong?

'I thought Anne and Raymond would give you a better life than I could,' her mother said, her back turned as she rooted around in a cupboard, squatting on her haunches, finally pulling out a large glass water jug. 'This ought to do,' she said. 'We're not really flower buyers in this family.' She must have realised what she'd said immediately, how cruel it sounded, because she straightened up, with a groan. 'I didn't mean it like that,' she said. 'I really appreciate that you've bought me some flowers. It's a lovely thought. Nobody buys me flowers these days.' She paused. 'Fiona,' she said, as if to herself.

Anne and Raymond. She's known all these years and done nothing. She knows their names but she didn't know mine. She must have not wanted to know. Well, now, thought Fiona, she has no choice. 'You're my mother,' she said, and was shamefully pleased when she saw the woman flinch. 'So who's my father?' she said, then – with a thrill of daring, and of fear – added 'Mum' to see how it would sound.

'Don't call me that, sweetheart,' her mother said. 'I feel old enough as it is.' She filled the jug from the tap, tipped some water out. 'Call me Heather.'

'Heather,' repeated Fiona. 'Is that what Maddy calls you?'

Heather laughed. She put the tulips into the jug, moved the stalks around in a clumsy attempt to arrange them. 'When she remembers.' Carrying the jug into the living room, she looked around her. 'Where shall I put them?'

'You could put them in your bedroom,' Fiona said. 'It gets all the light from outside. It's so dark in here.'

'Yes, it's not the sort of place you're used to, I know that.'

'That isn't what I meant,' said Fiona. She was waiting for Heather to answer her question. Who is my father? she wanted to ask again, although she suspected that Heather had already told her. I thought that Anne and Raymond would give you a good life, that was what she'd said. The man she had always thought of as her father really was her father? Is that what Heather meant? She wondered if Maddy knew. She wished that her sister – her twin – were here in this dark, stuffy room, wished that the three of them could sit down together and talk themselves into an understanding, a recognition of all they shared. This wasn't right, she thought, her sneaking here, knowing that Maddy would be away. But it wasn't her fault that Maddy had disappeared and taken Ludovico with her. It wasn't her fault if Maddy preferred Ludovico to her own flesh and blood. They were better off without her.

'Well, now you know who I am,' she said, undaunted, determined to be cheerful, walking across to Heather and taking the jug out of her mother's hands, putting it on the kitchen table and hugging her mother unexpectedly, so that the woman stiffened in shock and then relaxed into the embrace and returned it, wriggling her arms free a little to hold her daughter better, pressing her cheek against Fiona's, its warmth and softness surprising Fiona, who felt rather than heard the tiny sound of what seemed to be a catch in her mother's throat. 'Now you know who I am,' she said again when they had separated and were looking into each other's eyes for the first time as themselves, with the knowledge of that, 'maybe you'll let me take you out somewhere nice to have lunch?'

Heather chose a place just round the corner from the flat. Most of the tables were empty. The waiter took them to one near the back, beside a dresser with plates and a loaf on a breadboard. When he asked what they wanted to drink, she ordered water and a litre of red wine, pouring them both full glasses as soon as it arrived. There were no glasses for water; it wasn't that kind of place. She ordered minestrone to start with, and liver to follow.

'*E per la signorina?*' the waiter said.

'What are you having, Maddy?' Heather said, realising her mistake when Fiona sucked in her breath. 'Oh sweetheart, I'm so sorry,' she said. Fiona shook her head and picked up the menu, avoiding her mother's eyes. The waiter sighed.

'He's waiting, dear,' Heather said. She paused before saying her daughter's name. 'Fiona.'

Fiona raised her eyes, her gaze serious and accusing. 'Well,' she said, 'he is a waiter, isn't he?'

Her mother smiled, a smile at first cautious and then spontaneous as Fiona began to laugh. 'I'm forgiven?'

Fiona nodded. 'Yes,' she said. 'If you'll forgive me for that joke.' She ordered ravioli and a green salad, then waited for the waiter to move away before saying, in a voice that was almost hushed, 'I have so many questions.'

'Let's not rush,' Heather said, her voice as quiet as her daughter's. 'This is still so strange.' She sipped her wine. 'I never expected to see you again.' She paused. 'I know that sounds terrible, but I don't mean it to. It's just such a shock.'

'I understand,' said Fiona, feeling unexpectedly in control. 'Don't worry.'

Her mother took another long sip of wine. 'How long have you known?'

Fiona told her everything then, about the newspaper cutting – which brought a smile to Heather's lips – and the evasive way her adoptive mother had behaved, about the detective work at the library and her growing conviction that the likeness was more than just a coincidence, about Patrick's help, although she was more circumspect about that, and her decision to change subject and come to Rome. She told her about the day she had seen Maddy for the first time, and about the scarf. All the time, as she spoke, she saw Heather's face relax. She told her about the afternoon she'd seen a woman get knocked over and only realised later that the woman had been her mother.

'So you were looking for me?'

'Of course I was.'

'And Maddy didn't want you to find me,' she said in a low voice, as if to herself.

'I couldn't understand what Maddy wanted,' Fiona said cautiously.

'She's been so difficult recently,' Heather said. 'Maybe this explains it.'

'We mustn't blame Maddy,' said Fiona.

'No, of course not,' Heather said but it was obvious to Fiona that she did blame Maddy, and the satisfaction this gave her was unseemly, as Anne might have put it, because it gave her an edge over her sister that she didn't deserve. Besides, it was exactly the reaction she had hoped for.

'I didn't give you away willingly,' Heather said suddenly, after their first courses had arrived. 'You need to know that. I had no choice.'

Fiona nodded, but didn't speak.

Heather refilled her glass. 'I can't do this sober,' she said, with a forced laugh.

'You don't have to do anything,' said Fiona.

'Raymond made me,' Heather said, as if she hadn't heard. 'Well, he didn't make me as such. I mean he didn't physically force me or anything like that. It's just that he made it all sound so simple when he talked about it before you were born. He made it all sound so fair.'

'Talked about it?'

'About separating you,' Heather said. 'About having one each. Anne couldn't have babies and, I don't know, it seemed selfish to keep you both. He said he'd make sure you were both looked after whichever one they chose and, I don't know, I barely had enough to live on.'

'You sold me,' said Fiona.

'Don't put it like that,' said Heather, horrified. 'It wasn't like that. It was just, oh I don't know. It was all so long ago.' She seemed to be about to cry. She sniffed, stirred her minestrone around, lifted a spoonful from the bowl but then put it back with a surprisingly angry gesture. She stared at Fiona, her eyes brilliant with tears. 'I never wanted to have children in the first place. I was younger than you are now. I was a child myself. You know what he said when he saw the two of you together? He said that you were God's gift. Can you believe that? I was lying there, stitched up like a piece of meat after hours of agony. God's bloody gift. Did he strike you as a religious man?'

Fiona thought about her father, how he would watch his wife leave the house each Sunday morning to go to church, lowering the newspaper slightly – *The Telegraph* – looking over his glasses to acknowledge her as she crossed the hall. 'Do give my regards to whatsisname, you know, the vicar, my dear,' he would say and she would sniff and close the door firmly behind her.

'No,' she said, 'I wouldn't say he was religious.' But he hadn't helped her either. It had taken her years and endless battles to convince her mother she had no right to drag Fiona along with her. The woman was a bully and a hypocrite.

'I wanted you to be happy. Happy and safe,' Heather said, tearful again, her spasm of anger behind her. 'That's all I ever wanted.'

Fiona couldn't stop herself. 'Why didn't you want that for Maddy?'

Heather reached across the table and took Fiona's hand. Fiona still hadn't touched her food. 'Don't hate me. Please, that's all I ask. Don't hate me.'

The waiter came across. '*Tutto bene?*'

'You make it sound as though you were doing me a favour.'

Heather nodded briefly, watched the waiter walk away, Fiona's hand still trapped in hers.

'It's all so complicated,' she said, her voice slightly altered, muffled by the wine she had drunk. 'Can't we just be happy now? You've found me, we're together. Can't that be enough?'

Fiona nodded. She wanted to hold her mother, to reassure her, to reassure herself. For an instant, she wished she were somewhere else, thousands of miles from here, leading a life that was solely hers, no family, no friends. But this woman in front of her, alone, already drunk, needed her more than anyone had ever needed her before.

'Of course it can be enough,' she said.

CHAPTER THIRTY-NINE

Maddy didn't expect to find her sister at the flat, although on the drive back from Frascati she had done nothing but think about what she would do if Fiona was there. Sitting in the car beside a silent Ludovico, she had fiddled with the ring on her finger, feeling it tainted, wanting to take it off and hurl it through the window, wanting to lift her hand and press the twinned gold to her lips. Opening the door to the flat, she saw her mother sitting where she had left her, the television on, the ashtray as full as ever and what she felt most was sadness. The woman looked across as Maddy closed the door, confused until she saw her daughter's hair.

'You're back early,' she said. 'I didn't expect you.'

'Well, here I am,' Maddy said and looked around. The flat was as she'd left it, apart from a bunch of yellow tulips forced into a jug too small for them on the kitchen table.

'When did she go?' she said.

'She?' said her mother.

'Fiona.'

'That's better, Mad.' She paused. 'Don't be cruel to her, sweetheart. It's not like you to be cruel.'

She hadn't called her Mad in years, not since Maddy had burst into tears and told her that she wasn't mad, she was perfectly sane, and her mother had hugged her, laughing. That was when her mother listened to her, she thought, years ago now. But maybe she would listen again.

'She calls you Heather, I bet she does.'

Her mother smiled and nodded. 'It's easier for her. Easier than it is for you. You've known me since you were a baby. She's an adult by now, and so am I. She's never known me any other way.'

Whose fault is that? thought Maddy. She was filled with an anger she could barely control, or understand. Nothing had been taken from her, after all. Her mother seemed more loving now than she had been for months, maybe years. But it felt second-hand, as though intended for someone else.

'So when did Fiona go?' she said.

'Last night. After she'd made me something to eat.'

'Why didn't she stay, like the last time? My bed was free.' Maddy paused a moment. 'I wouldn't have minded.'

Her mother looked at her, doubtful. 'She has someone staying with her, she said. An old boyfriend. She needed to go home and make sure he was all right.'

'Did she say when she was coming back? She is coming back, isn't she?'

'I don't know, Maddy,' her mother said, irritated. 'Why don't you call her? Oh, by the way, where did you find the money to pay the phone bill?'

'That doesn't matter now,' Maddy said.

*

Fiona let herself into the flat, closing the door as quietly as she could. But Patrick must have been waiting, because he was in the corridor before she had time to take off her coat. He was wearing a pair of Ludovico's pyjamas, sleeves and legs rolled up to fit, which made him look smaller and younger than he was. He wagged an admonitory finger at her.

'I know,' she said. 'I know.'

'Don't worry. I've been sleeping mostly.' He walked over and kissed her, let his hands rest on her hips. He smelt of Ludo's aftershave, and of some other scent, characteristically Patrick. He took her hand and led her into the sitting room. There was no one there, with Ludovico in Frascati and the lovebirds God knows where. She wondered what he had been doing while she was with Heather, and felt a sudden stabbing need to be back with her mother in San Lorenzo. But Patrick took her to the sofa and she let herself sit down beside him, her hand still in his.

'Why are you here?' she said.

He didn't answer immediately. He released her hand and slumped back into the cushions behind him, then turned his head to face her, his eyes suddenly moist. 'I don't know,' he said, his voice quiet, almost hesitant. She'd never heard him speak like this before, as though the life force had been knocked out of him. 'I didn't know where else to go, I suppose.'

'Why didn't you want me to keep in touch with you?' she said.

'I was ashamed.'

'That wouldn't have mattered,' she said. 'You shut me out.'

'I thought you wouldn't want to know me any longer. I'd served my purpose.'

'What do you mean?'

He sighed. 'You know, finding your sister, your mother. I thought that was all you wanted from me.'

'I never said that.'

He looked at her, more intensely.

'So was I wrong?'

She didn't say anything. She touched his cheek, stroked away what might have been a tear. 'Come here,' she said.

Sometime later, she said, 'I would never have found her if it hadn't been for you. I'll always be grateful to you for that.'

'But that's not all, I hope.' He looked brighter now, more like the Patrick she knew.

'No, that's not all. You kept me company when I was lonely. You gave me an excuse to buy that wonderful silk dress. Do you remember?'

'Of course I do.'

'I brought it with me,' she said. 'I don't know why. I can't imagine when I'll want to wear it here.'

'We'll find a moment,' he said. 'Rome is the home of *la dolce vita*, after all.'

She laughed. When he took her hand again, she raised it to her lips and kissed his knuckles, one after the other. 'You're on my side,' she said. 'You don't know how much that means to me.'

They were on the sofa together in the half-dark of late afternoon when Ludovico returned to the flat. He shouted 'Ciao' from the hall while taking off his coat, then walked into the sitting room when Fiona shouted 'Ciao' back. Noticing Patrick, he nodded briefly and then looked at Fiona with a quizzical expression.

'Is your friend wearing my pyjamas?'

'I hope you don't mind,' said Patrick, standing up from the sofa and holding out his hand. Ludovico considered it for a moment before giving it a perfunctory shake.

'Most of my own clothes don't fit any longer,' Patrick said, following this with a nervous laugh. 'I lost weight when I was in prison.'

'Ah yes,' said Ludovico. 'Prison food can't be very appetising.'

'You know all about it, I imagine,' said Patrick. 'About my time in prison, I mean.'

'I know what Fiona has told me,' said Ludovico, visibly

annoyed. He turned to leave the room. On the way out, he glanced at Fiona. 'I think you need to talk to your sister,' he said. 'You owe her that, at least.'

*

Later in bed, Fiona stroked the hair on Patrick's forearm. 'Instinct,' she said. 'As soon as I saw her I knew she was my mother. My body knew. It sounds crazy, but it's the truth.'

'You pretended to be your sister, and she didn't realise?'

'I think she knew as well, but it was just too much for her. I mean, how could I possibly not be Maddy? She needed time to process it, that's all. But it's true what they say. Blood is thicker than water.'

Patrick was silent for a moment. 'And Maddy? Did you feel it with Maddy? You've hardly talked about her at all. You were looking for your twin sister and you've found your mother. Is that what matters now?'

Fiona sighed. She put her arm beneath the duvet and snuggled into Patrick. 'I did feel it with her, I really did. But I don't think she felt it with me. She held off, Patrick. It was awful.'

'Why would she do that?'

'I don't know. It's not as if her life is perfect. It's anything but. They're stuck in this miserable little flat near the station. I don't think they've got much money either. I think she resents me.'

'You could help her if you wanted.'

'How could I do that?'

'With money, silly. You're going to be rich.'

'I suppose I am.'

'Maybe Ludovico is right. Maybe you should talk to her.'

She slid her hand down over his stomach, tugged gently at

318

a tuft of hair. 'Am I going to be very rich?' she said, her voice babyish, teasing.

'Oh yes, my little rich girl,' he said, turning over in bed to face her. 'You're going to be so rich you'll be able to keep us all in luxury.' He smiled, kissed her, then lifted her until she was lying on top of him. 'But now's not the moment to talk about money.'

CHAPTER FORTY

Maddy and Fiona were sitting outside Bar Marani, drinking cappuccinos. A cold wind was blowing and both of them wore coats and scarves. Maddy's was the pale-blue one that had once belonged to Fiona; Fiona's was striped and borrowed from Ludovico without his knowledge. Maddy recognised it, but said nothing. They had decided to meet before their mother joined them, to talk to each other. Now, sitting at the only occupied table, neither of them knew what to do. Neither of them wanted to be there. They were cold, but they would rather be outside, without the restrictions of walls and doors, where all one had to do if the need to leave became irresistible was to stand up and walk away. To see them now, to look at the way they were sitting, legs crossed, shoulders hunched against the easterly wind, both of them playing with their spoons, identical apart from their hair, it was laughably obvious that they were twins. The truth was that they had never been so close, both on the same wavelength, although they couldn't know this, they couldn't know how their separate paths had brought them to this single place, this table at this bar, with their mother only fifty yards away from them, fussing with her hair and feeling nervous – no, more than nervous, frightened – because the last time she had seen her daughters together was almost twenty-one years ago and she had no idea how they would treat her, no way of knowing if they would act together or be divided, be allies against her or enemies against each other.

After they had drunk their cappuccinos and commented once more on the bitterness of the wind, and Fiona had insisted that short hair suited Maddy, their silence became impossible to sustain and Fiona turned to the only subject that mattered. Their mother.

'How is she?'

'Who?'

'Heather.'

'She's fine.'

'Has she forgiven me, do you think? For not telling her who I was right away?'

'Oh yes,' said Maddy. She smiled wryly. 'She forgives very quickly.'

After a moment, Fiona tried again. 'She loved the flowers.'

'Yes. She doesn't get many flowers.'

'That's what she said. She was so touched.'

Maddy looked at her sharply. 'Is that a dig at me? That I don't buy my mother flowers?'

'Please, Maddy,' said Fiona hurriedly. 'I didn't mean anything. It's just that I miss her. I haven't seen her for forty-eight hours and it's crazy how much I miss her. I've got so many years to catch up. So many years you've had her all to yourself. Please, don't let's argue.' She sighed. 'All I've ever wanted is for us to be friends.'

'Not sisters then?' said Maddy. 'Not twin sisters.' She emphasised the word 'twin'. 'Just friends?'

Fiona sighed again, not sure if Maddy was teasing or hostile, furious and frustrated that she couldn't read her. 'Oh, both. Both.' She stared into Maddy's eyes, held them, wouldn't let her sister look away. 'I don't want to take anything away from you. I love you, I do, honestly. I want to love you and I want you to love me. How can I make you understand that? I don't want anything that's yours. I just want what's mine.'

'I thought they were the same.'

'Well, they aren't.'

'So what about Ludovico? Is he yours?'

So is that what it's all about? Fiona wondered. Ludovico? She shook her head. 'Ludovico doesn't want me. Ludovico has nothing to do with this.'

Now it was Maddy's turn to hold the gaze of the other girl. 'And me? Does he want me?'

So I was right, thought Fiona. 'I think he does.'

'And you're OK with that?'

'I told you. Ludovico doesn't want me. But I expect you know that already. He's bound to have told you.'

Maddy shrugged. 'We haven't really talked about you,' she said, and this time the intent to hurt was painfully obvious.

Fiona, stung, drew in her breath. She'd been so good, she thought, she'd tried so hard to be open with Maddy, to be honest with her, and all she got in return was spitefulness. Well, she could be spiteful too. 'Really?' she said. 'You know what, I don't believe you. I bet you talk about me all the time. I mean, why shouldn't you? I talked about you with Ludo before you'd even met him, never mind all the rest. I wonder how that makes you feel. Being talked about by someone you've never met, by someone who knows something about you that you don't know.'

'It makes me feel sick to the stomach, if you really want to know.' Maddy stubbed out her half-smoked cigarette. 'This whole fucking story does.' She spoke as if reading from a card. 'Twins. Sisters. Separated at birth. You say you want to be friends and then you say something like that. You've been spying on me for years and now I'm supposed to love you like a sister? Do you know just how creepy that is? Well, just fuck off. You're mad, you know that? You're totally off the wall.'

She stood up, her chair scraping on the floor as she pushed it away, and was about to leave when her mother appeared at the gate.

'Please don't go,' said Fiona quietly. *Creepy*. That awful word again. 'It'll only upset her.'

Slowly, Maddy sat down again.

'It's freezing out here,' their mother said, walking across to the table. 'We'll catch our deaths.'

'Sit down, Heather,' said Fiona. Maddy winced.

Heather shook her head, shivered. 'It's too cold. Seriously. Let's go back to the flat, all three of us. We can have a cup of coffee there. Or something stronger.'

Fiona got to her feet but Maddy didn't budge. Fiona prodded her arm.

'I'm not ready for this,' Maddy said. 'Not yet.' She stood up. 'I'm not ready for the family reunion, Heather.'

'Don't do this to me, Maddy,' pleaded Fiona, but Maddy ignored her and walked out onto the street, without turning back.

'She's impossible,' said Heather. She pulled her coat about her. 'I'm freezing to death.' She slipped her arm through her daughter's. 'Come on,' she said, and hugged Fiona's arm to her side. 'I've got just what we need back at the flat. A hot toddy. How does that sound?'

'That sounds lovely,' said Fiona.

*

As soon as Maddy was out of sight of Bar Marani, she ran to the nearest phone and called Ludovico, but a man whose voice she didn't recognise answered the phone, in English.

'Can you pass me Ludovico?' she said.

'He isn't here,' the man said, then added, 'You're Maddy, aren't you?'

Surprised, she said, yes, she was.

'I'm a friend of Fiona's,' he said, before she could ask. 'I need to speak to you.'

'I don't know who you are,' she said. 'How do you know my name?'

'You'll have to meet up with me if you want to know that,' he said, and laughed.

'And if I don't?'

'If you don't you'll never know what you've missed,' he said.

'All right,' she said after a moment. 'Where do you want to meet?'

He named a place near Piazza Navona. Naima. She'd never heard of it, but said, yes, she'd be there in half an hour. She was intrigued and, more than intrigued, fired with resentment, Fiona's use of 'Heather' and her mother's gratified smile rankling more than anything.

Naima was a small, narrow bar, empty apart from a couple at the far end of the room and a man, about her age or a little older, sitting a few tables away from the door, holding a glass in his hand. He stood up as soon as he saw her, put the glass down and beckoned her across.

'Short hair suits you,' he said, with a smile. She was startled, then realised that, of course, he knew Fiona, which meant that he also, in a way, knew her, or thought he did. 'What can I get you to drink?'

'I don't know,' she said, hesitating. She didn't want to lose control.

'They do a pretty good Manhattan,' he said. He glanced down at the table. 'That's what I'm drinking.'

'Look, who are you exactly?'

'I'm a good friend of Fiona's,' he said. He winked at her. 'A very good friend.' Before she could respond he walked over to the bar and ordered, in English, two Manhattans.

'I know who you are,' she said when he came back with the drinks. 'You're the friend of hers who's been in prison.'

'That's very astute of you,' he said, sitting down and watching her in an appraising way. 'Do I look like a jailbird?'

'I don't know what jailbirds look like,' she said.

'Well, now you do.' He smiled. He was good-looking, nicely cut hair, nice mouth. She wasn't attracted to him, although she could see why Fiona might have been. There was something too neat about him, too composed.

'What's your name?' she said. 'I've forgotten.'

'So you have talked about me?'

She sipped her drink. She didn't plan to play his game, whatever it was. He didn't need to know that she had indeed talked about him, but not with Fiona. With Ludovico.

'You said you needed to speak to me,' she said. 'What about?'

'Patrick.' He offered her his hand. She shook it, surprised by the sudden formality of the gesture, a little perturbed by the strength of his grip.

'So how do you feel about having a twin sister?' he said.

She looked at him. 'Fine. I feel fine. Why shouldn't I?'

'Seriously? You don't feel she's just muscled in on your life? I don't think I'd have been that thrilled, to be honest. A sibling turning up out of the blue after twenty-odd years. After all, you knew nothing at all about her, did you?' He offered her a cigarette. She let him light it, his hand curling around hers. Again she felt that sense of almost menace. He didn't take one himself. 'Or did you?'

She shook her head.

'She just turned up and moved in?'

'You could say that.'

'And where is she now?' Before she could answer, he continued. 'I thought the two of you were going to have the great reunion scene with your mother this evening.'

He knows everything, she thought. Fiona must have told him every single thing about us. Why should I keep secrets from him? It's only fair he hears my side of the story too. 'We were,' she said. 'But things went a bit wrong.'

'So you wanted to weep on Ludovico's shoulder.'

'Not weep exactly.'

He laughed. 'Well, revenge is sweet,' he said, 'whatever form it comes in.'

'My relationship with Ludovico doesn't have anything to do with revenge,' she said sharply.

'Of course it doesn't,' he said. He finished the half-drunk Manhattan on the table and started the new one. She took a second, cautious sip from hers. 'Although I often wonder how close the two of them still are.'

Still, she noticed. 'You went out with Fiona, didn't you, in Oxford? Before you were arrested.'

He smiled.

'It'll be your birthday soon,' he said. 'Any plans?'

She shook her head.

'Twenty-one and no plans? That's awful. I'll have to see what I can do.' He paused. 'I wonder what Fiona plans to do to celebrate. After all, it's a special day for both of you, but a very special day for her.'

'What do you mean?'

'She hasn't told you? About the fortune she's due to inherit?'

'I know she's going to get some money, yes.'

'Some money?' He laughed. 'Is that what she said?'

'We haven't really talked about it.'

Patrick finished his drink and called across to the bar for another two.

'Do you have any idea how rich her father was?'

'Our father,' she said before she had time to think.

'But of course,' he said. 'How stupid of me. If he was Fiona's father, he was your father too.' He leant forward, then back when the girl who served behind the bar arrived with two more Manhattans, carried away Patrick's empty glass, casting a curious, apprehensive glance at Maddy, whose own glass was still almost full. 'You know what that means, don't you?'

'No,' she said.

'It means that half the money is rightfully yours.'

On their way out, Patrick touched her shoulder. 'I think it might be best if we kept this little meeting to ourselves, don't you?'

Maddy nodded. 'Not a word,' she said.

CHAPTER FORTY-ONE

Maddy couldn't sleep. Nothing she thought about made any difference. She tried not to hear her mother breathing through the partition wall that separated their two bedrooms, but it was there constantly, like a tap dripping in the silence, like a rat scratching behind the skirting board. It was three and then four o'clock in the morning, and every time she felt she might be on the point of attaining the oblivion she craved some unwanted thought shook her back into wakefulness.

She imagined what it must be like to have been a twin all your life and to have known it. To know another life, your sister's life, outside, as like yours as two peas are in a pod. To have had that intimacy, that oneness against the world. How could she hope to have that with Fiona, someone she barely knew, and didn't trust? And then there was the money, Fiona's inheritance, because her thoughts relentlessly returned to that, and to what Patrick had said. Because he was right, it was half hers. If her father hadn't thought to include her, well, that just proved what a bastard he'd been, she thought, her eyes wide open in the dark that was never really dark, in the silence that was never really silence, the noise of traffic never that far away. She wondered what kind of house Fiona had grown up in, somewhere in the countryside, she supposed, somewhere quiet, the sky at night full of stars. Like Ludovico's place in Frascati, she thought, but bigger, better.

And that reminded her of Ludovico, and the time they had spent there together, which seemed so long ago, although so little time had passed. They'd barely touched each other since then; there had been people around, or she had been angry with him. She was ready to forgive him now, she thought. He'd told her that Fiona meant nothing to him and she believed him, despite the insinuations of Patrick. And yes, Patrick, because he was there as well, in her sleeplessness; the things he'd said about righting wrongs were there, and revenge, and how to have it.

She was on the point of turning the light on to read – *Sophie's Choice*, lent to her by Matteo, who seemed, in his innocence, to think it might help her to understand – when she heard a hoarse cry from the next room. She got up, pulled on a jumper over her pyjamas. 'I'm coming,' she said, but not loud enough to be heard in case her mother was talking in her sleep. She didn't want to wake her.

Her mother had kicked her blankets to the floor. Visible in the light from the living room, she was sitting up, reaching out into space, a look of anguish on her face, her eyes open wide, staring at the wall in front of her, but Maddy could tell she was still, somehow, asleep. She was mumbling, a stream of sounds more than words but there were words within the stream if only Maddy could catch them. Then, with startling clarity, the way a radio station can leap out of the general buzz and crackle, she heard her mother say 'Give her back to me, she's mine,' her arms stretching out even further than before, a terrible strain in her features. 'Give her back to me, she's mine,' she said again, then fell back. She lay still as Maddy adjusted the blankets around her, scared to wake her, wondering who she'd meant; not really wondering at all.

*

Ludovico and Patrick were talking in the kitchen, to Fiona's relief. Fiona didn't want to interrupt them. She wanted Patrick to feel that he had been accepted in the flat for as long as he needed to stay. He'd told her about his time in jail, the bullying. A couple of mornings ago, she'd found him in the kitchen before anyone else was up, sitting in front of a cup of lukewarm coffee, and she'd sat beside him and held his hand while he told her about his cellmate and what the man had done. He'd been evasive with her at first, but then his voice cracked and she saw that his eyes were wet with tears. It was awful, he said. I was scared, so scared. He thought he had a right to me, he made me do stuff, oh, I don't know. It wasn't just the sex. God knows, that was bad enough. It was being powerless. I've never been scared like that, and I felt so dirty. So dirty. He looked at her then. You'd understand. You're a woman. You know what men can do. They violate you. He was sobbing by now, it was hard to follow what he said. She put her arm around him and hugged him as his whole body shook, trying to calm him. That's all right, she said. You're safe now, crying herself at that point. I'm sorry, he said. I'm sorry. She held him for as long as it took, then led him to bed and held him again until he had fallen finally asleep.

Later that morning, when they were both awake, he was sheepish with her, as though he'd opened up too much and regretted it, which touched her more than she would ever have imagined. She took him with her to the market, they had coffee together in a place that served cappuccino in deep white bowls and they'd talked about Paris, and how lovely it would be to go there one weekend. The longer they talked the more she realised that she'd found a Patrick she'd only dared dream of at Oxford, attentive, loving. If he had to leave now, with Ludovico's loyalty in doubt, it would be too hard to bear. If Ludovico were responsible for his leaving she would never forgive him.

She was preparing her weekly lesson in Maddy's faculty, although she had never been less keen on teaching than today. She yearned to be in San Lorenzo, with her mother, not half a mile away in front of a bunch of unenthusiastic, judgemental students whose names she couldn't learn. She didn't expect to see Maddy there, what point would there be? In any case, Maddy's place was with their mother, not wasting her time in an underheated classroom. Heather needed to be cared for and loved, she'd been neglected, she'd had an awful life in one way, but an enviable one too. She'd been free to make mistakes in a way Fiona's other mother, the adoptive one, the surrogate, never had been, or had chosen not to be, out of cowardice or greed. She had been a rebel, she had used that freedom for better and for worse. Fiona admired her so much, although admiration didn't even come close to describing what she felt for Heather, the tangle of need and love and loss at what they hadn't been allowed to share. She saw her as battle-scarred but alive, a survivor. It was inexplicable to Fiona that Maddy, who had shared so much of that freedom, who had lived in two countries and a dozen different flats, who had been given room to move and air to breathe in a way Fiona could barely imagine, didn't seem to understand how lucky she'd been. She couldn't forgive Maddy that.

Packing into her bag the material she planned to use, Fiona thought back to the photograph that had started it all, of the concert in Hyde Park and the toffee-nosed journalist's comments, the way the girl, who might so easily have been her, was smiling up at the camera, curled on her mother's lap, the two of them like a perverse Madonna and child, the child wrapped in nothing but an oversized grubby T-shirt, with a crown of wilting daisies on her head, like a badge of honour. It must be possible to live like that still, she thought. We must be able to do that if we really try.

She was in the hall and lifting her coat from the hook when

she heard raised voices from the kitchen. Ludovico was telling Patrick to get out of the flat, to fuck off, and leave them alone. She put down her bag and went into the kitchen.

'I've just told him he has to leave,' said Ludovico. 'We don't want him here.'

'That isn't your decision to make,' Fiona said. 'I live here too.' She touched Patrick's shoulder, a touch that was both reassuring and a caress. 'In any case, who is this we? He's my friend, not yours, and he's sleeping in my room. It's got nothing to do with you. I don't try and tell you what friends you can have.'

'Are you talking about Maddy?' said Ludovico, and she could hear the fury in his voice, which gave her power.

'If you want to make everything about you and Maddy, yes.'

'I gather you and Maddy have an understanding,' said Patrick.

'Fuck off,' said Ludovico.

'I have to go to work,' said Fiona coldly. 'We'll talk about this later.' She threw a warning glance at Ludovico. '*E mi raccomando. Non fare lo stronzo*,' she said.

'*Io non faccio lo stronzo*,' he said. He swept out of the kitchen and went to his room, slamming the door behind him.

Patrick followed her into the hall. When she put on her coat, he put on his. When she picked up her tote bag, he picked up a small expensive-looking leather rucksack she hadn't seen before and slung it over one shoulder. 'I'll come with you,' he said, opening the door for them both. 'And thank you for defending me.'

'I told him not to be a shit, that's all.' She walked past him. 'I don't like men who behave like shits.'

Patrick walked with her to the bus. He didn't speak, but she could feel his presence at every step, mirroring and attuned to hers, and she was glad of it. At the bus stop she turned, looked into his eyes for the first time and asked him with a smile what he intended to do, and he smiled back and said he'd like to come with her and see her teach, if that was all right with her. The bus arrived before she had time to think of an answer and they pushed their way onto it together. The bus was so crammed there was barely room for them both, they were separated almost immediately. She turned and saw Patrick near the rear door, grinning bravely, his hand pressed against the inside wall of the bus as it swung out of Largo Argentina. She shook her head and he mouthed 'Crazy' at her, and she nodded because it was crazy to travel like this, with people pressed so close to her she could feel the heat of them, the buckle of someone's bag strap in the small of her back, the garlic stink of some man's breath. Beside her, a Filipino nun was muttering under her breath and what Fiona first took for irritation was the reciting, she realised, of the rosary.

The bus half emptied at the station and Patrick reached her finally. 'Wow,' he said. 'Talk about cattle trucks. I don't know why you don't get a taxi.'

'I don't know why you've come with me,' she said. 'I can't believe you want to see me teach.'

'I love work,' he said. 'I could watch it for hours. Now who said that?'

'Oscar Wilde, I expect. It usually is when you say something witty.'

'Ouch.' He touched her cheek. 'Don't be cruel to me,' he said, with such a pitiful expression she couldn't stop herself laughing.

'For God's sake, Patrick.'

'You don't really need to go to work, do you? I mean, really?'

'Of course I do.'

'Hey, but what if you're kidnapped? Isn't that what people do to heiresses in Italy? Kidnap them and hide them in some cave, and then post bits of them back to the family?'

'I'm not an heiress.'

'Yes, you are.'

'I have to get off here,' she said.

He followed her as she left the bus. When they walked past a bar, he caught her arm.

'Just a coffee,' he said. 'There's something I really need to say.'

She sighed. 'OK. Five minutes.'

She felt guilty about missing her lesson, and then put it out of her mind, although a nagging anxiety stayed with her. Ever since she'd spoken to Maddy, she'd had the sense of impending catastrophe. It felt as though the wind had changed, or a light been extinguished. Everything was the same, and different. Everything before this had been leading up to this.

Sitting at a table in the bar, he took her hand in his.

'I need to talk to you,' he said.

'I'm listening.' She felt uncomfortable, as though the old Patrick, cynical, demanding, had suddenly reappeared. She tried to ease her hand away, but he wouldn't let her, and it was obvious to them both that he knew how much she wanted her hand to be released and how determined he was to stop that happening.

'What I said about you being an heiress.'

'You need to talk to me about money,' she said.

He lowered his voice. 'You can't pretend it doesn't exist.'

'I told you,' she said. 'I don't want to think about it. And it really doesn't have anything to do with you, Patrick.'

He let go of her hand. 'I'm sorry, I thought we were, well, together.'

And there he was again, hesitant, unassuming, gentle. 'We are together, Patrick. At least, I hope we are. But what does that have to do with money?'

'Nothing. Of course, it means nothing.'

Neither of them spoke for a moment. Finally, Fiona said: 'There's something I've been meaning to ask you.'

He smiled, but his smile was apprehensive. 'Ask away,' he said.

'Why did you visit my mother?'

'Who told you that? Jennifer? I thought you two had fallen out.'

She shook her head.

'Your mother, then?'

Fiona nodded. 'She is my mother.'

He seemed momentarily lost for words.

'What did she tell you?' he said eventually.

'You talked to her about my inheritance.'

He gave a wry smile. 'I thought you weren't interested.'

She brushed this to one side with a rapid gesture of her hand. 'What did she say?'

He looked behind her, at the street outside, as if seeking the words he needed there, and then at her. 'Let's just say she's thought about it a lot more than you have. Your father understood how money worked. That's why he tried to make sure you'd get everything with no strings attached. He had some clever accountants. And now they're working for your mother.'

'You're telling me she's trying to stop me getting my money.'

'It's really none of my business,' he said.

'You started this, Patrick,' she said. 'Tell me what you know.'

'I just think you need to be careful, that's all,' he said.

'How can I be careful?' she said. 'I don't know anything about money.' She looked at him, then took his hand. 'You're the expert.'

'If I can help you in any way,' he said, 'of course I will. You know that.'

*

335

'She didn't turn up,' said Matteo. 'That's the second time she's missed a class. I don't expect anyone will come next week.'

Maddy sighed. She was tempted to tell Matteo about what Patrick had said, about the money and how half of it should be hers, but some scruple about her promise to him to tell no one, or simply not wanting to seem covetous, stopped her. 'I just wish all this was over, Matteo. Mum goes on and on about her. She doesn't realise but it's just so obvious that Fiona's all she thinks about. I don't know whether to feel neglected or relieved.'

'Relieved?'

'To have someone else to share the burden.'

'You think your mother's a burden?'

'Don't go all Italian on me, Matteo. Not all mothers are perfect, you know.'

'I didn't say that.'

'It's what you meant.'

'I've never even met her,' he said, plaintively. 'You've never let me.'

'I'm not part of some package, you know,' she said, irritated. 'You don't have to meet the whole family. I've never met your parents either, but I'm not complaining.'

'How long have you known Ludovico?'

She was startled. 'Are you all right?'

'What?'

'This curiosity about my private life. I don't get it.'

'So Ludovico is your private life?' He stressed the word 'private'.

'Would you mind if he was?' She was genuinely curious.

He sighed, then reached across and pulled the collar of her coat around her as if he was worried she'd catch cold, his eyes not leaving hers. They were standing outside the faculty building, students milling around them, the sun almost set, and what little light there was transported her back, for some reason she didn't understand, to the weekend in Frascati, a memory now, and then a sensation, an unsettledness that she couldn't put into words.

'I don't know,' he said.

CHAPTER FORTY-TWO

Fiona was curled up half asleep on her bed, already in pyjamas although it was still early evening, the rag doll clutched to her belly. She was humming a song Ludovico's mother would sing to her when she was still a child and didn't want to take a siesta – '*Stella stellina*', it was called, she'd never forgotten it – when she heard the phone. She counted the number of rings, holding her breath, hoping someone else would answer it, hoping the call would be for Ludovico or one of the other two. Patrick had left her half an hour earlier on some mysterious errand. They had made love, the sheets were still tangled beneath her but she didn't want to move from the bed, to get up and sort them out. She felt guilty about having missed her class, although she knew no one cared apart from her. She was an awful teacher. When the call went unanswered, she let her breath out in a rush. She must be alone in the flat. She was relieved, but there was an element of disquiet as well, as though the world had been spirited away and left her behind, overlooked. The ringing stopped at twenty – a moment's silence, the time it took to redial – and then began again. With a start of hope, astounded this hadn't occurred to her immediately, she realised that it might be Heather. She kissed the rag doll and laid it carefully on the pillow, where her own head had been, its stiff yellow plaits sticking out at each side. 'I'll be right back,' she said. '"*Ognuno ha il suo bambino*,"' she sang as quietly as she could, hurrying out of the room. "*Ognuno ha la sua mamma.*"

It was her mother, phoning from England. It didn't take her long, a flurry of pleasantries about the weather and how much more pleasant the climate was at home, to arrive at the reason for her call.

'You will be coming home for your birthday, won't you, Fiona? I know I've asked you before, but you're always so evasive.'

'I hadn't planned to.'

'Oh dear.' Her mother sighed. Fiona waited for her to continue. 'I was hoping you wouldn't say that.'

'I'm sorry I've disappointed you.'

'Are you, Fiona?' Her voice had an edge of irritation. 'People will expect you to be here. They won't understand.'

Your awful friends, thought Fiona.

'Because it's such a significant event, isn't it? You aren't twenty-one every day. I thought we might even run to a marquee.'

Have you ever said anything that hasn't been worn so threadbare there isn't a shred of thought or sincerity left in it? wondered Fiona. And a marquee? She didn't have enough friends to fill a tent.

'Are you listening to me, Fiona? I hope I'm not just wasting my breath. You are *so* exasperating.'

She sighed. 'Yes.'

'Because there are also several things that we need to discuss. Important things that won't wait any longer.'

'I suppose you're talking about money.' The money you plan to steal, she thought. My money.

'There's no need to take that tone, Fiona. Your father certainly wouldn't have appreciated it.'

'Why bring my father into this?'

'Because everything he did, he did for you. He worked his fingers to the bone for you. You wouldn't have an inheritance at all if it hadn't been for him. You may not appreciate the effort I've put into making sure you're fed and clothed and educated, especially since he was taken from us, but you can at least show some appreciation for him. The poor, dear man.'

Fiona sighed again. She loved her father, despite everything. Why couldn't he be left out of this? Why did she have to lie? Did she have no shame?

'He wanted you to be happy and not have to worry about money, just as I do.'

'But I'm not worried,' said Fiona. 'I'm not the least bit worried.'

'There you are, you see. That's exactly my point. You don't seem to have any idea of the importance of it.'

'It? What's it?'

'Your inheritance. For heaven's sake, Fiona! Are you on drugs, or what?'

Finally, thought Fiona, I've got her goat. 'That's my business, surely?' she said, curious to see how she would react. With a rush of glee, she heard her mother draw in her breath before speaking.

'You're far too young to be responsible for such a large amount of money. Every word you say is proof of it. I can't just allow it to be handed over to you as though it meant nothing. Your father would never forgive me if I let that happen.'

'You can't stop it being handed over to me though, can you? I mean, the money's mine, isn't it?' She heard Patrick's voice in her head. *Your mother has clever accountants.*

'There's no need to react like that, Fiona. I've been talking to Mr Furling – you remember him, your father trusted him absolutely – and he agrees with me. I only have your best interests at heart.'

'Haven't you had it long enough?'

'What on earth do you mean?'

'You know what I mean.' She mimicked the woman's tone. '*It.*
My inheritance. It's my money, isn't it, not yours? I'll do what I
want with it.'

'Will you indeed? We'll have to see about that, young lady.'

'You can't stop me.'

'Can't I? I wouldn't be so sure.'

'Are you threatening me?'

Her mother didn't answer at once. Finally, her voice
determinedly level, she said: 'Don't be so touchy, Fiona dear. Of
course I'm not threatening you. I'm your mother. What an awful
word to use, when I only have your best interests at heart. I'm
sure we can find a way to talk about this calmly. Maybe this just
isn't the moment.'

Fiona didn't speak.

'Yes, well, let's have another chat about this in a few days'
time, dear, when we're both feeling a bit more, well, serene.' She
paused. 'Oh yes,' she said. 'Your friend, that bright young man
who came for Christmas.'

'What about him?'

'Do say hello to him for me, won't you?'

Shaking with rage, she stormed around the flat, banging on doors,
ready to talk to anyone who would listen, even the lovebirds. But
she was alone. Where the hell was Patrick, she thought, when she
needed him? Back in the sitting room, she poured herself a glass of
whisky, then picked up the phone. She was on the point of calling
her mother back and telling her what she knew, the lies and the
deceit, the life she'd been denied, of telling her about Maddy and
Heather, her real mother, her real family. But instinct told her
how unwise that would be. Any power she might have depended
on her keeping it secret for as long as she could. Thinking about

the conversation she had just had, she began to understand how badly she wanted not only to have her inheritance herself, as her father had intended, but also to make sure that her mother, his wife, had nothing. Nothing. Just as she had been denied her family, her real mother and sister, so would she deny her adoptive mother every last penny of the money left her, every last brick of the house the woman had thought of as hers since the day she'd married. Her husband had fucked another woman and given her the child, or one of them, to bring up as some sort of consolation prize because she was sterile, or because he couldn't bring himself to touch her, and now that child would reclaim everything that was rightfully hers, and that would be her consolation prize for not having had the childhood that was her birthright. And that way she would have it all.

I need to share this with Maddy, she thought. She had the number by heart. But Heather answered the phone. 'Maddy's gone out,' she said. 'I'm here, though. Why don't you come round and keep me company this evening?'

CHAPTER FORTY-THREE

Maddy and Matteo waited for their pizzas to arrive in silence. It was the first time he had taken her out to eat, and she wasn't sure if he thought this was a date or not. He was attentive, but distracted, as though his attention were the result of careful training and his mind were elsewhere. She didn't want to hurt him, she liked him too much for that, but any idea that he might be more than a friend, an idea she might have entertained a month ago when they first met, had been lost in the rush of her feeling for Ludovico, and she didn't know how to broach the subject. He fiddled with his knife, glanced out of the window at the traffic outside, smiled at her in a way that made her wonder if he knew who she was. 'This is nice,' she said finally, and he nodded, and said that yes, it was nice. It was very nice. And then she stood up. 'But I don't know why we're here,' she said. 'And I don't think you do either.'

'No, please,' he said, 'don't go.'

She sat down again. 'So what shall we talk about?'

'Our future?' he said.

She looked at him, startled. The pizzas arrived. He began to laugh.

'Don't worry,' he said. 'This isn't a proposal of marriage.'

'Maybe we should just eat our pizzas,' Maddy said.

'I was joking,' he said. 'But I shall tell you what I see. I see a brilliant future for you, and for me, and I hope we shall continue to be friends in our amazing careers, and with our amazing partners, whom we shall love with all our amazing hearts.' He cut into his pizza. 'There,' he said. 'How does that sound?'

'Amazing.' She cut and folded a slice of pizza and lifted it to her mouth. 'Seriously.'

'I seriously agree.' They began to laugh together.

And then, because she had to tell someone sooner or later, she said, 'I met Patrick.'

'Who's Patrick?'

'I never told you about him?'

'No.'

'He's Fiona's boyfriend, or he was Fiona's boyfriend. I'm not quite sure.'

'Fiona's boyfriends remain an enigma,' Matteo said.

Maddy let this pass. 'They were at Oxford together, and then he went to prison for fraud. They let him out and he moved here. He's living in Fiona's flat.'

'With Ludovico.'

'Yes, also with Ludovico.'

'And what does Ludovico think about this?'

'I've no idea. We haven't talked about it. He's working on something, some project at the research centre in Frascati. I don't really know what.' She paused. 'He asked me to go and stay with him there, but I didn't want to leave my mother.'

'You think Fiona might take your place?'

She nodded. 'I suppose I do.' She took another bite of pizza. 'That makes me sound awful, doesn't it?'

'Not really.'

'I ought to be pleased, I know that. I just can't bring myself to accept her.' She paused. 'She's going to be very rich.'

'I know. You told me.'

Maddy shook her head. 'No, richer than that. Richer than I ever imagined.' Pushing her half-eaten pizza to one side, she told Matteo what Patrick had told her, how she was entitled to half the money.

'Have you spoken to Fiona about this?'

She shook her head. 'Fiona doesn't know I've met Patrick. Not unless he's told her, of course, and somehow I don't think he has. Why would he? He's working against her interests, isn't he?'

'But not against yours. Why would he do that?'

She shook her head again.

'Why would he want to take money from his girlfriend and give it to you?'

'Perhaps because he thinks it's fair. I mean, the money *is* mine.'

'But your father left it to Fiona.'

She had no answer to this.

'Maybe we should go back to Plan A,' he said.

'What's that?'

'Don't you remember? Kidnap her. Hold her to ransom. Bury the body in a cave.' He finished his beer. 'Don't you want that pizza?'

She'd completely forgotten about the pizza. 'No, you eat it. I'm not hungry any longer.'

*

Fiona let herself into the flat. Heather was waiting for her. She'd put on some make-up: lipstick and the kind of mascara she'd worn at the rock concert all those years ago. Her hair was brushed, she was wearing a kaftan-style dress Fiona had never seen. She noticed all this immediately, and was touched. They kissed each other on the cheek, then fell into a long spontaneous hug. 'It's so good to see you,' Heather murmured in Fiona's ears, and Fiona felt tears start to her eyes. 'Look what I've brought for us to share,' she said, reaching into her bag and bringing out a bottle of champagne. 'Get the glasses,' she said. Heather went to the kitchen and came back with two tumblers. 'They're not exactly made for champagne,' she said, 'but everything else is dirty.'

'So what are we celebrating?' Heather said after they had both had their first sip.

'It's a little pre-birthday celebration,' said Fiona. 'Just for the two of us.' She took a second sip. 'It's not very good champagne. I got it from a bar on the way here.'

'It tastes fine to me,' said Heather. 'You're such a sweet girl.' She raised her glass. 'Happy pre-birthday!'

Two-thirds of the bottle had been drunk before Heather asked why Fiona had called. 'Did you want to speak to me,' she said, 'or to Maddy?'

'Either of you. Both of you. I just wanted to talk to someone.'

'I thought you shared your flat?'

'I do, but I was alone and, well, I'd just had a horrible conversation with my mother.' She caught herself. 'I mean, with Anne.'

'Why was it horrible?'

They sat down on the sofa while Fiona told her all that she could remember. Anne's cajoling, Anne's threats. Heather listened, her free hand gently stroking Fiona's knee. When Fiona stopped talking, she said, 'Anne was always about the money. She always thought people could be bought and sold. So did Raymond, in a way. He gave me a house for you, he said it would be Maddy's inheritance, but you know all about that, don't you? I mustn't grumble.' She filled her glass. 'I wonder what Anne thinks about me now. She knows about us, doesn't she? That must be why she's doing it. She doesn't want you to help me. She knows that's what you'll do once you have the money.'

Fiona shook her head. 'No.'

'No?'

'I haven't told her.'

'Why on earth not?'

'Because it's none of her business.'

'That's not really true though, is it?'

Fiona sighed. 'I suppose not.'

'Oh, well, who cares about her?' Heather hugged Fiona close. 'That's enough misery for one night. Let's enjoy our bubbly!'

When Fiona got back to her own flat two hours later, she found Patrick asleep on her bed, the rag doll on the pillow next to his head. He was still using Ludovico's pyjamas, rolled up to fit, and looked more like a boy than ever. She watched as he rolled over onto his side, then, still sleeping, lifted an arm and moved the doll closer to his face until one of her yellow plaits touched his cheek. She had the strangest sense that he needed to be protected. As quietly as she could, she undressed and, slipping on her nightie, lay down beside them.

Waking the next morning, she found Patrick sitting on the side of the bed, already dressed, with a cup of coffee for her. She sat up, took the coffee.

'You looked so sweet last night,' she said. 'I didn't want to disturb you. What did you do?'

He smiled. 'I must have just missed you. I read. I listened to music. I should be studying Italian, I suppose, if this is where we're going to live. What about you?'

'I went to see my mother.' *If this is where we're going to live*, she repeated to herself, startled, elated, puzzled, storing the thought away to be examined later.

He smiled again. 'And your sister? Was she there?'

Fiona shook her head.

'Would you have minded if she was?'

'I don't know. I wish I did.'

He reached into his pocket. 'I have something for you,' he said. He gave her a small box with a ribbon around it.

'What is it?' she said.

'Open it,' he said.

*

'Look what he gave me.' Fiona held out her wrist and shook it so that the bracelet shimmered in the light. 'Isn't it lovely?'

'It certainly looks expensive,' said Ludovico. 'I wonder where he found the money.'

'Shh,' she said. 'He'll hear.' She lowered her voice. 'He's bound to have had some money squirrelled away somewhere, that would be just like him. And I know his family has been giving him an allowance until he gets back on his feet.'

'And is that what he's doing here? Getting back on his feet?'

'You don't know what he's been through.'

'All I know is that he's lounging around here, contributing nothing, doing nothing but distract you. He's really won you over, hasn't he?'

'I don't understand you, Ludovico,' she said. 'Anyone would think you were jealous.'

'Jealous?'

'Because I'm not jealous, although I'd have every right to be.'

'Don't start that again.'

'Anyway, you'll be pleased to hear that Maddy went out for a pizza last night with her friend Matteo.'

'Is that intended to annoy me?'

'Do you want to know how I know?' Fiona said.

'Fiona spent yesterday evening with her mother,' said Patrick from the door.

'Thank you, Patrick,' said Ludovico. 'And now, if you'll excuse me, I have work to do.' He walked over to the door, pointedly waited for Patrick to move, then turned to Fiona. 'Oh, by the way, the lovebirds are moving out. In fact, they already have.' He looked at Patrick and then back at Fiona. 'They said there were too many people hanging around the place.'

Fiona smiled at Patrick. 'In that case, there's no reason at all for you to go. We have lots of room.'

As soon as Ludovico had left the kitchen, Patrick walked over to Fiona, lifted her hair from her neck and kissed her on the nape.

'What was that for?' she said.

'I love your hair,' he said. 'Promise me you'll never wear it short.'

'All right,' she said, amused. 'Maddy's cut hers short, you know.'

'Silly girl,' he said.

'I think she did it so that my mother would know who she was.'

'You never asked her?'

'We had other things to talk about,' Fiona said.

'Did you talk about me?'

'I don't remember.'

'Have you thought any more about your birthday?' he said.

'Don't you start!'

He looked at her, puzzled.

'I had my other mother on the phone yesterday, droning on and on about how I should go home. She even threatened to hire a marquee, can you imagine? I'd rather die.'

'Did she mention me?'

'Actually, she did. She said to say hello.'

'And the money? Did she have anything to say about that?'

'Yes. She said I didn't deserve it. She said it wasn't mine. She said my father would be very disappointed in me. She said I was incompetent. She said I was on drugs.' Her tone changed as she spoke, from flippancy to irritation to near-anger.

'On drugs? That's a new one.' He laughed. 'You know what you need to do. You need to take the money and run.'

'She'd never let me get away. She'd never leave me alone.'

'You've forgotten about Elizabeth,' he said.

Patrick clapped his hands with joy when Fiona told him that Elizabeth Bingham had not only been provided with a passport but also a national insurance number and a bank account. 'You've done a fantastic job,' he said. 'All we need to do now is shift the money into Elizabeth's account as soon as it's in yours and it's a done deal. We don't even need to be in the UK to do it. It's the last thing she'll expect.' He filled the coffee pot. 'There is just one thing, of course. If you really want to be left alone.'

'What?' she said.

'You'll have to disappear,' he said.

CHAPTER FORTY-FOUR

Fiona caught up with Ludovico as he was leaving the flat. 'Let me come with you,' she said. 'I need to talk.'

'We can talk here,' he said, putting down his briefcase.

'No,' she said, looking behind her. 'Let's go to a bar somewhere. And Ludo sweetheart, I don't want to argue. Be gentle with me, OK?'

Ten minutes later, they were sitting in a bar in Campo de' Fiori and Fiona was talking about her inheritance.

'I know it all sounds crazy,' she said, 'but I need to be where I feel I belong, and I don't belong in England, and I don't belong with Anne. She'll never let me go. If she finds out that I know about my real mother and Maddy I don't know what she'll do, but I don't trust her. It won't be good, I'm sure of that. You know how vindictive she can be. Don't you remember that time we were in your villa and she found me with a packet of cigarettes and she held a lit match under my palm until I cried out with the pain? She's a cruel woman and I want to be rid of her.'

'I don't remember that,' he said doubtfully.

'You don't need to remember it,' she said. 'I remember, and that's enough.'

'So you're going to make use of your invented identity, Elizabeth.'

'Yes.'

'And run off with Patrick, who will share your fortune.'

She sighed. 'It isn't like that,' she said.

'You need to convince me of that,' Ludovico said.

'I don't really need to convince you of anything,' she said hotly. 'I thought you wanted my advice, not my approval.'

'Will you let me finish?'

'I'm sorry,' he said.

She paused, in part to gather her thoughts, in part to let her anger pass. 'What I want to do is split it, all of it, with Maddy and our mother. It's as much her money as mine, after all. She's my father's daughter too. He would have wanted her to have her share of it, I'm sure.'

'Have you spoken about this to anyone else?'

'No, no one. Apart from Patrick. It was partly his idea.'

'Why doesn't that surprise me?' said Ludovico, his tone ironic. 'So what does he get out of it?'

'He's my boyfriend,' Fiona said with a touch of defiance. 'What he gets out of it, as you put it, is my business. I might as well ask you what you'll get out of it, as Maddy's boyfriend.'

'That's a stupid thing to say,' he snapped.

'Yes, well.' She stood up. 'I was hoping you'd understand, but obviously I was mistaken.'

'Sit down, you idiot,' he said. 'I think it's a beautiful idea. But I don't know how Maddy will feel about it.'

'Won't she be pleased?'

He looked thoughtful. 'I'm not sure. I don't know her well enough to say, not yet. I do know that she's very proud.' He paused. 'Obviously, she'd be glad to have the money. I've never met this new mother of yours, by the way. I've asked to be introduced and Maddy has always found an excuse not to invite me home. She's ashamed, and she has no reason to be. I don't care.' He stared into Fiona's eyes. 'You've been to the flat. You've met her. What's she like?'

'She's impulsive, and warm, and she responds to love,' said Fiona. 'She's everything Anne isn't, and I want her in my life more than I've wanted anyone ever before.'

'Does Patrick know this?'

She shrugged. 'If he doesn't he'll find out soon enough.'

Ludovico looked at his watch. 'I need to go,' he said.

'Work?'

'No,' he said. 'Later on, yes. Right now, I'm actually meeting Maddy for lunch.' He patted his stomach. 'I'm putting on weight with all these lunches and dinners. All we do is meet and eat. We're like teenagers on their first dates. I'm surprised we haven't booked into a hotel. She refuses to take me to her flat and I've never felt comfortable about bringing her back to ours, and don't tell me I'm being stupid because you wouldn't be happy to find her in the kitchen in the morning, so don't pretend you would.'

'Any more than you were to find Patrick,' she said, with a smile.

'Precisely.' He grinned. 'We go back a long way, Fiona. We have too much luggage.'

'Baggage, Ludo, baggage.' She watched him pay for their coffees, pick up his briefcase. 'Don't breathe a word of what I've said, will you?'

'Of course I won't.'

'Just try to make her like me, that's all.'

'I promise you that I'll do my best.'

When they were both outside, he said, 'By the way, be careful with that bracelet, won't you? You might find you need to take it back when Patrick's cheque bounces. That reminds me, you haven't seen a watch of mine lying around anywhere, have you? A Jacques Couture?'

Ludovico had lied about not having booked into a hotel. He and Maddy had spent a night together in a two-star *pensione* near the station a few days earlier. The room was bare but clean, the bed more than adequate for their needs. Maddy wondered if this was the first time he had brought a woman to a place like this and then decided she didn't care. They had eaten at a trattoria beneath the *pensione*, which was on the third floor and had no lift. He joked about carrying her over the threshold, that he would have done so if it hadn't involved six separate flights of stairs, and she found the remark both touching and slightly offensive. She thought of the man in the park, of the money slipped into her pocket, all of it irrevocably bound up with her feelings for Ludovico although she had tried to break the link. Over dinner, they talked about everything except Fiona and her mother. Ludovico listened to Maddy as she told him of her plans for the future, the kind of work she wanted to do with her degree, about international cooperation and the role she saw for herself in it, about travel and how little she'd seen of the world, about what she could give when she was free. She didn't say what prevented her from being free. He knew as well as she did what that was. She didn't worry that he might be bored, because he so obviously wasn't. He loves me, she thought, and she believed, with a sense of falling, that she loved him. In bed, they joked about their illicit affair and the eroticism of anonymity, and then made love in a bed that creaked under their weight, which made them both laugh and then be more careful as a nearby door was closed and they realised that everything that happened could be overheard. Eventually, spent, they fell asleep. Maddy woke during the night with Ludovico's right arm thrown across her breasts and lay there with the heft of it on her, wishing that she could stay like that for ever until it became too heavy and she eased herself from under it. The following morning, leaving the *pensione* before the winter dawn, with the lights of the traffic of the station all around them and a buzz of early-risen travellers, Maddy had grabbed his coat sleeve with an urgency she couldn't explain, holding on to it as though she would never see him again. He had laughed, and kissed her, and they had said goodbye.

Maddy hadn't been to a class for two weeks now; she relied on Matteo to keep her up to date. He passed her his notes and she read them in a hurried, distracted way, asking the occasional question so that he would feel that the effort he had made to share them with her had been repaid.

She thought, as she had done a hundred times every day, about what Patrick had said, about the inheritance, half of which should be hers. The injustice of it tore at her, an internal thorn, a splinter she had swallowed but not absorbed, that continued to rend her from within. It was too good to be true, she told herself. Fiona hated her or distrusted her, she could feel it, however much she denied it. Why would she want to give away half of what she owned? But that didn't make the thought go away. And then there was that other thought, for which Matteo was responsible, that thought of kidnap and ransom. It had been no more than a stupid joke, but even so, she'd had a dream about the woods behind the house in Frascati and she'd been staring into a hole, and the hole had been empty but she'd woken up knowing for whom it had been made.

They met at the same trattoria for lunch, at Ludovico's suggestion. 'It's romantic, like a rendezvous,' he'd said. Maddy was unconvinced by this but went along with the idea, because Ludovico was paying. What she felt for Ludovico was confused, and powerful, and tinged with an anxiety she couldn't shake off, an anxiety that overwhelmed her. He had so much to offer; she had so little. One day, she told herself, I shall have enough money to decide where to go and what to eat and I shall be beholden to no one. One day.

Ludovico was waiting for her at the door. 'Hungry?' he said. She nodded, let him hold the door open for her, help her out of her coat, small gestures of attention that touched and excited her in equal measure, gallantry as foreplay, she thought later, remembering. As soon as they had ordered, he leant forward, his elbows on the table, his hands linked under his chin. He scared her slightly, as though he were about to interrogate her or tell her something she didn't want to hear. She broke off a piece of bread. He caught her hand.

'Are you all right?' she said.

He let her go. 'Yes. Why do you ask?'

'Because you seem, well, tense.'

He sat back, whatever he had been about to say or do apparently forgotten. 'No, I'm fine,' he said.

'Is there something you want to say to me?' she said, suddenly sick with fear.

'I was talking to Fiona this morning.'

Not Fiona, she wanted to scream. Anything but Fiona.

'And?'

'She wanted to know how you were, that's all. She misses you. You haven't seen each other in ages.'

'Well, more like days than ages.'

'That's not how she sees it.'

'Are we here so that you can defend her?' For God's sake, stop, she thought. Just stop. Any appetite she might have had when she entered the trattoria had drained away.

'Of course not,' he said. 'It's just that I think you've misunderstood her.'

'So it's my fault?'

'It's nobody's fault.' He sighed. 'There are always two sides,' he said.

She took her napkin off her lap and slapped it down on the table. 'I've had enough of this. So it is my fault.'

'That isn't what I said. You know that.'

'So what did you say?'

'Please let me speak,' he said, plaintively.

But it isn't you speaking, she wanted to cry out, it's her. 'OK,' she said. 'I'm listening.'

'She wants to spend time with you,' he said. 'She wants to share your life, she wants to share her life with you. It isn't her fault, or yours, that you didn't have the opportunity to grow up together. More than anything, she wants to be part of a family. You, her, your mother. She's lonely, Maddy. When she was younger and staying with us in the summer, with my family, she always looked as though she wanted to belong but couldn't. She used to cry whenever she had to leave. Her mother's a mean, selfish woman. Her mother in England, I mean. My mother despises her.'

Maddy felt herself soften, and resented it, saw it as weakness. 'Go on,' she said.

'She's been looking for you for years. She came to Rome specifically to find you,' he said.

Maddy gasped. Ludovico covered his mouth with his hand, but it was too late. 'What do you mean? She knew I was here?'

He nodded. 'I shouldn't have said that.'

'She never told me. My God, I believed her. She's lied to me from the start then?'

'Don't put it like that. It was partly my idea. She wanted to be honest with you.'

The food arrived. Maddy pushed her plate away from her. 'All that pantomime about bumping into each other, and swapping dates of birth. Lies, all of it lies. That's why she decided to teach that fucking stupid useless course in my faculty? She knew she'd see me sooner or later. She tracked me down.'

He nodded again. 'I'm sorry,' he said. 'I've said too much.'

'And you've known this all along and you've never said a word.' She paused for a moment. She felt his hands on her, and shivered with disgust at the memory. 'You helped her,' she said. 'You make me sick, both of you.'

She stood up, grabbed her coat from the back of her chair, began to put it on. Ludovico grabbed her arm but she pulled away from him, stumbled out of the trattoria. She stood in the street and cried until she heard the door behind her open. Without turning round, she broke into a run.

CHAPTER FORTY-FIVE

'But I don't mind,' said Heather.

'How can you say that?' cried Maddy. 'She's done nothing but lie to me. And to you.'

Heather shook her head. 'She's never lied to me.'

'For God's sake! She spent an entire weekend pretending to be me.'

'That was my fault. I should have recognised her at once.'

'But you didn't, did you?'

Heather thought for a moment. 'I'm not sure. Sometimes I think I did. Part of me did.'

'Which part? The sober part? If there was one.'

'How can you be so cruel?' Heather paused. 'Fiona would never say anything like that to me.'

'Of course she wouldn't. She's all sweetness and light, isn't she? Can't you see what she's doing? She's trying to wheedle her way into our lives.'

Heather sighed. 'Where's all this anger coming from, Maddy? This negativity. You need to open yourself up to her.'

'Don't give me that hippie shit, Mum.'

'Is it so awful to have a sister? All three of us happy together? What is it that frightens you so much?'

Maddy picked up her coat. 'I've had enough of this. I'm off.'

'That's right, run away.'

'How dare you say that to me? You've spent your whole life running away, and dragging me along with you.'

'And believe me, there are times I wish I hadn't,' Heather said, then gave a little shriek, barely more than an intake of breath, and covered her mouth with her hand. 'Oh sweetheart,' she said. 'I didn't mean that. Honestly I didn't. Don't go. Don't leave me like this.'

But it was too late. Maddy had already closed the door behind her.

She found Matteo in the faculty library. She gestured to him to gather his books together and to follow her. Five minutes later, they were sitting in the campus bar and Maddy had told him what Ludovico had told her.

'So what are you going to do?' he said.

'I wish I knew. I feel as though I've lost everything.' She felt tears coming and wished she hadn't spoken.

'Are you talking about Ludovico?'

'He knew all along,' she said, her voice breaking. 'Do you realise what that means?'

'Or about the money?'

'What?'

'The money,' he said, gently.

'My mother told me I was cruel,' she said, crying openly now. 'And I was. I am. I wish I was dead.'

'That wouldn't solve anything,' Matteo said.

'I wish she was dead.'

'Your mother?'

'Idiot. Fiona.'

'That's a much better idea,' he said.

'My mother wouldn't agree with you,' said Maddy, sniffing. 'She loves her more than she's ever loved me. I know she does.'

And now I'm wallowing in self-pity, she thought. But it was true, Heather did seem to love Fiona more than she loved Maddy.

Matteo pulled a paper tissue from the dispenser and gave it to her.

'Blow your nose,' he said.

'Thank you, Daddy.'

'That's better. A little respect at last.'

She looked at him.

'You do me good,' she said.

'So how are we going to do it?' he said.

'Well, she needs to inherit first,' said Maddy, leaning forward and lowering her voice, playing along. 'She needs to actually have the money. Otherwise there'd be no point in killing her and taking her place.'

'So we're ruling out kidnapping in favour of murder?'

'Yes, I think so,' she said. 'Less risky in the long run.' She touched her hair. 'But I'll need to grow my hair long again.' She thought for a moment. 'I suppose I could always get a wig.'

Matteo snapped his fingers. 'Damn, I knew there was something I'd forgotten. It's these little details that betray the unprepared assassin, isn't it?'

'Maybe we're not cut out for it,' she said.

'Well, let's see what we'll need to do to make it work.' He took a notebook out of his rucksack, uncapped a pen. 'Ready?' he said.

*

'I can't believe you told her,' Fiona screamed, pummelling Ludovico's chest. 'You stupid, stupid fool.' He grabbed both arms and forced them to her side. She struggled against him briefly, then went limp. 'You've ruined everything,' she said. 'She'll never let me get close now. I'll never forgive you.'

He hugged her to him. 'I'm sorry,' he said. 'I never imagined you hadn't told her.'

'What good does being sorry do?' she said.

'No good at all, I know.'

She pulled away from him. 'So what are you going to do to put things right?'

The phone rang in the sitting room. 'Whoever it is, I don't want to speak to them,' she said urgently. She stared around the kitchen as though some implement might be found there to protect her from the call. Ludovico moved towards the door but the ringing stopped almost at once. When they heard a man's voice, they looked at each other.

'I thought Patrick had gone out,' he said.

'So did I. He must have been in the lovebirds' old room. He's moved his stuff into it. He said he might as well use it while he can.'

'He said what?'

'Shh.'

They listened but the kitchen was too far away from the phone for them to do any more than realise that he was speaking to someone he knew. He laughed once, and then again. Fiona would have gone into the corridor to listen to what he said, but Ludovico's presence constrained her. When the conversation came to an end, they heard him cross the sitting room and walk along the corridor towards them.

'That was your mother,' he said to Fiona. 'I told her you were out teaching.'

'What else did you tell her?' said Ludovico.

'Oh hello,' said Patrick. 'I didn't see you there.'

'What did she want?' Fiona said.

'She's still trying to persuade you to go home for your birthday. And now she's roped me in as well.'

'I hope you told her to push off.'

'Well, not in so many words.'

'You sounded as though you were enjoying yourself,' said Ludovico.

'I was,' said Patrick. 'She always makes me laugh.'

'Oh, by the way,' Ludovico said, 'you haven't seen a watch of mine lying around anywhere, have you? It's rather a good one.'

'Yes, I've noticed you like rather flashy watches,' Patrick said. 'You had a Rolex on a couple of days ago, didn't you?'

'Did I? I don't remember.' Ludovico paused. 'So have you?'

'Seen it? No, I'm sorry, I haven't. But I'll be sure to tell you if I do.'

'Oh, and while we're on the subject,' Ludovico said, 'Robert called earlier.'

'Robert?' said Patrick.

'The lovebird,' said Fiona.

'Apparently a cheque of his has gone missing.'

'Oh dear,' said Patrick, with a smile.

'That's enough, Ludo,' said Fiona, putting a hand on his arm. She looked at Patrick, her expression half pleading, half apologetic. 'Actually, Patrick, we're just in the middle of something. You wouldn't mind leaving us alone for a bit?'

He smiled again. 'Not at all. I think I'll go for a walk. *À bientôt.*'

As soon as Patrick was out of the flat, Ludovico said, 'I'll sort this out somehow, I promise you.'

'Maybe you should leave it to me,' Fiona said. 'You've done enough damage already.'

*

Fiona and Maddy bumped into each other on the campus the following week, or so Maddy thought. The truth was that Fiona had finished her lesson and followed Matteo as he crossed to the bar. She foresaw that he'd be meeting Maddy there and her foresight was rewarded. Unnoticed outside the door, she waited until the two of them had taken their coffees and carried them across to a table. As soon as they were seated she walked across and put her bag on one of the two empty chairs, then sat down on the other one.

'Hello,' she said.

Matteo, looking uncomfortable, stood up. 'Coffee?'

She nodded. 'Thanks. That would be great. No sugar.'

Maddy caught his arm, as if to stop him, then let it go.

'Just let me talk,' Fiona said as soon as they were alone.

'So talk.'

'We've made a mess of everything,' Fiona said.

'We have?'

'All right. I have.'

'I can't believe you didn't tell me.'

'I was stupid. I was scared. You have to trust me. I know you think I'm creepy. But that's why, don't you see? Because I lied to you from the start and then I didn't know how to put things right. But the last thing I ever wanted was to hurt you.'

Maddy stirred her coffee.

'Creepy, you said. *I think you're creepy*. I've never said that I think you're creepy.'

'I heard you, Maddy. I heard you say it.'

Maddy nodded. 'Oh, right. When you were spying on us that time, outside the bar. That *is* creepy.'

'I wasn't spying on you. I was coming in and then I heard you say what you said, and I was so upset I had to go away.'

'So what do you think we should do about this mess we've made?'

Fiona took a deep breath.

'Ludovico wants us to get together, make peace. He's got this idea we'll all be happy if we just talk things through.'

'Ah, Ludovico.' Maddy played with her spoon for a moment, then stared out through the window towards the almost empty campus. 'Good old Ludovico. Everyone's best friend. And you agree with him?'

'I don't know,' said Fiona. 'Do you?'

Maddy gave a small, wry smile and shook her head. 'I don't know either.' She looked straight at Fiona. 'I'm not that fond of Ludovico these days, but I suppose you know all about that. Anyway, it's none of your business, although it's probably your fault.' Like everything else, she thought. She picked up her coffee, which was cold by now, and put it down again, untouched. 'I suppose we could try.'

'Start again?' said Fiona, with a hopeful smile, holding out her hand.

'Start again,' said Maddy, taking the offered hand and shaking it.

'I love our mother,' said Fiona.

'Wow,' said Maddy. 'That didn't take long.'

'I want to spend as much time with her as I can.'

'I'm sorry?'

'You've had her all your life. I've had, what, three days with her.'

Matteo came back with a cup of coffee. 'I can leave you alone if you prefer,' he said, putting it down in front of Fiona. Fiona was about to say, yes, that would be the best thing, but Maddy spoke first.

'Don't be silly.' She patted his empty chair. 'Just sit down and listen to this.' She looked at Fiona and then at Matteo. 'She wants my mother.'

'I didn't say that.' Fiona was indignant.

'As good as,' said Maddy. 'And you know what?'

'What?'

'You're welcome to her.'

'You don't mean that,' said Matteo.

'You stay out of this,' snapped Maddy. 'This has got absolutely nothing to do with you.' She turned to Fiona. 'Shall I tell you what I had to do for her this morning, before I left the flat? I had to change her sheets, and get her to take her pyjamas off so that I could wash them and make her have a shower. Why? Because she'd wet the fucking bed. And she didn't even realise she'd done it until I woke her up. So, yes. If you want her you can have her.'

'That's awful,' said Fiona quietly. 'But I can help you with her, don't you see? She needs to be cared for.' She paused. 'I mean, I know you care for her, but maybe that isn't enough.'

'And you would be? You'd be enough?'

'I can help with money,' she said.

'I think your mother is often worried about money,' said Matteo, hesitantly. 'Maybe she drinks too much from worry?'

'That's it,' said Maddy, starting to her feet, pushing her chair back until it banged into a neighbouring table. 'You know nothing about my mother,' she said, bending down and prodding Matteo in the chest, her face inches from his face, twisted with rage. 'Not one fucking thing,' she said. She straightened up. 'I don't believe this,' she said, then burst into tears and ran out of the bar. Matteo glared at Fiona before following Maddy out. Fiona finished her coffee. I know I'm right, she told herself. I'll get what I want and do what's right in the end, you'll see. You'll all see. She watched the two of them outside, Matteo putting his arms around Maddy, Maddy pushing him away, relenting and allowing him to hug her, him trying to lead her away and Maddy resisting, breaking away from him. Fiona sat and watched the two of them talking, slowly at first and then more urgently until finally it seemed that some sort of agreement had been reached. Maddy wriggled free from Matteo. She'll go now, back to her mother, Fiona thought, but she was wrong. To her astonishment, Maddy pushed open the door and walked over to the table.

'You're right,' she said. 'I'm being selfish.'

Maddy spoke to her mother that evening. She told her what Fiona had said, more or less, and what she had said, in more detail, as people do when they report conversations they have had. She told her mother that they had argued and then made peace, and that she was speaking not only on her own behalf but also on Fiona's. Her mother listened intently, nodding and looking anxious and then, as the conversation finally turned to money, relieved. When Maddy had finished talking, she struggled up from the sofa and walked to where Maddy was sitting. She bent over and kissed her forehead, then straightened up and smiled.

'I love you too,' she said. Or was it *two*?

PART SIX

CHAPTER FORTY-SIX

A week later, Liz and Aldo have still not quite forgiven each other. Their disagreements generally last an hour or two and never more than a night, but this time some small, untreated wound continues to rankle. Perhaps because what was wrong remained unsaid, thought Liz, as the days passed and they barely spoke, or spoke with a painstaking caution she'd decided she couldn't stand any longer. When Aldo comes home from work the evening of the programme, she's already decided to apologise, implicitly, by treating him with all the affection she can muster. She's spent all day working on a translation of a book she doesn't think worth publishing in any language, and is happy to put it to one side and prepare an aubergine parmigiana, one of Aldo's favourite dishes. She fries the aubergine, makes a sauce of fresh tomatoes, slices the mozzarella, goes into the garden to pick some basil, assembles the parmigiana, distracted by the task, humming quietly to herself, with the radio tuned to the BBC, a habit she has never lost. When Aldo comes home and throws his briefcase on the sofa in the kitchen, she walks across and hugs him, then takes his jacket and hangs it up. She sees herself from outside, the perfect wife, and would have blushed if anyone else had been there, but Aldo takes it as it's intended. He hugs her back, kisses her with more passion than he's shown in weeks, then crosses to the fridge and takes out the bottle of wine she opened ten minutes earlier, topping up her glass and filling a second glass for himself. 'Another day, another dollar,' he says, a phrase she taught him when they first met, which amused him then and amuses him now, she's never quite known why. 'A bit more than a dollar, I hope,' she says, as she usually does, and they clink their glasses.

The programme begins straight after the news, which they watch in a distracted way on the TV in the kitchen while the parmigiana is in the oven. By the time it starts, they are seated with their trays, side by side, on the sofa. Liz has convinced herself that the risk is over, the story of the missing girl is dead in the water, and she watches the first hour of the programme with a wilfully detached interest, only getting up to carry away their trays. The parmigiana has been a success, she's glad to see. She takes a second bottle of wine out of the fridge and is twisting the cork off the corkscrew when Aldo calls her.

There is the record card again. Name, age, height. The last place she was seen. But San Lorenzo is no longer there. Someone has called in and said Frascati. She was seen in Frascati three days after her supposed disappearance. This horrifies Liz; she almost cries out in shock. Almost forty years have passed and some busybody with nothing better to do has remembered seeing a girl he, or she, has never met, and has bothered to phone a TV programme. And this is taken as proof that the girl was there when everyone knows an eyewitness is already unreliable only minutes after the event. It's madness. Absolute madness.

She says this to Aldo, expecting him to agree with her, perhaps to laugh reassuringly, to dismiss the whole thing as nonsense. But he is leaning forward, absorbed. He turns his head only once, to gauge her reaction, perhaps sensing her shock, then looks away as though he hasn't much liked what he's seen. The intensity of his interest disturbs her. He's still unconvinced, she thinks. She watches the information from a fortnight before as it's recycled, an extract from the interview with the woman sandwiched between two photographs she can't remember having seen before. The presenter says that the woman has declined to comment on the theory that the girl was one of a pair of twins. There is a computerised image of what the girl might look like now, with the long hair of that time and a new short bob of the kind favoured by middle-aged Italian women, and Liz is relieved to see how inaccurate both are. Then, to her horror, Ludovico comes on and Aldo edges forward a little further in his seat. At first she thinks the piece is merely a replay of the original interview, with Ludovico sitting behind his desk in what has to be his study, until she sees his expression change from a detached, rather weary concern to awkwardness. The reporter asks him about the twin theory and he says, yes, there might be something in it, he recalls being introduced to a girl who looked very much like the missing girl, a student of hers, he thinks but can't be sure. The reporter asks him about Frascati, about the sighting there of the girl, and if he has anything to say about that. Aldo glances across at her once again, an odd look of triumph on his face, as if she, not Ludovico, has been put on the spot. Ludovico pauses and then nods. My family had the use of a house there, he says. We went there once or twice, I don't remember exactly when. The reporter asks him if they went there alone or with others. He shakes his head.

'I knew it,' says Aldo.

'Knew what?'

'This guy is the answer,' he says. 'If anything bad happened, and I'm sure something is fishy here – a rich girl disappearing only days after she's inherited a fortune – I'd bet that he's responsible. I've never liked him. These television experts drive me mad.'

She's silent. She feels that anything she says might give her away.

'Look at him,' Aldo says. 'Come on, Liz. What do you think?' She looks and what she sees on the screen is the man she thought she once loved, and maybe did, despite everything. How can I tell him that? she asks herself. Aldo has always imagined he's the first man I've ever really loved.

As they watch, Ludovico's study is replaced by the TV studio, Ludovico's evasive, still handsome face by the face of the presenter and another desperate case, a woman in her fifties who set out on her bicycle one morning just outside Modena, no more than forty miles from their house, and has never been seen again. Thank God they haven't gone back to interview Matteo, she thinks, although what else could he say that he hasn't already said. And the inheritance hasn't been mentioned either, the emptied account, the friend who's clever with money. It could have been a lot worse. Maybe now, they'll leave us alone. A mystery unsolved, like so many other mysteries.

Aldo slumps back on the sofa, no longer interested in what he's watching, absorbed by the story he has heard. It has all the ingredients, she has to admit, of the kind of novel he likes to read. An heiress, just twenty-one. A mysterious disappearance. A possible culprit. All it lacks is a happy ending, although perhaps he doesn't need that. Perhaps a happy ending is the last thing he needs. At least he hasn't remarked on how much she looked like the girl in the photograph this week, and Liz begins to hope that the identity of the girl no longer interests him in that way.

'It's obvious he did it,' says Aldo.

'Who?'

'That guy with the house in Frascati. The last person to see her alive.'

'You don't know that.'

'And you do?'

'Don't be ridiculous, sweetheart,' she says. 'Of course I don't. I just mean that he never said that, did he? Someone else said she'd been seen in Frascati, not him. I thought you always said people were innocent until proven guilty.'

'Legally, yes,' he says. 'But that doesn't mean I have to believe every word they say.'

She's about to answer when something in the voice of the journalist, some change of tone, attracts their attention. The photograph of the girl appears again and this time Aldo looks at her in a way that feels like an accusation. You see, his eyes say. It's useless to lie. The journalist has a sheet of paper in her hand and is reading it silently, as though the information it contains has only just been given to her and she needs to decide whether it should be broadcast or not. The credits are already running across the bottom of the screen when she makes up her mind. She looks up dramatically before casting her eyes back to the paper and beginning to read.

'A body, the age and sex of which remains to be established, has been discovered in the grounds of an historic villa in Frascati. The body was buried in a shallow grave, but has recently been partially unearthed, probably by wild boar, and was found by a group of German hikers yesterday morning. From the physical condition of the body, it has been estimated that it may have been there for anything up to forty years, and certainly for more than thirty years. Further information will be made available after the post-mortem scheduled for next week has been conducted.'

The following morning, when Aldo has left the house and Liz finally sits down to work on the translation, her cell phone rings. It's a number she doesn't know. She hesitates for a moment, then takes the call.

'*Pronto*.'

She listens to the voice, its tone of affection still familiar to her after all these years, until it has finished, then sighs.

'I was wondering how long it would be before you got in touch,' she says.

PART SEVEN

CHAPTER FORTY-SEVEN

It was Ludovico who suggested Frascati. A fresh start, he said to Fiona over the first coffee of the day. A moment of healing on neutral ground. Barely glancing up from the magazine she was reading, she agreed that this would be a good thing. Encouraged, he suggested they celebrate her birthday, and Maddy's birthday, there, with everyone else. She closed the magazine and said she'd need to think about that. 'Why don't you ask Maddy?' she said. 'See how she feels about the idea.'

Their birthday was just under two weeks away and Fiona still hadn't decided what to do. Patrick wanted to take her out for a special dinner, just the two of them somewhere nice, by which he meant expensive, but the business about Ludovico's watch and Robert's cheque had shaken her new-found faith in his reformed character. She was happy to spend time with him, she enjoyed his company, she enjoyed making love with him, she liked the way he was somehow apart from everything else in her life, from Maddy and Heather – her little secret, in a life that didn't seem to have any secrets left. She loved the way he talked about Anne, with amused contempt. He was so clearly on her side when the business of money came up, and he'd shown her how to transfer the money to the new account when the time came, simple enough when you knew how, but she hadn't, and she was grateful. 'All Anne will know is that the money has disappeared,' he said. 'She won't know where it is, and she won't want people to know that, because it would make her look foolish and greedy. She'll get her share, after all. And she won't know where you are either, unless you want her to.' She'd asked him what percentage he expected for all his help, and he'd behaved in an offended way. 'I thought I was your boyfriend,' he'd said, 'not a paid hand,' then adding, with a smile and a kiss, 'Whatever you think I'm worth.' When she finally dared to ask him about the watch and the missing cheque, because she couldn't not ask him, he looked at her reproachfully. 'Give a dog a bad name and hang him, is that how it works with you too?' he said. 'I thought you were better than that.' She softened towards him, as she always did. 'I didn't mean it,' she said, and kissed his nose. It wasn't her affair, in any case. If Robert was stupid enough to leave cheques lying about, that was his business. She felt that everything was falling into place. Heather, Maddy, the money. Even Patrick. All of it was beginning to make sense.

*

Maddy was easier to convince. 'Not that there's any need. Fiona and I have already made a fresh start,' she said. She'd ignored Ludovico's calls for days and then finally answered, and he'd taken her back to the same trattoria as though his intention had been to wind back time, to erase the disaster of the earlier lunch. He told her how stupid he'd been and she let him make his excuses long after they were necessary because she wanted him to suffer for a little while longer and because she *understood* Fiona. After the hurt and rage Fiona's subterfuge had unleashed were finally absorbed, Maddy understood why it had made more sense for her to lie at first, and how that lie had then become the only workable truth. She'd used the same tactics herself, with school friends, with Matteo even. For the first time, almost without realising it, she found herself on Fiona's side. She found herself forgiving her. Two weeks before their birthday, Fiona suggested they spend some sister time together – a phrase Maddy would have detested only days before – and Maddy, despite an inward wince, agreed at once. Because, of course, as Matteo had pointed out, there was also the inheritance to be considered.

They met in Largo Argentina, outside the theatre, neutral ground for them both. For the first time, in this new spirit of forgiveness, they discovered they could enjoy each other's company; a sort of complicity bound them together. Fiona took Maddy to a hairdresser in the centre, who transformed her chopped-up bonnet into a gleaming cap. They went shopping for dresses on Fiona's credit card, and picked out the same dress more than once, which confirmed the truth of their twinhood; a truth that Maddy was gradually being forced to acknowledge. In the end, after trying on dresses in half a dozen designer shops – Patrick would be proud of us, thought Fiona – and sizing each other up surreptitiously in the changing rooms to discover that, yes, they were identical down to the last square inch of bare skin, they chose the same model in different colours. Maddy cornflower blue, Fiona olive green. 'Now shoes,' Fiona said, 'we need new shoes,' and once again Maddy let herself be treated. She had never known that shoes could cost so much, or be bought with such ease. 'It's *our* money,' Fiona insisted, and Maddy, initially reluctant, eventually agreed.

They took a taxi to Trastevere to a wine bar as narrow as a corridor, a stone's throw from Santa Cecilia. Fiona ordered a bottle of champagne, describing it as the real thing. 'Much better than the one I took round to Heather's that night,' she said, carefully watching Maddy's face, checking that she hadn't gone too far. They toasted each other with a giggling sort of intimacy, as though they were two girls on the town and nothing else, as though they would get drunk and then go on the razzle, as their mother used to say. It was a favourite expression of hers. Fiona hooted with joy when Maddy told her. 'How wonderful,' she said. 'I love her so much,' she said and they toasted their absent mother, and Maddy let it pass because why shouldn't Fiona love her mother? She loved her too, in her way. She'll learn soon enough, Maddy thought.

When the bottle was empty and Fiona had ordered another, they began to talk about love.

'Do you think Daddy loved her?' Fiona said.

'She never mentioned him,' said Maddy. 'Not once.' She sipped the champagne. 'I always thought my real father was this friend of hers who used to hang around when I was a kid, before we came to Italy. He used to take me to this Chinese place, and then he just disappeared. I didn't mind, I don't think. I don't remember minding. There were others, but I used to call them all by their first names. I've never called anyone Dad, let alone Daddy, in my whole life. Did you really call him Daddy?'

Fiona ignored this. She was getting used to being teased by Maddy. 'He did look after her, though, in a way.'

'Giving her the house, you mean? Yes, I suppose he did. He bought her off, in any case.'

'And you. He looked after you?'

Maddy felt abruptly tearful. 'He left it up to Mum to do that.'

'I suppose he did.'

'And she didn't exactly make a brilliant job of it.'

'You've turned out all right though, haven't you?' She tapped her glass against Maddy's. 'Well done!'

Maddy gave a brief laugh. 'Oh God. You sound like my – I don't know – my grandmother, the grandmother I never had. I

382

feel as though you just patted my head and slipped a five-pound note into my hand.'

'Still, when you look at us, I mean seriously look at us, we've both turned out all right, haven't we?' said Fiona, grinning, a little drunk by now. 'More than all right. I think our parents – our real parents – should be very proud of us because we're bloody wonderful.' She raised her glass. 'I think we deserve another toast.'

'What's it got to do with toast anyway?' said Maddy. 'I've never understood that. It's not as though there's any bread involved, is there?'

Fiona began to giggle. 'I think we both need some fresh air.'

Half an hour later, sitting on the edge of the embankment beneath Porta Portese, watching the ink-black Tiber flow past only feet away below their dangling legs, Fiona told Maddy about Elizabeth, and Maddy said, 'That makes three of us, though, and three's a crowd. So which one of us is going to have to disappear?'

*

The next day, nursing a hangover, Maddy agreed with Ludovico that it would be wonderful to celebrate their birthday in the house at Frascati.

'It's only right we do it together,' she said. 'And you'll finally get to meet my mother.'

'And you'll get a chance to meet Patrick.'

'I already have,' she said, without thinking.

'Really?'

'No, not really,' she said hurriedly.

'You have, you haven't. Not really.' Ludovico drummed his fingers on the table. 'Confess,' he said.

She sighed, furious for not having stopped herself in time. 'Oh, all right. Nobody's perfect.' She told him about the conversation she'd had with Patrick, the Manhattans, his insistence that she had a right to half Fiona's inheritance. 'I'd never have thought of it if he hadn't.' But I've thought about it a lot since, she almost added.

'Now why would he do that?' said Ludovico. 'Why would he want to work against Fiona's interests, and his, for that matter?'

'But it's what she wants too.'

'Yes, she told me what she plans to do. I think it's very good of her.'

'You don't think I'm entitled to it?' Maddy said, bridling.

He reached across the table and laid his hand on hers. 'That isn't what I said, Maddy, and it isn't what I think,' he said gently. 'Can we start giving each other the benefit of the doubt a little more? I think what she is doing is the right thing to do, and I'm happy that she agrees with me. Does that sound better?'

'I'm sorry. I don't want you to think that I'm just after the money, that's all.'

'I don't.' He paused. 'I think Patrick is.' He stroked her forearm. 'I think he's a serpent. A toxic serpent.'

She smiled. 'I think we'd say venomous, but I like toxic better.'

'What impression did you have?'

'I didn't like him much. I thought he was a bit slimy.'

He nodded. 'And dishonest. Things have disappeared in the flat recently.' He told her about the watch, the cheque. 'Has Fiona shown you her new bracelet?'

Maddy shook her head.

'I'm not an expert on gems, but I think they are emerald. How can a man who has just been released from jail afford an emerald bracelet?'

'Have you spoken to Fiona about it?'

'She refuses to listen. She thinks I have a – what's the word? – grudge against him. Maybe you can talk to her, try to persuade her?'

'She doesn't know I've met him. I'd rather she didn't find out now, after my accusing her of lying and all that.' She smiled anxiously. 'It's all going so well.'

'Maybe Patrick shouldn't come to Frascati after all.'

'No,' she said, 'that would only make it worse. I don't think he wants her to know we've met either. Otherwise, he would have said something.'

'You're probably right. Enough of Patrick.' He glanced towards the kitchen. 'They've forgotten us.'

'Maybe they think we're going to have another row.'

He laughed. The waiter arrived with a half-litre of white wine and a basket of bread. Ludovico filled their glasses, raised his.

'To Frascati,' he said. 'And to being twenty-one.'

Maddy raised hers. 'To Frascati.'

CHAPTER FORTY-EIGHT

They took two cars; Fiona and Patrick in one, and Ludovico, Maddy and Heather in another. Ludovico hadn't wanted Patrick in his car. Maddy and Fiona had chosen not to travel together; like members of the royal family, Heather had commented. She had needed to be persuaded to come by both of her daughters, separately and together. To start with, she wanted to know who Ludovico was. Fiona said he was an old family friend. Maddy was more circumspect. She said she'd met him at Fiona's, which was true but gave her mother the impression that they barely knew each other. This was confirmed by her behaviour towards Ludovico as they drove out of Rome, with Heather in the front seat and Maddy behind; her tone with him was distant, even distracted, to such an extent that Maddy saw him searching her eyes out in the rear-view mirror, his face a mask of bewildered amusement. But all her subterfuge was ruined as the two cars arrived together. Carrying groceries into the house, Fiona reminded Maddy that this wasn't her first visit to Frascati. 'You left your ring here,' she said, holding her free hand high in the air to show hers off. 'Don't you remember?' Maddy didn't answer; she had thought the brief loss of her ring was her and Ludovico's secret. Heather, who had a shopping trolley filled with bottles, came to a halt and looked at Maddy.

'Sly boots,' she said. As soon as they were in the kitchen, she took Maddy to one side. 'This is where you came for that dirty weekend, isn't it? He's your astro-whatsit, isn't he? I don't know why you can't be honest with me.'

'Let's get these bottles in the fridge,' Maddy said. Her mother was looking around her, impressed.

'And this belongs to his family?'

Maddy nodded.

'Not bad,' she said. 'Not bad at all. Well trapped.'

Maddy ignored this.

'I remember when I was twenty.' She sat down at the table and lit a cigarette. 'Sorry, forgot it's your birthday. Twenty-one.'

'My birthday's tomorrow.' She closed the fridge door. 'When you were twenty-one you already had me. And Fiona.'

Heather sighed. 'Don't remind me.'

'That's not a very nice thing to say,' said Fiona from the door.

Heather looked embarrassed. 'You know what I mean, sweetheart.'

Ludovico walked in with an armful of cut wood. He stamped his feet on the mat as Fiona took off her coat, then helped her mother off with hers while Maddy stood and watched, wishing she'd thought to do this first. In a spirit of self-inflicted suffering, she didn't take off her own coat. 'I thought we'd grill the sausages we brought for lunch,' Ludovico said, carrying the wood across the room and stacking it to one side of the fireplace. 'How does that sound?'

Patrick came in empty-handed and took a cigarette from Heather's packet on the table. 'Sounds good to me.' He waved the cigarette at Heather as though it had only just occurred to him that it might be hers. 'You don't mind?' he said.

'Be my guest.' She looked at him, curious, mildly hostile. 'So let me try and sort things out. You're Fiona's boyfriend, right?'

He laughed. 'You should ask Fiona that,' he said.

Fiona nodded. 'If that's what he says, it must be true. Patrick always tells the truth.'

'Ouch,' said Patrick.

Fiona smiled. 'Just joking.'

Heather shivered. 'Bit chilly here, isn't it?'

'We'll soon be nice and warm, Heather,' said Fiona, kneeling beside the fireplace and twisting sheets of newspapers into knots. Maddy flinched; she couldn't help herself. She tried to call her mother Heather but it felt so false to her, so forced. She watched Fiona make the fire, touch a struck match to the knotted paper, sit back on her haunches, her face lighting up as the flames rose through the tangle of small branches Ludovico had given her as kindling. She looked across at Patrick, who had opened a bottle of wine and was pouring some into a glass for her mother.

'This is nice, isn't it?' she said lamely. 'All of us here together.'

'It's still bloody cold,' said Heather. She stood up and moved her chair nearer to the fire while Fiona balanced a couple of split logs in an arch above the fiercely burning tinder. As Heather adjusted her chair, she spilt the glass of wine Patrick had just given her. 'Oh shit,' she said and looked to Maddy for help. But before Maddy had time to move, Fiona had taken the half-empty glass away from her mother and pulled a clean tea towel from a drawer under the table. She knows where everything is, thought Maddy, as Fiona mopped up, then held out the glass for Patrick to refill while her mother settled down as if nothing had happened. Well, of course she does, she's been here a hundred times, long before Ludovico even knew I existed. I'm the newcomer, the intruder. My mother and I are the ones that don't belong here. Even Patrick has known her longer than we have. She blushed with shame for her mother, who had already emptied her glass and was looking hopefully at the bottle, and then at Patrick. If she could, she'd walk out of this room and never see a single person in it again, including her mother. And that wouldn't be awful, although most people would judge her harshly, she knew that. It would just be what she wanted. She would do anything to have that independence, that invisibility.

She was about to leave the room to get some air when her mother said in a loud, already slightly slurred voice, 'So when do the celebrations start? That's why we've dragged ourselves away from our nice, comfy homes, isn't it? We're not just here to light fires and eat sausages.'

'Our birthday's tomorrow, Heather,' Fiona said, smiling at her mother. 'We'll start celebrating a bit later on.'

'There is a reason we're here,' said Fiona. 'Another reason.' She looked around, at Maddy first and then at Patrick. Ludovico was staring out of the window and refused to meet her eye. 'I want to talk about our future.'

'That sounds ominous,' said Heather. 'I think I need a refill.' She looked at Patrick. 'You can see to that for me, can't you?'

Patrick grinned and made a little bow from the waist.

'As I think all of you know, I'm coming into rather a lot of money,' said Fiona, her voice tight as Patrick filled her mother's glass again. 'And I want to make sure that I do the right thing with it.' She paused. 'I want you all here because I need your help.'

'Can't we do this after lunch?' said Ludovico. He rubbed his hands together. 'I'm hungry.'

'I agree,' said Maddy. 'Let's relax and have something to eat first.'

Fiona looked at her, surprised. 'I thought this mattered to you as much as it does to me,' she said.

'It does,' said Maddy. 'It's just that, I don't know—' The truth was that she was scared. None of what was about to happen seemed real to her, and there was refuge in that unreality.

'My adoptive mother has control of the money my father left me until my birthday,' Fiona said, her tone determined. 'Patrick told me she was doing everything she could to maintain that control.' She glanced gratefully at Patrick. 'He's helping me make sure that doesn't happen by moving it to a place she can't get to.'

'Patrick is a financial genius,' said Ludovico wryly.

Fiona ignored this. 'The thing is,' she said, 'my father wasn't just my father. He was Maddy's father too.' She looked at Heather, who had put down her glass and was staring at her with an anxious, doubtful expression on her face. 'And he was your lover, he gave you two children. He gave you a house in exchange for me. He must have loved you both, so why did he leave it all to me? Because he thought a house was enough? Well, it wasn't.' She sighed. Her voice was shaking when she continued. 'Anyway, I want to put things right,' she said. 'I want us all to be happy.'

'Happy how?' said Heather.

'I don't want all the money,' Fiona said. 'I've already talked about this with Maddy. I want to share it with Maddy. And with you.'

'And what does Anne have to say about that?'

'She doesn't know,' said Patrick. 'She'll go berserk,' he added, with a grin.

'I'm talking to Fiona,' Heather said.

'Anne isn't my mother,' said Fiona. 'You are.' She tossed her head. 'What she says doesn't matter. As far as I'm concerned she's dead.'

'You can't mean that,' Heather said, abruptly sober. 'Anne brought you up.' She paused. 'She wanted you.' She looked at Fiona and then at Maddy. 'She really did. So badly. She wanted you more than I wanted either of you.'

'You can't mean that,' Fiona said, shocked.

'I was twenty years old. I didn't want children. I wanted to live my own life. I was a fucking hippie.'

'I'm surprised you didn't give me away as well,' Maddy said.

Heather looked at the floor, then raised her eyes. 'I tried to, if you really want to know,' she said, 'but Anne only wanted one. She said that no one would believe she'd been carrying twins. And Raymond agreed with her, because he always did.' She turned her head to look at Fiona again. 'It isn't the money Anne wants, you stupid girl. It's you.' She glanced at Patrick, and then back at Fiona. 'Isn't he the one that's done time for fraud? He is, isn't he? Why is he so keen to help? He's probably ripping you off.'

Patrick put his arm around Fiona's waist.

'Don't be a fool,' Heather said, anticlimactically. 'I was, I know that. But you don't have to be.'

Fiona pulled away from Patrick and sank to her knees by Heather's chair. She looked up, imploring. 'You had no choice. You said it yourself. You were a child.'

'Good God,' said Maddy. 'Didn't you hear what she just said? She said she didn't want either of us. She didn't want us. Why are you making excuses for her? She was no more a child than you are now, than I am now. I'm not a child.'

'I think we all need to calm down,' said Ludovico. He walked over and took Maddy's hand. 'All of us,' he said.

'You're right,' she said, surprised to feel so grateful. She pulled her coat about her. 'I need to get some fresh air,' she said. 'Are you coming?'

Ludovico nodded.

CHAPTER FORTY-NINE

They took the path that led away from the villa. They walked side by side, silently at first, Maddy's hand still in Ludovico's. Finally, Maddy spoke.

'You remember telling me about the Demon Star,' she said, 'the first time you took me out?'

'Algol?' he said. 'Of course I do.'

'And how it wasn't two stars, but three?'

'Three or more. That's right.'

'Did you know about Elizabeth then?'

'Yes,' he said.

Maddy sat down on a fallen trunk and waited until Ludovico was sitting beside her before she spoke again.

'Do you trust Patrick?'

Ludovico laughed. 'Of course I don't. And I have good reason not to. You'll see.'

'You think Mum was right then? He's trying to swindle her?'

'Swindle?'

'You know, cheat her out of her money.'

'I'm sure of it.'

Maddy picked up a dry leaf, crushed it in her hand. 'You knew about all this before, didn't you?'

Ludovico was silent. She felt that he was counting to ten before he spoke. 'I knew,' he said finally, 'what she just told us.

That she intends to divide the money between you.'

'Well, yes, that's one way of putting it.'

'What other way is there?'

'She didn't say anything specific to you about our mother? About Heather?'

He shook his head.

'She didn't tell you that she wants to buy her off me.'

Ludovico laughed again. 'She what?'

'That's what it comes down to. She wants to take Mum on. Basically, she wants to be me, but rich. She wants to be Madeleine Thomsett, with Heather Thomsett in tow.'

'And what would you be if she becomes you? I mean, you can't be her, can you? You can't be Fiona Conway. Her mother would realise immediately, and I don't think she'd be very happy about it.'

'I'd be Elizabeth.'

She looked at him, waiting to see what he would do.

'She's giving you a new identity and half her money in exchange for your mother?'

'Yes.'

'Why on earth would she do that?'

This time Maddy laughed. 'Come on, Mum's not that awful.'

'I didn't say she was. It just seems such a crazy thing to want to do.'

'I think she's lonely,' Maddy said. 'I think she wants someone to love.'

'And you? Are you lonely?'

She shook her head. 'I can think of nothing I'd rather do than start again, start a new life, be free of all the shit I've had to put up with.'

'Am I part of that?'

She looked at him. 'I don't know,' she said.

When they got back to the house, Fiona was alone in the kitchen, sitting in the armchair by the fire, poking desultorily at a fresh log that hadn't taken and was threatening to stifle the flames beneath it. She looked at them as they walked in, then back at the fire. 'Heather's gone home,' she said.

'How come?'

'She said she was cold and she didn't know why we'd brought her here. Patrick took her down to the station.'

'Where is he now?' said Ludovico.

'Upstairs. He said he wanted a lie-down after all the excitement.' She sighed. 'I don't understand. I thought she'd be so pleased.'

'There's something I need to tell you, Fiona,' Ludovico said. 'About Patrick.'

'Don't you start,' said Fiona. 'It was bad enough hearing Heather have a go at him. I hope she thanked him properly for getting her to the train.'

'She can be a bit selfish sometimes,' said Maddy.

Fiona poked at the log. 'Nobody's perfect,' she said. 'She hugged me before she left. You weren't here, you didn't see.' She cast an imploring glance at Maddy. 'She does love me, doesn't she? You know her, Maddy.' She sniffed. 'I don't.' She rattled the poker along the front of the grate. 'I can't even get this bloody fire to work.'

Maddy was the first to notice Patrick. She touched Ludovico's arm, then gestured with her head towards the stairs.

'So what do you need to tell her about me?' Patrick said.

Ludovico turned to look at him. 'You little shit,' he said. 'You don't think you're going to get away with it, do you?'

Patrick came down the stairs and walked towards the door. 'Come on, Fee. We don't need this.'

Fiona didn't move.

'Come on, sweetheart,' Patrick said. 'Don't pay any attention to him. He's just jealous.'

Ludovico ignored this. 'Why don't you show her the letters she's been getting from her bank?' he said.

'What letters?' Fiona said. 'I haven't had any letters.'

'Oh no, that's right,' said Ludovico. 'They weren't addressed to you. Were they, Patrick?'

'Will you just mind your own fucking business?' Patrick said. He walked over to Fiona, crouched down beside her, stroking her fingers until they loosened, then easing the poker from her grasp. She turned her face away from him, but he took her chin in his hand and forced her to look at him. 'Don't listen to him, sweetheart. I'm on your side. I've always been on your side,' he said, his tone wheedling. 'You'd have nothing without me. Nothing. Nothing and no one. Your real mother's a drunk. She doesn't want you. She said so, in the car. All you have is me. Don't ever forget that.'

'Those letters addressed to Elizabeth Bingham,' Ludovico said. 'The letters replying to Ms Bingham's request that Patrick Appleton be added to her bank account, with full rights of withdrawal. The letters you hid in the lovebirds' room along with the rest of your trophies.'

Fiona pulled his hand from her face, looked back at the fire. The new wood had finally caught and bright flames leapt up into the darkness of the flue. She picked up the poker again. 'Get away from me,' she said dully. Maddy felt her heart go out to the girl, her sister, her other half, collapsed into herself somehow, as thoroughly as someone beaten physically into acquiescence. A wave of anger rose within her. She stepped forward, but Ludovico caught her arm. 'No,' he said quietly. 'Not yet.'

Patrick reached out to take the poker a second time, but Fiona stumbled to her feet, holding its glowing tip within inches of

Patrick's chest. Something had woken in her. 'Just stay away from me,' she said. 'How dare you talk about my mother like that? How dare you! You liar. She loves me!' He tried to bat the poker to one side, yelping with pain as the scalding metal caught his hand. 'You little cunt,' he said. Beside herself with rage and hurt, she moved to poke him in the stomach but he leapt back, then stared around him wildly.

'I think we all need to calm down,' said Ludovico.

'You can just fuck off,' said Patrick. 'You started this.' He pointed at Maddy. 'And you can take her with you.'

'You seem to forget whose house this is.' Ludovico held up both hands in a peace-making gesture. 'If anyone needs to leave, it's you.'

Patrick grabbed Fiona's arm and yanked her to her feet. 'If I leave, she leaves with me.'

'That's for her to decide,' said Maddy.

'Stay out of this, Maddy,' said Ludovico. He was about to say more but was interrupted by Patrick's squeal as Fiona lifted the poker from the fire and jabbed it at his face. He let her go and stepped back, his hands flying up but she moved with him and jabbed a second time, and then a third, each time with greater force and precision. Ludovico called out to her to stop, stepped forward, but was blocked by Patrick's flailing arms as he tried to fight Fiona off. Patrick sank to his knees. 'Make her stop,' he sobbed. 'For God's sake, help me.' Ludovico moved a step towards Fiona, but she was out of control. 'I'll burn you too,' she cried, and waved the poker in the air. Maddy began to cry. Ludovico, his hands held out before him, in a gesture of supplication and self-protection, edged slowly closer to the enraged, hysterical girl.

He had almost reached her when Patrick rose to his feet and pushed them both to one side to get to the table. He picked up a bread knife from the board and lunged at Fiona or Ludovico

– it didn't seem to matter which – his face a mask of blood and seared flesh; his left cheek was an open wound, it looked as though one of his eyes had been put out. Fiona brought the poker down a final time on his wrist. He dropped the knife and she darted down to grab hold of it before anyone else could. She held it out before her as Patrick struggled to his feet. When he moved towards her it wasn't clear whether he intended to hurt her or restrain her, prevent her from hurting him any more, but none of that mattered in the end, his intentions were without importance, because the knife sank into his chest as soon as he was close enough and she put all her weight behind it, because she had had enough, he had gone too far, she told Maddy later, when the body had been dragged out of the house and a suitable place found for its burial. I'd had enough, she said, and Maddy had nodded; they had understood each other. When their hands touched by accident as they pushed their spades into the damp earth, they let the spades fall to the ground and fell into each other's arms, with Ludovico looking on, their bodies encircled and curved into a mutual embrace, their heads pressed together, cheek against cheek, long hair and short hair indistinguishable, until they were finally one again.

PART EIGHT

CHAPTER FIFTY

Ludovico has his head down and is reading something on his cell phone when she arrives. She's reached the table before he looks up and sees her and then, a half-second later, recognises her. She's amused, but also disappointed, to watch him as he adjusts his expression from shock that she is no longer twenty years old, and has grey hair, to relief that she is who she is. The girl he knew and loved, or so she hopes, putting her bag down on one of the two spare chairs, looking at him with less surprise, because she did after all see him on television only ten days ago, but with a pleasure as genuine as the one she hopes he feels.

He stands up, kisses both cheeks and then embraces her awkwardly. She slips her hands around his waist, slimmer than she remembered, too slim to be quite healthy; if she squeezed, she feels, she might snap him in two. He is dressed in the same way he always dressed, a tailored shirt and jeans, expensive as ever. She looks at his face, properly this time.

'I'm not as young as I was,' he says, then laughs wryly. 'Unnecessary to say that, I know.'

She shakes her head. 'You haven't changed,' she says.

'You're a much more accomplished liar than you used to be,' he says, then laughs again, with less edge to the laugh.

'I mean it,' she says, sitting down. 'I thought you had when I saw you on that awful bullying programme, but you're the same as ever.' She pauses. 'It's your turn now.'

'You look wonderful,' he says. 'I was just about to tell you.' He takes her hand. 'But you have changed.'

'Really?'

He nods. 'You're no longer afraid of the world.'

She smiles. 'Is that how you saw me?'

He squeezes her hand, lets it go, sits back in his chair. 'You had a great deal to be afraid of,' he says.

'And apparently I still do.'

'That awful bullying programme. Is that what you just called it?'

'Why on earth did you let them interview you?' she says, abruptly angry, or rather finally revealing the anger she has felt, intermittently, since that first time she saw him, talking about Fiona, with that air of sincerity she knows better than to trust.

'I had no choice.'

'I don't understand.'

'Fiona's mother is dying. She doesn't have much time left and she wants to say goodbye. She wants closure. She actually said that. Closure. I wouldn't have expected it of her. It's such a modern word.'

'You've been in touch?'

'We've always been in touch. Or she has with me. It's been the hardest thing all these years. Not to tell her, I mean. She isn't that bad a woman. Fiona had her reasons, of course, but Anne wasn't the ogre Fiona always said she was. She loved Fiona, in her way, and she still does. I think if she had loved her less she would have looked harder for her. Does that make sense?'

Liz nods. 'I suppose it does. Leaving her alone, letting her escape, was the only gift she could give her.'

He pauses. 'I've never regretted it, you know.'

'Not even now?'

He shakes his head. 'He destroyed lives, or tried to. He was evil, Maddy. He lied to Fiona about almost everything.'

'No one's called me Maddy for almost forty years,' she says.

'What does your husband call you?'

'You know I'm married?'

'You forget, Maddy. I'm an important man now.'

'I was wondering how you found my number.'

He smiles, then shrugs. 'I'm an important man,' he says again.

'He calls me Liz. Everyone does.'

'So tell me about yourself,' he says.

A girl arrives with a tray. She puts two glasses of prosecco on their table, a bowl of olives, some peanuts.

'I took the liberty of ordering,' he says.

'Well, I'm married, as you know. He's an engineer coming up to retirement. Aldo. He's from Bologna, well, just outside it. He's a good man. Honest, straightforward. We're happy together. We have two boys, twins as a matter of fact, although I imagine you know that as well.' She sips her prosecco, takes a spoonful of peanuts from the bowl but doesn't eat them. 'I've made a life for myself, Ludovico. It wasn't easy to start with; I thought it would be easier to give up my mother but I missed her terribly the first few months, years even. I missed everyone.'

'And you gave it all up for the money,' he says.

She looks at him. 'Did I? I've often wondered about that. I think I did it to get away, that was all. Fiona had more reason to do it than me. She had the money in any case, whatever happened. What Fiona wanted was to love our mother, I think, and to be loved by her. All I wanted was to get out.' She sighs. 'I wonder if she managed in the end.'

'They went to live in Cyprus, you know.'

'No, I didn't know that. I told her we needed a clean break. Anything else would have been intolerable.' She stares at the peanuts in her hand. 'I wonder why they chose Cyprus.'

Neither of them speaks for a moment. Maddy looks around the bar. It's the same as ever, the light filtering through the vine, the zinc-topped tables, the bohemian feel of the place accentuated by the casual manner of the girl who brought the tray. But not everything is the same. They have closed the door to the street, she's noticed. She had to pass through the bar in order to reach the patio. There is less trust in the world, she thinks.

Then Ludovico says, 'So you missed your mother most?'

She knows what he wants to hear. She could tell him the truth, that she has never entirely believed in him, never been entirely convinced that he wasn't involved in some complicated private double game, playing one off against the other, playing with their love. She could say that, that she has never quite trusted him. Maybe there has never been enough trust, she thinks.

'No,' she says. 'I missed you most.'

This seems to satisfy him. 'So here we are,' he says.

But she isn't satisfied. 'Can I ask you something?'

'Of course you can.'

'Did you love either of us? I mean, seriously.'

He smiles. 'I loved you both,' he says.

'I don't believe that's possible.'

'I'm a shallow man. It hurts me to admit it, but it's true. I loved the one I was with, and fought for her and defended her. I saw the woman in front of me, and loved her, and did what I could to help her. And sometimes it was you, and sometimes it was Fiona. Which put me in an impossible situation. I'm not proud of myself. Believe me, you couldn't think worse of me than I have done. In the end I lost you both. I deserved to, I know that, but that didn't make it any easier.'

She nods, satisfied. 'I told my husband everything, I think you should know that. After the programme last week, when they said that the body was an unidentified young man. I told him the truth. It wasn't easy. I'd lied to him for so long.' Although it never felt like lying. She has never seen their life together as a lie.

'And how did he react?'

'Angrily at first.' She stops herself, thinks for a moment. 'Or no, he wasn't really angry. He was more, I don't know, stupefied, I suppose. I think he may even have been a little impressed.'

'He never suspected anything? I mean, you haven't changed that much. Even if the photograph was of Fiona.'

'Oh yes, to start with, yes. But the funny thing is that he suspected you,' she says. 'Immediately the body was found. How convenient that was, by the way. Before I said anything he'd decided you were the guilty one.'

Ludovico laughs. 'They'd known about the body for days, the police tipped them off. You know how television works. The essential element of surprise.' He pauses, before continuing, with an edge of apprehension: 'And you told him that I had nothing to do with it, I hope.'

'I didn't say that you were there, obviously. I told him Fiona and I did it.' She pauses again. 'The oddest thing was that he didn't seem to care that I'd helped to kill someone and then hide the body.' She smiles. 'I think he watches too much television. You know, crime investigation, all that stuff.' Her face becomes serious again. 'He said he had loved me for almost forty years, and he saw no reason to stop just because I'd had another name at some point in the past. That was how he saw it. He loved me,' she repeats, with emphasis. 'The person I am. And he's right.'

'Maddy,' Ludovico begins, but she interrupts him.

'No, don't call me that. Call me Liz.'

He shakes his head. 'I can't do that. You'll always be Maddy for me.'

'Maddy lives in Cyprus, with her mother.'

'Her mother's dead.'

'You didn't need to tell me that.'

He looks ashamed. 'I know. I'm sorry.'

'And you?'

'Me?'

'I know you're a public figure,' she says, with a hint of scorn. 'But that's all I know.'

'What else do you need to know?'

There is something else she needs to ask. 'Do you know why she brought the whole thing up again?'

'Who?'

'Fiona's mother. Why now?'

'She's dying too. Cancer. She's an old woman, alone in the world, and she's dying and she feels responsible. I think she wants the chance to say she's sorry. She still has no idea Fiona knows the truth about you and your mother. She can't believe her daughter would treat her like this, I suppose. Deep down, I think she hopes that Fiona is dead. Nothing else would explain her silence.'

How cruel we've been, thinks Liz, her fingers worrying at a hangnail. And soon it will be too late. Perhaps it already is. 'I see,' she says. Neither speaks for a moment. She has a sense of panic, as though all she has ever had is sliding away, slipping out of her grasp. 'I'm sorry,' she says, looking up from her hands and into his eyes. 'You were going to tell me about yourself.'

He gives one of his little bows and she is taken back to when they first met. Her heart skips a beat.

'I've been married twice. One divorce, one premature death. I have no children. I have important friends, sufficiently important for the inquiry into the body to be quietly shelved. I'm currently involved with a colleague at the Institute. She's younger than I am and wants to keep our relationship a private matter. I think she may be ashamed of me. She may be right to be ashamed, although not for the reason she thinks. She thinks my appearing on television means that I've sold out.'

'And have you?'

'Not at all. I've never intended to abandon my academic career for the bright lights of late-night television.'

She smiles. He is still charming, she can't deny it.

'So what are you studying now?'

He empties his glass and calls across to the girl for another, then turns back to the woman in front of him.

'I'm still trying to figure out Algol.'

'Algol?' she says.

He smiles.

'The Demon Star,' he says.

Acknowledgements

Birthright is set in Rome in the early 1980s and many details reflect my own experiences in the city. I arrived in 1982 with the promise of a university teaching job but no contract, a month's salary in my pocket, knowing no one. I was lonely, sleeping in a *pensione* near the station, eating in the cheapest trattorias, checking each day to see if my contract had come through. I remember one afternoon, watching a film being made near Piazza Venezia – Tarkovsky's *Nostalghia* – and striking up conversation with a cameraman. When he returned to work I realized that he was the first person I'd spoken to in days and I found myself on the steps to the Campidoglio, crying my eyes out. The following morning, I was told that I could start work and I was saved. I was saved because my colleagues became my friends, and I would like to finally take this opportunity to thank them. You know who you are. Clarissa, Jenny, Giuliana, Danny, Brenda, David. You fed me, and housed me, and made me laugh, and it is a privilege to have known you and to have woven tiny, almost irretrievable fragments of you, and of us, and of the lives we led, into the texture of this novel.

A Q&A with Chales Lambert

• How long have you been writing? Why did you start?

I started writing when I was around 14. We were living in a cottage in the Pennines, the location for much of my first novel *Little Monsters,* and isolation encouraged my already highly developed reading habit, which is, as everyone knows, the gateway drug to believing oneself to be a writer. I started with rhyming sonnets (seriously) and by the time I was at university I'd moved onto the harder stuff of narrative.

• What were your favourite books growing up? How do they influence your writing now?

As with many people of my generation the foundations were laid by Enid Blyton, from *Noddy* through the *Secret Seven* and the *Famous Five* to the more demanding *Adventure of...* series, which unearthed in me a lasting complex about being trapped underground. I had a thing about fantasy from early on, and have vivid memories of E Nesbit's *Five Children and It* and her wonderful creation, the Psammead, and, of course, C.S. Lewis's Narnia books, which taught me that anything that can be written can be made to happen, in this world or elsewhere, and which provided the spirit that lurks, perhaps perversely, behind my own *The Children's Home.* But that's just skimming the surface. I was a full-time book-borrower (which reminds me, I also loved *The Borrowers* when I was very small) and I have a stronger recollection of standing among the bookshelves of Lichfield Public Library, greedy with desire, than I do of any schoolroom. School interrupted my reading, and I have never quite forgiven it for that.

• What inspired you to write *Birthright*?

It was originally inspired by a long-running programme on Italian state television called *Chi L'ha Visto?* (Who has seen him/her?), the ostensible aim of which is to help people find loved ones, frequently grown-up children, that have disappeared. A noble aim, but one that has always irritated me, because surely one of the human rights that cannot be denied is the right to disappear, to move on, to escape, and if this involves a certain amount of cruelty, well, so be it. The rest of the novel grew out of this conviction that not only can we make our lives but that we can remake them as well.

• You moved to Rome at the start of the 1980s, which is where and when the main action of *Birthright* is set. How did your experience of the city at that time shape the writing of the novel?

Very much. I had a similar job to Fiona's, working at the university as a language teacher for students who were not that much younger than I was and treated me with either diffidence or an extremely casual respect. Both Fiona and Maddy live in apartments based on apartments I lived in at different times during those early years in Rome, when my income careered vertiginously from high to low. In many ways the day-to-day experiences of both Fiona and Maddy, despite their obvious differences, were mine. Setting the novel in a city and context that I knew, and know, so well, meant that I had to resist several temptations as I wrote. The strongest was probably the desire to describe the dreadful conditions language teachers had to put up with (and still do, but that's another story). The urge to dwell on extraneous details about the city, details that meant a great deal to me but were totally inessential to the plot, was almost as strong and I thank my agent, Isobel Dixon, and editor, Rich Arcus, for helping me bring it under control.

• The two sisters react very differently to the discovery of the other's existence. Do you sympathise with one more than the other?

In the first draft of the novel I began with Maddy's story, with Fiona as predator and Maddy as prey, and my sympathy was inevitably with Maddy. A second draft moved Fiona to the forefront and, feckless as I am, I shifted my affections to Fiona and listened to what she had to tell me about her life and her needs. By the third draft I felt that I had the measure of them both and my sympathies were divided equally between the two. It was important to me that the reaction of both sisters was equally credible, and allowing myself into their separate lives as I did by, effectively, writing the novel twice, and then a third time, made that possible.

• Fiona and Maddy each covet what the other has. Were you deliberately playing on the idea of 'the grass is always greener'?

Not really. There's something unexplored and irrational about the notion of the grass being greener elsewhere, with perfect greenness a fleeting and finally unobtainable quality. I think both Maddy and Fiona knew exactly what they wanted, and didn't want, long before their meeting gave them the opportunity to have it.

• What are you currently reading?

For reasons I won't go into here, I've spent the last couple of months relying on my Kindle and books I'd uploaded but never got round to reading. The most recent were *The House of Brede* by Rumer Godden and *The Animal Factory* by Edward Bunker. Godden is an author I've admired since I read *The Greengage Summer* a couple of years ago and Bunker is someone I'd been planning to read since I came across James Ellroy's praise of his work. Only when I'd finished did it dawn on me that both novels are set in closed rule-bound communities – a convent and a prison – and that, although stylistically they couldn't be more different, the strength of the narrative came precisely from that sense of constriction, something that many of us have experienced during the COVID pandemic as a sort of unwished-for refinement. I've always been fascinated by constraints, and how people deal with them, and both these novels are masterworks in that sense. On a lighter note, I recently reread, and re-loved, Armistead Maupin's *Tales of the City* series from beginning to end. But I'm anticipating your next question!

• Are there any books or authors you reread and return to?

See above! I'm not a great re-reader, although I'm planning to become one, if only because I already have far too many books and really need to start culling rather than accumulating. Apart from Maupin, whose work renews my faith in human nature, the comedy of manners and the tactics of survival, I go back to several authors, for various reasons. Relatively recent re-reads include work by Elizabeth Strout, Stephen King, Antoine Laurain, Mary Renault, Rose Tremain and Georges Simenon. I pick up *The Lord of the Rings* every few years, and lose myself in it as totally as I did when I was 15. I also dip into Eleanor Farjeon's wonderful *Martin Pippin* books (and I should have mentioned her in my answer to your second question!). And, of course, D. H. Lawrence and Anthony Trollope. So I do actually re-read quite a lot!

• What does your writing routine look like?

I don't really have one. Every book seems to impose its own rhythm and I just go along with it as far as I humanly can. *Prodigal* was written during early morning shifts (from 7 to 9) on the canonical 1000-word-a-day basis. *The Children's Home* took seven years, in crazy dream-inspired bursts. *The Bone Flower* was the product of an idea, a chapter breakdown and six weeks of solid writing. *Birthright*, as I've already said, went through several drafts until I found the book I wanted. Who knows what the next one will require of me? Which leads me neatly to your final question.

• What are you working on right now?

Right now, nothing. I have three or four ideas for books, and I'm waiting to see which one takes hold. In the meantime, I'm revising a novel I wrote some years ago, but didn't feel I'd got quite right. It's a dystopian fantasy, currently called *The Raven's Mark*, so, given the current state of the world, its time has probably come!